The Wood Nymph And The Cranky Saint

C. Dale Brittain

THE WOOD NYMPH AND THE CRANKY SAINT

Copyright © 1993 by C. Dale Brittain

A Baen Books Original

Baen Publishing Enterprises
P.O. Box 1403
Riverdale, N.Y. 10471

ISBN: 0-671-72156-9

Cover art by Dean Morrissey

First printing, February 1993

Distributed by
SIMON & SCHUSTER
1230 Avenue of the Americas
New York, N.Y. 10020

Printed in the United States of America

GREAT BIG FANGS

As I strapped up my saddlebag, I caught a glimpse of motion from the corner of my eye and turned slowly.

There were *two* of the creatures, the size of small dogs but shaped like rabbits. My first hope was that they were some bizarre illusion, but they were very real. They came hopping awkwardly along the edge of the stream, ignoring my presence. Rather than ears, they had long, pointed horns. I stepped back involuntarily. Instead of broad rabbits' teeth, they had protruding fangs and instead of wide, placid rabbit eyes, they had small, red nasty eyes. And those horns looked sharp.

One flicked its red eyes toward me and emitted a cry—a low, hooting sound, almost like an owl. The other creature responded with the same cry. Both redoubled their speed, made a sharp turn and disappeared rapidly across the meadow toward the base of the cliff.

I stood idiotically, just watching them go. They looked so ridiculous that I felt I ought to laugh. But that hooting, haunting call had stifled any laugh within me.

I hurried across the meadow, putting together a probing spell to help me find them. As soon as I opened myself to it, I found that the valley was thick with magic, making it virtually impossible to probe for anything. And yet— Somewhere behind me, in the grove, I thought I could sense the presence of a powerful spell.

This was even worse than I had thought. The denseness of magical forces made me lose track of the spell that had seemed so strong a moment ago. I walked swiftly along the little paths between the springs, without seeing anything but trees. But then something caught my eye in the muddy earth.

It was a footprint, about the size of a man's foot, even roughly the right shape, but somehow wrong. I knelt down for a closer look, but I already knew. That print had been made by nothing human.

CONTENTS

Part One: THE HERMITAGE   1

Part Two: THE YOUNG WIZARD   37

Part Three: THE OLD WIZARD   77

Part Four: THE WOOD NYMPH   113

Part Five: THE DUCHESS   151

Part Six: PRINCE ASCELIN   191

Part Seven: THE CAVE   225

Part Eight: THE MONSTER   267

PART ONE
The Hermitage

I

When it was over, the living back where they belonged—or someplace else—and the dead buried, I thought again of the day it all began. I wanted to keep Yurt the charming, bucolic, little out-of-the-way kingdom it was, but I had also wished for a little excitement.

A wizard should know better than to wish for something. Sometimes wishes come true.

As Royal Wizard, arrayed in midnight-blue velvet, I was supposed to give an air of deep wisdom to the court proceedings. But I no longer had the slightest idea what that day's case was about.

My king, however, seemed to have an excellent grasp of the details. I leaned against the wall and watched him. King Haimeric bent forward on the throne, pulling his ermine-trimmed cloak tighter around his thin shoulders as the late afternoon breeze came in the open doors and windows of the great hall.

He settled his spectacles more firmly on his nose

and looked at the people before him with shrewd eyes. "So even though he struck you, he didn't try to deny that you had a right to bring your cows into the field?"

"Of course he didn't deny it!" "I only struck him when he started beating me with his stick!" "Don't listen to him! You can't believe someone who'd dig up a grave!" "Listen to his lies!" "Look at my leg; the bruises are there yet!" "His wife was the worst, and she knew she could thump me all she wanted because I wouldn't hit a woman!" "Anyone can tell you I cleared every stump out of that field with my own hands!"

Two dozen men and women, all from a village located five miles away, stood in front of the throne. I still hadn't sorted out which were the claimants, which members of their families, and which the character witnesses they had brought along. A young woman with straight flaxen hair was crying openly. Over to one side, apart from the rest, a man with very broad shoulders was moodily examining the tiles of the fireplace as though trying to dissociate himself from the whole quarrel.

The knights of Yurt, ranged along the wall to help give authority to the proceedings, looked both bored and tired, with an air of having long ago stopped hearing what anyone said. Even the king's burly nephew Dominic, who used to pay very close attention to legal cases, had wandered off, but then he had been acting somewhat distracted lately anyway.

During pauses in the arguments, I could hear faint clangings from the kitchen. The smells of supper gradually became more pronounced. Several times already a servant had peeked around the door to see if we were done yet.

Abruptly, King Haimeric pushed aside his lap robe and stood up. "I've heard enough!" he exclaimed. The excited arguing of the group before him stopped short.

"You brought this to me as a property dispute," he said sternly. "But both your documents of property rights and your witnesses are highly suspect and highly contradictory."

"We already told you, Your Highness, that they stole our deed and substituted a lying fake!" one woman put in bravely.

"And it's become clear," the king continued, not even pausing for the interruption, "that much more than property is involved. This field has become the excuse for verbal abuse and for physical violence, which you know I consider intolerable. Some of you have even claimed that others have dug up somebody's relative and hidden the body—don't interrupt me! And now you've told me that the quarrel over this field has even been the cause of a serious breach of promise."

I had missed this final detail amid everything else, but it explained the weeping young woman.

"If those of you who were in the wrong originally," the king continued, "hoped that by utter confusion you would avoid a ruling against you, you are mistaken." All of the principal disputants looked jubilant, as though secure in the knowledge that not they but the others had originally been in the wrong.

But the king's next words took the smiles from their faces. "*All* of you are in the wrong. This case cannot be settled by a simple determination of right."

I certainly agreed with him there. I even had to abandon what would have been my own solution, to divide the field down the middle between the two claimants—if indeed there were only two.

The king crossed his arms and glared. "I have only one option left to me. I am going to swear you to peace!"

The knights all straightened to attention and slapped their sword hilts ritually.

"But in that case—" someone began.

Again the king paid no attention. "You will have to work out for yourselves who has the right to plow and gather, who to pasture cows on the stubble, where your cousin is buried now, and who will marry whom, but you will have to do it without violence!"

He turned and motioned toward Joachim, the Royal Chaplain, who had been standing on the other side of the throne from me. A dissatisfied murmuring and shuffling began with the king's words but stopped immediately as the chaplain came forward, carrying a heavy Bible in both hands.

He was as young as I and didn't even have my wizardly white beard to give an aura of mysterious wisdom. But the absolute seriousness of his gaunt face and his enormous and compelling black eyes always gave him an air of dignity and authority that I knew I would never be able to equal. This was made even worse by the knowledge that in his case the effect was entirely unintentional.

The chaplain set the Bible on a table beside the king. "Come forward!" the king commanded. "Each of you, put your right hand on the Bible. Swear before God and the saints that you will practice violence no more, but that you will seek peace with these your neighbors."

With covert glances at the tall and silent chaplain, all the disputants and all their witnesses came forward, abashed, and swore individually. The broad-shouldered young man came over from the fireplace to swear last of all.

"Now take each other by the hands in fellowship," the king continued. "All of you. Take each one's hand to symbolize the peace that now exists between you."

The flaxen-haired woman, her cheeks still wet but no longer weeping, went at once to the young man. She stopped as though abruptly shy two feet short of him, but he reached for her hands and said something to her. She slowly started to smile. While the rest went back and forth, shaking each other's hands, sometimes with what I thought unnecessary firmness, the two stood silently, looking at each other's faces.

When the whole group left a moment later, they were still holding hands.

The king, the chaplain, and I went out into the courtyard with them and through the gates, to watch them walk down the hill from the royal castle of Yurt. The sun was low and red in the west. The king continued to stare sternly after them until they were out of sight.

"Well," said King Haimeric in satisfaction, his usual good humor reappearing as soon as they were gone, "I don't think we'll hear from *them* again. And that's the last of this month's cases. I don't know about you two, but I find giving justice hungry work. It's hard for an old man to have to wait for supper!"

We went back into the great hall where, just in the few moments we had been gone, the servants had illuminated the magic lamps that dated back to my predecessor's time and brought out the trestle tables for supper. Now they were spreading the tablecloths and lighting the fire in the fireplace. In the little balcony high on the wall, the castle's brass choir tuned their instruments.

"In fact," said the king, "there shouldn't be any more urgent cases this summer. I think I deserve a vacation, say for a month or six weeks. How would you two like to try running the kingdom?"

The chaplain and I exchanged surprised glances. In the two years I had been wizard of Yurt, I had never known the king to leave his castle for more than a few days at a time.

"You mean," I said, "exercising royal authority—" I had only recently managed to make myself into a passably competent wizard, and it would certainly be a challenge to become a competent substitute for a king.

The king smiled. "No, I wouldn't really make you two act as regents. But I *am* serious about taking a vacation."

The knights and ladies of the royal court were

assembling in the hall. The queen came in, carrying the baby boy all of us considered the most important person in the castle. His nurse hurried behind, frustrated as usual because the queen kept stepping in to do things the nurse felt were her proper duties.

"So you finished up the last case?" said the queen, smiling at the king affectionately. She was less than half his age and the most beautiful woman I had ever met in my life. "I'm sure you handled them all with justice and wisdom."

She set the little prince down on the flagstone floor. He crawled determinedly to the table, took hold of a table leg, and started cautiously pulling himself to a standing position. His face carried an expression of intense concentration.

The queen caught him just before he reached the tablecloth. Holding onto one of her hands with both of his, the prince swayed a little but remained standing and gave a wide smile of triumph. He already had four teeth. "Dwrg," he said.

"Did you hear that?" asked the queen in delight. "He called you 'Daddy.' "

The king seemed happy to believe it. I decided not to mention that just the day before the little prince had looked directly at me and indubitably said, "Gizward."

Above us, the brass choir began to play and we went to our seats, the king at the head of the main table and the queen, with the prince in her lap, at the foot.

The king had said nothing to the queen in my hearing about a vacation. I glanced again toward the chaplain, whose place was directly across the table from mine. He gave a slight shrug, with no better idea than I. Could the king really be planning to leave Yurt?

Servants brought steaming trays from the kitchen and we all began to eat, too hungry for more than minimal conversation. It was early summer when the days are longest, and yet the sun was setting outside.

But as we reached dessert, people settled back more comfortably to talk. I sat at the table, as I always did, with the queen's aunt on my right side and the king's nephew on my left.

Dominic, royal nephew and presumptive heir until the birth of the baby prince, was built along the lines of a bear, large and solid. The layer of fat that had begun to replace his muscles did not conceal the fact that plenty of muscle still remained. Like a bear, too, he moved slowly—these last few months especially— but there was always the suggestion that he could move very rapidly if he wanted to.

The Lady Maria, on the other hand, gave an impression of constant motion even when quite still. Although, in the two years since I had come to Yurt, her golden curls had turned a rather attractive ash gray and she had given up lacy gowns for dark colors and severe styles, her manner still verged on the girlish.

"I'm always so *impressed* with King Haimeric when he gives judgment," she told me. "He cuts right through to the truth!"

"He certainly had a complicated case this afternoon," I agreed.

"I'm sure it's a *great* help to him to have the assistance of a Royal Wizard at his side!" she added with a smile. "Our old wizard hardly ever assisted in legal affairs."

The implied insult to my predecessor, I realized, was actually supposed to be a compliment to me. "I can claim no credit, my lady; the settlement today was all the king's idea." It was interesting to hear that my predecessor had not stood, as I had, through long afternoons of complicated quarrels. I could appreciate his point of view. Listening to dull court cases was not the challenge to my magical powers I had anticipated when becoming a royal wizard.

The old wizard, who had been Royal Wizard of Yurt for a hundred and eighty years before me, through five generations of kings, was still alive. He lived by himself with his magical roots and herbs in a little green house down in the woods. Although when I first came to Yurt I had negotiated a truce with him, which is about the best one can hope for between young and old wizards, and he had taught me some of his herbal magic, there were still a large number of things about him I did not know.

But the Lady Maria moved on to other topics. As dinner ended, people rose and stood talking around the fireplace. The evening air, coming through the hall doors laden with the scent of roses, was just cool enough to make the fire's warmth welcome.

The king said to me, "How about some of your illusions to round out the evening, Wizard? I may not get a chance to see many more of them for a while."

So he really did mean to go. As I put together the words of the Hidden Language to shape my spells and produced a few simple but effective illusions—a golden egg that pulsated with fire and hatched into a phoenix and then a twenty-foot giant who strode the length of the hall while waving its club and roaring silently—I wondered how he could bear to leave. I couldn't imagine wanting to go anywhere else.

II

And yet I also surprised myself by envying him. Wherever the king was going, he would see new people, new sights. Yurt was a wonderful place, but sometimes I had to admit, very quietly to myself, that it could be a little dull.

I went to talk to him the next morning. Every morning that the weather was fair King Haimeric spent a few hours in his rose garden outside the castle walls, weeding, pruning, trimming off faded blossoms, examining the bushes for slugs and insects, and planning which varieties to plant or breed next. It was hard to imagine the castle without the king in it. As I came across the drawbridge, I saw that the barred garden gate was swung open and could hear his and the queen's voices at the far end of the garden. I proceeded slowly along the grassy paths, taking time to admire the roses.

Some bushes were tall and robust, others propped against tiny trellises. Some blossoms had scores of petals and were as big as saucers, while other bushes were covered with tiny blooms no bigger than my thumbnail. Every shade of white, pink and red was represented. At the far end, where the voices came from, was a section of yellow roses. The king had begun his rose garden when a young prince, but he had only started on the yellows within the last eight or ten years. The mingled scents from the different blossoms were almost overwhelming.

I spotted the king and queen sitting together on a bench. He looked happy and not at all regal, with a broad-brimmed straw hat on his white head and grass stains on his knees. A bowl of cut roses and his garden shears were beside him. The queen had put the baby prince down on a blanket, but he kept crawling off it. As I watched, he reached for her skirts to try to pull himself upright. She reached down and lifted him into her lap with a smile of affection and maternal solicitude that made my heart turn over.

I had been in love with the queen since the first moment I saw her. As a mother, she seemed even more beautiful to me than ever. However, this was certainly something I had never felt appropriate to tell the king. For that matter, my feelings had also never been something to tell a woman so obviously in love with her husband as the queen—even if he *was* more than twice her age.

"I thought I saw you come in, Wizard," said King Haimeric. "Come join us. We were just talking about our trip. And look at my new bush; the buds started opening today."

It was one of his yellows, with pale blooms almost the color of parchment but tinged very delicately with red on the edges. I bent down to get a faint whiff of scent. "So where are you going?"

"To visit my parents," the queen answered. "I think Baby Buttons here is old enough to travel safely."

The castle without the queen in it would be even worse. "Why can't your parents come visit us?" I asked.

The queen laughed. "They visited here last year when their grandson was born. And you know they hate traveling. I think they got their fill six or seven years ago, going around the western kingdoms trying to find someone appropriate to marry me to—until I found someone myself!" with a smile for the king.

"I'm still a little concerned about my garden," said the king. "You know, I've never been away from the roses in June. Some of the bushes haven't bloomed yet, and I'm starting to worry about them."

The little prince looked up at me from his mother's lap. He had startlingly bright emerald eyes, the same shade as hers. He gave an unexpected chortle. "Gizward," he said.

"Did you hear that?" asked the queen, so quickly that I almost wondered if he might *not* have said what had seemed so clear. "He just said 'Wizard'!"

In spite of the king's concerns about leaving his rose bushes in June, the trip almost immediately became something for which the whole castle was preparing. The king and queen would travel with a relatively small party: the baby's nurse, the queen's Aunt Maria, a few ladies, and a half dozen knights. The king was leaving his chaplain and me behind, although we had often accompanied him on short trips.

"You'd be bored silly in two days," he told me with a conspiratorial smile. "The queen's parents are very dear people, but . . . besides, I trust you to keep an eye on Dominic."

Since they planned to be gone over a month, the king took the precaution of appointing his burly nephew as regent. Prince Dominic listened to the announcement without any apparent emotion. He merely nodded and slowly twisted the ruby ring he always wore on his second finger. The ring's setting was a golden snake, with the jewel resting on its coils, and I had always felt it would be a much better ring for a wizard than for a prince. This regency, I thought, might be the closest Dominic would ever come to being king of Yurt, and I would have expected more reaction from him.

I had sometimes wondered at Dominic's calm acceptance of the birth of his young cousin. After all, the royal nephew had probably spent most of his life, until the baby was born, assuming he would someday be king. I wondered if he planned to revolutionize the running of the castle while the king was away and rather hoped he didn't, for, if so, I might be the first to go.

Less than two weeks after the king and queen first announced they were going, they were gone, riding off in the cool of the early morning accompanied by a fanfare of trumpets. The whole party rode white horses with bells on their harnesses.

Everyone had come out to say good-bye and, for several minutes as the riders mounted, there was a great deal of laughing and calling final messages and instructions. The baby prince, riding in a pack on his nurse's back, frowned at us all. Dominic alone stood stolid and dignified, as though already feeling the weight of his responsibilities and wanting to be sure we all knew it.

The king reined in his horse just as they all started down the hill. "Be sure to cut the roses every day," he told the constable. "As I already told you, it's better to cut them in the bud than to have the blossoms all fade on the bushes."

"Yes, you already told me, sire," said the constable respectfully, but with a hint of an indulgent smile.

"All right, all right," said the king, who did smile before hurrying to catch up to the rest.

They reached the edge of the woods below the castle's hill and disappeared from sight with a final ringing of harness bells. The morning suddenly seemed extremely quiet and extremely empty.

"Well, it looks like you're in charge of the castle now, Prince Dominic," I said to break the silence. "At least until the royal family comes back."

The regent was juggling something heavy in his hand which I recognized as the royal seal of Yurt. "But it's not my castle, and they're not my wife and child," he growled, turned on his heel, and stomped across the drawbridge into the castle.

The staff and the knights and ladies who were staying behind drifted back inside, but I didn't feel like going in yet. The day had gone flat, and it would be at least three more days before we could expect a telephone call, telling us that the royal party had arrived safely at the castle of the queen's parents.

My biggest wizardly accomplishment since coming to Yurt had been the installation of magic telephones. They were not like the magic telephones common down in the great City, but then, very little of my magic seemed to be like anyone else's. This was largely due to the fact that I often had to improvise to compensate for all the courses at the wizards' school where I had not paid proper attention—in this case I had managed to avoid courses in the technical division completely—but I preferred to think it demonstrated my unique flair and creativity.

In the meantime, I didn't want to mope for three days, waiting for the telephone to ring, imagining the royal family attacked by bandits or dragons without their wizard there to protect them.

"Joachim," I said to the chaplain, who was also still

looking off across the green fields of Yurt, "let's go sit in the king's garden for a moment."

He gave a start, as though he had forgotten my presence, but answered calmly. "All right, Daimbert."

We were the only people in the castle who used each other's names, being Father and Wizard to everyone else. We didn't always understand each other and I had long since despaired of giving him a proper sense of humor, but we had managed to become friends, at least most of the time, though traditionally priests and wizards do not get along at all. For that matter, wizards don't usually get along with other wizards.

We sat on the bench by the king's yellow roses. The king had been up at dawn, pruning everything one last time before he left, so the only blooms on the bushes were the buds that were just opening.

"Do you know what's bothering Dominic?" I asked. "I'd expected he'd be delighted to have a chance to act as king of Yurt."

"I think that's his problem precisely," said the chaplain. "He loves the little prince—everyone must love him—but Dominic had been heir apparent to the kingdom his entire life, and now he isn't. Being named temporary regent must emphasize for him that the future he'd always thought he was preparing for will never come to pass."

If Dominic was undergoing some sort of emotional crisis, I just hoped he didn't bother me with it. "Well, at least it's not us," I said cheerfully. "What shall we do first while the king is gone? How about if I try to discover a spell to raise up armed men from dragons' teeth?"

Joachim stretched his long legs out in front of him and glanced at me from deep-set eyes. "I'm afraid we have no dragons' teeth," he said, perfectly serious. "But I have a task of my own. I received a message from the bishop yesterday, asking me to investigate the situation at a hermitage at the far eastern end of the kingdom."

This sounded deadly dull to me. One advantage of being a wizard rather than a priest was that the wizards' school wasn't always giving us the responsibility of carrying out uninteresting tasks.

But something about this message had bothered Joachim. There was a faint note of concern in his voice that no one who did not know him as well as I did would have noticed. "What's the problem?"

"I don't understand why the bishop asked *me*," he said, turning his huge dark eyes fully on me. Even after two years, the effect was still intimidating. "Why didn't he just send one of the priests from the cathedral?"

"Maybe because the hermitage is here in the kingdom of Yurt," I suggested, puzzled why this was important. "You're Royal Chaplain, but the cathedral is located in the next kingdom."

Joachim shook his head. "That shouldn't make any difference. Both kingdoms are in the bishop's diocese."

"Maybe the bishop thinks you'd do the best job."

He frowned at this. "The bishop should realize I have no special merits."

I expected the bishop thought the exact opposite but didn't say so. I was still wondering why being asked to do something which sounded simple and dull should bother Joachim so much, when the constable appeared, walking briskly down the grassy path between the roses.

"I thought I'd find you here, Wizard," he said. "A message just came in on the pigeons for you. It's from the count."

I took the tiny cylinder from him, all that carrier pigeons could handle. Since the royal castle still had the only telephone in Yurt, the rest of the kingdom had to communicate with us via pigeons. I unrolled the little piece of paper. Yurt had two counts and a duchess; this message was from the older of the two counts. The message was, by necessity, brief.

"Have strange magical creature here. Don't think it represents immediate danger, but wish you would look at it, soon as possible."

I read it again. It made no more sense the second time.

"Look at this," I said, handing Joachim the piece of paper. "What do you think he means? If they 'have' a magical creature, does that mean that they've captured it? Or does he mean that some nixie is flitting around the castle at night? *Any* magical creature poses potential danger, yet he claims this one doesn't—or at least not immediately. But if it's not dangerous, why was he concerned enough to write me?"

Joachim shook his head, with no better idea than I.

"The count's castle is over at the eastern end of the kingdom," I said, "so it must be quite near your hermitage. If we go together, we can investigate both at the same time. All right then," turning to the constable without giving Joachim a chance to object. "Send the count a message to expect us. We'll leave for his castle as soon as I tell the regent we're going."

If nothing else, this certainly solved the problem of what to do while waiting to hear from the king and queen.

III

We sat under a beech tree, eating bread and cheese. Our horses, their saddles off, grazed before us. If I had been going alone, it would have been faster to fly, but flying is hard mental and physical work, and I still wasn't as good at it as a qualified wizard really ought to be. Besides, I was glad of Joachim's company.

"You had been starting to tell me about this hermitage," I said, brushing crumbs from my lap and leaning back against the tree trunk, which rose smooth and white above us.

"Yes, but I'm beginning to wonder if I am wrong to bring a wizard into the affairs of the church without consulting the bishop," Joachim said slowly.

I was glad I wasn't a priest. There seemed to be all sorts of things over which one could have moral dilemmas, none of which would have bothered me in the slightest.

"But perhaps it's best that I have," he continued after a moment, "for the hermitage has a magical creature of its own. The hermitage is built in a grove at the source of a little river. There has always been a wood nymph living there."

I sat up straight. "How very exciting! I had no idea we had a wood nymph in Yurt. I've never seen one before—I'll definitely have to visit this grove. So how do she and the hermit get along? Is that what you're going to investigate? I wonder if it's the nymph who is annoying the count?"

He looked at me and looked away, seeming to find the idea of a wood nymph much less exciting than I did.

"The old wizard, my predecessor, must know about the nymph," I continued. "I'll ask him when we get home again. There's a lot of the old magic of wood and earth that he knows but which they don't teach at the school."

"My investigations have nothing to do with the nymph directly," said Joachim. "But with you along, it may be easier to deal with her if she appears—I've never seen a nymph myself. The bishop has sent me to the hermitage on a matter concerning the saint's relics kept there." This sounded dull again. But apparently it was not dull to the chaplain. "Why would the bishop send me on such an important commission?" he burst out.

I lay back again with my legs crossed, looking into the leaves above us. Very high up, hidden from view, a bird was singing gloriously. "You've been Royal Chaplain of Yurt," I said, "what is it, five years now? And I know you were at the cathedral for a year or two after leaving the seminary before becoming chaplain. The bishop has had plenty of time to see your abilities. Maybe he trusts your judgment more than that of the priests in his cathedral chapter."

"If he's giving me this kind of responsibility," said Joachim gloomily, "I'm afraid he may even be thinking of *making* me a member of the cathedral chapter."

I sat up abruptly. This gloom I could understand. "But if he did, you'd have to leave Yurt! How could you bear to leave the king and queen and the little prince?"

His huge dark eyes were turned toward me, but did not seem to see me. "That's not the real issue. The issue is that I know I am not worthy of such an honor."

"Wait a minute," I said. "I don't understand. Why would it be such an honor to be a cathedral priest? I thought you had been one already."

Joachim looked at me soberly. "You really don't know how the church works, do you?"

"Not me! We wizards prefer to have as little to do as possible with the details of organized religion." If I had been the chaplain, I would have rolled my eyes at me. So far, I had never managed to make Joachim roll his eyes, but I still had hopes.

"I'll explain it to you again," he said patiently. "I went from the seminary where I was trained, two kingdoms away from here, to the cathedral of Caelrhon, the cathedral that also serves Yurt. The bishop who headed my seminary knew the bishop here and recommended me to him. Young priests are always sent away from the dioceses where they are trained."

"I already knew that," I said promptly.

"But I was never a member of the cathedral chapter, just one of the many young priests attached to the church. Only the most senior and spiritual priests of the diocese are chosen to join the chapter."

"But the bishop of Caelrhon appointed you Royal Chaplain," I objected. "Isn't that more of an honor than being a priest in his cathedral chapter?"

His eyes became intense and distant again, no chance now of getting him to roll them. "To serve the cathedral is a much greater honor and a much greater responsibility. As chaplain, I am only responsible for the souls of the royal court, but the bishop and his cathedral chapter must mediate between God and all the people of the twin kingdoms of Yurt and Caelrhon. I fear I do not have a heart and mind pure enough to take on such a burden."

I wanted to ask who did, in that case, but he went on without giving me a chance.

"And at the same time as I think this, I am filled with doubt, whether it is only my pride that even makes me imagine the bishop has such a plan. If I were truly humble, I would take the duties God sends me without worrying either about a possible promotion or my ability to carry out those duties."

"So leaving Yurt wouldn't bother you," I said, highly irritated. To me, having Joachim leave the kingdom permanently would be almost as bad as having the royal family leave. Apparently he saw it differently. "All that bothers you is some moral dilemma."

Now his eyes did focus on me again. "I shouldn't have tried to explain it to you," he said stiffly. "I should have realized a wizard wouldn't appreciate moral concerns."

The bird had stopped singing. We resaddled our horses and rode on toward the count's castle.

"It runs like a rabbit," the count told us as we ate dinner. So far, I thought, this did not sound like a particularly frightening magical creature. The count was a little younger than the king, but not by much. He had the same wispy white hair, but otherwise was built very differently, being round and jolly-looking. "But it's much bigger than a rabbit—closer to the size of a fox, or even a small hound."

"So you've seen it?" I asked, setting down my fork.

"I saw it yesterday, just once," the count said, "but my men have seen it several times in the last two days. It has, how can I describe this, an *unfinished* appearance. It moves awkwardly, almost as though it was about to fall apart. But the strangest thing about it," he paused and I felt a cold finger touch the back of my neck, "is that instead of rabbits' ears, it has horns."

"*Horns?*"

"That's right. Long, straight horns. Almost like a young sheep."

I caught Joachim's eye across the table. He frowned as though wondering if this could be something diabolical.

"And don't forget to tell him about the strange sound it makes," said the countess.

"What kind of sound?"

The count hesitated. "A strange sound. Not like you'd expect a rabbit to make, even a horned rabbit. It sounded almost more like an owl." He turned slightly pink, then smiled half-apologetically. "I'll make the sound for you." He raised his hands to his mouth and gave a long, low hoot. An awkward cross between a rabbit, a sheep, and an owl should have seemed funny, but somehow it didn't.

"What has it done so far?" I asked.

"Well," said the count slowly, "it hasn't actually *done* anything. A little girl said she saw it late yesterday afternoon, heading east, up toward the high plateau. If she was right, we may not see it again. But I don't like it. It's not right for strange unnatural creatures to roam around the land of men."

"Don't call it unnatural," I said absently. "Magic is a perfectly natural force. But I do agree with you on the key point," I continued more forcibly. "I don't like

it either. Great horned rabbits don't belong here. I've
never heard of one before, and if I had, I would have
expected it to be thousands of miles north of here, up
in the land of dragons and wild magic. Modern wizardry usually tries to keep such creatures there."

"I hope you don't mind," said the count, again apol-
ogetic, "but since I wasn't sure if you'd be able to
come right away—"

"Yes?" I prompted when he hesitated.

"At the same time as I sent you a message, I also
sent one to the duchess. I thought perhaps she could
help us hunt the horned rabbit." The duchess, whose
castle was about five miles from the old count's, was
a noted huntress. "She sent a message back that she
would be here tomorrow. I'd hoped she and her
huntsmen could find its trail and track it up onto the
plateau, or wherever it's gone."

Joachim had said nothing so far, but he suddenly
put in, with a look toward me, "I'm going to the high
plateau tomorrow myself."

"Good," I said. "We'll go together. While you talk
to the hermit, I'll search for this magical horned rabbit
there. A wood nymph's grove might even attract it. At
the same time, the duchess and her hunters can be
looking for its trail down here. Between all of us, we
should catch it."

IV

In the early morning, the high plateau was half hidden by mist, but the sun rising behind it gave the rows
of trees against the sky a halo of light. When the
count's stable boy led our horses into the courtyard, I
saw at once that he had switched the harnesses. The
rangy bay Joachim had been riding had the correct
saddle, but its bridle had bells, whereas my old white
mare had no bells.

Joachim did not actually become angry; he never

did. "I'm a priest and a representative of the cathedral," he said. "I can't go visit a hermit while riding a horse with bells," and he proceeded to lengthen the stirrups on my mare.

"Wait a minute, Father, I can change the bridles," said the mortified stable boy.

"It's not your fault," the chaplain said quietly. "I have no time to wait, but think no more of it." His long legs reaching well below the mare's belly, he rode out through the gates while I scrambled up on the bay, hastily tugged up the stirrups, and hurried to catch him.

We rode in silence, through a woods where dark pines stood tall on either hand, then slowly up and out of the pines as the road ascended toward the plateau. Our horses were breathing hard when we emerged at the top.

Joachim pulled the mare over to the side to rest and sat stroking her mane. Here the wind blew across pastures thick with wild flowers. A mile away, I could see a group of brown and white cows and a stone barn, but otherwise we seemed to have the plateau to ourselves. In the bright sun and air, it did not seem the place for a great horned rabbit.

It also did not seem a place to be quarreling with the chaplain. "We'll want to rest the horses for a few minutes anyway," I said. "Why don't we change the harnesses now?"

He turned his dark eyes on me, then unexpectedly smiled, a genuine smile that worked its way up from his mouth to his cheekbones and eyebrows. "You're right," he said. "I'm being both silly and stubborn." He swung down off the mare. "I wanted to arrive early at the hermitage, but fifteen minutes isn't going to make any difference. Let's give the horses a rest, and I can tell you what we're likely to find."

Whether the chaplain felt he needed a wizard's protection against the horned rabbit or he was worried about the wood nymph, I was pleased he might still want the company of someone who didn't appreciate moral issues.

But he hesitated for a moment before beginning. "As you may know," he said at last, "there is a deep limestone valley cut into this plateau. The hermitage is located in a grove at the upper end, where the valley's river is born. I visited it once when I first came to Yurt, before you became Royal Wizard. The hermitage is also a shrine, sacred to the memory of Saint Eusebius." He paused for a long look at me. "Did you ever hear of Saint Eusebius of Yurt?"

I shook my head. Wizards don't learn very much about saints.

"I know you," he said slowly, "so I feel I should warn you. There's a special relic of the saint at the shrine, and the hermit will not appreciate it if you laugh at the relic."

"But why should I laugh at a relic?" I protested.

"Because," he answered, almost reluctantly, "because it's the saint's big toe." He had turned away, but for a moment, I half imagined he might find this funny himself.

"The saint's big *toe*? But what happened to the rest of the saint?"

"Eusebius was eaten by a dragon," said Joachim, looking at me as soberly as if it had never occurred to him that a saint's toe could be amusing.

"When was this?" I was amazed that I had never heard the story.

"It must be," he hesitated as though calculating, "a good fifteen hundred years ago, long before the kingdom of Yurt or the rest of the western kingdoms even existed, back in the latter days of the Empire." That explained why I had never heard of Saint Eusebius; I had never been strong on history, especially ancient history.

The morning sun shone on our heads, and what looked like a hawk soared high above. It was hard to believe in either saints or dragons—or, for that matter, in great horned rabbits—on a lovely June day like this.

"Saint Eusebius himself was living in the grove, then," Joachim continued. "He lived alone, spending his days in devotion and contemplation. But when a dragon appeared up on the plateau and started eating the people's flocks, he felt he had to do something."

"He should have called on a wizard," I provided. "I know there were wizards, even back then."

Other than giving me a quick look, he paid no attention to my interruption. "Saint Eusebius took his crucifix and went to face the dragon, to command it in the name of Christ to leave the area."

"But, Joachim, you know that wouldn't work. It might work with a demon, but dragons aren't inherently evil, just magic."

It was harder this time for him to ignore my interruption, but he managed. "Inspired by the devil, the dragon began to eat the holy man. But a desperate group of peasants had banded together, armed with spears and meat hooks. When the dragon tried to swallow the saint, it miraculously began to gag and choke on him. While the dragon was thus occupied, the peasants burst out of hiding and attacked it. One of them got in a lucky stroke with a meat hook and pierced the dragon's throat at the one spot where it was vulnerable."

He paused as though the horror of it were almost too much. "But they were too late to save Saint Eusebius. All that remained of him was his left big toe."

I felt rather proud that I did not even smile. "And so they preserved the relic at the hermitage where he had lived," I said, "and subsequent generations of hermits have succeeded Eusebius there ever since. Is that it? But what do you have to investigate *now*?"

"Saint Eusebius was always a rather, well, difficult—if holy—man, even while he was alive. Now, fifteen hundred years after his death, some say he's a difficult saint."

"What do you mean, difficult?"

"Well," said Joachim after an almost imperceptible pause, "here's an example. A lady, a very lovely and vain one, went to his shrine to pray for help in overcoming her faults. The saint began with her vanity, by putting a giant wart on her nose."

I could see the problem. What was the church supposed to do when the forces of good turned out to be a real pain?

Joachim hurried on without waiting for a response. "His, uh, difficult nature is why the bishop sent me here. Certain priests, in a church two hundred miles from here, have written to the bishop. They say that Eusebius appeared to them in a vision, saying that he was 'fed up' with having his relics at this shrine, and that he wanted his toe to be preserved at *their* church."

Although a saint who induced giant warts had seemed to have promising possibilities, the situation now sounded like the confusing and dangerous churchly concerns they used to warn us against at the wizards' school. "If he's been dead so long, why does it matter where his toe is?" I asked irritably.

Joachim answered with infuriating patience. "The saints are still here with us on earth at the same time as they are in heaven. Even you must know that."

"But why would priests in a distant city want an old dead saint's toe anyway?"

Joachim sighed. "This may be hard for you to understand. Their church, the church where Eusebius originally made his profession, has wanted his relics for fifteen hundred years. He was a priest in their city, the son I believe of a provincial administrator under the empire, before he came to this valley to become a hermit."

A city boy like me, I thought, or at least like I used to be.

"After the saint was martyred," Joachim continued, "the priests there rededicated their church in his name."

"But that was all so long ago!"

Joachim shook his head with the air of someone who had known all along that I wouldn't understand. "Individuals forget and individuals die. But churches are undying institutions and they never forget." He took a deep breath. "But you don't need to worry about either the saint or the hermit who lives there now. That's my responsibility. I want you to worry about the wood nymph."

He stood up and took the offending bridle with bells off his horse. In a few moments, with our harnesses where they should be and the stirrups readjusted, we continued on across the plateau.

In another mile, the road turned abruptly to the left. Ahead of us was a low stone wall. Rather than turning, Joachim rode his bay up to the wall. "Look at this."

Although one could not see it until almost on top of it, before us was a narrow and very deep valley. I pulled my mare's head up more sharply than necessary when I realized we were standing at the very edge of a cliff, with only the low wall between us and an abrupt drop. The morning mists still lingered below in the shadow of the valley walls. Beneath the vertical white cliffs, an intensely green valley curved away, a narrow river rushing down its center.

"Directly below us," said Joachim, pointing downward, "hidden by those trees, is the hermitage, built at the source of the river. There is a direct path down or, I should rather say, steps cut into the cliff just a little farther along, but the road itself takes two more miles to get down to the valley floor." Off to our left, at a spot where the cliffs were not quite so steep, I could see the white line of the road winding its way sharply down into the valley, appearing and disappearing among the beeches.

Joachim shook his horse's reins and started along the road. I followed after one more look down. I could have flown down myself easily enough, but I would not want to try it carrying the mare.

We had gone less than a hundred yards when Joachim stopped again, pulling up the reins so hard that his normally gentle bay half reared and gave a protesting whinney. Wondering if it might be the mysterious horned rabbit, I hurried my horse to join him, then stared with equal surprise.

Before us was a little wooden booth. No one was inside, but a large brightly colored sign proclaimed, "See the Holy Toe! Five pennies on foot, fifteen pennies in the basket."

I was trying to work out what this could mean, if perhaps whoever had painted the sign was offering us a chance to see the holy toe on someone else's foot, and why a toe in a basket should be more valuable, when there was movement under a nearby tree. A young man in a feathered cap stood up and came out from the shadows.

"Greetings, my fine gentlemen!" he said in the hearty tones of someone manning a booth at a fair. "Are you here to see the Holy Toe of Saint Eusebius the Cranky? I'm afraid we don't have the basket ready quite yet, but if you want to go down on foot, it's not a bad climb—and cheaper, too!"

Joachim dismounted and looked sternly at him. "So you're charging people just for the privilege of climbing down the cliff to the Holy Grove?"

The man gave a start, as though feeling the impact of the chaplain's eyes, but he recovered almost immediately. "Excuse me, Father, I didn't notice your vestments at first. If you're worried that we're restricting access to the relics, you needn't be; people can still go around by the road for free. We're just providing an extra service."

"Charging them to climb down the steps is an extra service?"

"Ah, but we've improved the path!" said the man proudly. "And our *real* service is going to be the basket. As I said, we don't have it ready quite yet, but we should in a few weeks."

"What *is* this basket?" I asked.

The man looked at me properly for the first time. "Excuse me," he said with a delighted smile, "but are you a wizard? You are? This is wonderful! You have no idea how much we'd been hoping to be able to attract a wizard.

"You see," he went on, "the basket is all very well, but it would be so much better if we could have a wizard working with us. Wouldn't it be more exciting and appealing to have people carried up and down the cliff by magic than lowered in a big basket at the end of a pulley? I'm sure we could charge more, too. We'd give you a fair cut of the profits; you needn't worry about that. You wouldn't even need to be here! Just set up the spell and teach us how to keep it working and we'll do the rest."

There were so many things wrong with his assumptions I scarcely knew where to begin. "I'm afraid a spell to lower people down the cliff couldn't just be 'set up' and then kept working with no wizard here," I said at last.

He looked thoughtful. "That might be a problem. But maybe you'd prefer to be here yourself, at least during the summer months when business will be best! I'm sure this will be enormously profitable once word gets out. Do you have a post at the moment?"

"I'm Royal Wizard of the kingdom of Yurt," I said gravely, "and this is the Royal Chaplain. I don't need any extra income."

The man was taken aback for a moment, but he seemed to have quick powers of recovery. "Well, then, maybe you know some other wizard who might be interested. Or maybe you'd even like to lend a hand yourself when the king doesn't need you! I should put the proposition up to him myself, explain that this will really make Yurt a well-known place, not just a novelty as one of the smallest of the western kingdoms."

"We'll take the road down to the Holy Grove," said Joachim, abruptly swinging back up into the saddle.

"But I haven't even had a chance yet to tell you about all our souvenirs, Father!" the man said eagerly. "As you can see, we're not quite ready for business yet, but in the next week or two we hope to have reproductions of the Holy Toe itself, figurines of a dragon—children always like things like that—and booklets telling of the life and miracles of the Cranky Saint."

Joachim's shoulders stiffened into rigidity, but he made no answer. Instead he kicked his horse sharply into a trot. I was right behind him. The man in the feathered cap waved cheerfully after us.

After three-quarters of a mile, as the road left the level plateau and began its steep descent toward the valley floor, I had suppressed silent laugher enough that I dared ask a question. Even for me, originally the son of a city merchant, this seemed to have gone much too far. "Had you known about all this?"

"The bishop made a brief reference to 'some inappropriate activities' at the site," said Joachim, looking straight ahead. "But I hadn't realized it was this bad. No wonder Saint Eusebius wants to leave."

V

For the next twenty minutes, we had to give all our attention to our horses, keeping them at a slow walk as the steep road wound and twisted its way down the side of the valley. The road leveled out at last and we rode back toward the grove at the head of the valley, parallel to the road we had followed at the top of the cliffs. There were some stone huts near the road, but we saw no people. A few goats, feeding in the meadows along the merrily running stream, lifted their heads to look at us in surprise—apparently travelers to the Holy Grove were not all that frequent. The air was fresh and cool, the valley and the trees intensely lovely.

"Can't you, as the bishop's representative, just make them stop?" I ventured at last.

Joachim shook his head. "As long as they do not impede the free access of the faithful to the Holy Grove and the saint's relics, they're not actually doing anything sinful. It's shameful, of course, to be trying to make money from Saint Eusebius as though he were a two-headed calf at a fair, but it isn't evil or even against church law. But if the saint was 'fed up' to begin with, this must make him furious."

He shot me a quick, worried glance. "I'd assumed that we, the bishop and I, would try to persuade those priests two hundred miles away that they had no right to the saint's holy relics. Now I'm not so sure. And it may be difficult to break that news to the hermit."

As we rode, the sound of rushing water became louder and louder in front of us. We came around a corner to see a waterfall, white water splashing in the sunlight. Long grass and dark green ferns festooned the edges of the falls.

At the top of the falls I could see a small level area, dense with trees. Beyond the trees, the white cliff face rose abruptly. My eyes traveled to the top. That was where we had stood looking down; the cliff appeared even higher and steeper from below than it had from above.

Looking to the right, I was able to spot the steps that had been cut into the cliff for a quicker descent than we and the horses had taken. They were still little more than toeholds in spite of the entrepreneurs' "improvements." Here, presumably, was where they were planning to set up a pulley and a basket to lower the pious, if less agile, pilgrim and the adventurous tourist.

"If you don't mind," said Joachim, "I'd like to introduce you to the hermit. He and I will have a lot to discuss after that, but you might be interested in trying to find the wood nymph."

We tied our horses' reins to a branch and scrambled up a steep track at the side of the waterfall. At the top, the stream emerged from the dark shadow of a grove of trees. We continued along its edge, ducking our heads where the branches swung low. Here, the water course widened into a swirling pool. In a few more yards, I saw what seemed to be a stone hut, like those we had seen further down the valley.

But I was more interested in the river. When Joachim had spoken of its source, I had visualized a spring where water gurgled up from the earth, and I was wondering how the river could carry so much water and so rapidly. I went a little further, with Joachim following, and then spotted the real source.

The river did not gurgle up from the earth but rather poured out of the face of the cliff. A cave mouth, only a few feet high but at least twenty feet broad, opened in the limestone, and the water boiled from it. A faint but steady wind accompanied the rushing river. After emerging and making a quick eddy under the branches of the grove, the water rushed over the edge of the falls and disappeared down the valley.

"Has anyone ever gone into the cave to follow the river back further?" I asked. There seemed to be a low, damp ledge along one side of the river, along which it might be possible to walk or crawl.

"I don't think so. The cave's too small and there's too much water," said Joachim absently. We walked back to the stone hut and he went down on one knee before it, dropping his head reverently.

I saw then that it was not merely a hut, but that the side toward us contained a stone altar, only partially protected from the elements by protruding stone walls. Next to the rough wooden crucifix on the altar was a reliquary, a shining box where the saint's relics would be kept. From where I stood, it looked as though it was made of pure gold. It was indubitably made in the shape of a giant toe.

I hung back, having no intention of going down on my knees before the preserved toe of a long-dead saint who had not even had the sense to ask a wizard for help against a dragon.

Joachim rose again after a minute. At the same time, I caught a flicker of motion in the shadows beyond the hut. I turned toward it quickly, hoping it was the great horned rabbit—or, even better, the wood nymph.

Instead, it was an old man in a coarse brown robe that reached to his ankles. Below the robe, his feet were bare; I noticed that he himself had very large and horny toes.

This, then, was the hermit. My eyes had become adjusted to the dim light in the grove and I could see that the hut, beyond the altar, would make an adequate shelter for someone who had deliberately given up comfort. The old hermit had a ropy beard that reached nearly to his knees and a beatific smile that he turned on both of us.

"Greetings, my son," he said to me, and "Bless me, Father," to Joachim and knelt before him.

Joachim blessed him in evident embarrassment and helped him back to his feet. "I should rather kneel to you, Father," he said. "Priests who are busy with the sins and affairs of the world have much to learn from hermits whose days are spent in contemplation and prayer."

The hermit looked at him more closely. "You're the Royal Chaplain, aren't you? I thought I recognized you."

Joachim beckoned to me. "Let me present Daimbert, Royal Wizard of Yurt and my close friend."

Mollified at being called the chaplain's close friend, I made the hermit the full formal bow, first the dipping of the head, then the widespread arms, finishing by dropping to both knees. I reassured myself that to kneel in this way to a living holy hermit, as a wizard might to a superior wizard or to his king, would not be a discredit to the position of institutionalized magic. Besides, Joachim looked pleased.

"Have you come to see the wood nymph?" the hermit asked me. I rose and met his eyes. I had somehow expected them to be distant and dreamy, but they were surprisingly sharp under long, shaggy eyebrows.

"That's right," I said, deciding not to worry him with the horned rabbit.

"It's those poor souls up on the top of the cliff who are worrying you?" the hermit asked Joachim with another smile.

"That and a letter the bishop has received." I could hear the unease in the chaplain's voice and realized that the hermit must not yet know that certain priests were insisting the Holy Toe be taken two hundred miles from his grove. Since I didn't particularly want to be there when he received the news, I excused myself as they sat down on mossy stones beside the pool.

The area around the pool itself, next to the shrine, seemed an unlikely place to find a nymph, but the grove stretched further along the bottom of the cliff. I walked slowly on spongy soil, following slightly drier paths marked with rows of tiny white stones. Here, there did seem to be several springs of the sort I had originally expected, sending smaller trickles of water to join the larger stream.

I picked my way across an especially muddy patch of ground and looked up. A young woman stood directly before me, carefully trimming dead twigs from a small tree.

It took only the briefest glance to realize that this was not some local village girl.

She turned toward me. Her face was perfectly still, with the intense beauty of a pastoral landscape. She leaned back against the pale trunk of a beech, one arm stretched above her head, and watched me with no apparent expression. Her only clothes were a few strategically placed leaves. Her skin and her hair were dusky, the color of shadows deep within the woods, and her eyes a brilliant violet. Her unbound hair, which hung to her waist, looked incredibly soft.

"Excuse me," I faltered. "I didn't mean to disturb you. I'm the Royal Wizard of Yurt. Are you the wood nymph of this grove?"

She moved her head slightly, neither nodding in affirmation nor denying it.

"I'd been hoping to meet you," I pushed on. My heart began beating rapidly and I felt much more flustered than I should have. Still she did not answer.

"Have you lived here long?" I asked inanely.

This time, she did more than not answer. She disappeared. One second she was standing before me, and the next she was gone. It seemed as though she might have slipped quickly around the tree, but when I looked, there was no one behind it. I glanced up. Far above me, I saw for one second a motion that might have been the leaves on the tree or might have been a swift form among the branches.

I spent the next fifteen minutes walking through the grove, seeing all the little upwellings of water and all the smooth-trunked trees, but no more sign of the nymph.

I returned to where Joachim and the hermit were sitting. "But the saint often appears to me," the hermit was saying to the chaplain with a pleasant smile. "I know some people have nicknamed him 'the Cranky Saint,' but I have always been blessed by seeing his gentle side. He came to this grove originally, as a young hermit, because he wanted to put the city behind him. And he's never told me he wanted to leave."

I continued past them, following the path back down along the waterfall to where we had left the horses. They were grazing industriously, unbothered by entrepreneurs, saints or nymphs.

I reached into my saddlebag and pulled out the packet of lunch the count's cook had prepared for us, not so much because I was hungry, as because eating would give me time to consider.

There was more happening here, I could sense, than I had yet been told. Negotiating with a holy old hermit who, from his demeanor, might be declared a saint himself one day, and finding a way to deal with souvenir sellers who might not be doing anything illegal but who still seemed scandalous, even to me, could turn out to be more serious responsibilities than I had originally thought. Joachim might well be right that the bishop was testing him to see if he was the sort of priest they wanted in the cathedral chapter.

I didn't like this any more than the chaplain did, although for different reasons, but right now I had responsibilities of my own which I'd been neglecting. To maintain the good name of wizardry, I should set about finding and coping with the strange magical creature the count and his men had seen.

As I strapped up my saddlebag, I caught a glimpse of motion from the corner of my eye and turned slowly.

And there were *two* of the creatures, the size of small dogs but shaped like rabbits. My first hope was that they were some bizarre illusion, but they were very real. They came hopping awkwardly along the edge of the stream, ignoring my presence. Rather than ears, they had long, pointed horns.

I stepped back involuntarily. Instead of broad rabbits' teeth, they had protruding fangs, and instead of wide, placid rabbit eyes, they had small, red nasty eyes. And those horns looked sharp.

One flicked its red eyes toward me and gave a much higher hop. At the same time, it emitted a cry—a low, hooting sound, almost like an owl. The other creature responded with the same cry. Both redoubled their speed, made a sharp turn and disappeared rapidly across the meadow toward the base of the cliff.

I stood idiotically, just watching them go. The count had only spoken of one great horned rabbit, not of two. They looked so ridiculous that I felt I ought to laugh. But that hooting, haunting call had stifled any laugh within me.

I shook my head hard. I should be trying to catch them, not staring after them. I hurried across the meadow, putting together a probing spell to help me find them.

As soon as I opened myself to it, I found that the valley was thick with magic, making it virtually impossible to probe for anything. Most of the magic seemed unfocused, which meant that it was wild, unchanneled by wizardry. And yet— Somewhere behind me, in the grove, I thought I could sense the presence of a powerful spell.

I clenched my jaw. This was even worse than I had thought. If the rabbits were the product of that spell, then they were not magical creatures from the land of dragons, which would have been bad enough, but rather the creations of a renegade wizard. Since neither of the counts nor the duchess kept a wizard and my predecessor was retired, I was, I had thought, the only active wizard in Yurt.

As I started back toward the grove, I hesitated again. This was not where I had seen the rabbits disappear. How many of them might there be?

When I came back into the grove, the denseness of magical forces made me lose track of the spell that had seemed so strong a moment ago. I walked swiftly along the little paths between the springs, without seeing anything but trees. But then something caught my eye in the muddy earth.

It was a footprint, about the size of a man's foot, even roughly the right shape, but somehow wrong. I knelt down for a closer look, but I already knew. That print had been made by nothing human.

PART TWO
The Young Wizard

I

Back at the shrine, Joachim and the hermit were still talking. I hesitated, not liking to mention the wood nymph before the hermit, and certainly not wanting to terrify him with the horned rabbits or that inhuman footprint.

But the hermit beckoned me to join them. "Your chaplain's been trying to tell me that Saint Eusebius has appeared to some priests in a vision, asking to leave the grove, but I'm sure they're mistaken. Perhaps they are not aware of the miracle that occurred only a year after the saint's death."

I sat down at the hermit's feet, willing to listen while waiting for my mind to come up with better ideas than I had now.

"You've doubtless heard that a reliquary was made immediately after the saint's death," continued the hermit, "to contain all of his mortal remains that had not been eaten by the dragon. You *do* know about the dragon?"

"Yes, I know that story."

37

He smiled approvingly. "One sometimes hears that wizards are too dismissive toward concerns of the church, or even laugh at them, but I've never felt that myself."

I tried not to meet either his eyes or Joachim's.

"And so for a year," the hermit continued, "the holy toe was peacefully kept here, at a shrine built onto the side of the little hermitage where the saint had spent his days—in fact, this very hermitage where I now live. One of Eusebius's pupils lived there as a hermit in obedience to his master's precepts.

"But one day three priests arrived in the grove. They said they had come from the church where Eusebius had originally been made a priest and that they intended to take his holy relics back with them! The young hermit, as you can imagine, almost went mad with despair. He fell on his face in the mud before the shrine and begged Saint Eusebius, his old master, not to leave him.

"And the saint heard his prayer. For when the three priests tried to lift the reliquary, they found it so heavy they could not budge it. They went for a block and tackle and tried again, but they themselves were hurled into the pool from the strain. And yet when the young hermit lifted the reliquary, it was as light as a feather in his hand. And thus the saint showed that he wanted to stay here, rather than going back to the city he had purposely left behind him. And after all these centuries, after generations of hermits of which I am the last and the least worthy, he has not changed his mind."

I nodded, impressed in spite of myself.

"As I already told you," Joachim said quietly, "he seems to have changed his mind now. The letter the bishop received said that the saint was 'fed up' with having his relics here."

The hermit turned his smile on the chaplain. "Excuse me, Father, if I tend to discount the testimony of priests who spend their days on secular concerns. I'm sure they mistook his meaning. I realize the saint expresses himself forcibly at times—and error must always be rebuked firmly, as our Lord showed when He drove the money-changers from the Temple—but when he has appeared to me, it has always been with a gentle face and a willingness to be my guide."

"Then I'll tell this to the bishop," said Joachim, rising to his feet. I was glad of the excuse to stand up as well; the damp moss on which I was sitting had started soaking through my trousers.

After the chaplain and the hermit exchanged final expressions of esteem and reverence, we picked our way back down the steep path by the waterfall to where we had left the horses. I surreptitiously looked for footprints in the mud and saw none but our own.

"Will this settle it?" I asked. "Will the priests who wanted the saint's relics take the hermit's word that the saint doesn't want to leave?"

"It depends on whether the bishop takes the hermit's word for it," said Joachim distractedly. He pulled the lunch out of his saddlebag and started eating, but not as though he tasted it. "Did you find the wood nymph, then?"

"I found her and even tried to speak to her, but she wouldn't answer."

"That's something else the bishop was worried about. He feels that it has been a mistake having both a saint's shrine and a nymph share the same grove all these centuries. The modern church needs to eradicate all remnants of superstition, and the uneducated may find it a stumbling block to their faith if they come to worship God and His saints and find themselves in the realm of a wood nymph."

"Especially one as lovely as she is," I provided.

Joachim gave me a quick look. "I think the bishop knows better than that," he said, answering a question I had not directly asked. "There has never been the least doubt about the moral purity of this hermit—or any of his predecessors. But wood nymphs, as I understand it, are immortal and, thus, they are outside of the human drama of sin and salvation."

And so, I thought, was whatever had made that footprint.

Joachim hesitated for a moment before continuing. "I've mentioned before," he said at last, "that the bishop is very uneasy about my friendship with a wizard. But I wrote him that, in this case, it could be advantageous to have access to someone who might be able to influence a nymph. Therefore," with a sideways glance from his enormous eyes, "I do hope you can do something."

I said nothing for a moment but thought about this. The bishop seemed to have issued the chaplain a veiled threat: Either I proved my ability and willingness to help the church or else the bishop would pressure Joachim to end our friendship. I thought of suggesting that if the bishop became angry with him, then he could stop worrying about being asked to join the cathedral chapter, but decided this would push him too far.

Instead I said, "I'll try my best, but it may be hard if the nymph won't even talk to me. I'll want to consult my books back at the royal castle, perhaps talk to my predecessor about her, and maybe even telephone the wizards' school. They don't want young wizards calling them up with every little problem, but if my books don't give me much help, I may have no choice."

Joachim had started to mount his horse, but he seemed to hear something in my voice I had not meant him to hear. He swung back down and looked at me. "I'm sorry. I was thinking of the need to get back to the count's castle, to send the bishop a message by the pigeons immediately. But he can wait a little while longer. What's really bothering you about the wood nymph?"

"It's not the nymph," I said. "It's something else I saw." And I told him about the horned rabbits, the footprint that was almost, but not quite, a man's, and the strange sense of renegade spells lurking amid the magic of the valley.

"So I know now the horned rabbits aren't creatures from the land of wild magic," I finished. "It looks as though someone took dead rabbits, attached sheeps' horns, and then, I don't know how, brought them back to life. Some wizard must have made them. But my predecessor and I are the only wizards in the kingdom."

"Do you think the old wizard's practicing black magic?" asked Joachim quietly.

"I don't know *what* to think," I said in despair. "I'll have to go talk to him at once. He would have been almost the last person I'd suspect of dealing with the powers of darkness, but if he's able to create life, he's gotten supernatural help from somewhere."

Joachim nodded thoughtfully. "That's the shortcoming of wizardry, isn't it. Because it's a natural power, you can't use unaided magic to alter the earth's natural cycle of birth and death."

"But why would he do it?" I burst out. "He's retired, he doesn't have to prove anything to anyone any more."

"When he decided to retire, back before you came to Yurt, he told all of us that he wanted to spend more time on his research. Maybe this is what he's been researching."

"I still can't understand it," I said gloomily, catching Joachim's intense gaze for a second and looking away again. "He knows as well as anyone the perils of dealing with the forces of evil."

"Do you want me to talk to him?"

I actually considered this for a moment. It was certainly appealing to contemplate someone else going down to the little green house at the edge of the woods to confront my cantankerous predecessor. But he had never liked Joachim; "young whippersnapper" was about his most flattering term for the chaplain.

"I'm afraid he wouldn't say anything to you," I said. "It will have to be me."

"But isn't it my duty, as Royal Chaplain, to talk to someone who might be imperiling his soul?"

This was the difficulty of having a conversation with Joachim. Sooner or later I always ran up against the fact that he was a priest. I shook my head. "This is a magical problem."

"Then let's get under way."

We had ridden only a short distance down the valley when a young man suddenly ran out from behind the trees toward us. Between the nymph and the great horned rabbits, my ability to see sudden motion without jerking convulsively was limited.

Joachim, however, reined in and turned calmly toward the young man. "What is it, my son?"

He was very young, not much more than a boy. His head was shaved and he wore scraps of rough, dark cloth held together by safety pins. He dropped on his knees before the chaplain, holding up clasped hands. "Oh, Father, please forgive me, and please tell me. Are you going to take our holy master from us?"

"The hermit?" said Joachim in surprise. "I have no intention of taking him from you. Why did you think I might?"

The young man flushed but pushed on determinedly. I noticed, back under the trees near the stone huts, several others with shaved heads watching warily from a distance. "Ever since those people built their booth at the top of the cliff, we've feared that someone from the cathedral would be here sooner or later," he said breathlessly.

"At least for now," said the chaplain gently, "I see no reason why the hermit should leave Saint Eusebius's shrine, at least until God summons him home."

The boy's face was transformed by a sudden smile. "Thank you, thank you!" He jumped up and ran like a deer back into the trees. As we turned back down the valley, I could see him and the other ragged young men talking excitedly.

Apprentice hermits, I thought. Wizards, too, used

to be trained as apprentices. It would have been hard enough being trained under my predecessor; these young men's apprenticeship must be made even more difficult by the fact that a hermit rarely speaks to anyone, including his apprentices.

Joachim suddenly seemed to remember he was in a hurry to send the bishop a message. He slapped his legs against his horse's flanks and, in a moment, the apprentices were far behind. We rode at a trot until the road started the steep climb out of the valley.

"What do you think?" I asked as our horses slowed to a walk. "Is it just coincidence that the entrepreneurs decided to set up their booth at precisely the same time as somebody wrote the bishop to ask for Eusebius's toe? And why do you think they don't have their basket or their souvenirs ready yet?"

Joachim looked at me sharply, but the ghost of a smile was on his lips. "You have a suspicious mind," he said. "I thought of it, too. Since Eusebius is widely considered to be a, well, troublesome saint, one could suspect that those priests in the distant city thought the easiest way to get his relics was to be sure he became irritated with life in Yurt."

"Do *you* suspect it?"

"I don't know." His dark eyes grew troubled. "According to the bishop, the priests were very positive that the saint wanted to move his relics to their city, yet the hermit here is equally positive that the saint wants to remain. The difficulty is that I don't know which came first. Did Eusebius appear in a vision to the priests *after* these entrepreneurs decided to make money off him and that's why the priests have written the bishop now? Or did the priests first decide they wanted him and then tried to ensure by devious means that he'd be happy to go?"

"We'd better speak again to the man at the booth," I said. "We'll find out how recently they set up and if they really plan to put in this elaborate basket-on-a-pulley contraption—it sounds horribly dangerous to me, I must say. If the talk of baskets and souvenirs is no more than talk, then we'll know it's only a façade, designed to make the saint angry."

But when we reached the top and rode back along the rim of the valley, we did not see the man in the feathered cap. The sign on the empty booth still invited us to see the Holy Toe.

"I hope I can get my whole message to the bishop on a small enough piece of paper," said Joachim.

II

We came over a rise and saw the count's castle before us, its shadow stretching long over the grassy meadows around it. As soon as we were inside the walls, the chaplain hurried up to the pigeon loft in the tower to send his message.

The count's constable took our horses and the count came out to meet me with his jolly smile. "Did you even get up onto the plateau, or did you spend all your time tracking the horned rabbit?"

"I saw the horned rabbit, or rather two of them, in the valley cut into the plateau," I said, puzzled.

His smile dropped away. "That means there are at least three of them. I'd hoped there was only the one. Almost immediately after you left, one of my men reported seeing a great horned rabbit just west of here and we spent several hours, without success, trying to pick up its trail. We were actually rather surprised not to see you there, too, because we'd assumed you would have spotted it."

The expression, "multiplying like rabbits," flitted through my mind, but it seemed best not to say it.

Joachim returned from the tower. "It took three pigeons for my whole message to the bishop," he said. He looked relieved. He did have one advantage over me in not being a wizard, though I wasn't going to tell him this. Once he had told the bishop about his visit to the Holy Grove, it was, at least for the moment, out of his hands. But there was no one to whom I could pass the responsibility for the wood nymph, the great horned rabbits, and whatever had made that footprint.

As we came into the great hall for dinner, I saw a slim woman's figure silhouetted against the fire. She came toward me, holding out her hands to take mine. It was the Duchess Diana.

I had always liked the duchess. She had ruled in solitary splendor for over twenty-five years, ever since the old duke, her father, died when she was still a girl. When not treating my wizardly abilities with respect— something that didn't happen very often—she enjoyed teasing me as if I had been a friend's favorite younger brother.

Duchess Diana prided herself on the knowledge that a number of people considered her outrageous. She was wearing a long dress the color of marigolds, which even I could recognize as hopelessly out of fashion. She and the queen were distant cousins and had the same midnight black hair, but Diana was some ten years older. Other than their hair, the two women were very dissimilar.

"I'm delighted to see you," she said with a wide smile. "I've got a surprise for you!"

"A surprise?"

"Well, you know you've been telling me for over a year that I ought to hire my own ducal wizard. I finally decided to do so!"

"About time, my lady! How will you find one?"

"I found him by writing to your wizards' school, of course. After all, I'd met the Master of the school the other Christmas. I said that I wanted someone as much like you as possible."

"You don't really want someone like me, my lady," I began, but she wasn't listening.

"My father always kept a wizard, back when I was

little, so I decided it was high time the duchy had one again." She smiled up at me, her gray eyes dancing.

"This is very good news," I said, wondering if the school would send her one of the young wizards I knew. They would not send a wizard who had been first in his class to a post in a small ducal court, but then I had been far from first in my class myself. "What made you decide at last?"

She stopped smiling for a moment. "I think it was the baby prince. If my young cousin the queen can have a baby who'll be walking soon, I should certainly be able to set up a proper establishment myself, and the first thing I needed was my own wizard."

I was oddly reminded of Dominic. But I didn't want to worry about why the baby prince should make apparently sensible people feel discontented.

Abruptly, I found myself looking forward enormously to the arrival of the duchess' wizard. Even though Joachim and I managed to be friends much of the time, the differences between us kept coming up and always would. Another wizard would not continually be disturbed by deadly serious moral dilemmas that wouldn't bother me for a moment. And he should have more recent memories than mine of some of the lectures in the advanced courses and might have all sorts of ideas on what spells would work in the problem of the great horned rabbits. Since Diana had asked the school for someone like me, her wizard should even have a sense of humor.

"When will he be coming to Yurt?"

"That's the real surprise—here he is!"

She turned and beckoned, and someone broke away from the small group by the fire. I had assumed, without looking, they were all members of the count's court. This one was no young lord—this was a wizard.

I was struck first by his hair. It was so thoroughly auburn that it glowed nearly carrot-colored in the fire-light. His cheeks were spattered with freckles below wide-set and very light blue eyes. At first I thought he was clean-shaven, as were most wizardry students, but then I spotted a few rather half-hearted red wisps on his chin. He wore a black velvet jacket, embroidered all over with moons and stars.

"Evrard," said the duchess, "I'd like to introduce you to Daimbert, Royal Wizard of Yurt."

He turned to me with an amazed grin and wrung my hand. "You're Daimbert? Of course you are! What an honor! We learned all about how you invented the far-seeing telephone—and within just a few months of taking your first post. Let me tell you, it's a real inspiration to the rest of us!"

I smiled modestly.

"Especially you're an inspiration to all of us who've never worked very hard, because we know that you spent as much time in the city taverns as with your books. And of course, in transformations class, old Zahlfast always uses your experiences that time with the frogs as a warning!"

My smile faded.

He looked at me with his head cocked for a minute. "I knew who you were—or thought I did—when you were still at school, even though I'm not sure I ever talked to you. But I don't know if I would have recognized you now. You look a lot older than the person I thought I remembered."

"I remember sometimes seeing you in the halls," I said, "but I'm afraid that's it. You probably don't recognize me because of the white beard."

He tugged in disgust at one of the wisps on his own chin. "Your beard looks very wizardly. Mine is coming in red, so I'm afraid I'm going to look more like a bandit than a wizard. If it ever grows in, maybe I'll try bleaching mine, too."

My hair and beard were, in fact, not bleached; they had turned white overnight, six months after I first came to Yurt, but I didn't want to go into that rather harrowing episode now. "How is Zahlfast?" I asked instead.

"Doing fine. He and the rest of the teachers always seem to be above the problems and the worries of all the students. He warned me, which I'd expected, that I was on my own now, that I couldn't expect the school to come help me with 'every little problem.' He did ask to be remembered to you and said you'd probably see him later this summer."

Every year or so, one of the teachers would visit the young wizards at their posts throughout the western kingdoms. With luck, I would be able to present Zahlfast, when he arrived, with a tidy solution to the problem of the great horned rabbits.

"You know," Evrard continued, "I've always rather liked old Zahlfast, but after what happened to me in the transformations practical, I didn't dare meet his eye for the rest of the semester." In spite of being highly curious about what had happened to *him*, I didn't dare ask for fear he'd allude to the frogs again and in more detail. "Therefore, I was shocked when he called me in to tell me he had a post for me—I'd been afraid he was going to tell me the school had decided to take my diploma back!"

We both laughed. "But I *did* pay more attention in my classes this last year," continued Evrard. "Did you know, Elerius came back to teach a course?"

"Elerius? You mean they've put him on the faculty *already*?" Elerius, three years ahead of me, was generally rumored to have been the best student the school had ever had.

"No, no, he's still Royal Wizard in that big kingdom way off at the base of the eastern mountains. He just taught the one course. It was very interesting, some of the old-fashioned magic of earth and stone the school doesn't teach any more. He said he'd learned it from an old magic-worker who lived high up in the mountains and who taught it to Elerius just before he died."

I was jealous at once. I had thought I was rather unusual in learning herbal magic from my predecessor at Yurt, and here Elerius had not only learned some of the old magic, but was actually being invited to teach it.

But I couldn't say that to Evrard. "So have you just arrived here in Yurt?" I asked.

"No, I've been here for two weeks."

I turned to the duchess, who was following our conversation with her hands on her hips and a pleased expression on her face. "Why didn't you tell me, my lady?"

"I scarcely needed permission from the Royal Wizard to hire my own wizard, did I?" she said with a laugh. "Besides, I wanted to wait until after King Haimeric had gotten safely off on his trip before I distracted the royal court with anything else. So, how do you like my wizard? As someone who's been in Yurt longer, do you have any recommendations? Are there certain books I should buy? Should I get in some crucibles and pestles and special herbs?"

"Ask Evrard himself what he needs," I said, but the smile froze on my lips. This likeable young wizard had been in the kingdom for two weeks. Could he be responsible for the great horned rabbits?

I did a little, very rapid, magic probing, which I hoped he wouldn't notice, and felt my shoulders relax. If he had made the rabbits, it was certainly not with supernatural aid. I could understand a school-trained wizard, even one I had barely met, better than anyone else, and there was nothing about Evrard which suggested a plunge into black magic.

At this point, dinner was announced. As we moved toward the table, I noticed the chaplain standing by himself. I had almost forgotten him.

"Joachim," I said, "let me introduce you to Evrard, the duchess' new wizard." His dark eyes had been distant, but at once they came back into focus. "Evrard, this is my very good friend, the Royal Chaplain of Yurt."

"I am glad to meet you," said Joachim gravely, shaking Evrard's hand.

The young wizard winced; Joachim's grip was strong. "I'm happy to meet you, too," he said.

Joachim smiled then, which he had not done when he first met *me*. "I think Daimbert will be pleased to have another young wizard in the kingdom."

At dinner, the count asked us about our trip to the high plateau. I merely mentioned the Holy Grove, because I wasn't sure how much of the situation Joachim wanted generally known, talked a little more about the horned rabbits, and did not mention at all the strange footprint or the spell I had sensed.

I would have expected that the duchess would be most interested in the horned rabbits, especially since she had come here at the count's request to hunt them, but instead she started talking about the shrine. "That's where the toe of Saint Eusebius, the Cranky Saint, is kept, isn't it?" she said. "He's not a saint to trifle with! Who was that man," turning to the count, "your great-grandfather?"

"Great-great-grandfather," he said as though embarrassed.

"Anyway," continued Diana, "our present count's ancestor was a noted rapscallion and sinner." It was hard to imagine anyone related to the white-haired count as a rapscallion. "But when he was dying, he started worrying about his soul at last, and he asked to be buried in the Holy Grove, near the shrine. But the Cranky Saint didn't want someone with so many sins on his soul buried that close. So he rerouted the river so it flowed between the grave and his shrine!"

Everyone but Joachim laughed. The count nodded sheepishly. "That's right. That count's son, my own great-grandfather, was so embarrassed he had him dug up and reburied in our castle cemetery. The next day, the river was back in its normal bed."

I wondered briefly if the Cranky Saint himself might have made the horned rabbits, but realized that someone with that sort of supernatural power would need no spells. If Evrard hadn't made the rabbits, there might be still another wizard wandering around Yurt. I wasn't going to let that go on in *my* kingdom. Or, as I had thought earlier, the retired Royal Wizard had lost all his good sense and summoned the powers of evil.

I was awakened from an uneasy sleep by a voice in the room with me. "Dear God."

Abruptly awake, I lay still for a moment in the darkness, trying to remember where I was. There was rapid, shallow breathing from the far side of the room.

Then I remembered that we were still in the count's castle, not home in the royal castle, which was why my bed felt so unfamiliar. I sat up and lit a candle. "Joachim? Are you all right?"

He pushed himself up on one elbow and looked toward me. The flickering light and shadow from the candle flame made his eye sockets black and empty. But then he turned his head slightly and his eyes came back. "I had a dream."

"I was dreaming, too," I said. "A nightmare about the great horned rabbits. But you're awake now and it's not real."

He flopped back down without speaking. I reached for the candle to extinguish it, but my hand froze as he spoke. "It was real."

He was silent so long that I thought he would say nothing more, but I wasn't at all sure I wanted to hear it anyway. I felt suddenly that there were not enough blankets on the narrow beds in the count's second-best guest chamber.

"It wasn't a dream," he said at last. "It was a vision. Saint Eusebius appeared to me."

My immediate reaction was highly interested curiosity. I had never had a vision in my life. I wondered how Joachim had known it was the saint and if he had had the sense to ask what the saint knew about the entrepreneurs on the top of the cliff. I thought of asking if the entire saint had appeared to him or just the toe, but decided against it. From the strain in Joachim's voice, seeing a saint had been a deeply disturbing experience. "What did he say?" I contented myself with asking.

There was another long pause. "He doesn't want to stay at the hermitage," said Joachim at last. He sounded distant, almost as if he were no longer in the room with me, although I could see his back in the candlelight. "He was very clear on that point. But he wouldn't tell me where he wanted to go instead."

He rolled abruptly around to face me. "It was horrible, Daimbert! I've never been addressed like that. His face was like a living flame. Yet there is nothing evil in him, only the overwhelming power of good. The sin is in me, not to be able to bear it."

He put his hands over his face. I blew out the candle and slowly stretched back out in my bed. He said nothing more. After a while I fell asleep again, although my dreams were more troubled than ever.

III

Diana was surprisingly unwilling to have me help her search for the great horned rabbits. Even though it was the count, not the duchess herself, who had summoned me from the royal castle, I would have expected her to welcome any magical assistance.

"My own wizard and my huntsmen will be plenty," she told me firmly the next morning. She wore a man's leather tunic now and a disreputable old stained cloak, her only ornaments the wide gold bracelets she always wore. She realized she usually did not look like a woman of the high aristocracy and enjoyed people's reactions to her refusal to be conventional. "You can go home and keep an eye on Dominic."

I was about to protest, to tell her that if there was someone casting a powerful spell in this end of the kingdom, then Evrard might need another wizard's assistance, but I stopped myself in time. He should have a chance to show his new employer his abilities unimpeded. Besides, although I would have liked to put it off, I needed to talk to my predecessor as soon as possible.

The count and countess thanked us for coming and waved from their gate as we all left their little castle. We had gone only a half mile, and Diana had just said she and Evrard would turn off the road in search of tracks, when she abruptly reined in. She started to speak, stopped, and merely pointed.

A man was coming toward us on foot, walking easily with long strides. He wore a green cloak and had a heavy bow slung on his back. He would have looked entirely normal except for his height: He must have been over seven feet tall.

I probed quickly with words of the Hidden Language, suspecting another magic creature. But there was nothing about him that suggested he was other than fully human.

He continued toward us, his long blond hair blowing out behind him. Though his hair was unkempt, his beard was neatly trimmed. Ten feet short of the duchess' horse, he stopped and went gracefully down on one knee.

"Greetings, my lady. I hear you need a huntsman." His voice was surprisingly cultured and very deep.

The duchess looked flustered, which was surprising in her. "Where did you hear that?"

He looked up and smiled. He had a slow smile that lit up his face like the sun. "It's scarcely a secret that you're trying to track some magic creatures. Horned rabbits, aren't they?"

"And you think you could help?" She almost sounded nervous, but not as though she felt any fear of this huntsman—rather, if it had been anyone but the duchess, I would have called it girlish shyness.

He stood up and came over to her horse, where he faced her nearly at eye level. "I've never failed as a hunter and tracker," he said, still smiling. "Call me Nimrod."

"And Nimrod was a mighty hunter before the Lord," quoted Joachim in a low voice next to me.

Diana studied him in silence for thirty seconds. "All right, Nimrod," she said abruptly, almost triumphantly. "I'll give you a chance to prove your ability. We've spotted the great horned rabbits several times. But we've never been able to catch one."

"Then let's begin. I'll leave you to place your huntsmen and your hounds." He strode off purposefully toward the woods.

"All right," said the duchess. "Well, good-bye, and thanks again for your offer of help!" she added to me, then kicked her horse into motion. Evrard waved at us and galloped after her.

Joachim and I looked at each other a moment in silence, then started up again for the long ride back to the royal castle. We had ridden a mile when Joachim asked, "Do you think he might have made the great horned rabbits himself?"

"I don't think so," I said. "It would take a wizard, and one wizard should always be able to recognize another. But he certainly seemed fully informed about them. Do you think the duchess already knew him?"

"It seems unlikely," said the chaplain. "After all, he had to tell her his name."

"I must say," I answered slowly, "there seems to be a whole lot going on in this end of the kingdom that I don't yet understand."

We had gotten a late start from the count's castle. The sun was setting by the time we came up the hill to the royal castle. In the courtyard, the staff was just finishing a volleyball game.

"I think you should probably wait until morning to go see the old wizard," said Joachim.

"Of course," I said, startled at the implication that I might not. I had no intention of going into a black forest, full of creatures composed of dead bones and magic life, to face a wizard who might be growing senile or might have sold his soul to the devil, or both.

But the next morning saw me flying down the hill from the castle and into the woods below. In daylight, what I might find at the wizard's cottage seemed at least slightly less terrifying than it had the night before.

For a relatively brief distance, I was always happy to fly. The rush of air past my face was exhilarating now that I had become good enough that I no longer had to give constant attention to my spells, and I liked the chance to show the old wizard that, even though I had been trained in the school he scorned, I was still perfectly competent. Not that he ever seemed fully convinced. . . .

I followed the brick road a few miles through the trees, gliding along five feet above it, turned off at a track marked by a little pile of white chalk, part of a giant protective pentagram the wizard had made for himself when he retired, and proceeded down his narrow green valley. As usual, an illusory lady and unicorn waited by a little bridge. The lady raised her sky-blue eyes to me as I passed over. Beyond, the wizard had a volley of magic arrows ready to repel the unwary, but the spell was tripped by someone walking down the valley floor and no arrows bothered me today.

Usually when I came to visit my predecessor, I found him sitting on a chair in front of his little green house, built under the spreading branches of an enormous oak. But today I saw no one and the door was closed. I dropped to the ground, remembering guiltily that it had been several months since I had last come to visit.

I thought again how strange it would be if someone who prided himself on being a wizard of light and air, who had even mocked me for the moon and stars on my belt buckle the first time I had met him, had descended into black magic.

The wizard's calico cat emerged from the long grass and pounced at my socks, making me jump. I squared my shoulders and raised my fist to knock at the door, expecting the old wizard to call for me to come in even before I had a chance to rap. Little happened in his valley of which he was unaware. But no voice called.

I did knock then and had to wait several moments for an answer, even though I immediately heard a loud crash inside. But then the door opened and the old wizard glared out at me.

"It's you," he said, as though highly disappointed. Where I had been steeling myself to face someone deeply sunk in evil, I found only an irritable old man.

"Excuse me, Master," I said. "I don't want to interrupt your experiments, but I need your wisdom and advice." He was not in fact my master, but I had always called him that, feeling it was appropriate for his superior age and experience.

"No wonder, being trained at that school," the old wizard snapped. He seemed unusually brusque, even for him. I wondered briefly how the Cranky Saint would hold up against him in a contest of irritable natures.

"I won't keep you very long." I glanced around surreptitiously, wondering how I could bring up the topic of the great horned rabbits. "But with your knowledge of the magic of earth and growing things, I thought you might be able to counsel me what do about the wood nymph."

To my surprise, his expression immediately softened. "The wood nymph," he said with a hint of a smile. "I haven't seen her in years."

Emboldened by his mood change, I asked, "May I come in?"

He scowled again at once, but then he nodded grudgingly. "You might as well."

I probed, very quickly, for supernatural influences and did not find them. There was nothing about him, any more than there had been about Evrard, that indicated the use of black magic. He turned and I followed him inside, enormously relieved but still wary.

I was shocked when I came through the green door into the cottage's single room. Even though it had always been full of herbs, books, mortars and pestles, and piles of dishes, he had managed to preserve some semblance of order, and the floor had always been swept clean. Now, mounds of decayed plant material were heaped on the floor and the furniture, amidst dirty crockery. There was an acrid smell to the place I could not identify. Shards of broken glass lay in front of the fireplace, the result, I guessed, of the crash I had heard. The calico cat sensibly refused to come in with me.

"Find a chair," said the old wizard with a vague wave of his hand. The word "find" seemed well chosen; it took a moment for me to identify which of the shapeless masses around me might be a chair at base. "I'm afraid the place has gotten a little messy."

I let this understatement pass and shifted a pile of dead leaves and a plate with the remains of what might once have been a fried egg. Having thus uncovered a chair, I pulled it up next to his rocking chair, the only piece of furniture not covered with debris.

He sat down and arranged his long white beard over his lap. It seemed full of twigs and bits of food, at which he picked as he rocked. Even his ring, shaped like an eagle in flight, was dirty and tarnished. But nothing here suggested he had been using diabolical power to bring dead rabbits back to life.

The old wizard had already been well past two hundred years old when he had abruptly decided to resign as Royal Wizard of Yurt. He was starting to feel himself old and even incapable two years ago, when he moved down here from the castle. I wondered uneasily if his decline might have been accelerated by living alone, with no one to talk to besides his cat.

He kicked half-heartedly at the broken glass and

continued to rock in front of his cold hearth. He seemed willing to let the silence stretch out until I finally decided to break it. "I need your advice," I began, "on how I might be able to shift the wood nymph out of her grove." If I started with her, I might be able to work around to the rabbits—and whatever had made that inhuman footprint. "I gather she's been there for generations. Is it even possible to shift a nymph?"

The old wizard smiled, quite pleasantly for him. "Are you sure you *want* to move her? Leave her where she is, treat her gently and with dignity, and she may agree to come down out of her trees so you can see her."

"I did see her," I said. "She was down from the trees at least for a moment, but when I tried to speak to her she disappeared at once, without saying anything."

"A nymph's conversation takes time," he answered, again with a reminiscent smile. "But it's worth it in the end." He leaned forward abruptly. "Why do you want to move her out of the grove?"

"Well," I said uneasily, "the bishop had asked the Royal Chaplain to ask me what I could do. The church considers that grove a holy grove, and they don't like having a nymph in it."

The old wizard stopped smiling and snorted as though thoroughly disgusted. "I thought I'd warned you about becoming too good friends with that chaplain. Why should you do errands for the Church anyway? They've always done their best to discredit wizardry, so we certainly don't owe *them* any favors. Why should a wood nymph have to leave the grove where she's always been happy, just because some bishop becomes fastidious about her proximity to an old hermit? Afraid she's going to corrupt him, is that it?"

I did not try to deny it. Clearly I would get no help from the old wizard here. I almost agreed with him anyway and would have agreed completely if Joachim had not seemed so troubled.

"I'm sure you're right, Master," I said hastily, trying to recover something from this conversation before he threw me out. "But I have another question for you. Some strange magic creatures have started appearing in the kingdom, and it looks as if they were made with wizardry."

"Strange magic creatures," he interrupted with another snort, "and you, a supposedly competent wizard, can't even deal with them yourself?"

I pushed ahead. "I had merely hoped, since you'd been in Yurt so long, you might have seen something similar before and would have some suggestions. They look like rabbits, but big rabbits, and they have horns."

"Horned rabbits," he said, looking at me thoughtfully. "So there are horned rabbits in the kingdom and you don't know what to do about them. I hope you weren't going to accuse *me* of making something so silly. Unless you created them yourself, eh? I suggest you talk to your fancy school. An apprentice wizard in the old days wouldn't have had these problems!"

I expected in fact that an apprentice wizard of a century or two earlier would have had just as much trouble, but I didn't say so. Rather, I decided I ought to leave before I did any more damage to our dubious relationship.

"And how many horned rabbits have you seen?" he asked as I stood up to go.

"There are at least three of them." I wondered if there had been great horned rabbits in Yurt before or if the old wizard was just pleased to see me facing— certainly not for the first time!—a problem I didn't know how to handle.

The old wizard smiled grimly. "If you've got a renegade wizard here in the kingdom making horned rabbits—*rabbits!*— there may be a lot more before you're through."

I left with this discouraging comment. As I flew

back home, I thought that at least the old wizard himself didn't seem to be creating great horned rabbits, or anything else at the moment, and certainly not with diabolical assistance. But that left me back at the beginning. Where had they come from, and why had they now appeared in Yurt?

IV

That evening, as I'd hoped, the telephone call came from the castle, halfway to the great City, where the queen's parents lived, telling us that the royal party had arrived safely. Dominic spoke to the king, but standing at his side, I could see the king with the queen and the baby prince behind him, tiny figures in the base of the glass telephone.

"Yes, we're all well," said the king. "Any problems yet you can't handle, Dominic?"

The royal nephew and regent took this comment entirely seriously. "Nothing I can't handle, sire."

I thought that, on the contrary, there was a great deal happening in Yurt over which Dominic had no control. I wondered if it could be pure coincidence that Nimrod and the great horned rabbits had both appeared in the kingdom at the very time the king left. I even wondered for a moment if Dominic himself might be responsible, if he had arranged for the kingdom to be invaded by magic creatures in the king's absence to demonstrate his ability to deal with them.

But this seemed a little far-fetched. There was no question, however, that Dominic was throwing himself into the role of royal regent. When we had reached home the day before, we had found him sitting on the throne in the great hall, gripping the arms and staring grimly at nothing in particular.

Hearing from the king made everyone more cheerful, except for Joachim, who was still waiting to hear from the bishop. He had hoped that an answer to his message of the preceding day would be here when we reached the royal castle yesterday, but no pigeons had arrived. The cathedral had never put in a telephone, probably afraid that to do so would be a concession to the forces of institutionalized wizardry, and Joachim could do nothing but mutter about pigeons being lost or caught by hawks—all of which was quite possible—before going up to bed early.

Perhaps the most cheerful person in the castle was Gwen, the assistant cook. She and I had been friends since I first arrived in Yurt, when she was still a kitchen maid. Not only was she glad the royal family was safe, she was pleased that they were at least temporarily out of the way. She and her husband, who played in the castle's brass choir, were the only people in Yurt who did *not* consider the baby prince the most important person in the kingdom. That honor they gave to their own baby daughter.

"I think she's going to start crawling soon," Gwen said to me. Her daughter was lying on a rug on the flagstone floor of the great hall. "Look at her kicking!"

The little girl, four months younger than the royal prince, was indeed kicking with great enthusiasm and pride of accomplishment.

I sat down on the floor next to her and patted her on her diapered bottom. She gave me a wide, toothless smile. "I like baby girls," I said to Gwen. "She's so full of energy; are you sure she isn't going to get into trouble once she starts moving around?"

Little Gwennie grabbed the hem of my trouser leg and tried to pull it toward her mouth. Gwen disengaged her. "There *is* a lot she could crawl into in the kitchens—they're much more dangerous than anything the little prince is likely to get into," she added pointedly.

We were interrupted at this point by Dominic coming toward us. I frequently had the uncomfortable feeling that, despite his silence and apparent slowness, he saw and recognized every one of my inadequacies—and probably a lot of inadequacies I didn't even have. But he was also capable of surprising me by speaking to me on occasion as though he had no doubts of my competence.

"It sounds as if the count and the duchess are having a great deal of trouble in their neighborhood these days," he said as I scrambled to my feet, "what with great horned rabbits and a troublesome nymph." I had, of course, given him a sketch of our trip as soon as we returned. From the stony look I had received then, I was rather surprised how much of it he'd understood, even though he didn't now mention the people trying to restrict access to the holy relics. "Do you think it would help if I rode over to that side of the kingdom tomorrow with a few knights?"

"Not for several days, anyway," I said. "Brute force won't be any good against the nymph. If any of our knights are good trackers, however, I'm sure the duchess would appreciate their help tracking the horned rabbits."

Dominic considered, as though wondering again why his uncle the king had even taken me on in the first place. "And are *you* doing anything about these strange events?"

"I'm checking what my books of magic have to say about such things," I said with dignity. Since I had been meaning to get to my books very soon, I didn't feel this was too great a prevarication.

Unexpectedly, Dominic's frown turned into a smile. "It was good to hear the royal family is well," he said, "especially the little prince."

I agreed wholeheartedly, although somewhat surprised, since Joachim had felt Dominic might be jealous.

"His hair is so light blond it's almost white," continued Dominic with a sentimental smile. "They tell me mine was just the same color when I was his age. Tell me, Wizard," with a sudden sharp look, "have you ever thought of getting married?"

"Me? Of course not," I said, startled by this sudden change of subject. "Wizards never marry."

"That's right," said Dominic and turned abruptly away, leaving me wondering what was really bothering the regent.

The next morning, I dug out the massive old books of spells that had once belonged to the wizard employed by the duchess' father. I had had them some time without ever looking at them and had almost forgotten about them, but meeting Evrard reminded me.

If there was no demon-assisted wizard in Yurt bringing dead bones back to life with supernatural power, then maybe it was possible, with unaided wizardry, to create new animals and give them the semblance of life if not life itself. I knew they had taught us nothing of the sort in school. But the night before, in reading through the books I had brought with me to Yurt, I found a brief mention in the first volume of *Ancient and Modern Necromancy* which hinted tantalizingly that such things might be possible.

The old ducal wizard, one of the last to be trained by the apprentice system, had retired thirty years earlier, even before Diana inherited the duchy, and when he went, he left a lot of his books behind. I had found these books and unabashedly stolen them on a visit to the duchess' castle a year and a half ago. Now I turned to them in the hope of finding something that the clean, printed pages of my books of modern magic did not cover.

The ink had faded and the spells were written down in no particular order, sometimes interspersed with what appeared to be chess puzzles or laundry lists. But the magic was fascinating. For two days I did little besides eat and work my way, page by page, through the volumes.

Much of it was herbal magic and rather ineffective herbal magic at that. I had learned enough of the magic of growing things from my predecessor during the last two years, during the interludes in which we were fairly friendly, at least to recognize spells that were unlikely to work. The spell to summon a swarm of honeybees looked as though it had promise, as did the spell to help heal a cow with a sore udder, but I did not have much faith in the spells which purported to be able to turn the moon black or put a burning cross on the forehead of a previously unsuspected murderer.

In the third volume I found a mention of the wood nymph. What started as a rather dry, scientific description of her attributes quickly disintegrated into a personal account. I smiled as I deciphered the cramped and faded handwriting. It seemed the old ducal wizard had thoroughly enjoyed himself. I remembered my predecessor's softening at the mention of the wood nymph and thought that she had certainly cut a romantic swath through the wizards of the kingdom of Yurt a generation ago. I wondered if the look she had given me when we met presaged a similar set of plans for me . . . an intriguing possibility. . . .

My thoughts were interrupted at this point by a knock at my door, and Joachim came in. He threw himself into a chair and came as close as he ever did to scowling. "Look at this."

"This" was a tiny square of paper. A quick glance showed that it was finally a message from the bishop—if you could call it a message. "Continue investigations. Gain more information. Pray for guidance."

I scowled, too. "So what does the bishop expect you to do?"

"I wish I knew." Joachim stopped, as though remembering that he probably ought not to be grumbling about the bishop to a wizard, and passed a hand over his eyes. "I'm sorry to bother you with this," he said and stood up to go. "I don't want to interrupt your research."

"Sit back down," I said. "I'm glad to take a break from reading."

I watched him make a deliberate effort to stop worrying about the bishop. "So, have you found anything useful so far?" he asked.

"Some of these books that used to belong to the old ducal wizard should help. I think I've figured out at last how to talk to a wood nymph. But I'd like to wait until it's clear whether the saint's relics and the old hermit will stay or go before I try to move her."

Joachim nodded slowly without answering.

"I already told you there's no indication that my predecessor is practicing black magic. I think, however, it might be possible with the old magic to make a horned rabbit that would move as though it were alive, even though it wasn't. I didn't see any immediate sign of the old wizard making anything, but he could have hidden all sorts of bones under the rubbish. It would mean he had lost his mind, rather than his soul—I guess that could be an improvement."

"Of course it would," said Joachim, surprised there could be any question.

"I'm a little worried about him. The condition of his house is appalling. But he may just have been concentrating so hard on the spells to create great horned rabbits—*if* he made them after all—that he had lost track of everything else."

"Are you sure you don't want me to go talk to him?" Joachim asked with a long look from his deep-set eyes.

"No, no," I said hastily. "I should have the spells worked out soon and then I'll visit him again. By the way," I went on, "has the saint appeared to you again with any clearer indication of what he wants?"

"No, he hasn't," he said, looking somewhere beyond my head.

"And I presume you can't summon a vision?"

"The bishop's right," said Joachim bleakly, standing up and opening my door. "I'd better pray for guidance."

I shook my head as the door closed, glad again I was not a priest. My own inclination would have been to leave the hermit and the toe in the Holy Grove with the apprentices, perhaps finding some way to get the entrepreneurs off the cliff top, but as nearly as I could tell Saint Eusebius had told three different sets of people three different things: He had told the hermit he wanted to stay where he was, the distant priests that he wanted to move to their church, and Joachim that he wanted to leave but not necessarily go there.

I shrugged and returned to the old ducal wizard's rather racy personal account of how one might deal with a wood nymph, but it had no more practical information than I had already been able to glean. I leaned back, stretching my stiff shoulder muscles. So far, I had found nothing that might in any way apply to great horned rabbits, much less creatures with semi-human footprints, and I had only one volume to go.

If Joachim had been waiting with eagerness and trepidation for his message from the bishop, I had been waiting to hear from the duchess. Someone as good at hunting as she had always been ought to have been able to capture one of the horned rabbits by now—especially if they were starting to multiply. And I would like a chance to talk more to Evrard, to find out if he knew any spells that might be useful. I wondered again, more uneasily, about Nimrod.

If I didn't hear from them soon, I'd create a magical excuse and go back to that end of the kingdom. Perhaps I could make it rain moles.

V

It was late in the afternoon. Dinner would be served shortly. I closed my books and went into the courtyard and out across the drawbridge to get some fresh air. If the old ducal wizard's last volume was not informative on strange magic creatures, I might have to swallow my pride and telephone the wizards' school.

A light breeze blew around my ears. The sky above was scaled with high, faint clouds. I thought somewhat wryly that, for someone who had spent all his life in the great City before becoming Royal Wizard of Yurt, I had certainly learned quickly how to find reassurance and repose in nature.

As I looked down toward the woods at the bottom of the castle's hill, a little group of horses and riders emerged. For two seconds I thought it might be the king and queen, back already, but then I realized it was the duchess.

She was accompanied by half a dozen mounted men, one of whom had bright red hair. Striding by her stirrup was a tall blond man in a green cloak. Nimrod appeared to have no trouble keeping up with the horses.

Evrard spotted me and waved. The riders kicked their horses for the last climb up the hill. "Well, here we are!" Diana said cheerfully, including both me and Nimrod in her smile.

I wasn't sure what evil I expected from the tall huntsman, but so far he and the duchess seemed to be getting on very well. She no longer appeared flustered as she had when she first met him, but her usual confident self.

"Did you catch one?" I asked. "One of the great horned rabbits?"

"I finally shot one this morning," said Nimrod with a grin for the duchess. "I've never before had to hunt something for three days before I caught it! Now we'll find out what it is, something from the land of wild magic or something supernatural. My lady Diana said that her wizard could analyze it, but I told her I wanted the best. Nothing would do but bringing it straight to the Royal Wizard of Yurt."

Diana interrupted before I could respond to this implied slur on Evrard's abilities. "I'm sorry you didn't get my message on the pigeon that we were coming," she said loudly. "A hawk must have gotten it!"

But she pulled me aside as the rest of her party, including Nimrod and Evrard, passed over the drawbridge and into the castle. "Actually, I didn't send you a message," she said with a wink. "I didn't want to give Dominic a chance to tell me to stay home. I don't trust him to do a good job as regent without someone like me to keep an eye on him."

The constable, with Dominic behind him, came out to greet the duchess with reasonably well-concealed surprise. She introduced Evrard and Nimrod and apologized for the loss or delay of the nonexistent carrier pigeon.

"I had been about to ride over to visit you and the count," said Dominic. "Have you made any progress?"

"Well, Nimrod's got a magic rabbit for your Royal Wizard to look at," she said. For a second I wondered if she was irritated he had brought it here. "I wouldn't have wanted you to bother yourself coming to my castle—I know you have *so* many responsibilities."

Dominic frowned as though suspecting flippancy and not quite seeing it.

"Let me see that horned rabbit," I said. Nimrod handed me his gamebag.

As I took the leather bag, I thought that it felt very strange, not at all the way a gamebag should feel. A chill touched me that was not caused by the late afternoon breeze. By feel alone, I would have guessed the bag held not a horned rabbit but sticks and bones.

"What's wrong?" asked Nimrod, catching my concern.

I had been about to take the bag into my chambers, but I now decided to open it here, in the middle of the courtyard. My apprehension became stronger as I slowly unbuckled it. "When did you put the rabbit in here?"

"Late this morning."

I had the bag open now; a powerful smell emerged in a wave, the smell of decay. Without reaching inside, I held the bag upside down and shook it. Scraps of fur, bones with bits of rotten flesh still clinging to them, and two long, straight horns fell out and clattered on the cobblestones.

Nimrod reached down and picked up a horn and a piece of bone. "These look like the bits and scraps someone might use if making some sort of artificial horned rabbit."

"That's my thought exactly," I said grimly.

Dinner was lively that evening with the addition of the duchess' party. Even Dominic, who kept looking thoughtfully at Diana, seemed to be making an attempt to be witty and charming. I remembered vaguely that there had been a story that Dominic had once intended to marry the duchess, back before the king and queen even met, but nothing had ever come of it. The mere thought of the stolid royal nephew trying to woo the lively duchess made this outcome easy to understand.

Nimrod, with his neatly trimmed beard and cultured speech, appeared to make the transition easily from a rough outdoor life to a royal court. I would have expected him to sit at the servants' table with the rest of the duchess' huntsmen, but she took his arm, laughed, and put him next to her at the main table.

"Have you heard the story about the peacock?" Evrard asked the youth next to whom he was seated.

Hugo was a young cousin of the queen's who was

doing some of his knighthood training at the royal castle. "No," he said, puzzled.

"You should have," replied Evrard with a grin. "It's a beautiful tale!"

"All right," replied Hugo with a grin of his own. Other conversation at the table had stopped. "What did the ocean say to the ship?"

"Nothing. It only waved! Why are flowers considered lazy?"

"Because they spend all their time in beds! At which of his battles did King Chalcior say, 'I die contented'?"

Evrard frowned. "King Chalcior? I remember him from history, but— Is this still a joke?"

"His last one!" cried Hugo, and the whole table, even Dominic, was convulsed.

I was the only one who did not feel lively. After spending two days persuading myself that I would, very soon, find a spell in the old ducal wizard's books that would give the semblance of life without supernatural aid, seeing the rotting rabbit's bones had made me again fear that someone in the kingdom was practicing black magic.

"Wizard!" called the duchess to Evrard over dessert. "How about entertaining us with a few illusions?"

Evrard gave a start and shot me a second's look of panic, then seemed to recover. He began muttering and moving his hands in the air, with far more flourishes than illusions actually required. In a moment, a fairly credible baby dragon appeared, about six inches long and colored bright blue. "There!" he said triumphantly.

He held it up for everyone to see and got a polite round of applause. It was not nearly as impressive an illusion as the last ones I had done to entertain the court, shortly before the king left, but no one was so ill-bred as to mention this. I hoped the duchess wasn't going to demand too much of Evrard too fast; I had been at Yurt three months before doing illusions before an audience. The baby dragon perched on Evrard's shoulder until it dissolved into air.

After dinner, he came back to my chambers with me. I had a couch in my outer chamber that folded into a bed; Evrard had happily agreed to sleep there.

It had started to rain gently and the evening air was cool. I kindled a fire, lit the magic lamps, and we drew our chairs up by the hearth. "I'm delighted to have another wizard here in Yurt," I said, "because we've got a serious magical problem."

Evrard looked at me attentively, then spoiled it by stifling a yawn.

"You and the duchess have been tracking the great horned rabbits for three days now," I said. "Do you have any idea what they are or how they could have been made? I haven't been able to find any indication of the supernatural about them, but those bones this afternoon didn't have any magic left clinging to them at all."

Evrard shook his head and smiled—he really did have a charming smile. "Not now, Daimbert! It's the end of a long day and I don't need this on top of everything!"

I apologized at once. "Of course. I've been looking forward so much to having you as a colleague that I'm afraid I've gotten over-eager." I reminded myself that a newly graduated wizard, especially one who had not been anywhere near first in his class, should not be pushed too much. I myself had not even bought all the books for my own second-year classes and still had gaps both in my library and in my knowledge as a result. If I didn't watch out, I would turn into a strict crank like my predecessor—though a much younger one.

In the morning, a steady rain was still falling—good for the crops, I firmly reminded the city boy I used to be. Evrard went off somewhere, but I settled down to finish the last of the old ducal wizard's books.

At first, it contained only the same mishmash of odd spells and herbal magic I had seen all along, but after several hours I found something else. I pulled the magic lamp closer and squinted at the handwriting. With growing excitement, I realized that the old ducal wizard had known—or thought he knew—a way to give dead flesh and bones motion and the semblance of life. It required no pacts with the devil, only a detailed knowledge of herbal magic and mastery of what looked like incredibly complicated spells.

Of course, spells which dated from before the advent of modern school magic were often more quirky and complicated than they needed to be— something that could also be said of some of my own spells.

I didn't have any herbs or bones in my chambers, but I decided to improvise. I pushed the chairs back to leave a clear place on the flagstone floor and assembled a pillow, the poker from the fireplace, and several pencils together in a vaguely reptilian shape. Standing well back, I read out the heavy syllables of the Hidden Language which should give my creature the semblance of life.

Not all the words in the book made any sense, some were illegible, and I had to add new sections to the spell to compensate for the lack of herbs, but in ten minutes I thought I had it. I said the final words, slammed the book shut, and looked hopefully toward my creature.

The pillow heaved itself up, tottered, and collapsed again. The poker clattered to the flagstones and rolled away. I walked over slowly to see what I had made.

At first I thought there had been no change at all. The poker certainly looked no different. But then I realized that all my pencils had turned pink and, when I picked up the pillow, I discovered it had grown what seemed to be three primordial feet at one end. I tickled them experimentally but got no response, not even a twitch.

Oh, well. I hadn't really expected it to work. I said the words that should have returned the pillow to itself, but the feet obstinately remained. I put it on Evrard's bed and sat down again.

Even if I couldn't work the spell—and I wasn't at all sure the old ducal wizard had been able to, either—this was what I had hoped to find. But though I knew now that a wizard could have made the great horned rabbits with natural magic, I still didn't know which wizard might have done so.

But I was going to find out. No other wizard could practice magic under my nose like this with impunity.

I caught glimpses through my rain-streaked windows of figures hurrying across the courtyard and realized it must be noon. But I was not hungry. I opened the book again but was interrupted almost immediately by a knock.

The door swung open before I had a chance to speak and Dominic's massive form stood blocking the doorway, dripping water on my floor. He closed his streaming umbrella. "I would like a word with you."

"Of course," I said in surprise and pulled up a straight wooden chair for him, not sure it would support his weight, but not wanting him soaking through the cushions on my bigger chairs. "Is it about the great horned rabbits?"

He glowered at me, pulled off his jacket, and sat down. The chair creaked but held. "It's about that huntsman with the duchess."

"Nimrod?"

"Clearly a false name," said Dominic without hesitation.

"What about him?"

Dominic looked out the window at the indistinct courtyard, then turned to glare at me again. If he had any confidence in my abilities, you couldn't have told it from that look. "Before the king left, he told me to consult with you or the chaplain on all important matters. I'm not sure why he wanted me as regent if he didn't trust my judgment, but I shall obey his commands, of course."

What a disappointment. And I had imagined the other day that he actually wanted my advice.

"And what important matter has come up now?"

"Isn't it obvious, even to you?" said Dominic with a scowl. It crossed my mind that far too many people had been scowling in my chambers lately, including me. "Duchess Diana acts toward that low-born giant like a flirtatious girl, and he's eating it up."

It had not been obvious to me, but then I had been too preoccupied with the question of how someone was making great horned rabbits to pay much attention. "Don't you think the duchess is old enough to take care of herself?" I asked.

Dominic made a sound that was half a snort and half a growl. "All I know is that she met some hunter out of the woods, took him home to her castle with her, and now has brought him here. If she wants to play fast and loose with her dignity at home that's one thing but, as regent of Yurt, I can't have her doing it here in the royal castle. That's why I want you to have a quiet conversation with her, tell her that her behavior has gone beyond respectable bounds."

"Me?"

"Of course you. Why do you think I came to talk to you? She's always seemed to like you, for some odd reason, whereas I'm afraid she might deliberately do the opposite of whatever I suggested, just to irritate me."

He had a point. "I'll try to find a chance sometime today," I said reluctantly.

"What's wrong with right now?" demanded Dominic. Being regent certainly seemed to have put steel resolve into his usually lethargic personality. "It's lunch time. You can observe her behavior at the

table for yourself and talk to her immediately
afterwards."

There seemed to be no way out of it. My wish for
new challenges was certainly being granted. I closed
the battered volume and got my umbrella off its hook.

PART THREE
The Old Wizard

-I

The chaplain and a few of the ladies had chambers from which they could reach the great hall without going into the courtyard; everyone else arrived for lunch dodging through the rain, and a line of wet umbrellas stood against the wall.

I still wasn't hungry and took only a little soup and none of the meat pie. Gwen gave me a concerned look from the servants' table, but I had no attention to spare for her. I was trying, as I had promised Dominic, to pay attention to the duchess and Nimrod.

I had to admit that Dominic was right. Nimrod and Diana sat with their heads bent together, talking about topics unrelated to whatever the rest of the table was discussing. During pauses in their conversation when the duchess was addressing a remark to someone else or busy eating, I saw the giant huntsman's blue eyes fixed on her almost caressingly.

The duchess had flirted with me as well when we first met, and my first thought was that this was just more of her teasing. But if so, it didn't seem fair to Nimrod, who was taking it quite seriously. She had never married because, as far as I could tell, she had never met a man who could keep up with her. I had sometimes wondered if Diana realized that her tendency to keep those around her off balance, to do or say things just to see the reaction she got, was in its own way highly predictable.

But now her behavior seemed oddly out of character, even for someone as determined to be outrageous as Diana. There had always before been limits. She enjoyed being a member of the aristocracy as much as she enjoyed behaving like no other duchess in the western kingdoms; she would no more have given up her castle and her authority than I would have given up magic. Dominic was right that Nimrod could not possibly aspire to be her social equal, despite his surprisingly cultivated speech and good manners. For that reason, I tried to reassure myself, whatever the regent might think, her obvious affection for a hunter without status or family would never lead to any permanent liaison or anything seriously harmful to her reputation.

As everyone stood up from lunch, I went over to her chair. It was one thing dealing with magical challenges in the king's absence, but it really would become complicated if I had to deal with everyone's personal problems as well. "Could I have a private word with you, my lady?"

Diana agreed at once. Nimrod smiled at her and walked away—I assumed things hadn't proceeded so far that they shared their chambers. Dominic caught my eye and nodded, an abrupt motion with his chin. For once, he approved.

The rain had let up enough that the duchess and I, our umbrellas spread over us, were able to walk, rather than run, to the door of her chamber and arrive relatively dry. "Have a seat," Diana said, taking off her cloak. "It's chilly enough that I'm going to start a fire."

She knelt at the hearth, put some twigs and wood shavings together against the front of a large log, and soon had a small blaze going—the duchess would never bother calling a servant for something like this. She added some slightly thicker twigs and, in a moment, the log was glowing red. Sitting down next to me, she said, "There. That should take the chill off the afternoon."

The fire had provided only a momentary distraction. I pushed aside my reluctance to speak. "I'd like to ask you something, my lady, and hope I don't offend you."

"You haven't managed to offend me yet," she said cheerfully.

"You seem to have become very friendly with Nimrod, considering that he just appeared out of the woods a few days ago. What have you learned about him?"

Her gray eyes narrowed slightly, but she was determined not to be offended. "I haven't been quizzing him about his ancestry and family wealth, if that's what you mean," she said, smiling to keep the comment mild. Something about the way she phrased it made me wonder if she might already have a good idea of his ancestry and family. "I know he's very intelligent as well as very handsome and he's a far better hunter than anyone I've ever seen. You probably haven't had a chance yet to see him use that enormous bow of his, but he's an absolute dead shot."

I had heard too little of Nimrod's conversation to be able to tell if he could keep up with her humor and often biting wit, but as a hunter I was sure she had met an equal.

"In fact, I even—" She stopped without finishing what might have been a very interesting sentence. Instead, she looked at me with a frown. "Your question doesn't really sound like you. Did Dominic tell you to talk to me?"

I nodded ruefully, rather glad in fact that she'd guessed the truth.

Fortunately, she seemed to find this highly amusing. "So he's worried that a member of the high aristocracy, the queen of Yurt's own third cousin, is flirting with a nobody? I ought to become really outrageous about it, just to teach Dominic a lesson."

"I'm sorry, my lady, I wouldn't have said anything if he hadn't insisted. In fact, well, Dominic has been acting a little strangely lately."

"In what way?"

"After the royal family called the other night, he was talking about the baby prince and asked *me* if I'd ever thought of getting married!"

She unexpectedly became serious. "So it's bothering Dominic, too," she said, which made no sense. But then her eyes twinkled. "I presume you told him that even an adorable little blond prince wasn't going to make you forget that wizards never marry?"

I took a deep breath. "The regent's going to ask me what you said."

She looked down her aristocratic nose. "Tell him," she said with a smile twitching the corner of her mouth, "tell him that I was deeply offended at your insult to my honor, that I told you I would always behave in the most honorable way possible and that, since I was sure of that point, I would always do exactly what I wanted."

Back in my own chambers, I found Evrard wearing my best dressing gown and sitting in my favorite chair with his feet up, leafing through the first volume of my copy of *Ancient and Modern Necromancy*.

I sat down across from him. "I need to talk to you."

"Fine," he said brightly. "I was just reading again about the Black Wars." When I cocked an eyebrow at him, he continued, "Surely you remember the end of the Black Wars." He waved the book in his hand. The first volume of *Ancient and Modern Necromancy*, which I'd never read very closely, was almost entirely devoted to history.

"I'm afraid I've never given very much attention to the history of wizardry," I answered. I was trying to remember if the Black Wars had come before or after the period in which Saint Eusebius was eaten by the dragon—after, I decided.

"You haven't? But I love history! Didn't you want to study all about how the wizards ended the fighting in the western kingdoms? Isn't that what made you decide to study wizardry in the first place?"

"No," I said sheepishly, thinking that maybe I could skim the book this evening after he was asleep. But I didn't want to be distracted by history. "You've taken courses at the school more recently than I, and some of them were different. I want to show you a spell I found this morning and ask if you've ever seen anything similar." I pulled the heavy volume onto my lap and found the place. "I don't think it is written down entirely correctly, but this gives the general outline."

"What *is* this book?" asked Evrard, sneezing from the dust.

"It used to belong to your predecessor, the old ducal wizard, thirty years ago," I said with a sideways glance. "There are four volumes. If you want them, you can have them once we're done."

"I guess so." He wrinkled his forehead at the handwriting. "I'd rather have a nicely printed book, but—" He stopped, and his forehead cleared. "But this is the same spell . . ."

"Yes?" I prompted.

"Nothing," he said quickly. "Nothing. I thought I recognized it, but of course I don't."

He sat back with a cheerful smile. I looked at him in silence, putting several things together. "In fact," I said at last, "I think you do."

At that moment we were interrupted by a hard knock on the door. Dominic, I thought resignedly, rising to my feet. "Yes, I talked to her," I started to say even before I had the door fully open.

But it was not Dominic. It was the chaplain, standing under an umbrella. In his hand was a small white square. He must have heard again from the bishop.

He turned to me without seeming to notice Evrard. "The priests are coming to Yurt."

"Which priests?"

"Priests from the church of Saint Eusebius, the church that asked for his relics." These were the ones, I recalled, whom Joachim almost suspected of trying to make the Cranky Saint cranky enough that he would leave the hermit's grove. "They want to examine the situation at first hand, according to the bishop." He glanced at the paper in his hand. "They're already on their way. The bishop has still given me no specific instructions, but the priests will be here in three days."

"It really does sound as though the bishop is giving you a free hand in all this," I said, just managing to meet the intense look on his face. "Clearly, he trusts you."

Evrard, behind me, cleared his throat.

"Let me know if I can help, but I don't know if I can," I said to Joachim.

"Of course. Sorry to interrupt you."

"So the chaplain's your very good friend?" asked Evrard as I closed the door again. "It sounds as though he's got plenty of problems of his own, what with bishops and priests and who knows what else. I guess it must be hard out here for you to find someone intelligent and interesting to talk to."

Although I had more than once thought the same thing, I didn't like the implications of what he had said and decided not to answer.

"He looks very dour," Evrard continued. "Somehow it's hard to imagine wild old Daimbert making friends with a priest!"

He would realize Joachim's merits when he got to know him better, I reassured myself. "Right now," I said, "I want to ask you why you made the great horned rabbits."

II

I had anticipated several reactions, from denial to angry pride. Instead, Evrard laughed. "I should have known I couldn't hide it from you indefinitely," he said with a broad smile. "When did you figure it out?"

"So you *did* make the horned rabbits?" I said, wanting to be sure of this point.

"Of course I did. Pretty good, weren't they?"

"It was something you learned in that class you took with Elerius," I said casually, not mentioning that it had taken me the better part of a week to work it out. "That class on the old magic. Did all the students make horned rabbits? I don't like to think of the western kingdoms overrun with those things."

"No, we all made something different. I thought of the rabbits myself," he added proudly. "It's hard magic, too! Elerius had to work with us individually to make sure we got the spells right and, as it is, the horns kept falling off mine. So when the duchess said she wanted me to make her magical creatures, I thought of the rabbits at once."

"Wait," I said sharply. "The duchess asked you to make them? You mean she's been chasing them across the kingdom these last few days, but they're something she wanted specifically?" I knew Diana loved hunting, but making something magical just for the purpose of hunting it seemed excessive, even for her.

"And she and I had to chase them earlier, too," Evrard said with a rueful expression. "I'd made three and gotten the horns to stay on fairly well. I wanted to test them to see if they'd move and hoot properly out in the wild. This was several days before I met you. We went up to a plateau a few miles from her castle and they moved so well, they escaped!"

"Escaped? And what did you do?" If strange magical creatures had been loose in the kingdom even longer than I thought, then I had clearly been derelict in my responsibilities as Royal Wizard.

"The duchess was terribly upset," said Evrard. "She said she didn't dare let anyone see them for a few more days—I don't know why. We managed to catch two of the three horned rabbits, though it took all afternoon. They'd gotten down into that deep valley that's cut into the plateau."

The valley of the Holy Grove. This must be what had made Saint Eusebius cranky enough to want to leave. The king had gone on vacation, the duchess had asked Evrard for horned rabbits, Nimrod had come out of the forest offering to hunt them, and the Cranky Saint had decided to leave Yurt, all within a very short period of time. At least some of these events had to be related.

But the more I thought about it, the less sense this made. The saint, with his relics in a grove shared with a wood nymph, must certainly have seen stranger magical creatures than Evrard's rabbits during the last fifteen hundred years. And I didn't think there had been enough time, between when the rabbits escaped and when Joachim first heard from the bishop, for the priests in the distant city to have had a vision of the saint, write to our bishop, and for him to write the chaplain.

Another thought struck me. "You didn't make any other magical creatures besides the great horned rabbits?"

"Of course not," said Evrard, his blue eyes round in innocence.

"But what did the duchess want the rabbits *for*?" I demanded.

"I wish I knew," said Evrard. For a moment, he actually looked troubled. "She never told me. Since they were my first assignment from my first employer, I didn't want to ask a lot of questions. Then, the afternoon before I met you at the count's castle, she said I should set free the ones we'd caught."

The day the king and queen left Yurt, I thought, the day before I had seen them hopping through the nymph's valley. The duchess had already told me she had wanted to wait until after King Haimeric had gone on his trip before letting the royal court know she had a wizard of her own. I hoped her only motive was not wanting to distract the king from his vacation.

"The count had sent us a message the same day, saying he'd seen one—the one we couldn't catch. So I guess she decided we might as well have all of them loose." Evrard smiled again. "When I first met you and we were talking about Elerius, I could barely resist telling you about my rabbits! But the duchess *had* said it was supposed to be a secret."

"A secret which I've now guessed. Don't worry. I'm not about to tell everybody else. But why," having a sudden thought, "if you were able to catch two horned rabbits in one day the first time, has it taken you three days to catch just one?"

"Well, *I* certainly could have caught it much faster than that," said Evrard self-righteously. "But the duchess told me this time that she didn't want them caught with magic. She wanted to use them as a test for her new huntsman."

No wonder she had refused my assistance back at the count's castle. Between having her wizard make horned rabbits and her huntsman hunt them, Diana was very busy lately testing the people around her. The queen had commented once that the duchess always did exactly what she liked.

"So you think she asked you for rabbits specifically as a test for him?"

"I doubt it," said Evrard with a shrug. Proud as he was of his rabbits, he was starting to find my questions about the duchess a little dull. "You saw how surprised she was when he first appeared, and I had started making the horned rabbits over a week earlier."

"Did you break the spell when Nimrod finally shot it?" I asked.

"I didn't have to. The spell only keeps all the different parts together as long as nothing happens to any of the parts. Even with Elerius's help, I couldn't make a rabbit that would hold together once it was trapped or shot."

"Who *is* Nimrod, anyway? Do you know?"

Evrard shrugged again. "Just some hunter. I guess she wanted to see how good he was before employing him." This didn't seem right, but Evrard didn't give me a chance to respond. He stretched his arms and smiled. "But that's enough about the duchess! You and I hardly had a chance to talk properly last week, and I've been eager to catch you up on all the news from the school."

I suddenly felt I had let this whole ridiculous matter of saints and horned rabbits become much too serious. I forced my hands and shoulders to relax. "Fine—but first, let me have my dressing gown back. If you don't have one of your own, tell the duchess you need money for 'personal purchases.'"

For the rest of the afternoon, Evrard and I swapped stories: exploits in the wizards' school, exams for which we had never studied, near escapes from the Guardians in the City down below the school, jokes played on other students and, in Evrard's case, even once on Zahlfast. After dinner, we decided to share a last glass of wine, which somehow became a whole bottle. I had not laughed so much or so long for two years. It was well past midnight by the time we turned out the magic lights.

But as I fell asleep—on the pillow with feet, which Evrard had switched back at some point—I remembered again the footprint, manlike yet inhuman, that I had seen in the Holy Grove.

Early the next day, Evrard and I rode out of the castle on old white mares. I'd assumed a fellow city boy would want a placid mount. We rode down the hill, past the cemetery, into the woods. Our saddles and harnesses creaked and the horses' hooves rang hollowly on the bricks of the road, but otherwise the summer morning was nearly silent.

"He's a fairly irritable old wizard," I told Evrard, "so try not to say anything that will upset him. For example, he doesn't like the wizards' school—he was trained under the old apprentice system, long before the school first opened."

Evrard stifled a yawn and grinned at me. "Now I'm going to be afraid to say anything."

"And call him Master. He likes that."

"But the Master of the school—" He stopped, laughed, and shook his head.

I gave Evrard an encouraging smile and wondered why I felt it so necessary to explain everything to him. I had come down alone to meet my predecessor two years ago, without the slightest idea what I would find, and managed fine—well, no, actually I hadn't managed very well at all.

"He's getting old," I said. "And he's started to lose control of his personal life. He no longer keeps his house tidy and he was even more offensive to me last week than usual, though it's hard to tell. If he's lost control in one area, he may also have had his magic get away from him."

Evrard glanced toward me, worried this time. "Then why are we going to see him?"

"Because I think something *has* gotten away from him. At the same time you were using some of the old magic to make horned rabbits, he may have been using similar spells to make something almost human."

He did not answer. We continued along the road in silence.

A half hour's ride through the fresh green of the forest brought us to the track, marked by the little pile of white stones, which led off from the main road and into the old wizard's valley. The trees hung low enough here that we walked our horses. After a few turns of the track, we could see the branches thinning ahead, and then we came out by the bridge.

"Did we really have to get up this early?" asked Evrard, yawning again. He had not yet seen what waited by the bridge. I smiled to myself and waited.

Then he turned his head and saw the illusory lady sitting on the bank, her golden hair spread across the grass and the unicorn resting its head in her lap. He was off his horse in a second and down on one knee before her. "Lady, let me put myself in your service. I am Evrard, the ducal wizard of Yurt."

As she always did when someone tried to talk to her, the illusory lady lifted her sky-blue eyes to him without answering, then rose and started down the valley, an arm around the unicorn's neck and her hair floating in a cloud behind her.

"Wait, Lady, I didn't mean to offend you!" Evrard called, still on his knee.

I laughed. "She's an illusion, young wizard." I paused, wondering why I had called him "young wizard," which is what the teachers tended to call us. "She fooled me the first time, too. Don't waste your time with someone that insubstantial."

He scrambled back up into the saddle, laughing. "If that's a sample of your crazy old predecessor's magic, I'm impressed! No one I've ever known could create a woman who looked that real, even the perfectly sane members of the illusions faculty. I wish she *was* real. She's the most beautiful woman I've ever seen."

"Wait until you meet the queen," I said confidently. The lady and the unicorn had disappeared; I started on down the valley.

But Evrard had stopped and his brow was wrinkled. "Daimbert, I think I ought to tell you something before we get to the old wizard's house."

I pulled up my horse, wondering what could be the problem now. "Yes?"

"You know you asked me if I'd made anything else besides the horned rabbits? Well, I did."

I took a deep breath, trying not to be angry. Having another young wizard in the kingdom was not turning out to be quite the help I'd hoped it would be. "You made a creature that has almost human footprints."

"Well, yes," said Evrard, not nearly as embarrassed as I thought he ought to be for having lied to me. "But it wasn't a very realistic creature. So, if your predecessor's magic is this good, I thought I'd better mention it to you before you accuse *him* of creating it."

"Would you like to tell me why you made it?" I asked very quietly.

Evrard gave his broad smile. "I was hoping to impress the duchess, of course. She laughed at my horned rabbits, even when I got the horns to stay on, and then she was angry with me for letting them escape, and then for only catching two of them again. I decided I had to do *something* or I would be out of my first job almost before it had started!"

I had to smile back, caught between irritation and sympathy. I recalled several of my own desperate magical improvisations two years ago, when my new royal employers had assumed I would know how to produce certain effects, where actually I had no idea. The duchess seemed to be expecting more of Evrard in his first two weeks in Yurt than had been expected of me in my first two months.

"So I decided to make something totally different to surprise her," he continued, his good humor restored, "something that might even be frightening. The duchess had gotten me rabbits' bones and sheep's horns, but I didn't have any human bones, of course. So I used some sticks and tried to extrapolate from the spell I'd learned in school."

"And what happened?" I asked, envious in spite of myself. It had taken me a long time to discover that such a spell was even possible, much less to make it work.

He shook his head ruefully. "I'm afraid it didn't

work very well. My creature wouldn't stand up straight and bits kept falling off. The legs and feet weren't bad, but the rest only looked human if you squinted right. And then when I'd given up, I couldn't get the spell to dissolve again!"

"You didn't try shooting it? That seemed to work with the rabbits." But as I spoke, I remembered the pillow that still had feet.

"Well, no. After all, it *did* look sort of human. And besides, I'd tried to make the spells a little stronger this time. But I certainly couldn't show it to the duchess! I decided I'd better just get it out of the way, and it would soon fall apart on its own."

"So you took it up on the plateau and set it loose," I provided when he seemed unwilling to continue, "where it went down into the valley and managed to terrify me thoroughly."

Evrard laughed. "It did? That's even better than I expected."

I forced myself to laugh as well. "I even thought someone in the kingdom was practicing black magic." Evrard, I thought, seemed much more than two years younger than I. But then, I reminded myself, he had not gone through the experiences of my first six months in Yurt, which I felt had aged me considerably.

"Come on," I said. "Since we've come this far, I might as well introduce you to the old wizard. He's the most senior wizard in the region and you really should call on him. And then I guess we'd better go over to the duchess' end of the kingdom and catch your creature before it terrifies anyone else."

III

We scrambled down a steep incline, leading our horses, and I paused at the bottom, looking ahead down the valley. Usually at this point, a shower of arrows began to fly across the path, but today there were no arrows, and some quick magic probing found no sign that they had ever been there. This made things easier because it meant we neither had to crawl under the arrows' flight nor fly over them, but I felt suddenly uneasy. If the old wizard was no longer doing the spells to maintain his defenses—especially since the arrows were also one of his best magic tricks—to what *was* he giving his attention?

But then I reminded myself that the strange magical creatures in the kingdom had been Evrard's all along. I relaxed and decided this was just one more instance of the old wizard letting everything go.

Evrard, who did not realize there ever had been arrows here, strolled casually in front of me, leading his mare. The grassy track led us around a few more turns and then into the clearing where stood the enormous oak which sheltered the old wizard's house. We dropped our horses' reins and walked slowly forward. I tried to decide if the ominous appearance the rather innocuous little green house seemed to have acquired in the last few days was only my imagination.

I jumped as the door swung open with a crash. The old wizard came out as though catapulted and slammed it behind him. Even at a distance of twenty yards, I could see he was breathing hard.

But he tried to appear casual. He looked shortly toward Evrard, then gave me his customary scowl. "So, I see young wizards are multiplying as fast as the great horned rabbits," he said. "And they're still as happily convinced, I'd say from this one's fancy jacket, that they can control the powers of darkness."

Evrard stepped forward and went into the full formal bow. "Greetings, Master. I am the duchess' new wizard."

The old wizard lifted shaggy eyebrows at me over Evrard's head. "What does the duchess want a wizard for? I'd have thought your example would have taught her that young wizards these days don't know any magic. But then the old duke's wizard, back over thirty years ago, was so incompetent that maybe she's thinking nothing could be worse."

Normally I would have been interested in his tacit admission that even a wizard trained under the old apprenticeship system could be incompetent. But I was distracted by wondering if the wizard had simply rushed out of his house to keep us from seeing whatever he might have inside, or whether something in there had physically thrown him out.

Evrard was still in the full bow, his arms outstretched. "Well, greetings, Wizard," the old wizard said to him grudgingly. "I doubt you'll like Yurt."

"But I think I'll like Yurt very much," said Evrard with a cheerful smile, standing up again. "It's a charming little kingdom."

The old wizard snorted. "Somebody used to the vain pleasures of the City won't be satisfied with country charm. Tell the duchess I warned her she won't have her fancy young wizard for very long."

"Oh, no," said Evrard seriously. "I'm planning to stay with the duchess for years and years."

"Maybe she'll learn a lesson at last, then."

Evrard was either working hard to maintain the old wizard's good temper or else he was too good-natured to take offense easily.

"But as for *you*, young whippersnapper," said the old wizard with a glare for me, "I'd like to know what you think you're playing at! First you came around here casting spells to reveal the supernatural, as though after all this time you thought I might be practicing black magic, and then I find out you're doing something similar yourself!"

I took a deep breath. "What are you talking about?"

"That creature made of sticks," he said brusquely. "Thought I wouldn't find out, did you? What happened, somebody made the horned rabbits under your nose and you got so jealous of your position as Royal Wizard of Yurt that you decided you'd try something of your own, eh?"

Evrard, I noticed, was wandering off in the direction of the old wizard's cottage with an air of not hearing our conversation.

"At least you made it with plain magic," continued my predecessor, almost grudgingly. "Nothing demonic about it, which may be why it was a pretty pathetic excuse for a magic creature."

"No, I didn't make it," I said loftily, stopping myself just in time from saying that Evrard had. "I know all about it, of course. But how did *you* find out?"

The old wizard glanced in Evrard's direction and snorted. But he didn't say what he seemed to have guessed. "I found it, of course. When you told me there were magical creatures roaming through the kingdom and that you didn't know what to do about them, I figured there ought to be at least *one* wizard in Yurt acting responsibly. I spotted the duchess and that giant chasing the horned rabbits—where did she find *him*, by the way?—so I decided to let them have their fun. I did improve the spells a little, though, to give them more of a challenge." He gave a malicious chuckle.

"But you brought the manlike creature back here with you," I said. Could Evrard's stick-creature have been what threw him out the door?

"What was left of it," said the old wizard. "It had dropped most of its sticks by the time it got here."

Then it was not Evrard's creature inside the house. That meant—

"So you decided to make a few improvements," I said with a glare to match his own. I pulled my eyebrows down into a frown that I knew would have been more impressive if they had been as shaggy as his. "When I came here today," I continued sternly, not giving him a chance to deny it, "I had not expected to find a wizard from whom age and isolation had taken his reason. But now I learn you've been giving old bones the form of life! You *know* only renegade wizards try to create life. As Royal Wizard, I demand that you dismantle the thing you're making!"

The old wizard was, for a few seconds, too taken aback to answer. I had never talked to him like this before—or, for that matter, to any older wizard. Then he bent over sharply, making creaking sounds. For a second I was afraid I had sent him into a fit. But then I realized he was laughing.

"It isn't funny," I said, trying to preserve at least some of my dignity.

The old wizard straightened up, wiping spit from his mouth and still chuckling. "*You're* certainly amusing, young wizard, trying to act as wise as though you were four times your age and actually knew some magic, and trying to face me down in my own valley."

"You *have* to tell me what you're doing," I said, refusing to be distracted. "I'm responsible for the oversight of any wizardry practiced in this kingdom. It's horribly complex magic. I would think a wizard of light and air had better things to do with his time than mutter long spells over dead bones."

The old wizard had started to turn away. Now he shot me a sharp, sideways glance from under his eyebrows. "And what do *you* know of complex spells and dead bones?" he asked.

"Look," I said, speaking to the old wizard directly, mind to mind, which I had never dared do before. I probed for magic, as I had down in the valley by the Holy Grove. And here, as there, were magic forces channeled by a powerful spell. "Don't deny it now!"

I felt rather than heard reluctant assent. But then the wizard turned his own mind toward me and I staggered back, my own spell disintegrating.

Anyone else's mind is always profoundly strange when met directly, even the mind of a friend. The old wizard's mind revealed both powers beyond what I had expected, as much as I had always respected his abilities, and a strange twist I could not identify but which terrified me.

Back in my own body, I stared at him. What had I felt there? Was it depravity, insanity, or just the strangeness of the old magic? His eyes held mine for five seconds, then he started to laugh again.

I tried to slow my heartbeat with calm breaths. "So you can't deny it," I said, speaking aloud. "You still haven't told me why."

Before the old wizard could answer, I heard a thin, sharp squeak. It sounded almost inhuman, but as I spun around I realized it was Evrard.

He had opened the green door of the wizard's house a crack and was staring within. A second squeak was forced from him as he took a backward step, and the door slowly began to swing open.

The old wizard leaped forward with a cry. He threw his body against the door and threw a powerful binding spell around the entire house. The door slammed shut again.

But not before I had had a glimpse of the creature inside. It was a creature out of nightmare. It was six feet tall and had arms and legs, but other than burning eyes it had no face. The eyes stared at me as though in comprehension. *This* was no botched student project. It looked as though it might once have been human.

Evrard clung to me, his head twisted to stare at the house. His face had gone dead white under the freckles. The old wizard, his dirty beard whipping around him, glared at us with eyes of fire. A whirlwind swirled around him and his whole house.

"Get out," said the old wizard, his voice magically amplified to carry over the roar of the wind. "Get out if you value your lives."

Evrard tugged at my shirt in evident agreement.

"But we can't!" I shouted. "Master, we have to help you!"

"With your weak school spells? Go, and go now!"

I took a step back. The whirlwind seemed to be

diminishing in power. The binding spell, I could tell, held firm.

It might have been my terrified imagination, but the old wizard seemed to be growing, as tall as his house, taller, until his head disappeared among the branches of the oak that leaned over the roof. Staring fascinated, I let Evrard pull me slowly away. Whatever might be beyond the door, the wizard clearly had the powers to deal with it.

Evrard turned and bolted, and I was right behind him. Our normally placid mares had retreated back up the valley, tangling their reins until forced to stop.

They rolled their eyes and bared their teeth as we approached. Evrard, who I had not expected to know much about horses, spoke to them softly and reassuringly, giving them confident shoves on their sweating flanks as he freed the reins.

Behind us, the sound of the whirlwind stopped. I looked back to see a bent, white-haired figure, restored to his normal size, calmly open his green door and disappear within.

I hesitated with one foot in the stirrup. "We have to go back and help him."

"Didn't you hear him? He doesn't want our help!" Exasperation mixed with fear in Evrard's voice. "Don't try to show off again."

I had not been showing off, but otherwise he was right. He kicked his horse into a rapid trot. I swung into the saddle and hurried to catch him. "How did you know how to calm the horses?" I asked. "Is it some new spell?"

"My father ran a livery stable in the City—didn't you know?"

After we crossed the bridge—no sign of the lady and her unicorn this time—we had to dismount to lead our horses under the low branches beyond. Evrard's light blue eyes were still nearly round. "What *was* that in the cottage?"

I shook my head. "You saw it better than I did." I

did not say that to me it looked like a dead human body, resurrected by a renegade wizard who had lost control of his own magic, then given living eyes.

"It looked almost human to me," said Evrard. "You should have warned me the old wizard knew such powerful magic."

I doubted I would ever know that much magic, even if I lived as long as the old wizard had. "I'd no idea anyone could work spells like that without the aid of the supernatural."

Unexpectedly, Evrard smiled. "After you'd warned me so carefully not to antagonize him, you certainly seemed to be trying to do so yourself!"

I decided I should feel relieved he could still smile after what he had just seen, but my immediate thought was that he was taking all this far too casually. "Evrard, I hope you realize you started this. He only decided to try to make that creature after he'd found yours."

"Come on, Daimbert, don't start talking like a schoolteacher! I'm sure you wanted to impress your king two years ago, just as I'm trying to impress the duchess."

He was right; I *was* starting to sound like a school-teacher. I tried to make my next comment sound like one student giving a friendly warning to another. "Sorry about that. But I should tell you something. The duchess' father, the old duke, once kept a wizard. Nearly everyone, as far as I can tell, considered him fairly incompetent. Yet it was in this fairly incompetent wizard's books that I first discovered the spell I think the old wizard is using."

Evrard shrugged and smiled. "Well, I can use it, too, even if I can't make anything that impressive. I bet your predecessor's never had problems like horns falling off!"

Not fifteen minutes ago he had been clinging to me in terror. I was irritated enough with his good humor that I let my mare fall behind, so conversation would be impossible. Wizardry students always played tricks on each other and wizards outside the school normally did not get along at all, but I had been hoping for better relations with the duchess' wizard.

As we came out of the woods half an hour later and started up the hill toward the castle, I glanced surreptitiously over the wall into the little cemetery where kings of Yurt and servants—and chaplains and wizards—of Yurt had been buried for generations. But I saw no sign that anyone had been digging among the quiet graves.

IV

We had left the castle early and it was not yet noon. The old wizard and his creature would need to be watched, but they were not the only strange events going on in Yurt these days. If I could first determine what the duchess was doing, I told myself, and why her tall huntsman had appeared now, then I'd be able to focus on my predecessor. Left alone for a few days, he might even become less furious with me. At lunch, I made a point of talking to Nimrod.

Sitting next to him was not the difficulty I had thought it might be for, as we all assembled in the great hall, Dominic announced that he had decided that our places ought to be moved around and he seated himself next to the duchess.

Nimrod hesitated, then came over when I motioned to him. He walked very gracefully in spite of his height, as if he were holding great strength in check. Sitting down, he no longer towered above me. His long hair was neatly pulled back and tied with a leather thong, and he had excellent table manners for someone who had emerged from the woods looking like a wild man.

The clattering of dishes and spoons made a good screen for private conversation. But Nimrod spoke before I could. "I'm glad I'm having a chance to talk to you properly at last, Wizard. What *are* those horned rabbits, anyway? I know every natural thing of woods and field, and there are none like these."

He spoke in a low voice. I glanced around the table and decided no one was listening to us. Dominic attentively served the duchess before himself and said something which, from his rather forced smile, was probably meant to be a joke. Knowing Dominic, I doubted it was very funny, but Diana laughed appreciatively.

"They were made by wizardry, but not mine," I said. I looked at Nimrod from under my eyebrows, wishing again they were shaggy. "You seemed to know about their existence already when you first appeared in Yurt and I'd like to hear how you knew."

Nimrod gave me a sharp look; then, unexpectedly, he grinned. The suntanned skin made little wrinkles at the corners of his eyes. "Did you suspect me of commissioning a wizard to create magic rabbits, just so I'd have an excuse to come into the kingdom?"

"No," I said although, in fact, at one point I had. I considered giving him an even sterner look and smiled instead. "You still haven't said how you first heard about them."

He hesitated, then said at last, "News of strange creatures travels fast among huntsmen, and I like to go where there's a challenge."

This rather cryptic statement raised more questions than it answered. I was about to ask him more when Dominic's voice, louder than normal, caught both our attentions.

"Perhaps we should have a ball in your honor, gracious lady," he was saying to the duchess. "I'm sure the king and queen would have wanted to take advantage of your extended stay in the royal castle to show you some sort of distinction."

For a second I thought this was meant to be a hint, rather subtle for Dominic, that she had already outstayed her welcome, but when he smiled again and rested his hand on hers it occurred to me that the royal nephew, in his own way, was trying to flirt with Diana.

I glanced quickly at Nimrod to see how he was taking it. He too was looking at the duchess and seemed thoroughly amused.

For a brief moment, Diana stiffened, but she did not pull her hand away. "That would be delightful," she said, with what looked like a genuine smile, warmly enough to make up for her hesitation.

"You know," said Dominic, leaning back as though comfortably relaxed, "I feel as though I've been blind all these years, not to realize before how lovely you are."

All other conversation at both tables had stopped. In both the chambers of knights and ladies and in the kitchens, I knew, there would later be extended speculation and discussion of what Dominic could be doing. But now everyone was too interested to see what he might say next—and how she would respond.

She gave a quick glance down the table, though I could not tell if she were looking toward Nimrod or me. "That's very dear of you to say, Dominic," she said, "but at our age, we scarcely need detain ourselves with these adolescent cooings, do we?"

Dominic took his hand back and frowned. The duchess, her head cocked, smiled sweetly at him. I knew she was teasing him, as apparently did Nimrod, but Dominic was still working it out. Given a choice between interpreting her words as a rejection or as a suggestion that he should speed up his courtship of her—which was indeed proceeding much too slowly for a couple past their first youth—he fell into silence. His silence became embarrassing when no one else at the table spoke, either.

"Did Daimbert tell you we visited the old wizard of Yurt today?" asked Evrard abruptly.

He was too far down the table for me to kick. I

tried speaking to him directly, mind to mind, but he had his thoughts well shielded.

It took the rest of the table a second to remember that I was named Daimbert, but then several seized on the conversational topic because, fascinating as the interchange between Dominic and Diana had been, it had also become very awkward.

"We haven't seen the old wizard since Christmas, I think," said one of the knights. "Is he still well?" The servants' table had given up any pretense of not listening to the head table.

I tried glaring at Evrard, but he was not looking in my direction. Turning him into a frog would certainly divert the conversation, but that seemed a little too drastic.

I did *not,* I told Evrard's unresponsive mind, want the royal court to hear how the old wizard was losing control at least of his housekeeping, probably of his magic, and perhaps of his mind. I certainly did not want to cast them into panic at the thought of an undead creature stalking the night. I'd calmed down enough to decide I should be able to handle the thing if, by chance, it did get loose, but a terrorized population could be very hard to deal with.

But Evrard, who perhaps could hear my silent shouts after all, initially fixed on a different aspect of our visit. "He's got some spectacular magic effects," he said. "Did you know that he has the most beautiful lady in the world sitting by the bridge into his valley?"

Most of the court had seen the illusory lady and her unicorn at some point. "Better than what they have at your school, Wizard?" the same knight asked.

"A lot better," said Evrard. Zahlfast would not have been pleased to hear a recent graduate running down the school so casually. "And he's working on something new, too." No, stop, you idiot! "He wouldn't let us have a real look at it because he's still hammering out the details, but this one's as frightening as his Lady is beautiful."

"He never used to create frightening illusions," one of the ladies said thoughtfully. "Sometimes they'd be amusing and sometimes dramatic, but mostly they'd be beautiful and even moving."

"It's our present Royal Wizard who creates frightening illusions!" said someone else and they all laughed, remembering how everyone—except of course themselves—had been thrown into a blind panic the first time I had made an enormous illusory dragon in the hall. Dominic glowered down the table without joining in the laughter; it was not one of his own better memories.

I relaxed a little, though still keeping my eyes on Evrard's face. He knew as well as I that whatever the old wizard had in his cottage was no illusion, but he seemed content to let the others think it was.

"Well, if old Daimbert's frightened you in the past," said Evrard, "he certainly learned his lesson today. You should have seen him run!"

"You ran first," I said, coldly and levelly, then realized from the looks I was getting that Evrard had succeeded even better than he might have intended in covering up an awkward silence. Speculation about why Dominic should suddenly start courting the duchess was one thing, but an open quarrel between two wizards was an even more titillating lunchtime entertainment for the court.

But Evrard answered good-naturedly. "Of course I did," he agreed with a laugh. "And I'm afraid I gave a very undignified shriek, too."

I would have called it a squeak rather than a shriek, but I let this pass. I smiled for the onlookers. Come to think of it, we *had* left in a very undignified hurry for two supposedly qualified wizards.

"That's the problem with being a new graduate," said Evrard, giving his charming smile. "When they hand you the diploma, you feel you know everything but, in just a few days, you're off at a new post and realize you don't know anything at all, compared to more experienced wizards."

The duchess, now giving Dominic no attention at all, leaned her elbows on the table and looked at her wizard in approval.

General conversation started again as the servants started gathering up the empty platters and bringing out the clean plates for dessert. "So the old wizard is starting work on a new and terrifying project," said Nimrod in a low voice next to my ear.

I jumped, having almost forgotten him.

"My guess is that two young wizards with the latest training wouldn't have been so frightened of something that was only an illusion," Nimrod added. He waited a moment for an answer but, when I said nothing, he took my silence for confirmation and continued. "Horned rabbits are bad enough, but I gather he's made something else. How big is it? Does it move like a man?"

I stared at him. "Have you seen anything like this before?"

He did not answer for a moment, as dessert was now being served. It was fresh raspberry pudding. I caught a pleased look from Gwen at the servants' table—she knew it was my favorite and had doubtless made it herself—and decided I had better not push it away untasted, my initial reaction. I plunged in my spoon determinedly and looked at Nimrod.

"Some years ago," he said, still in that voice just low enough that no one else could hear, but not so low that we might be thought to be whispering secrets, "in the mountains over toward the eastern kingdoms, a renegade wizard made a whole horde of soldiers out of hair and bones."

"And what happened?" I breathed.

"Some other wizards stopped him—ones from your school, as I recall." He ate half his pudding with apparent enjoyment. "I helped track down the horde," he added as though there had been no pause.

I considered his use of the term "renegade," which I was afraid might well be applicable to my predecessor at this point. Nimrod could have chosen the word even if he had never helped the school, but it *was* a term with a specific meaning among wizards. It meant someone whose magic had gone dangerously out of control because he had deliberately rejected the ethical principles of wizardry. There was clearly more to this huntsman than I'd first thought and that could be useful.

"Don't leave the kingdom," I said. "I may need you." I attacked my own pudding, relieved to think that wizards from the school might have dealt with something like this before, even though those creatures of hair and bone had doubtless been made by something closer to the spell with which Evrard had made his rabbits than whatever "improved" spell my predecessor had used. I felt much more cheerful, especially since the pudding really was delicious.

As the meal finished and everyone rose from the table, the chaplain touched me on the elbow. "Could you come to my room for a few minutes?"

As I followed him upstairs, I thought that during the last two years I had mostly discussed issues both weighty and trivial with Joachim. But only a few days of Evrard's company had reminded me that a priest and a wizard will never have much in common. Wizards may argue violently, but at least they agree on the fundamental issues. The chaplain, I feared, would have no interest in what I had glimpsed through the cottage door once he was reassured that the old wizard's spells had not put his soul in peril.

V

Joachim sat down on a hard chair across from me and looked at me thoughtfully. His eyes were so dark and deep-set that they merged with the shadows of the room.

"I gather from what your friend said that the old wizard has progressed beyond horned rabbits and is now making something far more serious," he said. He paused briefly, but when I did not reply, he continued as though in answer to my unspoken question, "I doubt two wizards would have been frightened by mere illusion."

I shook my head ruefully. "Nimrod said almost exactly the same thing. I'd hoped it wasn't that obvious."

"I think the rest of the court remembers your predecessor primarily for his illusions, and they're happy to believe that whatever frightening thing he's working on now is no more real than his winged horses at Christmas dinner."

"But if you and Nimrod saw through Evrard's dissembling at once, it may not take some of the others much longer. Even Dominic's not nearly as thick as he sometimes seems. By the way, the duchess seems to want to keep this secret, but it turns out she had asked Evrard to make her the horned rabbits."

"You still haven't told me what frightened you," the chaplain replied, uninterested in the duchess and in rabbits.

"Two things," I said slowly. "First was the creature that both Evrard and I glimpsed through the old wizard's cottage door. It was six feet tall and had human eyes. It moved, but it wasn't alive. It moved by magic," I added hastily as Joachim started to speak. "There was nothing supernatural about it. The old wizard may be acting very strangely, but he's not become evil."

"Surely you know," said Joachim quietly, "that fallen man is always capable of doing evil on his own, without invoking the supernatural powers of darkness. Tell me what else frightened you."

"This is something Evrard doesn't know about." I paused. The castle seemed nearly silent. Elsewhere, people were doubtless laughing and talking, but their voices did not carry to us. "I touched the old wizard's mind, very briefly. It's got a bend or a twist or, at any rate, something I've never seen. I hadn't tried before today communicating with him mind to mind, so I don't know whether he's always been like this, or if this is related to whatever mental breakdown he may be experiencing."

"Could it be a manifestation of an evil will?" asked the chaplain, his dark eyes burning.

"I just don't know," I said, thinking irritably that priests always seemed to want to turn magical problems into part of the struggle between good and evil.

Joachim said nothing more for a moment. "Something six feet tall with human eyes," he repeated at last. "If it's not alive or was never alive, it won't have a soul." That might reassure him somewhat, but I didn't find it much help.

"The old wizard does seem to have it very well locked up," I said. "Certainly there's a danger that it could turn on him but, at the moment, I'm hesitant to do anything that might distract him from what appears to be an excellent binding spell."

We were both silent for a moment. "But I still don't understand why he would do it, Joachim," I said then. "He's retired, highly respected. He has nothing more to prove. I know he's been acting rather peculiarly, but why should he want to make a monster?"

"Pride," said Joachim as though it explained it all. "Jealousy."

"Jealousy? Of whom? He's never had anything but scorn for my abilities and he thinks even less of Evrard."

"Isn't that a little strong?" asked Joachim with a slow smile. "I thought he'd been happy to teach you herbal magic."

"He's always been quick to point out my failings. I think he was only willing to teach me a little because he felt my school training had been so inadequate."

"I still think he is jealous of you," said Joachim, not

smiling any longer. "At first he was jealous of your youth, your ability to learn rapidly, the fact that you were Royal Wizard, a position in which he no longer felt competent. And then the one problem he couldn't solve, the one that made him decide to resign so abruptly, you came in with your own courage and wizardry and solved it."

I shivered. "With your help," I said. That experience was something else I didn't like to think about.

"And now there are not just one, but two, young wizards here in Yurt. He needs to do something to demonstrate, both to you and to himself, the superiority of his magic. And that's where he has been captured by the sin of pride."

Joachim, I thought, could bring any conversation back to sin.

"I know wizards have spells to give them long life," he said with a quick look in my direction. "But even a long life may not give a man the opportunity he needs to come to terms with his own mortality."

"But what does this have to do with pride?" I asked when Joachim paused.

"Since you're a wizard, too," he said after a moment, "I don't want to say anything that would sound like an accusation against you. But I think it must be even harder when one is used to wielding enormous power all one's life to realize that, at the end, one has no more power over one's life than does a newborn baby."

I was probably supposed to be gratified to hear that wizards could wield enormous power.

"Although one cannot live forever," Joachim went on, "someone may try to create something that will live on beyond one's short span. In one form, this desire for creation is God's power reflected in His creatures, the impetus to produce and cherish children, the basis for philosophy and art—even wizardry. But carried too far it becomes pride, the desire to become God's equal. In trying to duplicate God's act of creation, your predecessor endangered his soul.

"When facing his own death, when facing a young wizard with surprisingly good abilities, he needed to demonstrate that his powers of creation had not faltered. And he went beyond the limits ordained for mortal men because he tried to make a new living creature, to imitate God Himself."

"You've got all the answers," I said grumpily.

"You asked for my opinion," said Joachim reasonably.

We both fell silent again. I forced myself to consider what the chaplain had said.

It made sense. Stripped of the comments about sin, his explanation accorded fairly closely with what the school had taught us, one of the few lessons, in fact, that I had learned so well that I could no longer consciously remember first hearing it. Those who try the mightiest spells, delving deeply into the forces of magic, always do so at peril: theirs and others. And when such a spell is worked from base motives, from pride and envy, the peril is far greater.

Maybe I should try to explain to the old wizard that he had no reason to be jealous of Evrard and me— but I could think of no way to phrase it that wouldn't sound patronizing and, besides, he seemed to be in the process of demonstrating beyond any question that his magic was indeed much stronger than ours. I realized that everything Joachim had said could also apply to Evrard and the horned rabbits, but I dismissed this. My own attempts to impress my new employers were too recent for me to be able to think of another young wizard as driven by pride.

"Will you call your school?" Joachim asked. "Could you dismantle the creature? Is it likely to escape?"

"I don't know at the moment how to dismantle it, certainly not if my predecessor wanted to stop me. And I'm very reluctant to call the school. I don't get along very well with the old wizard as it is; if I brought in representatives of the school he despises to take away his magical creation, he'd never speak to me again. And it wouldn't do much good, anyway. The spell was out of the old magic of earth and herbs, unlike anything in modern scientific magic.

"At the moment, the creature doesn't seem at all likely to escape. In the next few days, I'm going to talk to the wood nymph now that I know how; I'll try to find out more about Nimrod; and I should probably catch the rest of Evrard's idiotic rabbits. Once I've gotten all the other distractions out of the way, I'll try to work out how to break the spell that holds my predecessor's creature together. What do you think?"

"You've already told me twice that this is a problem for a wizard, not for a priest." There was a hint of a smile in the angle of Joachim's cheekbones. "I think you're enjoying having another young wizard here." In spite of everything, he was right. "This seems like something the two of you should be able to handle."

"What do you think are Dominic's intentions with the duchess?" I asked abruptly, wanting to change the subject. Since half the castle was probably discussing the pair, I thought we might as well, too.

"I must admit to being surprised," said the chaplain. "To every indication, he has begun to court her in earnest, but one must wonder why his affections have become suddenly engaged after so many years of aquaintance. I would have hoped either one or both would have come to talk to me about their wedding plans, before these plans became so open."

For an intelligent and highly educated priest, Joachim could sometimes be startling obtuse. "I don't think Dominic has any wedding plans," I said, "and I'm sure Diana doesn't either. My own guess is that his courting just started today, and it has no more serious goal than keeping Nimrod and the duchess from carrying out what Dominic considers inappropriate flirtation."

"That could be," said Joachim, as though he found it highly unlikely. "But some of his gestures and comments were too explicit for him not to have had previous encouragement."

I laughed, glad to find something worth laughing at. "That's just Dominic. He's never had much finesse in his dealings—he has even less tact than you do." Joachim frowned at this. "I won't keep you longer," I said, standing up. "Have you heard anything more from those priests about the Holy Toe?"

"I won't hear anything more until they arrive," he said gravely.

Evrard was already back in my study, once again settled in my best chair. At least he wasn't wearing my dressing gown. "Why did you bring up the old wizard over lunch?" I asked him shortly.

"You didn't want me to?" he asked, so much remorse in his wide blue eyes it was almost comical.

"Certainly not," I said, sitting down in my second-best chair and refusing to be mollified. "Several people have already realized that if something was bad enough to make you squeak with terror, it was more than illusion. As soon as Dominic realizes it—or has one of the knights point it out to him—he's going to organize a military expedition to roust the creature out of the old wizard's cottage."

"But he couldn't do that," said Evrard, concerned. "The old wizard's magic would stop him."

"Of course. The most Dominic could accomplish with his knights would be to distract the old wizard enough that he would let down the binding spells containing his creature and it would escape."

I hadn't thought of this possibility until I said it, but it immediately seemed disturbingly likely.

Evrard smiled at me. "You're even more frightened of that creature than I am! But you don't need to worry about the old wizard. He has a powerful binding spell to hold it down."

"And what do *you* know about binding spells?"

"I can do many spells," he replied in a perfectly

sober voice, in spite of the twitching corners of his mouth. "Watch this."

I jumped up and interrupted the binding spell he started to put on my foot. "I don't think I need a demonstration. Besides, you have a word wrong in the Hidden Language—right *there*."

"Oh," he said in chagrin. "You're right. You would have gotten your foot free in no time." He smiled up at me and I sat down again. "At least now I know my mistake. You see, I almost never make the same mistake twice."

"That's good," I said, sounding surly even in my own ears. Since I was irritated with Joachim for being a priest and with Evrard for being a young wizard, maybe I should be irritated with myself for being me.

"Even aside from his binding spells," Evrard continued, "I'm certain the old wizard could stop Dominic. 'A competent wizard should always be victorious against an armed knight.' They taught us that in thaumaturgy class."

"And would *you* always be victorious?"

Evrard leaned forward and dropped his voice, though there was no one to overhear us. "Don't tell the duchess, but I was never very good at those spells. But I'm working on them!"

I tried to decide if I was good at the spells to stop armed knights. I had never had occasion to try. But Evrard was certainly right in one respect: a wizard who could grow thirty feet tall in the middle of a whirlwind would not find Dominic a problem.

PART FOUR
The Wood Nymph

I

Since I had told Evrard I really would turn him into a frog if he brought up the old wizard and his monster again, I expected dinner to be more quiet than lunch. Once again, Dominic seated Diana next to him and I ended up next to Nimrod.

The more I thought about it, the more I was sure that she must have known the huntsman earlier. For that matter, from his polished language and behavior, he must be other than what he at first seemed. It might explain a lot, even her surprising lack of ease when they first met, if she had last met him, say, in a very different context. I tried again to question him when dinner was almost over.

"So I understand the duchess is enjoying catching horned rabbits," I said casually. "Tell me, have you tried to track them down in the valley of Saint Eusebius? The valley seems to have strong powers of attraction for creatures of magic. I'm planning to go there tomorrow, to explore its magical properties more thoroughly, and I was wondering . . ."

But I never got a chance to say more. At that point,

Dominic rose to his feet. He looked pale, unusual in someone ruddy, and highly determined. He started to speak, got as far as "My lords and ladies—" and his voice cracked. Evrard smiled, but no one else dared.

Dominic tried again. "My lords and ladies of Yurt! I would like your attention. I have a special announcement to make. As you know, I have served King Haimeric of Yurt, my uncle, for most of my life, at present as his regent. But recently I have been thinking of doing something rather different."

There was a murmur of surprise. Dominic was as much a fixture of the castle as the king's rose garden.

"In fact, once the king and queen return and release me from my regency, I think I shall leave Yurt. I have not yet decided where I shall go."

My first startled thought—the thought of a city merchant's son—was to wonder what he would live on. He had all a prince could want as long as he was in Yurt, but his wealth was based on the revenues from the castle's own lands—really nothing more than a glorified allowance from the king.

The silence was broken by Hugo, the youth who had been training in knighthood under Dominic's direction. "You can come back to the City with me at the end of the summer if you like," he said. "Mother and Father won't mind."

Dominic smiled, almost affectionately. "I'll consider it," he said, then became determined again. "Before I go, there is something very important I want to settle."

He turned toward the duchess, on whom a horrible realization seemed to be dawning, and went down on one knee before her on the flagstones.

If I had determined to propose marriage to a woman I had already decided six years ago I didn't want to marry, then I would have done it in private. But that apparently wouldn't do for the royal regent.

He took a ring out of his pocket. From where I was sitting, I could see the firelight glint on the diamond. It was an enormous stone. We had in the castle treasury the jewelry that had once belonged to Dominic's mother and this must be from the collection.

Diana looked, for once in her life, completely nonplussed. I had the sickening feeling one sometimes has when seeing a bad accident about to happen, that everything is taking place very slowly but one is too paralyzed to do anything about it.

"My lady, I offer you this ring as a token," said the regent gravely. "A token of my love for you, which I dare to hope you may return. A token of my wish that you and I should become man and wife."

This had gone far beyond paying court to a woman to keep her from making a spectacle of herself with somebody else. Dominic, I thought, had simply lost his mind.

Diana took a deep breath. "Prince Dominic," she said in a high, clear voice, "you have set my maidenly heart aflutter." She did not take the ring held out to her.

I glanced toward Nimrod beside me and found his face stiff with tension.

"While I fully appreciate your sentiments," the duchess continued, "your proposal is so sudden that I will need at least a week to give you my answer." She gave a sudden, saucy smile. "After all, I've been single nearly as long as you have—that is, all my life—and it's hard to contemplate such a complete change so suddenly."

"Of course," said Dominic, watching her face as though searching for a hidden meaning.

I caught the chaplain's eye across the table. If he said, "I told you so," I would deserve it.

Diana rose to her feet with a swirl of the skirt she had put on for dinner. "Right now, I still need to concentrate on catching the last of those great horned rabbits. If you don't mind, Prince, I shall go to my room and plan tomorrow's hunt." Dominic nodded shortly.

As the duchess moved toward the door, she stopped

as though she had just thought of something and turned back. "Since I'm planning a hunt, I need my chief huntsman. Nimrod, could you join me?"

Nimrod smiled like the sun coming up and jumped to his feet so suddenly that his chair crashed over. He strode across the hall and he and the duchess left together. The rest of us retreated rapidly, almost in panic, not daring to look at the regent.

"We'd better stay out of Dominic's way for a while," I told Evrard that evening. "And it sounds as though the duchess won't want your help hunting the horned rabbits. Tomorrow I'll take you to the Holy Grove of Saint Eusebius so you can meet the wood nymph."

The next morning, I sent Evrard to the stables to supervise the saddling of our mares while I went to find the regent. If I could sort out the magical problems associated with the Holy Grove in the next day or two and if the duchess would just start behaving herself, then I could turn my full attention to the old wizard and his creature. Maybe by then I'd even have some ideas.

I would have liked to leave the castle without telling Dominic we were going, but he was, after all, regent. I squared my shoulders and hoped that by now he would be calm enough that I could talk to him coherently.

I expected to find the royal nephew in his chambers having breakfast, or already seated on the throne in the great hall. But I could not find him. When I returned to the stables, wondering uneasily where he could be, I noticed a number of horses were missing.

"That's right," said the stable boy I asked. "It seems like everyone has already gone somewhere this morning. The chaplain, Prince Dominic, a lot of the knights, the duchess and her new huntsman, they've all left."

"So what do you think?" asked Evrard, who seemed

to find the situation hilarious. "Have the duchess and Nimrod eloped and Dominic gone after them?"

As we rode out across the drawbridge, the clear sky promised another day of perfect weather. I asked myself how normally rational adults could act like this. And where could Joachim have possibly gone? I had enough to do solving magical problems in the kingdom without being responsible for everyone's emotional crises. For Dominic abruptly to decide to get married after all these years, for Diana to hire a wizard, commission horned rabbits, and flirt outrageously with a huntsman . . .

"Do you think Dominic will still want to marry her if she's run off with Nimrod?" asked Evrard. "I must say I was surprised he proposed. I wouldn't have thought their temperaments would be similar enough."

"If Dominic has decided it's finally time to get married, he may not have a lot of women to choose from. The only alternative I can think of is the queen's aunt Maria, and they would be even less compatible."

"But if Dominic and the duchess do get married, and he wants to leave Yurt, do you think she'll go with him? Will she still want a ducal wizard?"

I didn't answer. More relevant was the question of whether Dominic would murder Nimrod—and maybe Diana as well. She would have a lot to answer for if King Haimeric came home to find that his kingdom, as he knew it, no longer existed. For that matter, so would I.

Evrard broke into my thoughts again. "Are you going to try to make the wood nymph leave the hermit's grove?"

"I want to see if the old spell to talk to her really works," I said, "and you and I should catch the rest of your rabbits if they're still at that end of the kingdom—this business of creating magical animals just to hunt them has gone far enough. And while we're at it, I'm afraid we probably ought to find the duchess and Nimrod. As for the nymph, I told the chaplain I would talk to her and I really should do so before the priests of Saint Eusebius arrive."

I had been going to add that I also wanted to see if the entrepreneurs were still on the cliff above the Holy Grove, but Evrard interrupted me. "It seems to me, Daimbert," he said in exasperation, "that you let that priest boss you around much too much. Didn't they warn you at school about staying out of the Church's affairs?"

"I'm not being bossed around," I said, determined not to be angry. If Evrard and I didn't present a united front, the situation would become even worse. "As wizards, we need to examine all magical phenomena. I've never talked to a wood nymph before."

Evrard nodded, somewhat mollified, but he did not speak again. After a short distance, we passed the village from which the different claimants had come whose case the king had judged. The place was full of activity and the big wheel on the mill was turning. I thought of pointing it out to Evrard but decided to say nothing.

From two years of associating with Joachim, who had never been good at light chatter, I was accustomed to long silences. But it occurred to me that it would be a real effort of will for someone like Evrard not to say something. As we rode through the hills of Yurt, past high fields where hay was being raked and low meadows where cows raised their heads to look at us, past streams and sudden valleys and distant hilltops where a church spire rose from a cluster of houses, I considered the irony of the situation. The last time I had ridden this way, Joachim had felt constrained in talking to me because I had no interest in religious issues. This time, Evrard was behaving exactly the same way, but because I had too much interest in such issues.

But when we stopped to rest our horses, Evrard turned to me as though there had been no tension.

"Tell me more about the wood nymph. Is she as beautiful as that unicorn lady?"

"She *is* lovely," I said, "but she doesn't look anything like that lady. The nymph has violet eyes and dusky skin, the color of shadows in the deep forest. She's not human, even though she looks human—she may even be immortal. Apparently she's lived in the grove for centuries. Let me run through the spell to call a nymph."

He paid close attention and mastered the key elements far faster than I had although, I reminded myself, I had not had his advantage of having someone else organize and explain it all clearly.

As we remounted our mares, I was startled to feel a sudden constriction around my body. I could not move my arms or even keep my balance. My mare gave a little jump as she felt me starting to shift. I toppled slowly and majestically from the saddle. There was barely enough movement left in my lower legs to get my feet free of the stirrups in time and I was just able to snatch at a few words of the Hidden Language to break my fall.

Then I heard Evrard laughing. He reined up a few yards ahead and turned back. "So you don't think I can do a good binding spell? I *told* you I don't make the same mistake twice!"

It *was* a good binding spell. But I didn't give him the satisfaction of saying so, instead turning my attention to unravelling it. Someone else's spell always takes longer to break than one's own and, since he showed no signs of helping, it took me several minutes to get free.

Then I allowed myself to smile as I rubbed a bruised elbow and went to retrieve my mare, who had started once again to graze. "Not bad," I said with a guileless grin, swinging up into the saddle. "You really did surprise me. It might not equal the old wizard's spell, but you certainly had me tied tight."

"I'm sorry, Daimbert," said Evrard, still laughing

and sounding not at all penitent, "but you've been acting so serious about everything that I thought I should—"

He did not finish the sentence. He rose straight up from the saddle to a distance of about ten feet, shot sideways, and dropped. I managed to set him down quite lightly.

Now it was my turn to laugh, so hard that my mare turned her head around to look at me. After dusting himself off and giving me one truculent look, Evrard joined in.

Dominic and the duchess, I told myself, could take care of themselves. I was the wizard of this kingdom and my concerns were magical, not social.

"Let's call a truce," I said to Evrard. This was as good as being back in school. "If we keep binding and lifting each other, we'll never get to the wood nymph's grove."

"Truce it is," he said cheerfully. Just like back in school, I immediately and surreptitiously started preparing a new lifting spell, just in case. He approached his startled mare, making reassuring sounds, and remounted. "Did you ever hear the joke about the nun, the nixie, and the wood nymph?"

II

In mid-afternoon, we reached a fork in the trail. Turning one way would take us to the duchess' castle and the other way up onto the high plateau, toward the valley of the Holy Grove. The day had turned hot and the road dusty. I hesitated, taking a pull from my waterskin.

Evrard interrupted my thoughts. "Which road gets us to the wood nymph's grove the fastest?"

"This way," I said with sudden decision. It would be shadowy and refreshing down in the limestone valley where the hermit and the wood nymph lived. The duchess could wait.

The wind blew on top of the plateau, drying the sweat on our foreheads, as we approached the low wall where one could look down into the valley. Evrard looked thoughtfully at the view. "I didn't get a chance to ask the duchess when we were up here," he said. "Were there once castles in this valley?" pointing toward the rock formations. The white limestone, emerging in tall, tumbled shapes from the trees that clung to the valley walls, did indeed look like ruins.

"I think those are all natural. The stone weathers like that over the millennia." It was such a responsibility being burdened with Evrard's continuing education.

As we continued along the valley rim, I was surprised to see some raw wooden scaffolding, partially erected. It looked as though the entrepreneurs were going ahead with their plan to build a giant windlass to lower pilgrims to the Holy Grove. I had almost persuaded myself that it was all a façade, designed only to irritate Eusebius, the Cranky Saint, enough to make him leave. But it looked as though both Joachim and I were wrong on this point.

The young man in the feathered cap came out as we approached his booth. The sign was still there proclaiming, "See the Holy Toe! Five pennies on foot, fifteen pennies in the basket." But there was something different about the booth. On the little shelf in front, small shapes were clustered. As we came closer, I could see that they were ceramic figurines.

"Greetings, Wizard!" said the young man cheerfully, recognizing me at once. "Have you changed your mind? Do you want to join us? As you can see, we've got our figurines and brochures, including the story of how someone prayed to the saint to be healed of the pox after years of mocking him, and the saint only healed him along one side to teach him a lesson. We're going to add vials of water from the holy spring this week. And we're almost ready for the basket, though we still think it would be better if people could be raised and lowered by magic—certainly it would be more impressive!"

"And it might even be safer," said Evrard, looking dubiously at the scaffolding.

"Are you another wizard?" the young man cried in delight, noticing the moons and stars embroidered on the jacket slung over Evrard's saddlebag. "I knew it! The Royal Wizard has brought you here, hasn't he, to join in our enterprise. It's a wonderful opportunity, I assure you! Once the hordes of tourists and pilgrims start to arrive, the silver pennies will just pour in."

I had dismounted for a closer look at the figurines, but I froze when Evrard did not answer. I swiveled around toward him. Could he possibly be taking such a proposal seriously?

Still mounted, he turned his blue eyes ingenuously toward the young man. "I'll have to take it under advisement," he said gravely. "You realize, of course, that unless you were able to pay me at least five hundred silver pennies a week, it wouldn't be worth my while. That's what the duchess is paying me. And of course I'd need a month's advance before I could even consider beginning."

I turned my back to hide a sudden grin and picked up a figurine of a toe.

The young man gasped behind me. "But five hundred silver pennies—" He paused briefly. "Well," he continued then in a calculating tone, "if we charged them twenty-five pennies each for a *magic* ride and were able to get at least twenty pilgrims a week, we would gross that much. And although we'd been thinking of twenty-five pennies for the round trip, we might be able to charge them fifteen pennies to descend and twenty more for the ascent. But by the time we divided it . . ."

"How many ways were you planning to divide the money made by *my* magic?" asked Evrard.

I held my breath, listening.

"Well, five, counting you, although we need half the receipts for 'overhead,' and we'd also promised . . ." There was a long pause. "And we'll have to negotiate on the month's advance. Look, why don't you give me a chance to talk to the others and we'll be in touch. You say you're working with the duchess now?"

"Who *are* the others?" I demanded, turning sharply around. Joachim had said three priests were coming and I suddenly wondered if they might be this young man's still unseen associates.

His answer did nothing to dissuade me on this point. "Just some friends of mine," he said vaguely. "Keep in touch, Wizards!"

He stepped back under the shade of the big tree across from his booth, without even trying to persuade me to buy the ugly figurine of the Holy Toe I was still holding. I put it down next to a rather misshapen dragon and remounted.

When we had ridden a hundred yards from the booth, I turned to Evrard and said, "Try telling the duchess she's paying you five hundred silver pennies a week. You may be surprised at her answer."

The walls of the narrow valley stretched their shadows over us as we followed the river upstream toward the Holy Grove. The cooler air and the murmur of the flowing water took away the incipient headache which had been growing during our dusty ride, but I also realized how late in the day it had become.

"First we should set traps for the horned rabbits in case there are still any in the valley," I said. "How did you catch them before?"

"The first time," said Evrard with a frown, "I used a calling spell, flew up to them once they came near, and grabbed them. I had to get them by the rear end or they'd bite—and even so they kicked. I didn't try a trap for fear they would disintegrate. But these past few days, they were moving much faster and seemed much more cunning, so I'm not sure grabbing them will work anymore."

The results of the old wizard's improvements, I thought. "Well, let's try a trap now," I said. I found some string in my saddlebag from which I tried to weave a net.

"That doesn't look very effective," commented Evrard.

He was right; city boys never learn much about nets. But I wasn't going to say so. "It will be fine," I said loftily, "once I attach a paralysis spell."

I had actually made myself fairly good at attaching spells to objects. In a few more minutes, I had my net arranged under a bush, where I hoped a rabbit might hop. Anything that entered the net should immediately become paralyzed. I doubted the spell would last more than a short time, so any other creature that blundered in would soon be able to escape again, but with any luck the spell would cause a horned rabbit to disintegrate. "We can check later," I said, "and see how many we've caught."

Evrard gathered what he told me were especially tempting herbs for rabbits and dropped them into the net, from a height of several feet so as not to imprison his own hand.

"But since they're not alive, they don't eat," I objected.

"I think they still have the *habit* of eating," he said gravely, "laid down in the bones. I saw them nibbling on plants like this before."

As we started up the path toward the waterfall and the grove, I said, "Remember what I warned you. Even if we don't actually see the hermit, we shouldn't make any remark about the Holy Toe that he might overhear—we don't want to insult him." To sound less like a schoolteacher, I added, "It may be hard. It *is* awfully silly."

"From what you say," said Evrard, much more seriously than I expected, "the saint, the wood nymph, and a succession of hermits have all been living here together for generations. The hermits—and for that matter the saint himself—must have gotten used to the nymph. She can't always have made respectfully pious remarks yet, by now, they must be able to get along."

I glanced back toward the rough stone huts among the trees. Today I saw no sign of the hermit's apprentices. "But maybe some of her remarks have helped keep the saint cranky. And that still doesn't mean they are used to the comments of young wizards."

I paused, struck by a new idea. "But maybe it does! After all, both my predecessor and the old ducal wizard seem to have known the wood nymph quite well, a long time ago. If the hermits, the saint, and the nymph have made a threesome for generations, then maybe the wizards of Yurt have been a consistent fourth."

"Well, who else would keep a nymph entertained?" asked Evrard with a mischievous sideways glance from his wide blue eyes. "A hermit's not going to provide her with much action—and even less so a disembodied saint, when all that's left of him is his toe!"

But when we reached the grove, he seemed suitably respectful. "So—there it is," he said in a colorless voice, looking at the shrine of Saint Eusebius. If the detailing on the golden reliquary matched the saint's toe accurately, he had had an ingrown toenail. Perhaps that was one of the reasons he was cranky. "I don't see the hermit. Should we call him?"

"He's probably praying," I said. "We shouldn't disturb him. Last time I saw the nymph beyond those trees. Let's start over there."

We picked our way across the damp ground, following the faintly marked trails between the little springs. There was nothing in or behind the first dozen trees we looked at. In a short distance, the thick foliage and the smooth, silent trunks had managed to confuse me, so that I was no longer sure where I had come when I was here before. I was, however, fairly sure the nymph was teasing us deliberately. Several times we nearly lost our footing in the mud.

I had almost decided we should start for the duchess' castle before it became any later when I heard Evrard catch his breath. I turned my head very slowly.

She leaned against the pale trunk of a beech, as I had seen her before, her enormous violet eyes fixed on us but no expression on her face.

"Good day," said Evrard tentatively, which drew no response.

But I began at once with the words of the Hidden Language. When I finished the spell I paused, watching her. Her expression altered like ice breaking up in the spring. She began to smile, a smile both delighted and delightful.

"The spell worked!" I thought and just managed not to say it out loud.

"Greetings, Wizards!" she said. "It's been a long time since a wizard has been here, much less two!" Her eyes twinkled. "If I'm not mistaken, one of you is the new Royal Wizard of Yurt and the other, the new Ducal Wizard."

"Greetings, Lady," said Evrard, apparently perfectly at ease. "Daimbert has been Royal Wizard for two years, but he hasn't had a chance to meet you before. I'm Evrard, the duchess' wizard. I've just recently arrived in the kingdom."

She turned swiftly, smiling at us over her shoulder, and stepped behind a trunk. When we followed her a second later, we saw no one. But almost immediately a voice called from the branches above. "Come up!"

I put together the flying spell and rose slowly upwards. Evrard bit his lip, frowned, and then followed, without enough hesitation to make it worth commenting.

Forty feet up, a number of branches growing close together formed a hidden platform on which were spread rugs and cushions. Rustling green leaves formed a partial roof but from the platform one could also look out and up, toward the magnificent crown of the tree, the white limestone cliffs of the valley, and the deep blue of the sky beyond.

The wood nymph was already seated in the green shadows. As we arrived, she held out a wooden bowl toward us. "Have some raspberries." As she leaned toward us, offering the bowl, her hair fell over her shoulder and brushed my hand. It was just as soft as it looked. I almost expected the berries to vanish, but they stayed real and delicious all the way down my throat.

Evrard looked around thoughtfully. "Is this all there is to your house?"

She smiled. "It's all I need. It's humans, not wood nymphs, who try to build and create."

"What do you do when it rains?"

The nymph laughed, a charming sound like wind through the leaves. "I thought the necessary magic would be obvious to a wizard."

Evrard shook his head, almost blushing. "You live and breathe magic, Lady. We wizards have to learn it and I'm afraid I'm still learning. Have you lived here long?"

"I've lived here all my life," she said with another smile. Even Evrard knew better than to ask her how long that had been.

III

We sat on her cushions, eating raspberries and drinking spring water, while the blue slowly faded from the sky far above us. Tiny breaths of wind fluttered the leaves and touched our faces as gently as a caress. The water—or maybe the wood nymph's conversation—went to my head like fine wine. Sheltered as we were by branches above us and on either side, the broader world soon seemed very inconsequential.

The worrisome affairs of the duchess, Nimrod, and

Dominic shrank in importance, becoming something trivial they'd work out for themselves. It was clear that Saint Eusebius would never really want to leave such a lovely place—I could have stayed here forever myself.

The nymph asked us questions about the royal castle of Yurt, listened to our answers with her full attention, laughed approvingly at our jokes, and kept our water glasses full. Her own wit kept us teasingly at bay and invited further confidences. Every movement was graceful, every look and word from her as sensuous as a sunwarmed breeze.

If I had not already been in love with the queen, I would have been in love at once. I tore my eyes away from the nymph long enough to look toward Evrard. He had never even met the queen and he didn't have a chance.

With a start, I realized it was evening. I glanced upward to find that all the branches above us had lost their detail in darkness, and the sky beyond was only a somewhat lighter shade of gray. When I looked again toward Evrard and the wood nymph, they were invisible, hidden in shadows. I had been able to see perfectly until a glance upward, to the world outside of the nymph's cozy nest, showed me that it was so dark I shouldn't have been able to see for the last hour.

The nymph, too, knew it was late. I could hear her standing up. "Come see me again tomorrow," she said, the smile clear in her voice.

We floated slowly down toward the ground. Evrard was silent as we groped our way through the grove and then, once free of the trees, lifted to fly over the waterfall towards our mares, slightly paler gray shapes in the darkness. As we mounted, he gave a long, contented sigh. "She wants us to see her again tomorrow. I'd like to see her every day of my life."

"You can't bind yourself to a wood nymph," I said reprovingly. "She'll live forever or at least for many more centuries, whereas a wizard isn't good for more than two or three hundred years. And you know wizards don't marry, anyway."

Evrard's laugh came out of the darkness. "You're being a schoolteacher again, Daimbert."

He was right but, at the moment, I was more concerned about our horses' footing. My mare stopped, unwilling to go further on the uneven trail. I was not even sure we were still on the trail. I looked toward the sky, a slice of stars between the darkness of the cliffs.

"We need a light," I said. What we really needed was a magic lantern. I tried lighting up my mare's bit and bridle, which worked quite nicely to light up the path, but made her jerk her head so violently that I ended the spell at once.

"How far is it to the duchess' castle?" Evrard asked. "Do you think we'll be able to make it?"

I had been wondering the same thing. "Her castle must be nearly ten miles from here and the old count's isn't much closer. I think we'd better stay here."

"How about going back to the nymph's tree?"

I'd known he'd suggest that. "We can't very well impose on her. Besides, I don't want to grope around the grove, trying to find her. It was confusing enough in daylight."

Evrard gave another happy sigh. I realized with a shock that I had no clear idea what we and the nymph had discussed for the hours we had been in her tree, only the warm feeling that it had been a delightful conversation. If my purpose in coming to the valley was to persuade her to leave the Holy Grove, I was no closer to doing so than I had been before—in fact further, because I had as little wish as Evrard did to see her leave Yurt.

From the corner of my eye, I suddenly thought I saw a flash of light. There was a faint whispering sound that was not the whispering of the leaves. I probed quickly with magic and found several people moving toward us. After a startled second I remembered: the old hermit's apprentices.

The young men approached us, carrying a torch. One stepped out of the shadows next to my mare, making her jerk hard against the bit. The torchlight gave his badly shaved head the unreal quality of something out of a bad dream. But his voice was both polite and frightened.

"Excuse me, Father, but we heard your voices. Has something happened to the hermit?"

I realized he must think I was Joachim. "I'm not the Royal Chaplain," I said, "but the wizard who was with him when we saw you before. I've come to the valley with another wizard on a different mission entirely. As far as I know, no one is planning to take your master away from here."

There was a pause and one of the other apprentices whispered something. "It's the wood nymph, isn't it?" said the apprentice who had already spoken.

"What do you know about the wood nymph?" I asked quickly. But he shook his head without answering.

"Is there somewhere near we could stay tonight?" Evrard put in suddenly.

This seemed to delight the apprentices. All of them stared at us for a second and then began to grin. "Hospitality," said the one who appeared to be their leader. "We've had very little opportunity to practice hospitality and, yet, that is a duty of the solitary hermit. You can stay in our huts with us!"

The stone huts had never looked very appealing, but they had to be better than sleeping in the open. The apprentices lit our way with their torches.

I thought of saying, "Well done, young wizard," to Evrard but decided I had already sounded like a schoolteacher enough for one day. "Good work," I said instead. "But don't let them see any satisfied smirks if we talk to them about the nymph. We shouldn't shock their chaste sensibilities."

*　　*　　*

From the single blanket roll in the corner of the one-roomed hut, I assumed that only one of the apprentices lived here, probably the one who served as leader. Each of them must have his own hut in which to practice living in isolation. It didn't look as though being an apprentice hermit was anywhere near as entertaining as being a student wizard.

All five of the apprentices crowded in with us. "We need food for our guests," said our host and two disappeared into the night. In a minute they returned with some lettuces, an earthenware jug of goat's milk, and rather stale pieces of bread.

The wood nymph's raspberries, highly satisfying while we were eating them, now seemed to have made no impact, and we ate hungrily. The dense bread wasn't bad if eaten with enough lettuce and the goat's milk was better than I had feared.

The apprentice hermits made a small fire in the middle of the room and sat against the far wall from us, tugging their scraps of clothing around them as the evening air coming through the open doorway became cooler. I wondered where they had come from originally and, if one of them eventually replaced the hermit at the spring, what would happen to the rest.

"Have you ever seen the wood nymph?" Evrard asked conversationally, brushing crumbs from his lap.

The apprentices glanced at and nudged each other for a moment, then one spoke who I thought had not spoken before—although they all looked very similar with their rags and shaved heads. "We've seen her," he said slowly. "Up in the grove. I tried to talk to her once, but it was as though she didn't even hear me."

Evrard and I gave each other quick, complacent glances.

"But our master, the hermit, often talks to her," the apprentice continued. Evrard's eyes became round with surprise and mine may have done the same. "He told us that only wizards can attract the wood nymph's attention, unless she decides she wants to speak with someone anyway. She likes to talk to *him*. I think—I think our master and the nymph talk about the saint."

"Saint Eusebius?" I asked, managing not to refer to him as the Cranky Saint.

"The nymph knew the saint, you see," the apprentice continued in a burst of confidence. "When Eusebius came to this valley fifteen hundred years ago— You did know that the saint was the first hermit at the Holy Grove, didn't you?"

"Yes, yes," I said. "Go on." Maybe relations between the hermits of the Holy Grove and the wood nymph had been better all these years than I thought.

"When Saint Eusebius first came to this valley, the wood nymph was already here. I think her presence may at first have—bothered him, but our master has told us that she and the saint became friends and had many long conversations on spiritual issues. She had been a pagan, of course, but he was finally able to convert her to Christianity."

Evrard frowned at me. My first thought was to find this highly unlikely, but then it occurred to me that, since I had no clear recollection myself of what Evrard and I had discussed with the nymph a very short time ago, someone else might decide after an afternoon with her that they had conversed on spiritual issues.

"Why does the hermit want to talk to her about the saint?" I asked. I was quite sure he had said nothing of this to Joachim.

The apprentices gave each other troubled frowns. "Maybe we shouldn't have said anything."

"No, no," I said reassuringly. "I'm sure it's all for the best that you brought it up. My friend, the Royal Chaplain, specifically asked me to try to find out more about the wood nymph. Why does your master talk to her about the saint?"

"He told me—" started one of the other apprentices uneasily. "He told me he needs her help! Saint Eusebius sometimes, well, acts troublesome, and since she knew him when he was still alive, our master has hoped . . ."

He trailed off without finishing. If the old hermit felt this was an unsuitable topic to mention to the bishop's representative, then his apprentices must have begun worrying that it could be a further reason to take their master away from them. It was rather ironic that these young men, dedicated to austere Christianity, thought it safe to express their fears to a couple of wizards, just because they knew we had no prim and fixed ideas about what was or wasn't suitable behavior.

But in my attempt to assure them that I was Joachim's friend, I may have started them wondering again if they should have spoken at all. "Let's be clear and open with each other," I said. "Neither I nor the Royal Chaplain thinks the old hermit should leave the grove, unless for some reason he decides to leave himself. But the chaplain *is* very concerned that the old hermit not be distracted from his prayer and contemplation."

"No! No! Not at all! He's not distracted at all! He's a very holy hermit!" cried all the apprentice hermits together. "The wood nymph only comes to speak to him when he wants her to," added the one I assumed was the leader.

Joachim, I thought, might have trouble explaining this to the bishop but, if true, it certainly freed me from any responsibility of moving the nymph out of the grove.

"What have the hermit and the nymph decided about the Cranky Saint?" put in Evrard.

If they heard his flippant tone, they didn't respond to it. Instead they all shook their heads. "He doesn't tell us about their conversations. I think he believes we are not spiritually ready." Evrard shot me what I was afraid was a smirk, but I was able to ignore him.

"Have your master and the wood nymph discussed those entrepreneurs at the top of the cliff?" I asked.

To my surprise, this question made them fall silent as our other questions had not. "We don't really know," said an apprentice at last.

They must be afraid, I decided, that if a chaplain had come to accuse their master of consorting with a nymph, then two wizards must be here to accuse him of trying to make a quick profit. Before I could try to reassure them again, they all stood up hastily and their leader snatched up his blankets from the corner.

"We'll let you have this hut to yourselves," he said. "Thank you again for accepting our hospitality and God bless you. Good night!" All five rushed out, leaving Evrard and me looking at each other.

"Let's get the horse blankets," he said. "At first, when they started talking about their master having long discussions with the nymph, I was able to imagine all sorts of intriguing scenes, but I'm afraid it must in fact have been very dull and pure—if one could imagine the nymph being dull! I'm glad *I* never had any foolish ideas about studying to be a hermit. Can you imagine what my hair would look like as shaved red stubble?"

"Peach fuzz," I said. "On a particularly unappetizing peach."

There was no door to the hut, but we settled down close to the opposite wall. The small fire in the middle of the room had burned down to darkly glowing coals.

"It sounds as though making money off pilgrims as you lower them down the cliff," Evrard said thoughtfully, "may be shocking to religious sensibilities as well as, of course, extremely dangerous."

He fell silent for several minutes and I had thought he had fallen asleep, when he suddenly rolled over with a great rustling of his blanket. "Daimbert, how did you manage to get involved in all this in the first place? What does a wizard have to do with chaplains and bishops and hermits?"

"In the school," I said lightly, "they teach us about the supernatural power of demons and warn us against using black magic. Doesn't it make sense for a wizard to try the other side, to learn how to trick the supernatural power of good into helping us?"

But Evrard, for once, was not willing to be dismissed with a joke. "But how about *you*?" he demanded. "How did you become involved in the affairs of a Cranky Saint?"

"I sometimes wonder the same thing," I said slowly. Although he was only a foot or so away, I could sense him more than see him. "Yurt is important to me. If there are problems in the kingdom, no matter what kind of problems, I want to see what I can do about them. You've only been here a couple of weeks, but you'll see."

"So you've dedicated yourself, heart and soul, to this little kingdom?" His voice wasn't exactly scornful, but it was close.

I hesitated a long moment before answering. The royal court, I was sure, would find this a riveting conversation. "No," I said at last. "Not heart and soul. The only thing I belong to heart and soul is magic itself—and maybe not even that because, if I did, I'd probably be better at wizardry than I am. But freedom is useless unless it gives you the opportunity to choose, and I've chosen to try to help my friends in Yurt."

"But why these people?"

"Because I love them."

Evrard did not respond at once and after a moment's silence, I rather hoped he would not. But then a coal settled with a hiss, sending up a brief shower of golden sparks, and with the silence between us broken, Evrard, irrepressible, spoke again. "But how did you, a wizard, ever become such good friends with a chaplain?"

"Joachim saved my life."

"He did? When was this?"

"The first year I came to Yurt. I had an encounter with the *other* supernatural powers."

"Oh, Daimbert, I'm sorry!" said Evrard, at once

highly contrite. "I didn't know. But you hadn't said anything about it and I never heard anybody mention it at the school."

"They wouldn't have."

When the resulting pause seemed highly strained, I added, "I do hope you realize I have not become a pawn of organized religion. When I heard the duchess had hired you, I was delighted at the thought of having a wizard to talk to, someone whom I thought I would be able to understand better than I could any priest, and who might even understand me."

Silence fell again. Evrard did settle down at last and began to breathe deeply—doubtless dreaming of the wood nymph. I shifted, trying to find a less hard and bumpy patch of dirt on the hut floor, and pulled the scratchy blanket up around my ears.

I was drifting off to sleep at last when, abruptly, I was brought back to full consciousness by a distant, repeated call. It could have been an owl, a real owl, it could have been the horned rabbits, or it could have been something far worse. I lay perfectly still, but heard only Evrard's peaceful breathing and the strangely ominous rustle of leaves. Talking to the wood nymph had removed the terrors of my predecessor's cottage to a comfortable distance, but now they were back again in this dark hut, made worse by the winds of night and the slightly lighter rectangle that marked the open doorway. I listened for a long time, but the call did not come again.

IV

We did not wake until well into the morning. I sat up and looked across the hut to see Evrard just opening his eyes. He jumped up at once when he saw the sunlight outside. "It's late. The wood nymph is going to wonder where we are."

"And the apprentice hermits must be wondering when they'll be able to have their hut back."

"Do you think their hospitality extends to breakfast?"

But we didn't see the apprentices when we came out. We checked my net for horned rabbits, but it had caught nothing yet. I renewed the paralysis spell and Evrard dropped in some fresher herbs.

"Maybe the nymph will have something today besides berries," he said as we scrambled up beside the little waterfall toward the grove. "A doughnut and a cup of tea would be even nicer."

"I doubt the nymph does her own baking," I said. "For that matter, I wonder where the apprentices get their food."

"From the store," said the city-bred Evrard.

"Not out here," I said with a laugh. "They must grow their own lettuce and we saw their goats, but I didn't see a bake-oven."

Evrard suddenly pointed upward. "Who are *they*?"

I craned my neck to look. Tiny figures were descending the cliff, a short distance to our right. They seemed to be making their way down by handholds and toeholds. It made me dizzy just to look.

"Maybe," I said, "the entrepreneurs have their first five pennies at last—or I'd guess even more, if they're charging five apiece."

"It's going to take them a while to save enough to hire me if they can only manage pilgrims at this rate," said Evrard.

I didn't like to watch, but I couldn't look away. There were three figures on the rock face, all robed in light gray. They descended slowly but steadily. In a few moments, the first, then the second and third, reached the ground.

"Maybe they didn't want to go around by the road on foot because it's so much further," said Evrard.

"Well, they'd certainly reach the valley floor the fastest way possible if they fell off the cliff."

They walked toward us and I was able now to see

that the three men all had deep cowls pulled over their heads and crosses embroidered on the shoulders of their robes. Pilgrims, I decided.

They saw us and stopped, apparently surprised to see two wizards in a holy hermit's grove.

"Bless you, my children," said the pilgrim who appeared to be the oldest. Then all three seemed to forget us completely. "Do you have the bread and the little bottles?" the old pilgrim asked the others.

"Right here," said another. He pulled from his pocket a large loaf like the one we had eaten last night.

"Then let us proceed." They walked purposefully toward the shrine at the center of the grove.

"If the apprentices have to rely on occasional pilgrims for their bread," Evrard commented, "maybe it's just as well we didn't eat any more."

A gust of wind caught the pilgrims' robes, lifting them and wrapping them around their ankles. One had to stop and untangle his legs, shod in tall riding boots, before proceeding. But I was looking forward to seeing the nymph again and was nearly as uninterested in the pilgrims as they were in us. I glanced up to see pale tiny clouds coming in a thin but steady flock across the slice of blue sky above us.

Even though we had just been there yesterday, the wood nymph's tree seemed very difficult to find. I had begun again to wonder if she was deliberately hiding from us, when at last Evrard pointed to a deep footprint in the soft earth. "That's mine. I came down last night faster than I meant to."

I said again the spell to call the nymph and a tinkling laugh came from the tree above us. We caught a glimpse of violet eyes and a beckoning hand.

But when we started flying up toward her, the nymph darted away, leaping lightly through the air, catching branches just in time to break her fall, swinging through the canopy of the grove. Evrard and I flew after her, almost catching her a dozen times. But every time, laughing and with her hair swirling around her, she dodged or spun away at the last second. Much less agile among the branches than she was, we kept getting leaves in the face just when we thought we had cornered her at last. But finally she returned to her platform, and all of us dropped to the cushions, panting and laughing.

This morning she had strawberries and the same icy, invigorating water she had offered us the day before. Evrard did not mention that he would have preferred tea and doughtnuts. "Were you two sleepy-heads this morning?" she asked, which made me look suspiciously at my cup, wondering if she had put something in it.

But I did not ask, deciding instead to find out at once what she knew about the Cranky Saint. She might have some idea why Eusebius wanted to leave. Although I remembered scarcely any of our conversation of yesterday, I did remember the beginning. The sensation was that most of the rest had taken place years ago and had comfortably faded.

"Lady, I want to ask you something," I said, putting down my cup almost full, though I was thirsty. She bent gracefully to offer me more berries. "Do you speak to the hermit of this grove and to Saint Eusebius?"

She looked away, out across the tops of the trees, and an expression passed across her face that might have been a frown. Evrard lifted his eyebrows at me questioningly, but I shook my head at him.

The wood nymph looked back at us again, not quite smiling. "The hermit and I speak of mortality and of God."

I opened my mouth to speak and changed my mind. But she took my silence itself as a response.

"Yes, I have wondered sometimes," she said slowly, "what it would be like to be mortal. You humans are born and live for a period, trying to create something in this world to match your dreams, seeking to achieve something you never quite reach. And when you become old and weary, you die. But then, the hermit has told me, you come face to face with God."

Joachim, I thought, ought to hear this.

"You live for such a short period of time," she added, "that your goals and dreams can never all be fulfilled. Does facing God make up for this?"

I didn't know what answer to give but, fortunately, she didn't seem to expect one.

"I don't think I was ever born," she went on, so softly that I had to bend toward her to hear. "The world has changed and I have changed, but I do know I was here long before any humans first came to the valley." Her head drooped forward and her long hair almost hid her features. "I have lived in the grove forever, or at least as long as I can remember. The trees are mine to tend, but even they grow old and die eventually, in spite of my care. They take the only way that leads out of the ever-repeating cycle of life here on earth, but that way out is closed to me."

Her voice dropped even lower. "I know I don't think of time the way you humans do, although the hermit has tried to explain it to me. You go from a world of time to a world of timelessness when your souls are set free by death. But I am not sure I even *have* a soul. The hermit has told me that I will not meet God face to face, if I ever meet Him at all, until the end of infinite time, when the world itself shall end."

She lifted her head almost sharply and tossed her hair back over her shoulder, frowning at me in earnest. "I am immortal, but not with the immortality that the hermit tells me is reserved for mortal humans. While the world lives, I live, and I revere the God whom Eusebius taught me created it. But according to the hermit, I shall not pass on to spiritual immortality, nor even become weary of living and find rest in death. The saints, including my old friend Eusebius, may appear over the seasons to the hermits here, and even sometimes to other men, but they do not speak to me."

This took care of my hope that she might know what the Cranky Saint actually intended. "But—"

"But I have *not* become weary of the world," she said in her normal cheerful tone without giving me a chance to speak. There was now not even a trace of a shadow in her expression. For someone who never had to contemplate her own death, it must be hard to be serious for very long. "There are always surprises here in the world, such as young wizards."

"What was *that* all about?" Evrard asked me in an undertone, but I shook my head. I was even more convinced than I had been that there was no reason, whatever the bishop might think, to try to move the wood nymph out of the Holy Grove.

"Let me offer you some honey in which to dip the strawberries," said the nymph.

I took a sip from the cup in my hand and wondered if the nymph herself deliberately set out to forget some of the experiences of the uncounted millennia she had lived, either because they were unpleasant or just because there were too many of them. But if so, she managed to be selective in what she forgot, with an understanding of the magic involved that was certainly beyond me.

The conversation shifted at once to other topics and, nearly as quickly, I began to lose track of what we were discussing. The nymph's conversation was as unexpected, yet as internally consistent—and as difficult to remember—as the dreams one has when first drifting into sleep. The minutes could have been the seasons within a forest, each with its own events, but in retrospect all timeless and the same.

I looked down at the cup in my hand and realized I must have drunk a number of glasses of the nymph's icy water. In spite of the disconcerting effect of watching myself forget, talking to her was so pleasant that I would have been willing to continue indefinitely.

As each new topic arose, it was crystal clear; I thought with admiration that the nymph was not only charming, but witty and highly informed about the practice of magic. With each topic, as we laughed and traded quips, I thought I could not possibly forget *this* conversation. But as we turned to a new subject, even while that subject became brilliantly clear, I realized that the former was fading from my mind.

The only part of the day's conversation I was able to reconstruct afterwards was her attempt to explain the lives of birds to us. She whistled until finches and thrush flew from all over the grove to land on the branches nearby. They chirped to her and she to them in apparent perfect understanding. Although they all seemed to have nothing magical about them, their colors were more brilliant, their eyes brighter, their songs sweeter, than any birds I had ever seen.

"We'd better leave soon if we're going to the duchess' castle," I managed to say at last. I had only intended to stay in the nymph's tree for an hour or two and we must have been here far longer. Even suggesting we leave required a major effort of will.

I glanced upward to try to guess the time from the sky and was startled to see it was already dark. And then I realized it was raining, a light steady rain that tapped on the leaves around us but touched us not at all. I had the vague recollection that it had been raining for some time.

"You may leave if you wish," came the wood nymph's warm voice from the shadows, "or, if you like, you can spend the night here with me." I knew, even without seeing her, that she was not addressing herself to me, or even to both of us. She was speaking to Evrard.

He knew it, too. "I would very much like to stay, Lady. Daimbert, what will you do?"

"Evrard, I—"

"I am free," he said meaningfully, "and that means I am free to choose."

I knew better than to stay where I was not wanted. "I'll go back to the apprentice hermits," I said. "They can practice their hospitality some more."

Wrapping a protective spell against rain around me, I floated down from the tree, landing lightly next to Evrard's heavy footprint. Long ago, I had put a spell of light on my belt buckle. Because the buckle was made in the shape of the moon and stars, I had thought it appropriate to do so, but I had always been disappointed that it had never glowed very brightly. It would not have sufficed the night before to light the path for two mounted men but, when I turned it on now, it glowed softly, giving just enough light that I was able to grope through the grove amidst little swirls of mist, fly over the waterfall, and continue down the valley toward the stone huts.

Our mares were where we had left them, standing contentedly head to tail in the warm rain. I continued past them to the hut where Evrard and I had passed the previous night.

The light from my buckle showed a blanketed lump in the corner. It thrashed suddenly as I came in and the leader of the apprentices sat up, looking at me with startled eyes.

"I'm very sorry to disturb you," I said contritely, "but would it be possible to ask you for hospitality again tonight?"

Without answering, he jumped up, seized his blankets, and ran out into the night. I went to the doorway and was fairly sure I saw him enter another one of the huts. I would not have wanted him sleeping in the rain on my account.

I unfolded the saddle blankets we had left in the corner with our saddles. Tonight I had both mine and Evrard's, and the damp air made me glad I did. My stomach growled, but I did my best to ignore it. I felt surprisingly weary, as though I had run a great distance today, instead of sleeping late and then spending many delightful hours talking with the nymph. The steady drum of rain on the slate roof over my head lulled me quickly to sleep.

V

I awoke near dawn, unsure what had wakened me, but suddenly and abruptly fully conscious. The sound of rain had ceased. I breathed very quietly through my mouth, not daring to open my eyes or even move, but convinced that someone—or something—was in the hut with me.

Whatever it was, it seemed to be trying to be as silent as I. Very slowly, I opened my eyes, just far enough so that I could see through the lashes. The predawn light was still dim. Next to my face were two horny bare feet. The toes appeared unusually large.

Against my will, my heart pounded violently and my eyes flew open. Saint Eusebius, I thought, had appeared to me.

My eyes moved upward, to a long ropy beard and then to a face where sharp eyes looked back at me from beneath heavy white eyebrows. I realized after one dreadful second that this was not a vision of the saint. He smiled kindly. It was the old hermit.

He sat down companionably next to me. "I am sorry if I wakened you, my son," he said. "But I wanted, if possible, to speak with you before my apprentices arose."

I sat up slowly, pushing back the blankets. "What do you want to discuss?"

"I wanted to provide reassurance, to you and to your friend, the Royal Chaplain. That young man takes his spiritual responsibilities so seriously that I fear he may forget the words of Christ, 'My yoke is easy and my burden light.'"

I let this assessment of Joachim pass without comment. "Well, I'm hoping to reassure him myself," I said. "He and the bishop were worried that the wood nymph might be an inappropriate influence here at the Holy Grove but, when I talked to her yesterday, it was clear that she herself takes spiritual issues seriously."

As I spoke I realized, almost guiltily, that it was much easier talking to the hermit alone than it would have been with Evrard there.

The hermit smiled gently. "My daughter, the wood nymph, certainly does not distract me from my devotions, if that is what the chaplain has feared. I wish he had mentioned his concerns and then I could have eased his mind."

"I don't think I need any spiritual reassurance myself," I said, "but I did want to ask you something. What has the Cranky, I mean, what has Saint Eusebius said to you? He appeared to the chaplain in a vision and told him he wanted to leave this grove. Apparently he was fairly firm on that point."

"As I told you before," said the hermit, looking at me with bright eyes, "he will not want to leave the shrine where he worshipped when in the flesh, and where his relics have always been."

I hated to doubt the word of such an obviously holy hermit, but I knew he was prevaricating—either that or I would have to doubt the veracity of Joachim's vision.

"You mean," I said, lowering my eyebrows at him and trying to give an air of wizardly wisdom, "that your conversations with the wood nymph have persuaded you that the saint's cranky temper comes and goes. You are personally confident he will no longer be irritated with life in the valley if the entrepreneurs are removed from the top of the cliff."

"Those poor souls do seem somewhat confused," said the hermit, which I took as a confirmation of my guess. "Do you know," he added, cocking his head to one side, "they came to visit me yesterday?"

"They did?" This was a surprise.

"They came in disguise, of course, because they

were embarrassed at the spiritual inappropriateness of what they are doing. They hoped to find out, without actually asking, what was my opinion of their business and, even more importantly, if Saint Eusebius might be thinking of leaving the grove. From the point of view of their enterprise, I realize, the departure of the saint's relics would be disastrous."

"In disguise? But . . . of course. I saw them, too." I should have realized that the three men in gray robes were not really weary, footsore pilgrims. I had even seen their riding boots. "What did they say?"

"Very little. They offered me loaves of bread, as true pilgrims normally do, and they knelt in prayer at the shrine, although they seemed uncomfortable doing so. They took some water from the river in little bottles. But I know that Saint Eusebius will judge the spiritual impulse of their inner hearts, which made them ashamed of making money from the things of God."

"And what did you tell them about Saint Eusebius?"

"I merely told them that it is easier for a camel to go through the eye of a needle than for a rich man to enter the kingdom of heaven."

The hermit was fairly astute, but I had a different explanation for why three disguised entrepreneurs should have come to the shrine. If they had been hired to upset the Cranky Saint by the priests of the distant church who wanted the saint's relics, then they wanted to find out how well their plan was working.

But I recalled that, when Evrard and I had seen the half-constructed scaffolding, I had concluded they really must hope to make money from pilgrims coming to see the Holy Toe. This was rapidly becoming too confusing for me this early in the morning.

"You say that you do not need spiritual comfort yourself, my son," continued the hermit, his eyes resting on my face. "But I think that you do. Come back to the grove with me now. I was going to break my fast with some of the bread those poor souls left with me and I would be happy to share it with you."

I hesitated for a second, knowing that Joachim would be surprised if I did not go, knowing that Evrard would roll his eyes at me if I did, and wondering uneasily what my teachers at the school might say. But then I stood up. I could certainly have breakfast with an old hermit. Besides, I was hungry.

Early morning was just reaching the valley. We picked our way up the path beside the waterfall and went into the center of the grove, where the hermit's hut backed up to the shrine of the Holy Toe. The inside of the hut had the same dirt floor and rough walls as the huts of the apprentice hermits; if anything, it was a little smaller.

He gave me a slice of black bread and took a crust for himself. Having had nothing to eat the day before but the nymph's berries, I devoured it ravenously, washing it down with spring water that tasted exactly the same as the nymph's water.

"You seem hungry, my son," said the hermit with a small smile, and I realized with embarrassment that he had only taken a few small bites of his bread while I was polishing off mine.

"I thank you, Father," I said meekly. He wasn't my father any more than Joachim was, but I felt I had to show respect.

He put down the rest of his crust uneaten. "If you have finished satisfying your physical needs then, perhaps, I can help your spiritual needs."

I was still hungry, but it would have been rude to ask for more, especially since I doubted he always had enough himself.

He took me by the shoulders and turned me gently toward him. His touch was cool and very light. His bright eyes reminded me oddly of the deep pool in the center of the grove. "You are very confused, my son."

I started to deny it, then changed my mind.

"Surely your friend, the chaplain, has told you that God is the answer to confusion."

Actually, Joachim had never said this to me. Oh, well, I thought. Since I had eaten the hermit's bread, I would now have to listen to him.

But his next remark surprised me. "Have you ever thought of the origin of your magic?"

"Magic's a natural power, part of the same forces that shaped the earth," I said promptly. That every wizard knew.

The hermit smiled as though at a clever pupil. "And you know that the earth was formed by God. In performing magic, wizards touch the hem of His garment and take part, even if only in a very small way, in His power of creation."

This they had *not* taught us at the school.

"You have an awesome responsibility, my son. It would indeed be too heavy a burden for mortal man to bear, were it not for God's mercy."

I started to deny I had any awesome responsibility, then stopped. As I had told the old wizard, with an audacity that amazed me as I recalled it, I was Royal Wizard and responsible for any magical events in the kingdom.

"But God does not forget the sons and daughters of His creation, even when they forget Him."

I looked into the old hermit's bottomless eyes until I felt I was sinking into them. I felt almost as if in a trance, my breathing deep and regular and my heart-beat slow, though my mind felt unnaturally clear. I *could* leave confusion behind, I thought, if I gave up my own self-will and dedicated myself to powers far more important than myself, the kingdom, or even wizardry. For a moment I wondered if the hermit would be willing to accept me as an apprentice.

But then I remembered I had something important to tell him. I fought back to myself like someone swimming up from deep under water. I broke eye contact with him and mentally shook my head. Being trained in wizardry had always made me susceptible to powerful outside influences.

I was a wizard and the world needed wizardry as much as it needed priests and hermits. Here, I thought, the old hermit would agree with me.

"Did you know that three priests are on their way here," I asked, "to see if Saint Eusebius would be willing to have his relics leave with them? They come from some distant city—I forget its name—but it's where the saint was originally made a priest."

"On their way? When will they arrive?"

"The pigeon message from the bishop said they would reach the royal castle of Yurt—" I paused to calculate and was surprised at the answer I reached. "They should have reached there yesterday."

"Then I may see them today or tomorrow," said the hermit peacefully. "I am sorry they will have had such a long trip without result. But I must not say that. They will certainly find it spiritually refreshing to worship at the shrine. No priest from the church where the saint received his youthful training has been to the grove since I have been hermit."

I was not nearly as sanguine about the priests' arrival. But if Joachim was with them, I would at least have the opportunity to reassure him about the nymph.

Both of us stood up and I gave the hermit the formal bow as I thanked him for breakfast. But I walked quickly away from the hermitage without the slightest intention of going around to the other side and bending my knee before the Holy Toe.

The sun was still hidden behind the eastern valley wall, but the sky was bright overhead and birds were singing as though last evening's rain was only a distant memory. This was a lovely place and the past day had been extremely enjoyable but, if my predecessor's magic had gone renegade, then I had neglected for far too long my responsibility as a wizard to do something about it.

I wondered if it was too early to disturb Evrard. I

turned back toward the part of the grove where the wood nymph had her tree. This time I found the tree immediately. "Evrard!" I called softly.

A touseled red head emerged from the leaves far above me. "Good morning!" he called, as cheerful as I had ever seen him.

"I think we've done everything here we came to do."

"I certainly have!" said Evrard, with a grin I was glad the hermit had not seen.

"We need to get back to the royal castle of Yurt. First we should stop by the duchess' castle, even though I doubt they'd be there after two days, so—"

"Who's that?" called Evrard, interrupting me. "Is it more pilgrims?" High in the tree, he could see more clearly than I, but in a moment I, too, picked up the flicker of rapid movement among distant beeches. Someone was coming down the steep road into the valley.

I quickly began to put together a far-seeing spell, wondering if it were the priests come for the relics of the Cranky Saint. Then I stumbled on the words of the spell as I felt an icy and completely irrational conviction that I would see a manlike creature, not alive and not dead.

At last I had the spell functioning passably and was able to see that it was a single rider. By now the horse had reached the valley floor and was heading toward us. With a start, I recognized the duchess.

PART FIVE
The Duchess

I

A duchess should not be riding unaccompanied through the countryside. "Come on down. Hurry," I called sharply to Evrard. He floated down from the tree, and we flew over the waterfall and along the trail to meet her, while I imagined all sorts of alarming possibilities. Neither Nimrod nor Dominic was with her.

"There you are," said Diana with satisfaction. She reined in her horse and dismounted. "I thought I might find you here. You look as though you've been sleeping in the woods for days." I glanced down at myself and realized that I had been wearing the same clothes for three days now.

Evrard hurriedly tried to comb his hair with his fingers; he looked even worse than I did. I wanted to ask Diana what had happened, if she had really eloped with Nimrod, but I could not make myself do it. "The grove has powers of attraction I don't fully understand, my lady. We've been meaning to go to your castle for two days and, somehow, we've never gotten there."

"Well, we weren't there, anyway," she said absently.

In her stained riding cloak, she appeared nearly as little like an appropriate member of an aristocratic court as we did.

"But where were you? Is everyone all right?"

"Of course everyone's all right," she said, surprised. "But you're correct about the grove," she continued. "It's always had the power to draw people toward it. And not just the pilgrims who come to worship at the shrine of Saint Eusebius or to seek the hermit's wisdom. The story is that a wood nymph lives here. Thousands of years ago, back when everyone was still pagan, people came to worship *her*."

"She still lives here, my lady," said Evrard, speaking for the first time.

"Is that so?" said Diana slowly, as though understanding more than he had meant to tell her. He reddened under her steady gaze.

She turned back to me. "My father, the old duke, wanted to cut the grove down when I was a little girl. He even started making arrangements for the hermit to move somewhere else. My father said having a nymph's grove just encouraged women to practice secret rituals—fertility and the like, I presume. I think it was his chaplain's idea."

"But what happened?" If Dominic had murdered Nimrod, she seemed to be taking it remarkably calmly.

"King Haimeric wouldn't let him cut down the trees. I was just as pleased myself, though of course I couldn't say that to my father. The king adjudged that the grove was in royal territory, not ducal territory. I don't think he cared one way or the other about the wood nymph—or even the hermit. But he hated to see the beeches cut."

"You still haven't said why you're here alone, this early in the morning."

"Saddle your horses," said the duchess. "Nimrod should be down at the lower end of the valley by now. We were following what he thought was a trail left by a great horned rabbit up on the plateau. It just looked like an ordinary rabbit track to me, but he's even better at hunting than I am. The trail went straight down the slope into the valley and so did he, but I preferred to come around by the road. We caught one horned rabbit yesterday, so this one is the last." So my paralysis trap would never be tested—probably just as well.

Evrard and I retrieved our saddles and packs from the stone hut. There was no sign of the apprentices, but I scribbled a note thanking them for their hospitality. Our mares, content and well-fed after two days of eating the rich valley grass, looked at us grumpily as we approached but allowed Evrard to catch them.

"And where is Dominic?" I asked Diana as we rode down the valley.

"Last I knew," she said with a shrug, "he'd gone off to see the old retired Royal Wizard."

"I don't understand, my lady. I'd have thought Dominic would be more interested in where you and Nimrod had gone than in the old wizard."

The duchess burst into laughter. She seemed in an excellent mood this morning. "We hadn't left yet when he did. He was going to try to force the old wizard to dismantle his monster."

My heart gave a hard thump. "What?"

"A message I slipped under his door may have helped him decide he ought to go," said the duchess. She chuckled as she spoke, then turned to look at us gravely. "If you two plan to deceive either Nimrod or me, I'm afraid you're going to have to do much better. It was clear from what you said at dinner the other night that the former Royal Wizard of Yurt had created a new and terrifying creature."

My stomach knotted. I put a hand over my eyes, realized this probably wasn't safe when riding a narrow road immediately next to a river and, instead, glared at Diana. "So you sent him off to the old wizard's cottage to do goodness knows what, maybe even set the monster loose through his bumbling, just to make sure he didn't realize that you and Nimrod were leaving together?"

"It worked," she said mildly. "Besides, I'd already told him we were going hunting again."

Diana didn't care whom she irritated, but if she continued to flirt with Nimrod even after Dominic had proposed, Joachim and I would have to deal with a furious and humiliated regent for the rest of the king's absence—assuming he lived through his encounter with the monster. If I loved the people of Yurt as I had said to Evrard, then I could not pick and choose between them. To love Yurt meant not just the king and queen and baby prince, the chaplain and the constable and Gwen and little Gwennie, the queen's Aunt Maria and all the knights and ladies, but even—somehow—Prince Dominic.

But then I shook my head and tried to restore a little rationality to my thoughts. Considering how easily my predecessor had dealt with Evrard and me, two theoretically competent wizards, the regent would never be able to get past him and set the monster loose.

We rode several miles down the valley, farther than I had ever gone, to where it opened out into flowering pastureland. "By the way, Wizard," said the duchess to Evrard, "there's some sort of booth on the plateau at the head of the valley, and the man there said something very odd about how you might be working for them . . ."

Evrard interrupted her. "Excuse me, my lady, but might you have any food with you?" He had not, I realized, had anything to eat for nearly two days but the wood nymph's berries and, even then, it had only been stale bread and lettuce. In spite of my breakfast with the hermit, I was not much better off.

"I've got some hardboiled eggs you can have if you're hungry," she said, not quite grudgingly, and reined in to reach into her saddlebag. Neither Evrard, who ate three, nor I, who ate two, took time to worry about her tone.

Here, where the valley widened, a wind blew steadily and the flowers and shrubs swayed beneath a bright sky. Beyond, the valley walls closed in again, leaving only a very narrow gap just broad enough for the river to rush through and disappear with a faint roar. Through the gap, the hills were distant and blue; the plateau itself must drop off steeply here. It would have been nice to go on looking at the scenery, but I had responsibilities.

"Listen, my lady," I said. "The king asked me to keep an eye on the kingdom for him. I cannot have you upsetting the whole court while he is away."

Diana's expression softened. "Yes, you're certainly right. Nothing should happen that will distress Haimeric when he comes back. He's an excellent king, but he *is* an old man and he doesn't need shocks. Nimrod should be near here," she went on cheerfully. "I wonder if he's had any success yet."

A bush only a few feet from us suddenly stirred and the tall huntsman unfolded himself from behind it. "Didn't think I could hide behind such inadequate cover, my lady?" he asked with a grin.

Diana, who had jerked with surprise, burst into laughter. "No, I didn't. What luck have you had?"

"Nothing yet, but the track's still very fresh. I wouldn't be surprised to see that magic rabbit in my nets within the half hour."

"Take my wizard with you," said the duchess, "and go back to your nets. The Royal Wizard and I will stay here in case the rabbit gets by you."

The duchess and I sat our horses, watching Evrard and Nimrod in the distance. Now was my chance. If I was going to deal with the old wizard's monster, whether loose or locked up, I had to try to clear away everything else that kept distracting me: the Cranky Saint, the entrepreneurs, Dominic's strange behavior and, especially, what the duchess was doing in asking her wizard for horned rabbits and then carrying on with a hunter who appeared out of the woods to hunt them.

But she spoke before I could. "Tell me, Wizard," she said with a flash of gray eyes, "why this sudden prudish interest in my affairs?"

"You don't need to assure me of your honor, my lady. I just want you to realize what you're doing. Even though you put Dominic off with vaporings about maidenly uncertainty, the entire court, including the regent, knows you've never been uncertain in your life."

She did have the grace to look embarrassed then, but she let me keep on talking.

"And for you to refuse one man, and then immediately leave on a hunt with another ... And you camped out with him, I presume, if you weren't at your castle? You distracted Dominic by sending him down to the old wizard's cottage, but that doesn't mean you can forget him."

"You speak as though you thought I had become scandalous in my old age," the duchess said, coldly and evenly.

I had certainly never spoken to her like this before, but I did seem to have gained and kept her attention. "You *know* the royal court must be rife with speculation and rumor. It's well known that Dominic felt he would have to marry you, to continue the royal line, back before the king met the queen, and that he dropped the plan with relief when the king's marriage made it unnecessary. For him to propose to you now, without the slightest bit of encouragement in the years between, shows that he's willing to let himself be insulted and humiliated if he thinks it's necessary to stop the rumors."

"So that's *your* explanation?" she said icily. "That Dominic doesn't really want to marry me, he only wants to preserve the kingdom's reputation?"

"What's your explanation?"

She looked at me thoughtfully, her anger draining away. "Dominic's been living in the royal castle, as royal heir, since he was four years old and his father died. I'm not at all sure he really *wanted* to be king, but it was all he'd ever known."

For two years I had thought of Yurt as my kingdom. Yet at times like this, I was reminded that both the kingdom *itself* and the people in it had lived and had plans and agreements and quarrels long, long before I arrived.

"Dominic is a little slow sometimes," Diana continued, "but this last year it's finally sunk in that he's actually free, for the first time in his memory. But being Dominic, his first thought is to tie himself down again. He says he wants to leave Yurt, but he can't imagine doing so by himself." She laughed. "I guess even I look better to him than some girl from down in the village."

"But how could he support himself and his new wife?"

"I don't imagine he's thought that far," she said with a shrug.

This might answer some of my questions about the regent, but it still left the duchess' behavior inexplicable. She outranked me far too thoroughly for me to force her to tell me anything; all I could do was make her angry enough that she'd keep talking. "But how about Nimrod? You've been encouraging him, my lady, encouraging him as blatantly as any village flirt. When he finds out that you had no real interest in him, that you were only using him to provoke the regent, isn't *his* reaction going to be highly scandalous itself?"

The duchess' frown cleared unexpectedly at what I had thought was my worst accusation. But before I could react, I caught a sudden hint of something moving.

"The great horned rabbit!" Evrard shouted to us.

We rode quickly to where a net, almost invisible under some bushes, thrashed wildly. Nimrod, wearing enormous gloves, reached into the brush and pulled the net out.

Struggling against the cords was a real rabbit.

Nimrod laughed and freed it carefully. But as it flashed away, the duchess turned to Evrard with a look of irritation. "So your magic couldn't tell you the difference between a magical creature and an ordinary one? I'll tell you what. We're in a hurry so why don't you try a wizardly calling spell to bring the great horned rabbit into our nets?"

Evrard flushed deeply but started at once on a spell. It wasn't one I recognized; I wondered if it might be something else he had learned in Elerius's course.

The chirping of birds, which had been a constant background sound, was suddenly intensified. A flock of sparrows congregated from all over the valley and settled, with madly flapping wings and incessant chirps, on Evrard's head and arms. "Been taking some tips from the wood nymph?" I said sarcastically. Even *I* had never attracted sparrows by mistake. Evrard disappeared under a wave of brown feathers.

Laughing over the birds' voices, he said the words to end his spell. No longer drawn by magic, the sparrows hesitated, then shot off. Evrard reemerged into view and tried to brush off his sleeves. "But it should have worked—" he began, then stopped short.

Something was thrashing in the nets a little further down, something highly charged with magic, yet not alive.

A cry came, a cry that could have been an owl and could have been a soul in torment. It was no less bone-chilling because I knew what it was. My normally calm mare reared, setting all the bridle bells ringing and even Diana was, for a moment, hard-pressed to stay on her gelding. I kicked my feet out of the stirrups, dropped the reins and flew forward.

Nimrod was there before me. The netted creature's

tiny red eyes stared from beneath its sharp horns in what looked like living hate and long fangs snapped at him. I dropped to the ground and threw a binding spell onto the horned rabbit. I scarcely dared hope it would work, but the creature fell heavily to its side.

Nimrod leaped onto the still form at once, adding a cord to the binding properties of my spell. "Good work, Wizard," he said over his shoulder. "We've got it now."

But even as he spoke it began to disintegrate. The eyes went lifeless, and first one and then the second horn dropped from its head. The spell that had given the rabbit the appearance of life was breaking up. My binding spell was too much for something that was only held together precariously in the first place. In a moment there was nothing but horns and skin and the smell of decay.

Diana came up, leading my mare. "So you caught the last great horned rabbit?" she said to Nimrod. "Pretty good work, Hunter!" She seemed assiduously to be ignoring Evrard.

Nimrod smiled at her mischievously. "If you *do* decide to marry Dominic, the two of you will have a household even the royal court will envy. Not only will you have your own castle and your own wizard, but you'll have your own giant huntsman, something even the king doesn't have!"

II

Nimrod and Diana started winding up their nets. There were many more of them than I had at first realized, all carefully knotted from thin cords, almost invisible once in place although the spaces between the cords were so small that only a very powerful creature would have been able to escape. They were certainly much better constructed than my own attempt.

Nimrod moved off, getting the nets he had laid

down further away. Evrard went with him, carefully not looking at the duchess. They were soon well out of earshot.

The day had become hot and the sun made me squint. I eased nets free of shrubs and twigs, leaving the winding and packing to Diana and watching her out of the corner of my eye as we worked.

"My lady," I said suddenly and she gave a start as though her thoughts had been far away, "I know something you don't realize I know. The great horned rabbits were made by your ducal wizard, at your request."

"He told you?" she said, stopping and putting her fists on her hips. I didn't know if her steely glare was for me or Evrard.

"I'd worked it out for myself. But he doesn't know *why* you'd wanted them. Nimrod clearly thinks he knows. You heard him just now. He's treating the rabbits as a test—a test which he's now passed—with you as the prize at the end."

Diana had given up any pretense of winding the nets.

"And you don't know this either, but Evrard's horned rabbits—and something else he tried to make— were what decided the old wizard to shake off his lethargy and create a manlike creature. You've *got* to tell me: why did you want horned rabbits? I would even have thought you had known Nimrod before and were going to use the rabbits as an excuse to call on him for help, except that you were so surprised when he first appeared."

Her fury dissolved in one breath. Hands still on her hips, she slowly began to smile. "You know, Wizard, you're smarter than you like to appear."

I would try to appreciate later what was probably a compliment. I kept staring at her, trying to look severe and compelling.

She still did not answer my question, but began

again winding up the net she had dropped a minute before.

I tried another approach. "How about the old count? He was terrified by your horned rabbits."

"We stopped by his castle yesterday," she said with an amused look. She could be as stubborn as I. "We'd already caught the second rabbit and told him we'd soon have the third. He seemed relieved."

We were interrupted at this point as Evrard and Nimrod came back with the rest of the nets. The huntsman moved easily through the brush, like a giant cat.

I made a sudden decision. I had no more time to waste on the duchess and her games. "Evrard, you and I have to get back to the royal castle at once, to see what Dominic's been doing and find a way to make the old wizard dismantle his creature. Nimrod, I'd like you to come with us. If by any chance it gets loose, I'll need your help in tracking it."

"Of course," he said, with a smile for the duchess. "My lady enjoys watching me track things. But I should tell you, Wizard, that if the creature gets away from your predecessor, it may head this way. When I tracked those soldiers of hair and bone I told you about, up in the eastern mountains, we caught many of them on a peak that was locally reputed to be magical."

He paused and when he spoke again there was a hint of tension in what seemed an offhand request. "But before we go, as long as we're here, I'd like to see the Holy Grove."

"The grove?" I wanted to act now, not be a tour guide.

He gestured up the valley. "The ducal wizard was telling me about it while we rolled up the nets. I gather there's a hermitage, and a wood nymph, and a river that shoots directly out of the hillside."

I sensed something behind Nimrod's casual words— or thought I did. I wished I knew him better. His words did not, at any rate, seem to have any hidden meaning to the duchess. She smiled. "It's certainly worth seeing and we won't be closer anytime soon. Just wait until I get this last net wound up."

"I must get back to the royal castle," I said.

"We'll have to go within a quarter mile of the Holy Grove anyway to get out of the valley," said the duchess. "I at any rate have no intention of scrambling up these valley walls! It shouldn't take long to show the grove to Nimrod. He *is* my huntsman, Wizard. If you want his services, you'll have to wait until I'm done with him."

We rode back up toward the head of the valley, Nimrod striding at the duchess's stirrup. The sun had moved past noon and we seemed to be progressing very slowly. When we reached the open area below the waterfall, Diana pointed out the toeholds carved in the cliff face.

"It wouldn't be as dangerous as it looks," said Nimrod, looking upward with an interested frown. "The cliff is not perfectly vertical but angled, and the toeholds are well placed."

"As I know well," said the duchess. "When I was about fifteen, I climbed down here myself, just to see if I could do it. Be flattered," she said to all of us. "I've never told anyone about it before."

"You told me," said Nimrod with a smile. "That's part of the reason I'd been eager to see the valley."

"I told you?" Diana turned toward him with clear surprise. "But—" She recollected and laughed. "Of course I did. I'd just forgotten. All right, then, you already know that the young heiress to the duchy wanted to see the valley, but not to see it the way any ordinary girl would!"

Evrard appeared to have thought of a new way to impress his employer. "Wait until you meet the wood nymph!" he said to the duchess and Nimrod.

"I've only seen her once before," said the duchess. 'That is, I've always *hoped* it was the wood nymph, although I could never be certain. It was the time I just mentioned, when I climbed down. There was a girl in the grove, who seemed both to be my age and to be a thousand years old. She had remarkable violet eyes. She looked at me a moment without speaking, then disappeared."

"You have to be a wizard to be able to call a nymph," said Evrard confidently. "Or," he added after a second, "be someone to whom the nymph wants to talk, anyway."

We left our horses and walked up to the pool and the shrine of the Holy Toe. Diana and Nimrod went first, she swinging her riding crop and whistling, and he walking with very stiff shoulders and silent footfalls. Much as I wanted to be on our way, his behavior intrigued me. I glanced toward Evrard as we came along behind, but he did not seem interested in the pair before us. The hermit came out and blessed them, as Evrard and I waited a few yards away. Nimrod's face was very still and I could read no expression in it.

"You know," said Evrard, low enough I hoped that the hermit would not overhear, "I'm not very impressed with this Cranky Saint. Wouldn't a really powerful saint make it clear to everybody exactly what he wanted and then blast those entrepreneurs with lightning?"

This seemed more like a question for Joachim than for me, but I was spared from having to answer by the hermit. "I trust your day is going well, my sons, with God's help," he called to us with a smile.

In spite of the smile and friendly tone, I immediately felt guilty. I took his comment as a gentle reminder of the responsibilities with which he had earlier charged me. But at least he did not summon us to join Nimrod and Diana before the shrine.

They still knelt at the hermit's feet, his hands resting lightly on their hair. While the hermit looked toward me, I saw the duchess turn toward Nimrod.

Their eyes met and slowly he began to smile. In return she gave a sudden, secret grin.

I would have liked to conclude she was only mocking the old hermit and his piety. It was better than the alternative, which came with immediate if irrational conviction: that she had decided to treat this blessing as some sort of renegade marriage ceremony.

I shook my head. This was ridiculous. On top of everything else, I seemed to be losing my good sense. Diana and Nimrod thanked the hermit for his blessing, rose and came to join us.

At last, I thought, we could start for the castle. But now Nimrod appeared very interested in the spring, where the river shot out of the side of the cliff. He folded up his tall frame to crawl along the narrow, damp shelf at the edge of the river, back into the cliff. The rest of us watched and waited as his feet disappeared from view into the blackness.

In a moment we heard his voice, echoing hollowly. "I think it opens up a little back here. It's too dark to see well, but—" A splash cut off whatever else he might have intended to say. In a moment he reemerged, laughing and wet along one side. "Whew, that water's cold," he said as he stood up and wrung out his hair. "You'd need a torch to explore the cave properly. Even in the dim light from the entrance, the first big room looked as though it was festooned with colored icicles."

"There can't be anything in there very interesting besides rocks," said Evrard impatiently. "Come on, and you can meet the nymph."

Nimrod's short visit to the Holy Grove seemed to be growing longer and longer, but I felt powerless to do anything about it. For two days, the valley had beguiled me; now I only wanted to get out of it. I tried to persuade myself that Dominic had paid a short, friendly visit to the old wizard and was now safely back at the castle.

Evrard led the way, along the little pebble-marked

paths through the grove, to the tree that I thought was the nymph's tree. But here he hesitated. "I don't see my footprint."

"The ground's damp anyway and it's rained recently," I said. "A footprint won't last long."

"Or maybe it's the wrong tree."

Now he had me confused. "You should know better than I," I said pointedly. We moved back, looking at all the adjacent trees, then at other beeches further away. I caught the duchess giving Nimrod an amused smile.

"No, I think it must have been the first tree after all," said Evrard after ten minutes. But, somehow, none of the trees now seemed like the tree we had stood beneath only a short time before.

"Try using the spell to call her," I said in a low voice. The duchess would not find this amusing much longer.

Evrard frowned, bit his lip, frowned again and started on the spell. He finished with a flourish and looked up expectantly. There was a long silence, broken only by the soft murmur of the leaves and the rushing of the river.

"I thought you were going to introduce us to the wood nymph, Wizard," said Diana testily.

"Maybe she doesn't want to talk to so many people at the same time," I said, then realized that by speaking for Evrard I was giving the impression that he needed my protection.

"Daimbert," said Evrard, who seemed to realize this, too, "how about if you and Nimrod go back to the horses, and I'll see if the nymph will come out for the duchess and me alone." He moved to another tree and, with a good show of confidence, started on the spell again as Nimrod and I left the grove.

"The horned rabbits must have been frustrating prey," I commented as we scrambled down the path beside the waterfall, "since they disintegrate as soon as you catch them." I was no longer interested in the horned rabbits but, if he talked, I hoped to be able to see more of the edge of tension I thought I could feel running under the huntsman's apparent good humor.

He smiled unexpectedly. "For me, they've provided highly satisfactory hunting," he said. "But I must say, it's been more comfortable since I worked out they were neither monsters from the land of dragons, nor creatures made with black magic, but only something my lady, the duchess, requested from her ducal wizard."

I turned to stare at him. "Did she tell you that?"

"No, but I'm good at guessing," he answered easily.

We sat down on the grass near our horses. I glanced toward the grove, wondering if Evrard had had any luck. It was rapidly growing late, yet I hated to call him away from an opportunity to show off his magical abilities to his employer.

I turned back toward Nimrod's well-chiseled profile. He seemed deep in thought. "You still haven't told me why you came to Yurt," I said.

He took a sudden, sharp breath and then his eyes twinkled at me as his shoulders relaxed again. "Maybe I have private reasons for being interested. And, as I told you before, hunters keep track of what needs hunting."

"But you seemed to know about the great horned rabbits almost before we did."

He only smiled and shook his head.

If he wanted to be mysterious, I could do some guessing of my own. If he had known the duchess before, perhaps some years earlier when she had spent several seasons in the City, he might have wanted to enter the kingdom to reestablish their acquaintance, and have preferred for reasons of his own to come incognito. The appearance of the great horned rabbits would have provided a useful excuse for an excellent hunter. But I was still not sure what, if any, connection there might be between Nimrod, the Cranky

Saint, and the money-making enterprise at the top of the cliff.

"Had you learned about Saint Eusebius of Yurt before you came here?" I asked cautiously.

"The duchess told me a little about him," he replied, equally cautiously. "Why?"

His answer seemed deliberately to leave in doubt whether he knew anything beyond what she had said. Before I could formulate a response, I was distracted by movement on the road down into the valley.

My first wild thought, in spite of all my attempts at calm rationality, was that it was the old wizard's monster, but then I saw it was a group of horsemen. Nimrod had seen them, too, and stood up. With the aid of a far-seeing spell, I could tell that there were four mounted men, all dressed as priests and followed by a pack horse. The man riding at the head was Joachim.

III

I jumped at once to my feet, vastly relieved. With Joachim here, I could turn over the hermit, the Holy Toe, and the entrepreneurs to him. I realized that, somewhere in the back of my mind, I also hoped he would be able to help deal with the old wizard's monster, even though, as I had often told him myself, magic was much more efficient than religion if one had to face magical creatures. I only restrained myself from flying to meet him by the recollection that the priests from the church that wanted the Cranky Saint's relics might not look kindly on magic being practiced only a short distance from the Holy Grove.

"Who's coming?" asked the duchess behind me. I had not heard her approach.

"It's the Royal Chaplain and the priests he was expecting." I turned to see Evrard flash me a grin of triumph.

None of the others seemed interested in the arrival

of some priests in the valley. Diana started telling Nimrod about the nymph, who had apparently spoken briefly with them. Leaving them behind, I started down the road to meet the riders.

I prepared myself for a formal, even distant greeting. Joachim might not want to advertise his friendship with a wizard.

But then he lifted his head, gave a highly unexpected but quite genuine smile, and swung down off his horse. "I'm delighted to see you, Daimbert," he said, wringing my hand. "I'd assumed you were off chasing horned rabbits across the fields of Yurt. I didn't dare hope you might be here."

He turned to introduce me to the other priests who, as I expected, had come from the distant church where Saint Eusebius had originally made his vocation. I looked quickly at their faces, wondering if they might be the purported pilgrims who had climbed down the cliff to the grove. But they were completely unfamiliar. They did, however, all give me highly suspicious looks.

Joachim looped his horse's reins over his arms and walked beside me while the priests, still mounted, rode behind. He appeared much more at peace than when I had last seen him.

"I decided two mornings ago to meet these priests at the cathedral city," he said, "in order to have a chance to talk to the bishop. I'm afraid I slipped away very early and rather secretly. I wanted a fast horse, to be sure of reaching the cathedral city before the priests left there for Yurt."

His black eyes flashed at me with what in someone else would have been mischievous enjoyment. "The fastest horse in the stables, of course, used to be the queen's stallion until she sold it when the little prince was born. So I took Prince Dominic's new one. Naturally, I didn't tell him what I was doing. The stable boy was still too sleepy to give me an argument. When we all got back to the castle late last night, Dominic wasn't there."

This made it complete. The regent would now be furious with all of us. There were few horses in the royal stables that could carry him easily, now that he had gotten so heavy, and he had been inordinately proud of the enormous but light-footed chestnut he had bought that spring. And for the chaplain, of all people, to take it!

But this thought was driven out by another. Why had Dominic not been back at the castle? It was only a short distance to the old wizard's cottage in the woods. But if the royal regent and Yurt's best knights had come hammering on the green door, anything might have happened.

I didn't dare say anything to the chaplain about this with the priests so close behind. "That's not Dominic's stallion," I said instead, looking back at the mount Joachim was leading.

"Of course not. His is a wonderful stallion, very fast and nearly tireless, but it deserved a rest once the need for speed was over." He smiled again. At this rate he would soon break his previous record for most smiles in an hour. "It was good to see the bishop. I should have gone there before, rather than relying on messages."

By now we had reached the others. Joachim performed the introductions quickly. Nimrod appeared highly startled to see the priests. He stepped quickly back into the shadow of the trees, turning his face away, while they too stared at him in surprise.

"And I have a message you'll all be interested in," Joachim said. "Since almost everyone else in the castle was gone, the constable had me come to the telephone when the king and queen called last night. The baby prince has taken his first steps."

Evrard smiled politely and Diana said, "How sweet." I alone was as delighted to hear this news as Joachim. I was also intensely relieved the royal family was not here in Yurt but rather somewhere safe, where a baby's first steps could be the most exciting event.

The priests of Saint Eusebius left us and headed toward the shrine. The duchess glanced upward. The sun had long since passed from the narrow valley and the afternoon sky far above was a pale blue. "It's late," she said. "We'd better get started if we're heading back to the royal castle. We won't get there tonight, but I've got a tent big enough for at least four."

Before I could answer, Evrard said, "I don't know about Daimbert, but I'm staying here. Just leave me a little more to eat, my lady—the wood nymph's berries aren't very filling!"

I imagined five or six things that Diana might say in the short pause before she answered, but then she only said, very quietly, "I'd somehow imagined that my ducal wizard would be able to help me with magical problems and magical creatures."

Evrard refused to take the hint. "I thought I'd already helped you with magical creatures," he said with a wink.

Diana took a short breath through her nose, not quite a snort.

"I myself—" I started.

But Joachim didn't give me a chance to finish. "Will you stay with us this evening, Daimbert?" he asked, turning his enormous dark eyes on me. "The priests and I will pass the night near the hermitage and I'd very much like your counsel."

This was becoming like a frustrating dream in which one runs and runs but never reaches the goal. I had been trying to leave the valley since early this morning, but now I was trapped for another night. Joachim had never before, that I could recall, asked specifically for my counsel.

"Of course," I said. There was nothing else I could have said.

In a few minutes, Evrard had disappeared back

toward the nymph's end of the grove, carrying bread and cheese from the duchess' supplies; she and Nimrod had started along the road that would lead them out of the valley; and Joachim and I went up to the shrine of the Holy Toe.

The priests were kneeling at the altar and showed no immediate sign of seizing the golden reliquary of the toe and making a dash for it. Two of them were middle-aged and the third, who kept giving the others nervous glances, was younger, probably about the same age as Joachim and I. Once they and the old hermit had finished exchanging blessings, we all started back down the valley.

"We knew, of course," said one of the older priests, "that Saint Eusebius had retreated to a grove far from the bustle of the City when he decided to become a hermit." The priest was as round as an apple and he breathed hard after the scramble down the track by the falls, but his eyes did not have any of the good humor I had always associated with apples. "But somehow I had not expected that now, a full fifteen hundred years later, the site of his hermitage would still be located in such a God-forsaken wilderness."

"God never forsakes any land of His creation," said the other older priest, who was as thin as the other was round. He spoke intensely and his eyes seemed to gleam.

"We'll have to sleep rough tonight," continued the round priest, paying no attention to this comment. Then he held up a hand, as though to forestall a remark no one in fact had made. "But we must not grumble. God demands far harder of those dedicated to His service."

"And we must follow to the death," agreed the thin priest. He whirled on their younger colleague. "I hope you understand fully!"

"Fully!" the young priest cried in panic.

I didn't dare meet Joachim's eye. But he seemed calm and peaceful. I was quite sure I would not have

been as calm after more than two days in these priests'
company. I reflected how fortunate I was to have
come to a royal court where Joachim was the chaplain,
rather than someone like either of the older priests.
Whatever he wanted of me, I fervently hoped we
could finish our discussion tonight.

"Tomorrow," said the thin priest, "we shall pray that
the saint make his will unequivocally clear to us—that
is, his will that we take his relics back with us."

"I have no doubt Eusebius will be clear at the last,"
said Joachim. "This is, after all, the saint who responded,
when a man importuned him incessantly to straighten
his crooked arm, by resetting the bone so violently
that bone fragments flew out through the skin."

All three priests stared at him and so did I, but
none of them answered.

"I saw some stone huts further down the valley,"
said the round priest instead. "I'm sure they are provided for the crude comfort of pilgrims to the shrine."

"In fact," I put in, "they're the huts of the old hermit's apprentices." All three priests turned to look at
me as though surprised I would dare address them,
and the thin priest started to speak, but I went on
determinedly. "The apprentices like to practice hospitality. They may be willing to let us have one of their
huts for tonight."

"Ordained priests of the Church have precedence
over mere apprentice hermits," said the round priest.
"We shall take those huts that seem most appropriate
for our use."

"I'll ask the apprentices," said Joachim. Although he
spoke quietly, the others turned toward him sharply.
"Come with me, Daimbert," he added and we walked
together down the valley, leaving the other priests
looking thoughtfully after us.

I wondered hopefully if they were planning to
report Joachim to the bishop as someone who had
become dangerously friendly with a wizard, in which
case I need not worry about him being asked to go

join the cathedral chapter. I had several things I would have liked to ask, but the only one I ventured was, "What did the bishop say when you talked to him?"

"He reminded me that God does not give us responsibilities too heavy for us to bear, and that He is always there if we will only turn to Him."

This was almost exactly what the old hermit had said to me, although I found that it had eased my worries much less than it seemed to have eased Joachim's.

"All priests are called Father," he continued, "because we act as mediators between humanity and the One Father. But the bishop really *is* the father of all the Christian souls in two kingdoms. Even with his manifold duties and responsibilities, he still took time for a fatherly discussion with me."

"What did he suggest you do about the Cranky—about Saint Eusebius's relics?"

It was growing dim under the trees, but Joachim's eyes were even darker. "He told me that I had his full authority to act, that he was sure the saint would reveal his true purpose to me."

"And he told you this while these priests were there?"

"Of course," said Joachim in surprise.

This explained the three priests' deference to the Royal Chaplain. It also still sounded as though the bishop was testing him, to discover his true abilities before taking him away from Yurt.

The apprentices apparently expected us. All five stood together at the edge of the road, jostling and whispering as we approached. And all five dropped to their knees before Joachim. He blessed them calmly, resting his hand in turn on each of their shaved heads.

"Father, have they, have those priests, have they come to take away the hermit this time?" the apprentices' leader asked in a strained voice. My attempts to reassure them, two nights ago, had apparently not helped.

"They've not come for your master," said Joachim. "They've come for the relics of Saint Eusebius. I know," he continued, when all the apprentices gasped in dismay, "that he and you are dedicated to the saint's service. But it is not yet clear whether they will ultimately take the saint's relics away with them or leave those relics here. And, even if they do take them, you can follow the relics and the saint to their new home."

I tried, unsuccessfully, to imagine the old hermit and his ragged apprentices living in the comfortable urban environment from which I was sure the three priests had come. "For now," I put in, "we would very much appreciate it if you could let us have one of your huts for the night. I hate to keep turning you out. Don't you have an extra one you use for storage or something? One hut will do for all of us."

But as it turned out, we ended up turning two of the apprentices out of their huts. They did not sit with us around the fire, but pressed bread, lettuce and a jug of goat's milk into our hands and fled. After a supper made up both of the apprentices' food and some the priests had brought with them—Joachim drank the goat's milk but the others wouldn't—the priests of Saint Eusebius went off to the hut they were sharing, reminding each other that one must not grumble about the experiences God sends.

Joachim and I sat on our horse blankets, spread on the hut's dirt floor before the fire. I felt that sleeping in a bed and sitting on furniture were a dim memory, something I might once have done in my youth.

IV

It was going to be a dark night; there was no moon and clouds hid the stars. Yet, almost ashamedly, I felt safer, less as though trapped in a nightmare, with the chaplain there, even though I knew that the Church's normal reaction to magical problems was to leave them to the wizardry they claimed not even to respect.

Joachim sat staring silently at our small fire. The air from the open doorway made the flames flicker and cast tall, oddly twisted shadows on the wall behind us.

I was suddenly convinced that he was going to ask me if he should accept the bishop's invitation to leave Yurt and join the cathedral chapter. Because I didn't want to have to answer that question, I tried to forestall him with a completely different comment.

"Here's something you'll be interested in. I know you and the bishop were worried that it might not be suitable to have a wood nymph in a Holy Grove. It turns out that she was a good friend of Saint Eusebius, all those years ago, and that the saint converted her to Christianity."

Joachim gave me a long look as I pushed on. "It's actually rather poignant. She's worried that she may not have a soul. She seems to want to become human, with an immortal soul, even though being human means having to die. I'm afraid she really may not have a soul because she says her friend the saint has never appeared to her since his death."

"You know," said Joachim, "after two years of knowing you, I still don't understand your sense of humor."

At this I laughed. It was refreshing to be able to laugh. "Of course you don't understand why I would make a joke about something like this. It's because I'm not joking!"

Joachim lifted one eyebrow at my new-found seriousness.

"Even though she will not grow old or die as long as the world remains," I continued, "she seems to find something curiously appealing about breaking out of the earth's endless cycle through death."

"Of course," said Joachim, who did not find this attitude curious at all. He seemed suddenly absorbed by the issue of the wood nymph, although I was sure that was not what was really on his mind. "The world is God's creation and has enormous good and potential for good within it, but it is still a fallen world. All of us must find it wearying in the end and long for release into the realm of spirit."

I decided it was safest not to comment on this. I was very far from longing for release and wizards have a much longer life span than ordinary people—even though, from the wood nymph's point of view, there probably wasn't a lot of difference between any of us.

"At any rate," I said, "if the saint's relics stay in Yurt, I'm sure the bishop will understand why it won't be necessary to make her leave. But tell me. You said the saint would reveal his will clearly. Do you know what he really wants to do?"

Joachim hesitated. "Maybe I made a mistake discussing this with a wizard in the first place."

"Too late now," I said. "And you did say you wanted my counsel."

The firelight glinted in the chaplain's eye and he shifted his long frame in search of a more comfortable position. He was silent for a moment, looking at the fire rather than at me, and his face slowly went from almost smiling to completely sober.

"The saint's intention," he said at last, "will, I am certain, eventually become clear, but it is not clear yet." He paused for a moment. "He told me he wanted to leave Yurt, but he wouldn't say why, or where he wanted to go. The priests of the church of Saint Eusebius led my bishop to believe that he had also appeared in a vision to them, asking for his relics to be transferred to their church."

"But when you questioned the priests closely," I provided when Joachim again seemed to hesitate, "they admitted that the Cranky Saint had said he wanted to leave the grove, but hadn't specifically said that he wanted to go with them."

"But if he didn't want to go to their church, why should he have appeared to *them*?" demanded Joachim.

I decided that the old hermit was right in one thing,

that the Royal Chaplain did indeed seem to take his spiritual responsibilities much too seriously. "Because he was cranky," I suggested. "Because he knew he'd get a response out of them. Because he was angry at the hermit for not having done something about the entrepreneurs. That reminds me. I talked to the hermit this morning and he seems convinced that Saint Eusebius would want to stay if the entrepreneurs were gone."

"I didn't see anyone at the booth when we came by," said Joachim. "Yet it looks as though they're actually starting to build a windlass contraption to lower pilgrims down the cliff."

"Yesterday morning three men dressed as pilgrims—part of the entrepreneurial group in disguise—climbed down by way of the toeholds and came to visit the hermit."

"Maybe they've realized their error in trying to make money from the spiritual things of God," suggested Joachim.

I found this highly unlikely. "But are the priests planning to take the Holy Toe back with them now?"

"That's certainly how *they've* interpreted the will of the saint."

"By the way," I said, "Nimrod seemed surprised to see the three priests. He still won't say why he came to Yurt."

"I thought they were, instead, surprised to see him," said Joachim. "The sight of a seven-foot-tall hunstman would startle anyone."

"I'm fairly certain now that Nimrod and Diana had known each other previously. Otherwise, I don't think that even she would have left with him when Dominic had just proposed."

Outside the hut, the night made low rustling sounds that I told myself would not have sounded nearly as ominous by daylight. We had suddenly reached the topic of the old wizard.

"Joachim, I'm worried about the regent. He took a

group of knights down to the old wizard's house two days ago and he certainly should have been back to the castle by last night. Yet you say he wasn't."

"What do you think has happened to him?"

"Maybe the old wizard put a spell on him. Or maybe the wizard's monster escaped, and Dominic set off after it and hasn't been able to catch it."

"I told you I wanted your counsel," said Joachim quietly. "I've been trying to find a tactful way to say this because I don't want to seem to accuse you of neglecting your responsibilities." Maybe associating with the priests, who had even less tact than he did, was teaching him some at last. "But your predecessor's creature has gotten loose."

"It has?" I forced myself to say, in a voice that sounded loud and squeaky in my own ears. It was one thing to fear such a possibility, another to know it had actually happened.

"We heard of it today as we were riding toward this valley. The first word we had was in the village just a few miles from the castle." This would have been the same village from which the disputants had come, not long before the king left Yurt. It seemed years ago.

"The local priest came out to meet us, terrified. Something had come to the village yesterday. It was seen rummaging through a chicken house. They thought, of course, it was a thief and set the dogs on it."

Somehow, hearing this in Joachim's quiet voice made it worse.

"But the dogs wouldn't attack it and fled with their tails between their legs. By now they'd realized it wasn't just a common thief. Someone shot at it, though the priest told us that he, of course, tried to stop him. But it didn't make any difference. The creature walked off with three arrows stuck in its back."

Then even Nimrod might not be able to stop it.

"It killed five chickens."

"Five chickens," I repeated, thinking I should be grateful it was not five children.

"They belonged to a young couple who, I gather, had just set up housekeeping. I think I recognized them. The young woman was very blond, quite distinctive-looking. I believe they were among the disputants the king swore to peace."

King Haimeric's judgment, I thought bleakly, had brought them back together after what had probably been a major rift, but no sooner were they married than a monster had killed their chickens. A monster loose, I reminded myself, while the Royal Wizard of Yurt was engrossed in dreamy forgetfulness with the wood nymph.

"I guessed immediately it was the creature that you and the ducal wizard had seen," said Joachim. "But the village priest thought it might have been a demon." He gave me a sideways look. "You would have been proud of me. I told him that magic is not a supernatural force and that our best defense against a magical creature was to find a reliable wizard."

There were three wizards in the kingdom of Yurt, at the moment, and none of them reliable. Just a few days ago, the old wizard had appeared to have his creature very thoroughly imprisoned.

"There didn't seem to be anything we priests could do," Joachim continued, "so we went on. As you can imagine, I was even more eager than before to find you."

And where, all this time, was Dominic? "Did the villagers have any indication which direction it was heading?"

"The third village in which it was seen is located at the base of the plateau," said Joachim soberly. "It seems to be heading this way."

I was furious with myself. I had seen it in the wizard's cottage, seen it and been terrified of it, but I had persuaded myself and Joachim that it was safely constrained by the old wizard's magic. But I had not thought through what I already had good reason to know: The old wizard had lost control: of his mind, his soul, his good sense, or his magic.

It would be ironic if now, when I had at last persuaded Joachim that wizardry was not just an inferior and misapprehended version of religion, and when he and the old hermit both turned to me for aid, my magic turned out to be completely useless.

Evrard, in spite of taking Elerius's course, was not going to be any help. If the old wizard's monster was as good at hiding as Evrard's stick-creature, then I would need Nimrod, but he was camped somewhere between here and the royal castle and I'd never find him in the dark. I was more than ready to swallow my pride and ask for the school's assistance in spite of how my predecessor would react, but I was thirty miles from the nearest telephone and over five miles from the nearest pigeon loft.

I raised my eyes and found Joachim watching me soberly. "You could try praying for guidance," he suggested.

I restrained myself from saying that no saint would listen to a wizard. But his comment did give me an idea and, very briefly, hope. "Saint Eusebius," I said. "The Cranky Saint won't want a magical undead monster in his valley. The saint must like you or he wouldn't have appeared to you in the first place. Maybe he'll listen if you ask for his help."

"I constantly ask the saints for their help," said Joachim.

I considered asking Evrard's question, why the saint hadn't just blasted the entrepreneurs—and, by extension, the wizard's monster—with lightning if he didn't like them, but it seemed pointless.

Besides, it was only a guess that the entrepreneurs even bothered the saint. His cryptic demand to have his relics moved elsewhere could be based on almost anything—even a personal animosity toward the apprentice hermits. I wondered for a moment that if the saint didn't want to go with the three priests, he might show it by allowing the monster to eat them, but even I had to dismiss this thought as irreverent.

Maybe Joachim's prayers would keep the monster at bay until first light, when Evrard or I could fly back to the telephone at the royal castle without becoming hopelessly lost. "You told me the old wizard might have made his creature out of jealous pride," I said. "Having made it, do you think he set it loose intentionally? Is he trying to catch it himself or, in trying to catch it, will I have to fight him as well?"

"That I cannot tell you," said Joachim.

One thing I could not do tonight was sleep. I leaned my chin on my fist and tried to plan for tomorrow. If the monster did not appear in the valley tonight, then I would have to go looking for it. The fire had burned low, but the coals still glowed deep red.

Very early, I decided, I would fly out of the valley and find Nimrod, and then he and I would track the creature from where it had last been seen. First, though, I would roust Evrard out of the wood nymph's tree, whether he liked it or not, and send him back to the royal castle as fast as he could fly to telephone the school. Then he could start the search for Dominic from the old wizard's house and, for that matter, search for the old wizard, too. This implied, of course, that they weren't all lying dead there already.

I paused at this point in my deliberations, wondering if Evrard could fly that far. I knew I couldn't have when I first came to Yurt.

Joachim, who had been silent for several minutes, abruptly stirred, then rolled up in his blanket. "Let's get some sleep."

"I can't. Not with a monster loose. I must not have made this completely clear, Joachim, but the monster's escape—and, from what you said about the old wizard's jealousy, its very existence—are my fault. I have to find a way to stop it."

"You still need your sleep."

"No," I said obstinately. "You and I have often sat up most of the night talking and I'm always fine the next day."

"That is, you can still function," said Joachim mildly, leaning on an elbow and looking at me, "thanks to a spell that you've told me gives you a bad headache."

The problem was that the chaplain knew me too well.

"Lie down and close your eyes," said Joachim, as though he were my grandmother twenty years ago, tucking me into bed when I didn't want to go. "I'll sing you a hymn to make you sleepy."

I lay down obediently, knowing this wouldn't work. But I tried concentrating on the sound of his voice as he sang softly. Joachim had a very pleasant baritone. After a few minutes, I couldn't hear him any more. I opened my eyes to find that it was already morning.

V

Joachim had rebuilt the fire and was brewing tea. I could barely remember the last time I had had a cup. All my concerns of the night before abruptly took their proper place in the greater scheme of life: breakfast first, monsters second. I waited quietly until the tea was ready.

We dipped the remains of a loaf Joachim had brought with him from the royal castle into the scalding liquid. Even stale and tasting somewhat of a saddlebag, it was indubitably the product of Gwen's baking.

"I'll have to get Evrard away from the nymph first," I said.

Joachim looked at me over the rim of his cup but did not answer. He had somehow managed to appear clean, well-shaved and well-brushed, and even his vestments were much crisper than clothes might be expected to be after being slept in.

"You probably don't want to know what that young wizard's been doing."

"Probably not," he agreed. "His soul will be the responsibility of the duchess' chaplain."

"It would be best, I think, if you stay here in the valley," I went on, "and continue following your original plan, to determine what should happen to the saint's relics. Meanwhile—"

I stopped abruptly. Faint sounds of shouting and barking, then the high winding of a horn, drifted down the valley.

I gulped the last of my tea and scrambled out of the hut. The sounds were clearer, and now I could tell that they were coming from above the rim of the valley. Up on top of the plateau, someone—or something—was being hotly pursued.

I ran out from the trees a short distance toward the head of the valley, to a position from which I hoped to see. At the top of the cliff, near the entrepreneurs' booth, was a brightly colored and highly noisy confusion of what I took to be hounds and men on horseback. A dark shape broke away and began rapidly descending the cliff face.

I could hear the priests' voices a short distance away, saying their morning prayers loudly, either not hearing the noise or not concerned. But Joachim's voice was quiet at my shoulder. "Is it the monster?"

My heart was pounding so hard it took me nearly a minute to put the far-seeing spell together. But then I could see that the figure coming quickly and smoothly down the cliff was blond and wore a dark green cloak. My attention was jerked back up to the top of the cliff where, to my enormous relief, I saw Dominic very much alive and, from his gestures, furious. The duchess, just as furious, was beside him.

"It's not the monster," I said in bewilderment. "It's Nimrod."

*   *   *

We hurried up the valley to be there when he reached the bottom. Although the people at the top of the cliff were quickly cut off from view, from the sounds of shouting and barking I guessed that they were riding around by the road and, indeed, in a moment I saw them as they started down the steep incline. Dominic was in the lead, riding at a pace I was certain was not safe, and the duchess not far behind.

Joachim and I met Nimrod at the base of the cliff. But he rushed past without speaking or giving us a chance to speak and headed straight for the Holy Grove. He was breathing hard; his hands and his boots were heavily scratched as though, even before reaching the cliff, he had had to force his way through thorn bushes or fight off a pack of dogs.

The three priests emerged from the trees, down toward the apprentices' huts, and started sedately up the road. Evrard suddenly emerged from the grove and came over to join us. The young wizard looked more tousled than ever. His chin was covered in reddish fuzz; his beard had finally started to grow in.

The first of the riders reached the bottom of the steep road into the valley and galloped toward us. The priests, forgetting their dignity, dove for the edge of the road just in time.

Dominic was riding not his stallion but a long-boned gelding, the second biggest horse in the castle stables. It was heavily lathered and its eyes rolled wide and white. Neither rider nor mount looked as though they had enjoyed the last few days together.

The regent pulled up the horse, with a hard jerk on the reins that lifted its front feet from the ground, and leaped off. "Where is he?" he roared. He pounded up the track by the waterfall, slipped in the mud, landed on his face, and jumped up again without even seeming to notice. "Where is that coward hiding?" I stepped back nimbly or the regent might have run me over.

Nimrod stood just inside the grove, waiting impassively,

even though his shoulders rose and fell rapidly from heavy breathing. He had his bow and quiver in his hands.

"You're trapped now!" Dominic cried. The mud on his face and all down his front made him an inhuman monster himself. He wrenched his sword from its sheath as he advanced.

Nimrod spoke then for the first time. "Sanctuary!" he shouted, his voice ringing through the head of the valley. His face was set in grim lines. "I demand the right of sanctuary!" He threw his bow and arrows to the ground and stepped back under the trees.

Dominic stopped abruptly. "Coward!" he shouted. "You're nothing but a coward! You know I won't kill you if you're unarmed. Don't hide behind a saint's skirts! Come out and get what you deserve!"

I had not always taken Dominic seriously which, I now realized, was a mistake. Nimrod did not reply. He watched the regent from a few yards back in the grove.

Dominic unbuckled a long knife from his belt and threw it, scabbard and all, toward Nimrod. It clattered on the ground nearly at his feet, but he made no motion to pick it up. "What's the matter?" Dominic sneered. "My knife isn't good enough for you? Do you want a shield, too? Shall you wait while I go get you one?"

"I've thrown down my weapons," said Nimrod evenly, "not because I'm afraid of you, but because I have respect for Saint Eusebius. I do not wish to bring instruments of violence into his grove. I have asked for sanctuary, Prince!"

Dominic hesitated for a long minute, during which the rest of us barely breathed. Then, with a massive snort, he advanced toward the huntsman. Light glinted on the sword he held before him. But the old hermit emerged suddenly from the grove and stepped directly into the regent's path.

"You cannot bring a naked sword into the Holy

Grove," said the hermit with a gentle smile. "It is a place sanctified to God and His saints."

"But that man ... he's a despoiler, a polluter, a piece of low-born scum! He bribed the retired Royal Wizard of Yurt into making a monster and attacking me with it!" I was riveted at this, but Dominic gave me no chance to consider the implications. "He's ... he's a sinner!" His voice rose triumphantly, as though he had found the answer. "You can't give sanctuary to a sinner!"

The duchess' horse had not been able to keep up with Dominic's. She and a group of the royal knights of Yurt now rode up with a great clattering of hooves, the dogs swirling around them in a fit of frenzied barking. Diana was off her mount, up the track, and tugging at Dominic's sword arm almost before the horse had stopped.

"You can't ... this is my duchy ... don't you dare touch him!" she panted. Her hair had come unpinned and she was nearly as red as the regent.

The knights from Yurt did not immediately rush after her, but most of them were shouting. The peacefulness of the steep-walled valley was shattered.

"Put your sword down, my son," said the hermit gently, "and do not fight, my daughter." The duchess was not, at any rate, having much luck against Dominic. "Sinners most especially have the right to seek sanctuary, where they may repent and seek God's forgiveness."

Dominic shook the duchess off his arm but then hesitated. Nimrod still stood silently among the trees.

Diana stopped kicking the regent, looked at the knife and the bow lying on the ground, and turned to Nimrod in angry surprise. "You've sought sanctuary?"

"It was long ago adjudicated that this valley is under royal control, not ducal authority," Dominic said to her, but almost conversationally, no longer in a bellow. The deep red of his face lightened a little toward its ordinary hue.

Joachim stepped up beside Dominic and began talking quietly in his ear. He was as tall as the regent, even if only about half his mass. In a moment, Dominic turned grudgingly toward the track by the falls. The chaplain then put a hand on the duchess' shoulder and said a few calming words to her as well.

I shook off my amazement and hurried after Dominic. This was definitely not the best time for rational conversation with him, but I had no choice.

He swung around sharply when I touched him on the elbow. Now that the red of fury had faded from his face, he seemed oddly pale. "So you call yourself Royal Wizard, when—"

I interrupted without giving him a chance to make an accusation with which, in fact, I agreed. "I need your help. I'm sure you realize that Nimrod didn't commission any monster. But if there's a horrible creature loose in Yurt, I need to know what it is and what it's doing. Tell me everything that happened at the old wizard's cottage."

Dominic hesitated, anger and his normal sulky nature fighting with what looked like extreme exhaustion. He didn't even bother to scowl at me. "I decided I had to look at what that young wizard of the duchess' had tried to suggest was only an illusion. We got an even better 'look' than I expected."

"Yes?" I said impatiently when he paused. It would be entirely appropriate for him to decide, as regent, to fire me for gross neglect of wizardly duties.

"When I knocked at the old wizard's door," he continued slowly, "I saw him for just a second, then he stepped aside and this—this thing rushed out at us. It's almost human, but it didn't move like a human. And it has no face, only eyes."

Just two years ago, my predecessor had faithfully served the royal family of Yurt. The strange twist I had felt in his mind—or his soul—had gone even deeper than I thought. It didn't sound as though his monster had broken loose. It sounded as though he had set it on Dominic deliberately.

The regent gave me a long look. "I honestly don't know why anyone would want to study and train to deal with magical creatures. We got away, though it crippled one horse so badly we had to put it down. We've spent the last three days chasing it or else running from it. None of us have gotten much sleep. We must have lost it half a dozen times but, until now, it's always reappeared. We haven't seen it since yesterday afternoon."

He glared toward Nimrod. "Are you sure that huntsman didn't ask your predecessor for a monster? He was camping out unafraid, yet it showed no signs of attacking *him*."

"Quite sure," I said.

The three priests from the church of Saint Eusebius had begun an anxious conference while all this was happening. I glanced toward the hermit, who stood before his grove as though his thin body and smile of benediction could protect it from all physical violence. In a minute, I thought, the priests would announce loudly that a grove with such activities in it was no place for a saint's relics, snatch the golden reliquary and bolt for their horses

I excused myself from Dominic, who now looked only weary, and hurried toward the shrine on a collision course with the priests. The presence of a wizard might slow them down, I hoped, even if they seemed to have little respect for hermits.

Nimrod calmly watched the priests' approach, then flicked his eyes toward me. "I hope you don't think me a coward, Wizard," he said in a voice designed to carry. "But if I hadn't fled from Prince Dominic, I would have had to kill him, and I do not want to kill the royal regent of Yurt." He stepped out from the shelter of the trees to meet the priests and the sun shone with golden light on his hair.

Dominic turned around with a scowl. The duchess,

who had started down the track by the falls, froze for a second, then kept on walking. But Nimrod's words and appearance had their greatest impact on the three priests. They shook their heads and stared at him as though not believing what they saw.

"When we saw you last night, I didn't think it could be true," said the round priest, then paused as though feeling his words were inadequate.

"The Lord moves in mysterious ways," supplied the thin priest.

"Do you know Nimrod?" asked Joachim politely.

"Nimrod?" demanded the round priest. "Is that what he calls himself? We certainly do know this 'mighty hunter.'"

"We had thought him an obedient son of the Church, but his appearance here, an accused sinner under a false name, shows him to have been but a whited sepulcher," said the thin priest.

"Then who is he?" asked Joachim, when Nimrod said nothing.

"He is—or was—" said the thin priest witheringly, "the prince of our city."

PART SIX
Prince Ascelin

I

Somehow, Joachim managed to get rid of the priests. They retreated a little way down the valley highly indignant, but still unwilling to say anything openly against the chaplain and still not in possession of the Holy Toe. The shouting and barking had died down and it again seemed possible that, at some point, the valley's dreamy quiet might be restored.

Dominic, with the knights and the still excited dogs, settled down near the base of the waterfall, built a fire, and started making a late breakfast. Diana sat twenty yards away, combing her hair and pinning it up again, her back turned carefully to them.

This must be, I thought, very difficult for her. Nimrod, the man she might have loved in her own way, now appeared a coward and she had been thoroughly and publicly shamed before the knights of Yurt. Even for the duchess, this had gone beyond outrageous.

Joachim, Evrard, and I went into the grove with Nimrod. The old hermit had retreated to his hermitage. I should be, right now, trying to find the old wizard's monster. But even with my best magic, I feared I would not be able to track it unless I had the tall huntsman with me—I hadn't even been able to find Evrard's stick-man when I saw its footprint—and, for the moment, he couldn't leave the grove's sanctuary.

In the meantime, magical or not, I had a problem here that would thoroughly disrupt the kingdom if something wasn't done, and soon.

"So are you indeed a prince?" I asked Nimrod.

"It won't be much of a surprise to hear that I am," he said with a slow smile. "My true name is Ascelin. I know you realized all along that I was not simply a huntsman."

"And the duchess knew who you were?"

"Of course she did," he said, seeming much more amused than anyone should be when his life was in peril. "I won't try to pretend that part of my reason for coming into Yurt wasn't to see her again." He glanced in her direction. All that was visible was her hair and firmly set shoulders. "Although I'm afraid *that's* turned out very badly."

His next words showed how very precarious was his apparent calm. "Would she rather have me kill the regent and half the knights of Yurt than to run?" he demanded. It was quite clear he was not addressing any of us. "I could certainly outwrestle Dominic and I've got stag-arrows in my quiver. I could have picked off all of them one by one. Would her honor have been satisfied then?"

"I don't understand," said Evrard abruptly into the ensuing silence. "Why does Dominic want to kill you?"

"I thought that was fairly clear," said Nimrod or, rather, Prince Ascelin. "We'd camped on the plateau last night and were finishing breakfast outside our tent this morning, when Dominic and the knights came into view. Apparently, the regent didn't think my behavior toward my lady, the Duchess Diana, was the sort of behavior appropriate toward someone he'd planned to marry." He smiled briefly and bitterly. "If

I didn't intend to kill a lot of men, running seemed my best option."

I could see Joachim make a conscious decision not to lecture the prince on sin and virtue. "What do you know about Saint Eusebius?" he asked instead. "You said that seeing the duchess was only *part* of your reason for coming here."

At this question, Nimrod—as I couldn't help but think of him—became oddly flustered. I couldn't tell at first if it was just the change of subject or if the mention of the saint was disturbing. He would not meet Joachim's eyes but looked off, instead, toward the shrine and reliquary there. "The major church of my city is dedicated to Saint Eusebius," he answered slowly after a minute. "I've been devoted to the saint since boyhood."

Several things suddenly became clear to me. "Saint Eusebius appeared to you in a vision," I said. Joachim and Evrard stared at me, but I knew I was right. "He knew you for a remarkable huntsman and he wanted to get the great horned rabbits out of Yurt."

Nimrod looked at me almost with relief. "Yes, he did." He paused, then went on in a much lower voice. "But he'd never appeared to me before. It was . . . it was not what I'd expected." His face became distant and almost expressionless. A very short time ago, I had thought the forces of good were always gentle and pleasant, but it appeared I was wrong. Since seeing a saint seemed to be such a soul-searing experience, I was rather glad that saints did not appear to wizards.

"Eusebius has appeared to several people," said Joachim quietly.

"The Cranky Saint has said something different to every single person he's appeared to," I said. "When is he going to make his will clear?" But Joachim did not answer.

I tried to calculate when the saint might have appeared in a vision to Nimrod, counting from when

Evrard's horned rabbits had escaped. "But how did you get here so fast?"

"I set out, I think," said Nimrod, "within twenty-four hours of when the first horned rabbit reached this valley. I was here four days later." He managed a smile. "Fifty miles a day on foot was a push, even for me. I must say," he added after a brief pause, "that when I was asked to come defend the Holy Grove from magical creatures, I had expected something a little more, well, intimidating than great horned rabbits."

Whether the saint had told him or not, there was indeed something more intimidating in the kingdom now.

"What," put in Evrard, "do you have to do, Prince, with the entrepreneurs up on top of the cliff?"

"I don't know anything about them," said Nimrod.

I sat thinking rapidly. If the huntsman had come to Yurt in direct response to the horned rabbits, then many of the series of strange and coincidental events that had begun immediately upon the king's departure were linked. And Diana—even if in part unintentionally—was behind them all.

But I still didn't know what any of this had to do with lowering pilgrims in a basket to see the Holy Toe and I recalled I had already worked out that the horned rabbits had appeared too late to be behind the priests' vision, even if they had brought about Nimrod's. I wondered briefly if the "pilgrims" I had seen before had been the *real* priests of the church of Saint Eusebius and if these three were some other people in disguise.

I dismissed this thought as too elaborate. Besides, I doubted false priests could fool Joachim. But Evrard's horned rabbits—and the inhuman stick-man with which he had next tried to impress Diana—had also led to the monster. And I didn't have the slightest idea how I was going to catch it.

Too many other people, from the duchess to the

hermit to the priests to Dominic to Evrard, had had too many conflicting plans. And now everyone must be formulating new plans to get Prince Ascelin out of the grove. For all I knew, I might even be caught in some complicated scheme put together by the Cranky Saint. If I wanted to leave this perfectly charming valley within my lifetime, it was time to stop being a playing piece in other people's games and to have a plan of my own.

And the first priority was to end this deadly stand-off, before either Dominic or Nimrod killed each other, so that I could marshal my forces to go after the old wizard's creature. "Evrard," I said, rising resolutely to my feet, "we're going to find the monster as soon as I settle this impasse. I want you to start working on spells with which to bind it."

To my surprise, his face went white, making his freckles stand out sharply. "It's all my fault," he said as though he had just made a desperate decision.

"What do you mean?" I demanded.

"I made the stick-creature at the heart of the monster!"

I shook my head. "Whatever creature you made is long gone. It's all the old wizard's now. You're not a competent enough wizard to create a monster like that single-handed."

His face went, if possible, even whiter. "The duchess doesn't think I'm competent?" He turned desperately from me to Nimrod. "She doesn't think I'll make a good wizard?"

"I'm afraid she hasn't been very impressed so far," said Nimrod reluctantly.

"Then I'll have to catch the monster," said Evrard in tragic tones, "or die in the attempt."

"I think," I said witheringly, "the duchess has other things to worry about now than whether her ducal wizard meets her expectations." I certainly did. "Joachim," I continued, "I'll leave the Cranky Saint to you with pleasure, but first I need you to back me up."

"Of course," he said. The chaplain clearly trusted me to know what I was doing. I wondered if I actually did.

"We've got to make it safe for you to leave the sanctuary of the grove," I said to Nimrod. "I'll need your help to catch the monster. Joachim, come with me."

We walked to the top of the waterfall. The track had become churned and muddy from the many feet that had hurried up and down, but the water still gurgled icy and clear.

There was a spell I had learned in school, to make one's voice carry. After a moment's concentration, I thought I remembered it. "Listen to me," I said loudly, too worried to be as pleased as I normally would have been that the spell had indeed worked. "The Royal Chaplain and I speak to you as King Haimeric's representatives."

I certainly had everyone's attention. Even the duchess turned around. The dogs sat up expectantly, their tongues lolling.

Dominic heaved himself to his feet. The mud on his face and tunic had dried and he had made some ineffectual attempts to scrape it off, but the effect was still quite horrifying. "You can't act as the king's representative, Wizard," he said, frowning and crossing his massive arms. "*I* am the regent."

"But the king said he wanted us to help you while he was gone. And since this is a case that involves you personally, you cannot possibly act as judge.

"It is clear to everyone here," I continued, turning from Dominic to the knights and priests, "that a serious quarrel has taken place, disturbing the king's peace, a quarrel that requires a judicial decision." If I was not a particularly competent substitute for a king, I would be an even less competent justice giver, but I had no choice. "In the name of King Haimeric of Yurt, I declare this court in session!"

Joachim looked at me sideways and lifted his eyebrows fractionally. I hoped that meant he approved.

My audience stirred and whispered and the priests moved closer. Behind me, I almost thought I heard a soft laugh that could have come from the wood nymph. But no one else was laughing.

Under a sun far higher in the sky than I had hoped it would be by the time I finally got out of the valley, the knights of Yurt rose to their feet. They arranged themselves almost automatically into the relaxed but watchful stance they took when the king was dispensing justice. The regent gave me a black scowl but said nothing.

"Prince Dominic," I said formally, "step forward and state your case as complainant."

II

To my relief, the regent seemed willing to accept my highly irregular calling of a royal judicial court. This might even work. Dominic climbed up to stand before Joachim and me, then turned around to speak. Without a magic spell, his voice did not carry as well as mine, but no one had any trouble hearing him.

"I accuse Prince Ascelin, the man who has gone by the false name of Nimrod, of gross insult to the royal court of Yurt. He came to the court under false pretenses, disguised as a huntsman but secretly intending to woo my lady, the duchess. For an aristocrat to hide his real identity, to take advantage of a court's hospitality while lying at every turn, is to show himself no worthy prince!

"Then, even though I had asked the Duchess Diana to be my wife, and he knew that she would most likely agree, he lured her out of the castle. Here his behavior proved to be all that his earlier duplicity suggested, for last night he passed the entire night with her, in defiance of all laws of decency."

Diana became bright red, but I credited it more to fury than to maidenly modesty.

"When confronted with his shameful deeds, he fled to this grove like a coward. I demand that this court sentence him to death!"

"You can't 'demand' any particular sentence from a court," put in Joachim quietly. "You know that. And we have not yet heard evidence of any capital offense that would require the death penalty."

This stopped Dominic for a few seconds and, in the pause, the duchess marched determinedly up to stand beside him. She was still bright red.

But her voice was firm. "May I address the court?"

"Please do."

"Prince Dominic has made some accusations against me which I must deny at once," she said clearly. Those watching were completely silent, listening. "Prince Ascelin and I did indeed pass last night in the same tent together."

At this there was a faint murmur from the knights, which she ignored. "But our conduct was completely chaste! I am a duchess and the queen's own cousin; my standards of conduct are exactly the same whether camped rough during a hunt or entertaining elegantly in my own castle. For Prince Dominic to accuse me of acting in another way, in any way that would impugn my honor, is for me the grossest insult. Let me reassure him and all the court that, if he had spent the night lying between us, our relationship could not have been any purer."

Dominic winced at this. "He still came into Yurt in disguise," he said to her, "hoping to overcome your virtue, even if he hasn't yet succeeded."

Diana's eyes were almost wild in spite of the formality of her denial. It must be difficult being caught between fury toward Dominic and fury toward Nimrod. But her forthright nature did not fail her. "Concealing his true identity may have been a slight prevarication, but he did not come under completely false pretenses. I always knew perfectly well who he was."

This caused a sudden stir, silenced at once when she continued. "He came as a hunter because he wanted to help me as a hunter. If he'd come as himself, he would have had to come as a recognized suitor for my hand."

This certainly got everyone's attention.

"And what's wrong with that?" cried Dominic. "Do you discredit the possibility that anyone honorable could ask for your hand?"

"Not at all!" she replied haughtily. "But it was not a role he could play well. After all, I had rejected him five years ago."

This actually silenced Dominic. It took me a few seconds to recover my own voice. "I would like to summon the accused to testify for himself," I said.

Nimrod had been following my improvised legal hearings from just inside the Holy Grove. He looked toward Dominic, then back at me, but he made no move to emerge.

"Come, Prince Ascelin," I said, still in my magically amplified voice. "The royal court is its own sanctuary." I tried to remember the exact words I had once heard the king use. "I guarantee your safe conduct. The knights of Yurt are under orders to kill on the spot anyone who tries to harm you while under the court's summons."

The knights all slapped their sword hilts ritually. Dominic had about five seconds in which to overrule my offer of safe conduct. The knights would never have killed him, but once he let my statement stand, he would be bound by it.

He let the five seconds stand and the following thirty. Nimrod came out of the grove.

He walked forward slowly, as though consciously controlling his strength, his head held high. "Let me confirm," he said when standing before Joachim and me, "the purity of my relations with my lady, the duchess."

I was delighted to see with how much dignity the contestants stated their cases. Dominic, the duchess, and Prince Ascelin were well used to court hearings. If I had had a group before me like the villagers King Haimeric had heard before his trip, there was no way I could have persuaded them that this muddy patch of ground under a sunny sky was a place for formality.

"I came to Yurt to try to catch the horned rabbits," Nimrod continued. "I did indeed come under a false name, but only because I did not want to put the Duchess Diana under any sense of obligation to me." He paused as though bracing himself but, when he went on, his voice was clear. "She had, as she has already told this court, rejected my proposals when I met her and spent a season courting her in the great City. It was an unexpected advantage of hunting the horned rabbits that I was able to renew our acquaintance on a friendly basis." He shot her a quick glance as he finished speaking, but she was studiously not looking at him.

"But she'll never have you now!" cried Dominic triumphantly. "She won't love a coward!"

"You call me a coward for choosing not to kill you?"

"When the duchess' honor was in question, your only interest was your own skin!"

Nimrod tossed back his hair. The change in him was quite startling. He was furious and his strength no longer seemed controlled. "No one impugns a prince's courage like that and lives!"

"I don't give much credit to your courage. You slipped out of the royal castle and carried out your attacks on my lady's virtue where you thought I wouldn't see you!"

"And I don't give much credit to anything said by someone as hopelessly jealous as you are!"

"Come on!" the regent bellowed. "Come on, you overgrown sprat! Do you want to try your luck with your bare hands?" Nimrod dropped into a defensive pose as Dominic, his fists ready, began to advance.

Good. This was what I had been waiting for: a formal statement before everyone of what they were fighting over, followed by a new outbreak of unrestrained conflict. I hoped that the duchess would start beating Dominic again—or even Nimrod—but she stood to one side, frowning.

I didn't have time to wait for her. "Stop!" I shouted in a bellow of my own. It echoed up and down the valley, until a series of louder and fainter voices all seemed to be crying stop. "Stop your fighting before I must ask the knights to restore the order of this court!"

They both stopped and looked at me.

"This quarrel is now almost inextricably confused," I said with the best wizardly glare I could manage without shaggy eyebrows. "This quarrel has become an excuse for verbal abuse and for physical violence which the king—and we as the king's representatives—consider intolerable. If either one of you hoped that by utter confusion you would avoid a ruling against you, you are mistaken!"

I paused to give emphasis. "*All* of you are in the wrong. And that includes you, my lady. This case cannot be settled by a simple determination of right. I have only one option left to me. I am going to swear you to peace!"

For one second I caught Joachim's eye. He was smiling.

"You will have to work out for yourselves," I went on, "who has been accepted as a suitor and who rejected, who has impugned whose honor and who is a coward, but you will have to do it without violence!"

For almost a minute I didn't think it would work. The valley itself seemed to be watching and waiting for their response. But both Dominic and Nimrod had dropped their fists and, at last, Dominic said, "So what do you want us to do?"

I sent Joachim to get his Bible from his saddlebag so that they could swear on it. The hermitage was closer, but I had no intention of bringing out the relic of the Holy Toe. Even a saint who was not normally cranky might well be irritated by today's proceedings.

The three priests of the church of Saint Eusebius had started to confer again and Dominic went to join them. I wondered uneasily what the regent might have to say to them. For a brief moment, I wondered if it might also be possible to swear the hermit, the priests, the entrepreneurs, and even the saint to peace, but bringing in the supernatural was, I knew, beyond me.

Evrard came up beside me. "You continue to surprise me, Daimbert," he said, which I supposed was a compliment.

Joachim returned with his Bible and I had the unlikely triangle of Dominic, Nimrod, and Diana all swear to observe peace toward each other. They even managed to give each other the kiss of peace. I had rather hoped that Nimrod and the duchess might find this a way to break through the new coldness between them but, if so, it was not evident.

"Now that this case has been concluded," I said, "we as the king's representatives will end this—"

Dominic interrupted me. "Wait. I'm still regent. There is another urgent case that needs royal judgment."

Joachim and I looked at each other. Whatever Dominic wanted to do, I certainly hoped it did not involve me. "And so it shall be," I said formally to the regent. "We surrender the jurisdiction of this court to you. And now, if you'll excuse me—"

"I need the Royal Wizard while I'm giving judgment," said Dominic shortly. From the intimidating glare he gave me, I knew that I had no choice but to stay.

I had manipulated him into letting Nimrod leave the sanctuary of the Holy Grove and the regent was (rather generously, I thought) giving me one more chance to work with him. If I didn't take that chance, we would spend the rest of our lives living in the same castle but not speaking to each other. Of course, if the monster showed up and I couldn't find a way to control it, neither of our lives might last beyond today.

Once the knights realized Dominic meant to continue with more legal proceedings, they snapped back into their positions.

"Although my quarrel with Prince Ascelin has been so wisely concluded," the regent began, in a tone which left me wondering if he meant it as sarcastically as it sounded, "one issue remains. The honor and purity of the duchess, the leading woman of the kingdom in the queen's absence, has been cast into doubt. And we who are charged with protecting the kingdom of Yurt must sometimes make personal sacrifices to preserve the welfare and good name of the kingdom."

The three priests followed Dominic's words with serious and approving expressions. They had put him up to it, I thought. Diana, on the other hand, looked shocked beyond ready response.

"With doubts about the duchess go doubts about the entire kingdom of Yurt. Purity and morality must always come from the top." I wasn't sure if the silence of Dominic's audience was agreement, surprise at his sententiousness, or just attentiveness. "There is only one way to restore the honor and good name of the duchess and, with her, all our people. She must marry as soon as possible!"

Dominic, I thought, was desperate. Either he really did want to marry Diana, in spite of what she seemed to think, or he saw no way to take back his offer. But he also had to try to restore dignity to a proposal she had treated with public ridicule.

Diana began to laugh. For a second I feared it was hysteria, which would certainly have been my own reaction, but it appeared entirely genuine amusement.

"Is this the court's ruling then, sire?" she asked when she had recovered her breath.

"It is the court's ruling and will."

"Then I have a request to make," she said. Her head was held at an angle which, for reasons I could not have explained, appeared mischievous.

"Certainly, if it is consistent with the rulings of this court."

She smiled widely. "Then let me invite everyone here to my castle! It is not far away and we can all be more comfortable there than trying to camp here in the valley—especially since camping has taken on such a distinctly immoral tone in Yurt."

Dominic frowned as though trying to read some secret meaning into her words.

"Once there, I shall, of course, comply with the wishes of this court. I will be married by my own chaplain and we can all then proceed with the nuptial feast!"

Everything was happening so fast that the knights had trouble following it all, but they understood about the feast and raised a hurrah.

In my gratitude that the regent's "urgent case" had taken so little time, I was unable to concentrate on the amazing fact that the duchess seemed willing to accept Dominic. It would certainly be best for Nimrod not to be there for the wedding and, besides, I needed him. When everyone got under way, I would separate him from the rest.

III

Joachim said that he and the priests would stay at the Holy Grove for now, but everyone else began preparing for departure. This left only one more extraneous matter. I managed to draw Dominic aside.

I took a deep breath. "I've finally realized something,

sire," I said. "The entrepreneurs on top of the cliff—
you authorized them."

For a second the massive regent looked like a boy
caught out. "Why do you say that?"

"You reminded us all that this is royal territory, not
part of Diana's duchy. You would never have ignored
something like this money-making enterprise and yet
you seemed very uninterested when I first told you
about the booth and the basket. I'd been wondering
where you would get your income if you left Yurt. The
entrepreneurs told me they needed half their income
for 'overhead,' and I realize now that meant paying a
backer's share to you."

I held his eyes as I spoke and could see embarrassment and anger struggling for precedence. "Don't
worry," I said quickly. I had enough problems without
further worsening my relations with the regent. "I
won't say anything. Even the chaplain says it's not
actually illegal as long as people can still go around by
the road for free."

"I never imagined," he said coldly, "that you would
try to tell me what was and was not illegal."

"I hope you have other sources of income lined up
as well," I said. "Even if they get their basket working,
they're never going to get very many paying pilgrims."

Dominic twisted his mouth into a hard line but
turned away without answering. In a moment I saw
him talking to the duchess. She had a much friendlier
expression than I could possibly have foreseen an hour
earlier.

"So it looks as though she will marry Dominic after
all," commented Evrard. "I guess a woman's desire to
preserve her honor must overcome everything else."

This explanation didn't seem right, but I didn't have
time to worry about Diana. If we could find the monster quickly and somehow subdue it, we might arrive
in time for the last of the nuptial feast, and then we
would hear how it all had come out.

As Evrard and I went to get our mares, he asked,

"Do you think I have time to slip back and say good-bye to the wood nymph?"

"No," I said firmly. I felt an almost overwhelming need for haste and the slightest delay was now intolerable. "The knights are mounted already. It's time we—"

From the corner of my eye, I spotted someone moving on the top of the cliff. I jerked around so sharply I could feel the muscles in my shoulders popping. It was a human form, but I could not see if it was true human or monster. Before I could find the words of the Hidden Language to shape a far-seeing spell, the figure stepped to the edge and jumped.

Evrard gave a sharp cry. I threw together a spell that I hoped would slow the figure's descent, then realized it was already falling far slower than it should have been.

In fact, it was not falling at all but flying down the cliff face. With a start, I recognized the old wizard.

Leaving my indignant mare half-saddled, I flew to meet him. Evrard was right behind me, flying surprisingly well.

My predecessor stood calmly at the bottom of the line of toeholds. I expected to find an obvious renegade wizard, out of control, perhaps even emanating evil, but he looked no more out of control than when we last saw him.

"So you young whippersnappers are here, too," he said, straightening out a sleeve that had folded back during his descent. He looked toward the group of priests and knights for a moment, then dismissed them. "You might even be useful."

He seemed to have forgotten—or was willing to ignore—how rude I had been the last time I saw him. I was not going to remind him. "I know what's happened," I said instead. "Your monster's escaped."

His eyes flashed at me from under genuinely shaggy eyebrows. "Not escaped. And not a monster, but a living creature. I let it loose deliberately, but I'm having a little more trouble binding it again than I anticipated."

"But, Master, why did you even make it in the first place?"

"To confound young wizards who think they know more magic than they do," he said absently, looking down the valley. I attempted, very delicately, to reach his mind, but he had it well shielded. "I think it's down here in the valley somewhere. It may have gone around to the far end and be working its way back upstream."

"Coming, Wizards?" called the duchess.

"No," I called back. After trying so long to leave, I now had to stay. "Down here" could be anywhere, could be at the far end of the valley, could be the Holy Grove, could be the bushes beside us.

A branch above us bent suddenly, with a faint creak of wood and fluttering of leaves. I staggered backwards, but as I looked up I saw that it was the wood nymph.

The old wizard saw her, too. His stern expression changed at once. He called to her in the Hidden Language, not the spell I had derived from the old ducal wizard's books but something comparable. "How would you two young wizards like to meet a nymph?" he asked as she came further along the branch toward us, then looked over our heads.

"In fact, we've met her and even—" Evrard began, but he never had a chance to finish.

Someone screamed. I spun around. The creature I had wanted to seek for so long had come to me.

Or rather, not come to me, but come to the knights of Yurt. I could see it now much more clearly than I had seen it in the glimpse through the old wizard's door.

As tall as a man but twice as broad, it had a large blank oval for a face, its only feature its rapidly moving eyes. It rose from behind a bush almost directly in front of the duchess. Over its shoulder was flung a

ragged form which I identified as one of the apprentice hermits. From his choking cries, he was, for the
moment, still alive.

The duchess' gelding reared with a scream of its
own. Diana fought for and lost her seat. As she sailed
off, the monster threw the apprentice hermit away like
a bag of flour and snatched her instead out of the air.
Before any of us could move, it had raced up the track
toward the grove.

After a horrified second, everyone moved at once.
Nimrod grabbed his bow; Dominic forced his horse
toward the waterfall with the knights behind him; the
dogs foamed up the track; the old wizard, Evrard and
I flew after the creature.

It ran far faster than I had expected, darting at
much greater than human speed toward the grove. It
dodged in and under the trees, where Evrard smacked
into a trunk and sank to the ground, but the old wizard
and I veered desperately as we tried to keep up. At
least, on the basis of Diana's wild kicks, she was very
much alive.

The creature came to the pool at the center of the
grove, splashed straight through while the duchess
yelled, made a wide detour around the shrine of the
Holy Toe, where the amazed hermit stood watching
open-mouthed, and shot out again into the sunlight.

Flying as fast as I could, I could barely gain on the
creature. The duchess was in deadly peril, and both the
old wizard and this creature he had made, with a magic
much more powerful than anything I could imagine
wielding, filled me with horror. I even tried a prayer
to Saint Eusebius on the off chance he might listen.

Nimrod had his bow drawn, but I was very glad to
see him lower it again. From what Joachim had said
no arrow could harm the monster, but one of the
huntsman's stag arrows would certainly have a
devastating effect on the duchess.

The creature ran toward the cliff face without even

slowing down, altering its course at the last second. And then it headed straight toward the old wizard and me.

I threw both a binding spell and a paralysis spell at it, but my spells had no effect on the creature. Diana, however, stopped shouting and instantly became rigid. Wonderful. Now I'd made it easier for the monster to carry her. It held her motionless body high over its head while the dogs barked hysterically and snapped ineffectually at its ankles.

If the old wizard tried any spells, they had no more useful result than mine. Ten feet from us, the creature turned again, giving me a quick look from eyes I could have sworn were alive, and started scrambling down the tumbled rocks a short distance from the waterfall.

Dominic's horse had fallen and him with it, but Nimrod, who had dropped his bow, sprang to intercept the creature. It dodged yet again as it reached solid ground, but he made a desperate leap and seized it by the leg.

The creature lost its balance for a second and Diana dropped with a hard thump from its hands. It righted itself immediately, but Nimrod clawed his way up the creature's body and seized it around the neck. The two crashed back to the ground, rolling and grabbing at each other, Nimrod shouting and the creature absolutely silent.

The dogs caught up again and began biting both of them. The old wizard and I reached them only a second later. Leaving my predecessor to deal with his monster, I snatched at words of the Hidden Language in a desperate attempt to break the spells I had inadvertently put on the duchess. If she could run, she might escape.

I didn't know what the old wizard hoped to try, but he never had a chance. The creature lurched to its feet, thrust Nimrod effortlessly away, and raced up again toward the grove.

Diana came back to life with a start. "Christ!" she

burst out. "What happened?" Dominic reached us at that moment, fell to his knees and tried unsuccessfully to take her into his arms. Rather than tell her that I had paralyzed her myself, I took a quick five seconds to reassure myself that she was not badly hurt, then shot after the monster and the old wizard.

Evrard joined us near the shrine, rubbing his head somewhat woozily. But the creature was gone.

It was completely silent within the grove. Not even the leaves moved. "It came straight through here," Evrard said, showing no desire at all to pursue it further. "It was following the river."

I knew then where it had gone. I flew along the banks of the little river, out of the grove, and to the bottom of the cliff. The water poured sparkling out of the cave mouth as though nothing in particular had happened there, but there were a few deep scrambling marks in the gravel. A steady, whispering wind blew from the cave. I dropped down, looking into blackness, and probed with magic.

There was no question. My predecessor's monster had gone this way.

"He's back in the cave," I said as the old wizard and Evrard came out of the trees. Let them chase it now. I flew back down the valley to make sure the duchess really was all right.

She had pushed Dominic away and was sucking a barked knuckle. "I would have been able to rescue myself, without help from anyone," she said angrily, "if it hadn't put some sort of spell on me." As Diana was usually a rational person, I knew that this boast was a sign of how frightened she had been.

So far we had been enormously fortunate. The creature had let both the apprentice hermit and the duchess go without killing or even badly wounding them. Next time we might not be so lucky. Had it deliberately chosen these two out of all of us in the valley or would it seize randomly at different people—and maybe, or maybe not, let them go again—until it found some specific one it sought?

Nimrod—or Prince Ascelin—actually was in worse condition than the duchess. The priests and the knights had all come up and he sat in the middle of an attentive circle, picking grit out of a bloody knee. There were several marks of canine teeth in his lower legs. "None of those dogs had better be rabid," he said in irritation. "Don't you knights of Yurt train them better than to bite the person they're supposed to help?"

"But that's exactly what we *do* train them to do!" put in young Hugo with a wink.

The dogs now sat happily panting, not at all repentent. Diana was sitting beyond Nimrod. I was surprised to intercept an amused glance she aimed toward his hunched shoulders.

The apprentice hermit whom the creature had originally seized did not look physically damaged as a result of his adventure, but he sat a little apart from the others, his knees up to his chin and his eyes enormous. The youngest of the three priests unbent far enough to go sit beside him and say things which I hoped were reassuring.

For a brief moment, like the pause between two claps of thunder, peace had returned to the valley. "I always forget a wizard can fly," said one of the knights to me in what I hoped was admiration. In times of peace, which was now most of the time, Royal Wizards might do little more than illusions for months at a time. I didn't point out that flying had so far been useless against an undead monster running across the ground.

"I'm impressed you were able to get the better of the monster," I said to Nimrod, "even if only for a moment."

"I never did have the better of it. Wrestling it was like trying to wrestle a boulder! All I could do was throw it off balance for a second. Did you have any better luck with magic? Where is it now?"

"It's crawled back into the cave where the river comes out." He looked up briefly and nodded. "My predecessor and the ducal wizard are pursuing it." But the pursuers appeared a few minutes later, dripping wet and without a monster.

The old wizard took me aside, wringing out the hem of his cloak as he spoke. "It's far back in there now. We'd better get all these people out of the valley; then you and I can go in and get it."

His voice was quiet and he kept his eyes lowered. I was surprised and gratified he wanted my help, considering his usual opinion of my abilities. But I wondered how he could speak so calmly of catching a monster we had just pursued entirely unsuccessfully around the head of the valley. Then he looked up sharply and, for one second, I thought I saw a glimmer in his eye as twisted as the glimpse I had had before of his mind.

IV

I was afraid that Dominic or Nimrod or both would insist on leading the hunt for the monster, but they both seemed eager to escort Diana back to her castle. Her normal enthusiasm for hunting was greatly diminished, too.

Joachim and the priests, however, were still determined to stay in the valley. Although I tried suggesting to the hermit that he might want to leave, it was clear that even the dragon that had eaten Saint Eusebius would not budge him or the apprentice hermits.

"We came to assess the will of the saint and to remove his sanctified relics to a safer place, if necessary," said the thin priest. "What we have witnessed today may make our task even more needful. Those who fear the righteous wrath of God do not fear the terror by night or the destruction that wasteth at noonday."

My predecessor gave a snort and stamped off to watch the entrance to the cave; the hermit and his apprentices retreated to the shrine. Evrard and I unsaddled our mares again as the others rode up the steep road out of the valley. Dominic seemed badly shaken. I wasn't sure if he would insist, now, on the duchess marrying him immediately.

But I didn't have time to worry about that. The spells of three wizards had so far proved useless in catching the monster. Only brute force, Prince Ascelin's size and strength, had had any effect at all, and even that had been pitifully slight. I had known all along that catching the creature would be difficult. Now I was faced with the very real possibility that, even with the old wizard's help, it might be impossible.

For the sake of the priests' safety, I wished they had gone, too, but I was almost ashamedly glad that Joachim was staying. I needed all the support I could get; I felt that I would even welcome a discussion of sinful mortals or of complex moral dilemmas.

"You must be very grateful to have another young wizard here to help you," said Joachim. I didn't have the heart to tell him how wrong he was.

The knights, their horses, and the monster had torn up the ground above and below the waterfall and had broken branches from trees at the edge of the grove. I had just turned away from watching the duchess' party disappear when a branch creaked and dipped just above me. The wood nymph sprang lightly down, with a swirl of long soft hair, and began to attend to the broken branches.

The priests stared. They had clearly not expected to see a dusky-skinned girl dressed in nothing but leaves in their saint's grove. Evrard started to speak, but I motioned him to silence.

Not even seeming to notice us, the nymph worked quickly and efficiently on the broken branches.

Although I could not see quite how she did it, for she certainly had no pruning shears, she trimmed off dangling twigs quickly and evenly, passed her hand over the wounds so that they stopped dripping sap, and whistled to the birds until they came down from the tree tops and perched again near her. She was in constant motion, moving from branch to branch, springing lightly to higher ones with a flash of graceful legs, dropping to lower ones with no more than a dip and a swish of leaves.

Her violet eyes passed across us as though we were no more substantial than a bit of mist. But as she leaped up to a high branch, seemingly finished repairing the damage to her trees, she suddenly stopped. Her face changed as I had seen it change the first time she had heard my spell, but neither Evrard nor I had said any spells.

And she was not looking at us. She was looking at Joachim.

She swung down again and hung by one hand from a branch so that her face was at the same level as his. "Are you a hermit?" she asked with a delighted smile.

The three priests of Saint Eusebius seemed shocked beyond the ability to speak, but Joachim answered her calmly. "No, I am a priest. But like a hermit, I serve the will of God."

She dropped to the ground and looked at him as though puzzled. The rest of us might as well have not been there. "Are you a wizard?"

"No," said the chaplain. For one second, he caught my eye over her head. "Wizards work with the earth's natural powers, but I deal with the supernatural."

The wood nymph thought this over. Evrard frowned at me and I wondered if he was jealous.

"Would you like to come back to my tree with me?" she asked. "I would like to learn more about priests."

Now Evrard was definitely jealous.

"I don't think I had better, my daughter," said

Joachim. No one who didn't know him as well as I did would have realized he was smiling.

"But I have strawberries and the sweetest honey," she said, looking at him with dancing violet eyes. Soon, I thought, the round priest would explode, which would leave only two priests trying to appropriate Saint Eusebius's relics. "We could eat my berries and drink spring water while you explained the supernatural to me. Only humans, out of all of nature, have access to eternity, but only a few of you know very much about it."

"A visit with you sounds delightful, but I still must refuse. Thank you very much for an offer I am sure you have extended to few men."

"Isn't it only hermits who will refuse an invitation to a nymph's tree?"

"Priests, too, my daughter," said Joachim gently.

"And you aren't even in love with anyone," she said thoughtfully.

"I have taken an oath to foresake all sins of the flesh."

Her eyes danced again. "But Saint Eusebius explained that to me! Because I am not human, I have not fallen and, therefore, cannot sin any more than I can be saved."

It sounded to me as though she had a point. But the chaplain did not hesitate.

"You cannot sin, but I can." She nodded slowly but looked puzzled again. Joachim paused and then asked what I would have asked the nymph myself if there had been the slightest indication she would listen to anyone but him. "Is there a way you can help us catch the inhuman monster that is now in the valley?"

She shook her head so hard her hair swung in an arc behind her. "The magical creature that broke these branches? No! Trees I know, and hermits, and wizards, and now priests. But I do not know inhuman monsters." She leaped up and caught a branch. But just before she swung up and out of sight, she leaned forward, kissed Joachim lightly on the forehead, then was gone.

I watched the three priests fighting back a number of things they might have said. Disconcerting as they clearly found the bishop's representative, they just as clearly did not dare irritate him.

"Shall we join the hermit up at the shrine?" he said to them, perfectly soberly.

If they had business at the shrine, I thought, squaring my shoulders, I had business with an inhuman monster which the wood nymph might not know, but my predecessor knew all too well.

The old wizard was still standing by the cave entrance. "Was your creature drawn here by the magic forces of the valley, Master?" I asked. I didn't tell him he had just missed the wood nymph, not wanting him as well as Evrard jealous of a priest with no interest in what she offered.

"There certainly are magical forces here, as I thought you knew," he said grumpily. "In most of the western kingdoms, the forces that created the world in the first place are not very evident, unless wielded by a wizard. But in a few places they're still very strong: the northern land of wild magic especially, but also in a few pockets like this valley. That's why the wood nymph is here. And that's why I thought I'd better come here when my creature got loose."

"I know all about the magical forces here. They've kept me here for two days."

"Don't blame it on 'magical forces,'" said the old wizard with a snort. "A wizard may find the raw power of magic appealing or seductive, but this valley couldn't hold you against your will. You were just having too much fun with the wood nymph.

"The magical forces of the valley may make my creature a little harder to catch," he went on. "Did you see how fast it could run? Even my magic wouldn't give it that kind of speed anywhere else," he added regretfully.

This, I thought gloomily, was exactly what I needed to hear: First, my predecessor had made a creature almost too powerful for his own magic and certainly much stronger than either Evrard's or mine, and now its strength was increased dramatically.

"I'd better go see if I can find some herbs," said the old wizard. "I'll need them for my binding spell. You and the duchess' wizard could try putting some kind of barricade across the opening to the cave. I don't believe my creature will try to come out again during the day, after we all frightened it, but it might after dark. I'd ask you to help me, but you wouldn't recognize the right herbs."

His chief concern, I thought as I watched him stump off, was that we might have "frightened" his creature! This left it all up to Evrard and me—which meant, I was afraid, me.

Although I called the old wizard Master, he was not my real master. If I thought of anyone in the paternal role in which Joachim put his bishop, it was the Master of the wizards' school, who had been willing to take on—and even keep—a young man who must have been a very unpromising wizardry student. Since my own parents had died when I was young, the white-haired Master of the school had been the closest I had had to a father.

Yet in the two years I had been in Yurt, I had come to admire my predecessor, in spite of his crankiness. And I had certainly learned a tremendous amount from him, not just the herbal magic they did not teach at the school but, partly out of shame at his example, a lot of the school magic I had not learned properly the first time.

And now something had happened to him, whether he had been pushed into unwise new experiments by Evrard's creature, overcome by pride, or (quite unaccountably) made jealous of me. Even aside from catching up to his creature, I knew I had to catch *him*.

Meanwhile I'd better make sure of my only other ally. "When you and my predecessor followed the monster into the cave," I asked Evrard, "how far back did you pursue it?"

"Not far. He made a light on the end of his staff. It wasn't very bright, but better than I could do and enough for us to see. We got back to where the cave widened, the room that Nimrod mentioned—or, rather, Prince Ascelin. It's an enormous room and a lot of tunnels open off it. The monster must have taken one of them. I'm afraid, like the prince, we fell into the river on the way back out."

"I don't trust the old wizard," I said, "not his motivations, not even his magic. Catching this monster is going to be up to you and me."

"Oh, please, Daimbert!" cried Evrard. "Let me catch it myself! Don't you see, it's my last chance to impress the duchess, before she gets fed up with me and sends me back to the City in exchange for a different wizard. And since the monster tried to carry her off, it's my responsibility as ducal wizard to avenge her."

"Don't be silly," I said, feeling that Evrard was more like ten years younger than me rather than two. "Neither one of us could possibly capture it alone. Our only chance is to do it together."

"I guess you're right," said Evrard, but not as though convinced.

He would become convinced soon enough. "First," I said, "it would help if we knew what the monster is made out of. Since this creature is no illusion, it has to be made of *something*. And it's not sticks this time. Human bones, maybe?" In spite of keeping my voice remarkably calm, I could feel a thin trickle of sweat working its way down my back.

Evrard had clearly never thought about this. Now his eyes grew so wide that white showed all the way around the iris. "But where would he have gotten human bones?"

"That's what I'd like to know," I said grimly. "We've been worrying about the creature killing a person now that we know it's killed some chickens. But has the old wizard himself already killed someone?"

We both looked involuntarily down the valley where the wizard had gone. I thought I could see him a half mile away, where the valley started to curve, poking about on the river bank.

Evrard hugged himself as though standing in a bitterly cold wind. "But even the wizards trained under the old apprentice system must have taken the oath to help and guide mankind."

"Exactly. And that's why I can't let you even try to go after the monster by yourself."

Evrard shivered again and nodded. His desire to impress the duchess seemed greatly diminished. But then he looked at me with his head cocked to one side, his eyes almost back to normal. "I know what I can do," he said. "Your predecessor had a good idea when he suggested we barricade the cave. I can practice my lifting spells by lifting some rocks to block the opening. Once I have them in place, I'll put a binding spell on them, so that even a monster won't be able to push them aside."

"Good plan," I told him enthusiastically, though I didn't think this would work for long and there might be other exits to the cave. But it would keep him busy and give me a chance to walk and to think. Anything was better than waiting here, either for inspiration—which seemed increasingly unlikely—or for the old wizard to come back.

V

I jumped up and started down the valley. It was late afternoon and a soft white mist had begun to rise.

It hung over the river and sent long arms out over the water's grassy verges. As I walked downstream, I went into patches of fog so dense I could barely see ten feet in front of me and then went out again under a clear sky. The limestone formations on the valley walls looked even more like the ruins of old castles than usual.

The old wizard had still not told me why he had made such a creature in the first place and maybe he didn't know himself. I wished I could get word to the wizards' school but, with the creature actually here, I didn't dare leave the valley myself. Even Evrard's spells would be some help if the monster broke out.

I stopped in the middle of a patch of mist and looked around. I had not paid much attention to how far I had walked, but it was hard to tell distances with no landmarks. The only solid points in a white world were the road under my feet and the rushing river to my right. But where was the old wizard?

I came out of the mist again and saw him, standing under a tree, staring off down the valley. Heavy drops of moisture hung from the leaves above his head. He gave a start as I came up beside him. He looked as old as I had ever seen him, his full two hundred and fifty years, and much too weak ever to kill anybody.

"Did you find all the herbs you needed?" I asked.

"Herbs?" he said, as though coming back from a great distance and not sure what I could mean. Then he looked down at his hands which were clenched around a wad of drooping plants. "Oh, yes." He met my eyes briefly and turned away. "We can return now."

We walked back up the valley without speaking. The fog was growing thicker, so that we would have lost our way if we were not following a clearly marked road. Even the river beside us seemed to be running much more quietly. My predecessor, I thought with a sideways glance at him, might already have lost his way.

When the shape of the trees and clearings was again familiar enough that I knew we were close to the Holy Grove, I tried once more. "Maybe I can help you, Master," I began tentatively. "You know you've taught me a lot of herbal magic. I could help you put the spells together if I knew what you were trying to do. What's driving your creature now and how can we slow it down?"

"I already told you," he said, but without his normal irritated tone, "that it's the valley itself that's made it move so fast. As to what's driving it, I thought even you could recognize magic."

I kept my temper. "But what kind of magic? What purpose is the creature serving? After all, here in the valley it seized two people within two minutes. Did you make it in order to capture people?"

He looked at me fully for the first time since I had found him on the river bank. "No, that wasn't my purpose. But it does indeed like to put its hands on people." He gave a malevolent chuckle and went on more vigorously. "It certainly wanted to lay hold of Prince Dominic. You should have seen them all trying to get away! But of course, outside this valley, it couldn't run as fast as a horse."

We had stopped walking and were facing each other. I had always assumed he was taller than I and was surprised when I had to incline my head to meet his eyes. "And has it tried to seize you?"

"Yes. That always was a problem. That's why, young whippersnapper, I needed to give it my full attention the time your young wizard friend tried to let it out."

His magic must have gone even more badly out of control than I had thought if something he had created turned on him. "The great horned rabbits," I said, "dissolved when I put a binding spell on them or, for that matter, when they were shot. Is there any similar way we can dissolve your new creature?"

"You and that magic worker of the duchess' can

play children's games with rabbits if you like. This is different."

As I talked to the old wizard, he seemed almost the same as I had always known him—except marginally more civil. The aging, the loss of control over his own magic, I thought, were temporary, passing events. He would be himself for many more years to come as long as we were able to catch his monster successfully. I wished I believed it.

"I know that a simple binding spell won't dissolve your creature," I tried again, "because I already attempted one without success, but are there other spells that might work?"

"I'm not at all ready to 'dissolve' it, as you say. And don't get any bright ideas about trying to transform it into a fuzzy squirrel either; transformation spells won't work on a magical creature, as I hope you know. This is the best thing I've ever made, far better than those illusions that used to impress the royal court over dessert. I've got a spell that will hold it, all right, but it has to be standing still."

The sweat began again running down my back in spite of the cold mist around us. "Is there something from which you made this creature which might help account for its behavior?"

He turned abruptly. "I always did wonder about those bones." And he started up the valley again without giving me a chance to answer.

There was no mist around the Holy Grove and I did not at first see anyone. But then I spotted the youngest of the priests talking to an apprentice hermit. The other two priests, the old hermit, and Joachim were in prayer at the shrine. I didn't disturb them but went out of the grove again, following the river upstream. The water seemed much lower than I remembered. I decided to see how Evrard was coming with his lifting spells.

Even at this end of the valley, where the mist did

not yet reach, it was rapidly growing dark. The old wizard was outlined against the white of the valley wall, crouching over his herbs. These last two hours, the steep walls had begun to seem the walls of a prison.

I walked toward the mouth of the cave, where I could still see Evrard's flaming red hair in spite of the shadows.

But then there was a deep and hollow boom, a sharp grating of rock on rock, and a giant burst of water shot out from the cliff, propelling him in front of it.

"Evrard!" I shouted. He managed to find the magic to break his fall and landed on the soft ground near me. "What happened?" I cried. "Are you all right?"

"My plan didn't work," he said, dripping wet and in despair. I quickly determined he was more mortified than hurt. "But it seemed like such a good idea!"

"What didn't work?" I demanded.

"Blocking the cave mouth. It might have kept the monster in, but it also kept the river in. But now I find the river was stronger than my rocks!" He shook his head, sending drops of water flying, and started squeezing water from his clothes. "And I'd just gotten dry from falling in earlier."

That explained, then, why the river had seemed so low and quiet the last hour. Obviously, if Evrard tried to fill the entire cave mouth with boulders, the force of the river would push them aside. Even a former city boy like me knew something about the power of running water. I was about to try to explain it to him when I saw my predecessor approaching.

He had pulled up his hood so I could not see his face in the shadows, but his voice emerged with its old strength. "Trying to make a noise loud enough to frighten my creature, is that your plan?"

"Well, no, Master," Evrard began. "I didn't think it had ears anyway. And you see—"

The old wizard waved his explanations aside. "I have

the right herbs now and the right spell." I noticed then his fingers glowing with a pale blue light, as though the spell itself was held in his hands. "No more time for nonsense. We're going in after it."

Evrard, who had ducked behind me, pushed himself forward again in spite of obvious reluctance. "We're ready," he said, with a calmness I admired.

"Not you, young whippersnapper." I could sense Evrard wavering between indignation and relief. "This is a job for the Royal Wizard and me. That is," the old wizard added after a long pause, with unexpected gentleness, "we both think we need someone to stay at the entrance of the cave, to make sure my creature doesn't get past us and get out, and we think you'd be best for the job."

"Of course," said Evrard, still calmly.

"Find Joachim," I said. "He and the other priests are all at the shrine. Tell him we've gone."

Evrard patted me surreptitiously on the shoulder as I followed my predecessor toward the dark cave mouth. It felt as though he was saying good-bye.

PART SEVEN
The Cave

I

We had to pick our way around several small boulders that now littered the bank, and the limestone at the cave entrance was chipped, but the river flowed as swiftly as before. The evening light was at the point at which one imagines one can still see, but when the old wizard illuminated the silver ball at the end of his staff with magic, it showed how poorly I had been able to see a moment before. His face emerged from the shadow of his hood, looking determined and quite rational.

But his light also made all our surroundings darkly black, though seconds earlier they had only been dim. And where we were going it was black all the time.

"Don't slip," said the old wizard. He bent over and led the way along the narrow ledge that paralleled the river. I scrambled through the cave entrance after him, a hand on the rough wall to keep my balance, trying to find a footing in the crazy patchwork of light and shadows as the soft glow from his staff was repeatedly blocked by his body.

Now that we were in the cave, there could be no

return until we found the monster. The prison of the valley seemed wide open in comparison with the pressing walls around me now.

But our cautious, bent advance only continued for two dozen yards. Abruptly, the crouching figure before me straightened. "This is as far as the ducal wizard and I got before," he said. I reached cautiously over my head, felt only emptiness and stood up.

The magic light showed we were in a broad chamber that would have seemed tall if it had not been so very wide. Near at hand, I could see several tunnels leading away, but farther from us, the gravel floor and the smooth ceiling disappeared into darkness.

After a quick magic probe indicated that the monster was not nearby, I looked at the walls. As Nimrod had said, they were spectacular. The slow dripping of water over the eons had left behind what looked like waterfalls frozen into stone, colored with reds and blues that reflected and shot back the magic light. If the old wizard had told me the walls were covered with precious stones, I would have believed him.

"This is lovely," I said. "Can anything live here, without light?"

The old wizard was not interested in the walls. I wondered if he might, during his close to two centuries in Yurt, have come here many times. "Not much lives here," he said absently. "Deep in the cave there are blind fish in the river—not just with unseeing eyes, but with no eyes at all."

But he was also not interested in cave fish. "Now, which way did he go?" he added, half to me and half to himself.

He moved off across the chamber and I stayed close behind him and the light. I knew we were still very near to the entrance, that Nimrod, with the benefit of midday sun, had been able to come this far without any sort of light and still see well enough not only to find his way back out but to notice the walls. But outside it was now night and in darkness I could have blundered into a different tunnel, thinking it the entrance, and been lost forever.

I told myself firmly that I should be able to make a magic light as good as my predecessor's and that even in darkness I had only to follow the river. It helped a little.

But only for a moment. "This way," said the old wizard confidently. Leaving the river, the one reliable guide we had, he walked quickly across the chamber and into one of the wider tunnels. I had no choice but to follow him.

The tunnel descended slowly but steadily, heading, as well as I could tell, back into the heart of the plateau and away from the valley. The cave walls here were rough and plain, without any of the colors and fantastic shapes of the great chamber. I presumed that at some point in the ancient past a branch of the river had run here, too, but if so, it was long gone, leaving only a dampness on the walls.

We walked quickly for maybe a quarter hour, though almost immediately I began to feel that we were outside of time. The tunnel twisted, rising now, turning until I felt sure we would come back around on ourselves. I found myself staring into the blackness around us as intensely as if the force of my stare would make the dark dissolve into light.

Abruptly, the old wizard stopped. My heart accelerated, but then I realized he was only pausing to rest.

"I don't walk that much any more," he said, half under his breath. "And these last few days, between flying and walking and running—" He sank to the floor and I sat down beside him. The walls here were lined with crystals that shimmered like diamonds in the light of the old wizard's staff.

"You didn't bring any food, did you?" he asked after a few minutes of silence. "I should have known. No thought or consideration. One thing you'll have to do, young wizard, is learn more consideration for the other fellow."

I didn't answer. Now that I considered food, I too was hungry. As well as something to eat, we should have brought water; I didn't relish the idea of trying to lick moisture from the cave walls.

"You're sure it came this way?" I asked. Stumbling behind the old wizard, I had not had a chance to try my own magic.

He grunted in assent. His hands still glowed as if with blue fire.

There was a curious intimacy sitting here with him, the two of us maybe a mile from the cave entrance, perhaps a quarter mile below the surface of the plateau, but surrounded by a silent darkness that put as much distance between us and the rest of the world as though we were on the moon. I wondered how long one would have to be here before vision atrophied and one became as blind as a cave fish. The glow at the end of his staff could have been the only light in the universe.

I took advantage of the rest stop to try again to find out something about his creature. "You know, Master," I began, my voice bringing him back with a start from his own thoughts, "I'm especially impressed by your creature's eyes. It has almost no features, no nose, no mouth, no ears, and yet the eyes seem alive."

"Of course they do," he said but did not elaborate.

I tried a different angle. "You made it partly with herbal magic and the magic of the earth, didn't you? I haven't seen anything like it in any of my books of spells from the school."

He looked at me almost fiercely for a second. I should have known better. Every time I tried to compliment him by saying how much better a certain spell of his was than something I had learned at school, he seemed insulted that I would think so little of his abilities as to compare them with the obviously inferior school magic in the first place.

"And you won't find it there, either," he said, as though trying to impress this on me. "This is my *own* spell. In part, it's based on something my own master taught me two centuries ago and, in part, it's the result of research I've been carrying on for many years."

My predecessor had had a room for his experiments at the top of the north tower of the royal castle of Yurt, into which I heard he had sometimes disappeared for days. The room had not been used since his retirement. My own chambers opened directly onto the courtyard and I had yet to develop many startling new spells in them.

It wasn't worth telling him that the old ducal wizard had known that a spell something like his existed, and that Elerius had learned—and even taught at the school—a more rudimentary version. Except for the simplest spells, magic is more than a mere series of words of the Hidden Language said in the correct sequence. It is a combination of intellectual understanding and of the instinct that comes only from long experience, of a sequence of words integrated into a format that will vary with every wizard.

"Could you teach me the spell?" I asked timidly.

He gave me a look again, but this time almost kindly. "It's not the kind of spell I could teach you the way you learn a few words of the Hidden Language. Maybe when you're my age you'll be able to learn it properly."

But by that time, he would have been dead and gone for two hundred years. While I temporarily had him in a friendly mood, I had to try to learn more. "Did you find the bones you used in the woods?" I hazarded. "Deer bones, perhaps?"

But I knew they hadn't been the bones of a deer. Deer do not have hands.

I had expected him to keep a stony silence or, at best, to tell me it was none of my business. To my surprise he answered immediately. Perhaps he too had the feeling that we, with our conversation, were the only animate beings left in existence.

"No, they were human right enough, as I'm sure

you know. My guess is he might have been a bandit
once, wounded and then abandoned by his friends.
Or he could have been a hermit, one of those self-
proclaimed saintly fellows who wander around without
even the sense to find a shrine and settle down. They
never get enough to eat and the slightest illness will
carry them off. Whoever he'd been, he'd been dead
for quite some time when I found him. Flesh long
gone and the scattered bones bleached white. He
might once have had a black beard," he added
thoughtfully.

This monster had never been a hermit, I thought.
It had been a bandit, a murderer, someone who . . .
"My God," I said involuntarily, which earned me a
cold and stony look.

The soul, the spirit of a murderer should be long
gone by the time his bones were scattered by the
forest animals. If this creature had more than magic
motion without life, if it actually partook of the living
bandit's murderous spirit, then the old wizard had
summoned a demon to bring that bandit back from
hell. I inched backwards until my back was pressed
into the sharp crystals of the wall.

But then he laughed and it was not a demonic
laugh. "Imagining that I've been practicing black
magic, is that it, young whippersnapper?" he asked in
almost friendly tones. "No, I haven't tried to bring
back the soul that once went with my bones. As you
know perfectly well, I *am* aware of the dangers of
addressing demons." If I hadn't been afraid that he
had lost his mind, I would have agreed with him there.
"But I have started to wonder if the activities we do
in life might lay down a pattern in our bones that will
persist physically long after the spirit is gone."

When he spoke rationally like this, in the voice I
had grown to know well, I could believe him. Then I
remembered the claimants before the king, accusing
each other of having dug up somebody related to their
quarrel and hidden the body. If the old wizard had

found those bones, that might explain why his creature had gone first to the village.

"They probably have to warn you young wizards at the school against trying to get fancy results the quick way, by calling on the powers of darkness," the old wizard continued. "Even *you* still have the moon and stars on your belt buckle, though I cautioned you about that the first time I met you. But back when I was trained, we all knew that only a very weak wizard, one who can't get the forces of magic to respond to his own human powers, has to fall back on invoking the supernatural."

I was delighted to let myself be persuaded. He was, I knew, perfectly capable of lying to me, but he would never allow himself to be shamed, by boasting that he had not used the supernatural to assist his own magic if indeed he had, for I could check this at any time. I had, in fact, probed for the supernatural at his cottage and not found it.

Both of us relaxed and I felt again the closeness of sitting with him in a tiny circle of magic light, surrounded by stillness so profound that the sound of my own blood was a roar in my ears. I wished I had known him when he was younger, but when he was younger, he was Royal Wizard and, with him still in the castle, I would never have come to Yurt.

"Your creature," I began again, "always seems to be *searching*. Do you know what it's searching for? Will it know it when it finds it?"

But this was something he did not seem to want to answer, at least not at once. He snorted briefly but then began a rumbling hum, as though working himself up to speech. My foot had gone to sleep, but I did not dare move it while I waited for what he would say.

"Life," he said at last.

Death, I thought. I could not forget that this creature had killed. Not dead, not alive, in motion but without a human soul, it had taken on a direction of its own.

But might it indeed want life for itself? Like the wood nymph, at some level I didn't even want to consider, was it searching for a human life and soul? Was it going to kill someone in order to get it?

Below the surface of the earth, the air was cold, not growing any colder, but clearly not getting any warmer no matter how long we waited. While we sat, a tiny layer of warmer air formed around my body, which I was loath to break by moving. But on the inside, my blood felt like ice.

My predecessor shielded his eyes from the glow on his staff with one hand. "It's dark," he said distantly. "So dark. Nothing to see." My blood, if possible, went even colder.

II

Abruptly, he pushed himself to his feet. "We'll just get stiff and even hungrier sitting here," he said grumpily. "Only thing to do is to find my creature and bring it back out."

I jumped up as well, staggered on the foot that had gone to sleep, and hurried after him. He set a determined pace through the tunnel, whose roof seemed now to be sloping almost imperceptibly lower.

This was why, I thought, the monster had kept seizing at anything living and then—sometimes—letting it go. It was searching for the old wizard. The life it wanted was the life of its maker. This was also why it had seemed to have living eyes: The old wizard himself was looking through them.

The tunnel roof suddenly became very low, so that we had to go down on our hands and knees and crawl. I fought an irrational fear that we were going into a narrower and narrower space and would never be able to work free again.

Then the roof rose and we were back on our feet. "Watch your step," the old wizard said laconically. Almost directly in front of us, a shaft dropped away. As I worked my way around the rough edge, a dislodged pebble bounced into the hole. I listened but did not hear it hit.

We passed several more shafts which could have swallowed the unwary. Some, I thought as we corkscrewed upwards through narrow passages, must lead down to where we had been a few minutes before.

We continued for what could have been an hour and could have been weeks. Several times the old wizard turned abruptly into a side tunnel, sometimes climbing upwards, sometimes slithering down on loose gravel. At each intersection, I paused long enough to place a magical mark to show which way we had gone. I realized I should have been placing them all along, but there had been so few turnings since we left the great colored chamber that I hoped that would not be a problem. My predecessor either knew the cave intimately or was indifferent about finding our way out again but, if we were still alive after finding the monster, I at least wanted a chance to find our way home.

We had been walking for some time when I realized that part of the rushing in my ears was not just my own blood but the sound of running water. By circuitous routes, we were making our way back toward the river we had left behind near the cave entrance— either that, or we were approaching another river.

I realized I had been waiting unconsciously for the dawn, with the thought that we would be able to tell where we were once the light began to grow. But no dawn could be expected here, while earth and stone endured.

The old wizard stopped again, as abruptly as he had started forward. He sat down against the wall, pulled his cloak around him, and closed his eyes. His magic light became slowly dimmer, but the silver ball was close enough to his face that I could see all the deep lines the years had cut in it.

He had aged much more than two years in the time that I had known him. I had been highly impressed at the power of his whirlwind, but I had not before thought of the drain such magic must put on an old wizard.

I, too, was exhausted, but I didn't even dare think about sleep. If we slept, the old wizard could lose contact with his creature, which might then either attack us or burst back out into the valley.

"Master," I said softly and he opened his eyes. "Master, even if I couldn't understand the spell by which you made your creature in the first place, don't you think you should teach me a little of the spell by which we'll catch it?"

He grunted, opened his eyes reluctantly, then nodded. "The problem is," he said, "as I already told you, this binding spell only works when it's standing still."

He leaned forward, opening a hand to show that he clutched a few dead leaves in it. It was from the leaves that the blue glow came. First he started to explain it to me in words of the Hidden Language, but then he started to speak to me directly, mind to mind.

Here communication was much faster, although I had to concentrate much harder to be sure I missed nothing. I held my own thoughts, terrified, just out of reach of his touch, for I received not just the spells but the twist in his thinking.

The wizards at the school would have said that he was in danger of going renegade, Joachim that he was in danger of losing his soul. Neither seemed quite right. But I knew that his motivations, his assumptions, his purposes had all taken a turn somewhere, a turn I did not want to take and which left me, when he finally broke the mental contact, trembling and bathed with sweat in spite of the cold.

"I haven't determined yet if I can modify this spell to catch him while he's moving," the old wizard said.

"Now that you know the spell, maybe you can have a try with your fancy school magic."

School magic wouldn't work here. Whatever had been the case with the creatures Nimrod had once helped track, this particular monster had been made specifically to be able to walk through normal binding spells. It wouldn't have been any use even if I had been able to get word to Zahlfast. This creature was made with the combined magic of light and earth, and it would have to be caught the same way.

The old wizard pushed himself to his feet and his staff glowed brightly again. "This way," he said and started off in the direction from which I could have sworn we had just come. But almost immediately the passage narrowed, which I had not remembered it doing before. It was a good thing I was not trying to lead.

The passage became so tight we had to push and squeeze through. He went first and, immediately after the narrowest place, the passage turned, so that he and the light were gone.

For a second I felt completely lost, without direction, surrounded by darkness so profound it seemed to sear my eyeballs, crushed by a hundred million tons of rock. But then I was through, around the corner, and able again to see his light, bouncing slightly as he walked. I put a quick magic mark on the wall and hurried to catch up.

After the tight squeeze, the passage widened so that for the moment we could walk abreast. With a little more light, I did not stumble as often, even though I kept falling behind every time we passed a side turning and I paused to mark that we had continued to follow the straight way.

I glanced sideways at him as we continued, though he seemed almost to have forgotten my presence. His face was stern and his expression distant, as though he was still trying to see through his creature's eyes.

Pride, Joachim would have called it. They had

warned us against it in school, although most young wizards (including me) as I had come to realize, were still so marginally competent upon graduation that it was unlikely to be a problem. The Hidden Language did tap the human mind into enormous and elemental forces, but as long as one did only simple spells, one could stay as safe as a child wading in the tide pools of the western sea.

The truly idiotic young wizard might let himself be caught in an undertow, but the real danger was for the supremely good wizards. Their mastery of magic took them further and further out into it, until they tried a spell that brought magic breaking over them and their words of the Hidden Language with the force of the waves of a winter gale.

My predecessor had put spells from the old traditional magic together with spells he had created in years of study, to make not just something that could move and even look as though it were alive, but something as difficult to dissolve into its component elements as a real living being.

It had no face, other than its eyes, but at times he seemed able to see through those eyes. When it raced toward us out in the valley, carrying the duchess, it must have been a strange case of double vision for the old wizard: both seeing himself from the outside and seeing the creature running toward him. No wonder he had not been able to put any sort of binding spell together—even if the creature had slowed down long enough for a spell to work.

He stopped where the passage forked and, for a moment, I thought he wanted to rest again. Instead, he seemed to hesitate about the direction for the first time since we had started into the cave. I took the opportunity to make a few more magic marks.

"This way," he said, almost reluctantly, and not even as though he were addressing me, but then he started off again with renewed energy. I wondered if the monster were deliberately hiding from him.

There was much here that the old wizard had not yet told me, but I could guess. He had started by putting a true seeing power into his creature, something that I tried unsuccessfully to persuade myself should not seem frightening to someone like me who had invented a far-seeing telephone. The next, however, was even worse.

I caught up to him and glanced at his face. The magic light, from the silver ball held close in front of him, made his eyes gleam under his eyebrows. His next plan, I thought, was to go beyond seeing through his creature. He now intended to put his entire being into the creature's body.

A body shaped and held together by powerful magic would not be the rapidly weakening body of someone far past two hundred. Even if built originally from dead bones, it should not crumble while the spells held.

And here is where my predecessor had swum far out beyond his depth, even beyond sight of land. He had not yet found the spell to transfer his will into the creature's body, I guessed, but in attempting to give it the ability to receive true life, he had given it a generalized, unfocused search for life.

But it was still a monster without mind or volition of its own and all it could do was to seize upon living beings. And being enormously strong and incapable of reason, it could carry them, crush them and, quite unintentionally but quite thoroughly, kill them.

We squeezed through another narrow spot in the tunnel and then there could be no doubt that we were approaching the river. No longer a distant sound, the rushing was very near.

The old wizard stopped and held up his staff, and the silver ball on top burst forth in a new and brighter light. The passageway sloped down steeply before us and, at the bottom of the slope, just before the passage floor disappeared under water, stood the monster.

*   *   *

It watched us with glittering eyes but did not immediately move. Behind it the river, whose sound reverberated in the narrow tunnel, looked jet black. We had reached a dead end. The passage went no further than the river, which plunged downwards and out of sight. We and the monster would leave the way we had come or under water.

III

My predecessor took a deep breath, held out both hands and started on the binding spell. I mentally shook off paralyzing fear and added my magic to his. I had never used a spell like this before and, as the words of the Hidden Language drew me into magic's four dimensions, I felt the forces I touched tugging at me, as if I might be sucked down into magic just as a false step in this tunnel could drop us into the river.

But it seemed to be working. I fought free of engulfing magic to return to myself and found the old wizard staggering, but the monster was encased in magic and perfectly still.

I held out a hand to the old wizard. He took it; crumbled leaves were pressed into my palm. He turned his face blankly toward mine, then slowly seemed to recover. His magic light, which had dimmed to almost nothing, brightened again. "Magic is hard work for an old man," he said hoarsely. "I hope they warn you young wizards at the school how much it can drain out of you."

It was a good thing I had asked him to teach me the binding spell. I could not have done it completely on my own, certainly not in the short fifteen seconds it had probably taken us, and yet I was fairly sure three-quarters of the spell was mine.

He sat down on the sloping floor and considered his creature. The eyes still moved, but the limbs were motionless. "Let's get it away from the river," he said.

"No use having it topple in while we're working our spells."

Without asking if he needed my help, I used a lifting spell to raise the monster up and move it slowly toward us. I *knew* he needed my help. Our minds no longer touched, but I felt I could almost read his thoughts. And he was exhausted, not just the exhaustion of a night in the cave, or three days of chasing his creature across Yurt, but of a lifetime of magic.

I set his monster down prone on the slope below us. "Let's give it more features," he said. "The eyes work well, but it needs ears and nose and mouth. It will need to hear and need to speak, and it might as well be able to smell the spring flowers."

"Master," I said urgently, "don't you think we should try to dissolve it rather than improve it?"

"Of course not," he said with energy. "I already told you that. Now be quiet and let me work. I know they never taught you any of *these* spells."

They most certainly had not. The old wizard closed his eyes, then began to speak in a very deep voice that seemed to come from the rocks of the cave wall. The heavy syllables of the Hidden Language rolled and reverberated around us. I tried to follow it all and could not, in part because there were motions of the fingers also mixed in which sometimes went by too quickly for me to catch and, even when he paused, I was fairly sure he was continuing an aspect of the spell in his mind.

He stopped at last, his face gray and the lines in it more pronounced than ever. But the face of the monster lying before us had changed. The flesh on the sides of its head moved and shaped itself into ears; the center of the face twitched, grew, became a nose; and the lower portion of the face split and became a mouth.

As soon as the mouth was formed, it began to roar. The old wizard and I were nearly pushed backwards by the force of that roar. He recovered almost immediately, however, and added a few more loops to the binding spell.

The roaring stopped, though the eyes remained alive. I started surreptitously checking the binding spell with magic. It did not seem as strong or as thorough as I would have liked.

But my predecessor seemed perfectly content with it. "Well, that's that," he said in satisfaction. "You know, young whippersnapper, I'm glad you came with me. Even with your school training, you'll make a decent wizard someday."

I was too startled by the open compliment to respond.

He looked at me sideways. "You're surprised I never said anything of the sort before. Well, I didn't want to let it go to your head. And because I wanted to be sure you shaped up properly, I may once or twice have said something to you that the persnickety might find insulting.

"But you've not been a bad companion for an old man, in spite of what that school tried to teach you. You show me proper respect, but you've never gotten all crawling and obsequious about it. If you'd come along fifty years earlier, I might even have let you be my apprentice."

Again I did not answer, but I was quite sure I would not have wanted to learn the spells he was now working. For several moments we sat in silence.

"Well," he said at last, "now that we've got my creature, I guess we should start thinking about getting back out of this cave. But it's silly to take three bodies out when we've only got two minds between us, isn't it? And doesn't it make sense to leave the weakest body behind?"

'Master," I asked slowly, desperately trying to delay him until I could find some way to stop him, "what do you mean?"

"You know perfectly well what I mean," he said in

exasperation. "Why else do you think I brought you along, except to help me do it? You can make sure my creature doesn't move, while I——" His voice trailed away on a note of glee.

My only idea was to carry him bodily out of the cave—assuming I could find our way. I went so far as to throw the first loops of a normal binding spell onto him, but he broke it easily.

"None of that," he said sharply, but then, unexpectedly, he smiled. "Worried that if somehow it doesn't work, it will be all your fault, is that it, young wizard?" he went on more kindly. "Well, you can stop feeling so responsible, even if you *are* Royal Wizard now. I've been planning this for years. This old body of mine wouldn't be good for much more anyway, so this looks like my last chance to give my spell a try. I've already served five generations of kings of Yurt, so it won't matter if I don't see the new little prince grow up to succeed. If my spell doesn't work, nothing's lost—or nothing that wouldn't be lost soon anyway.

"But if it works! Then you can say you were there and took part in one of the world's greatest advances in magic, that you helped your old master do something no other wizard had ever done before!"

This didn't help. He wanted an appreciative audience to whom to demonstrate his power, but I could not simply watch. By being here at all, I had become responsible for him. I was madly searching for an argument, anything to say to talk him out of it, when my attention was caught by something else.

"Master, your creature—I think it's breaking out!"

"Nonsense. I cast that binding spell myself."

I had cast most of that binding spell and it was weakening fast. "When you changed its face, that must have interfered with the other spell and now——"

I stopped trying to talk, too busy trying to reconstruct my spells instead. For the monster was indeed beginning to move, slowly sitting up, leaning forward, watching us with avid eyes.

The spell wasn't working. I threw words of the Hidden Language together faster and faster, and then I realized what was wrong. This particular spell, a spell designed for a creature immune to normal binding spells, did not have an effect when that creature was moving.

I desperately tried to find a way to improvise something better, to bridge that gap in the old wizard's spell, expecting him the whole time to add his magic to mine. But he did not come to my aid.

Instead, the forces of magic were suddenly disturbed by a new and even more powerful spell. I came abruptly back to myself, to hear the narrow stone passage ring to words in the Hidden Language I had never heard before and did not want to hear again.

The wizard's staff blazed so bright that the passage and the river below were illuminated as though the stone had cracked and midday had reached us. The monster staggered backwards, throwing an arm across its eyes. My own eyes squeezed involuntarily shut.

There was the sound of something hard falling and I forced them open again. The old wizard's staff had fallen from his hands and rolled past the monster, halfway to the river. The silver ball continued to glow, but far less brightly.

He was still on his feet, his arms held out, but wavering. The creature was motionless at last, frozen with one hand reached toward the wizard.

I scrambled to find the spell again, to try to imprison the creature in the seconds before it moved. But the old wizard stopped me. "Let it come," he said as though choking. "Let it come to me."

I hesitated, not knowing if I would do more harm or good by obeying him. Ignoring me, the creature took one step toward the old wizard. For five seconds they stood face to face, their extended hands touching.

Then the silver ball on the wizard's staff flashed a brilliant white and his body crumpled to the cave floor beside me.

The monster bent over it while I sprang forward, horrified and unsure which spirit animated this creature of magic and dead bones. It poked at the tangled beard and cloak for a second, then suddenly seized the body and lifted it high.

I grabbed at the old wizard, both with my hands and with magic, but I was helpless before the monster's strength. It glared at me in mindless fury, and from its mouth came a wordless roar. It whirled the wizard's limp form over its head, dashed it to the ground, and raced past me, down the tunnel.

The silver ball on the wizard's staff still glowed just enough for me to be able to see him. His limbs lay twisted and bent at unnatural angles. I attempted to gather him up and put his head in my lap.

For a second I thought it was my imagination, but then his eyes moved beneath his eyelids and slowly opened. "I should have thought of that," he whispered, highly irritated, but irritated with himself.

I tried to silence him with a hand on his lips, but he clearly found it important to talk. "That spell's too powerful to be worked by any but the youngest and strongest wizard. And even then I should have realized I'd need something completely empty into which to transfer. I knew it had no mind of its own, so I thought I should be able to transfer my own mind directly into its body."

He paused and the breath rattled in his throat. He had not even tried to move anything except his eyelids and his lips. He went on in a moment, even more softly, so that I had to bend my face close to his to hear him.

"No mind was there, but there was still the motive force. My own spell. There was no room in him for my spell and my spirit at the same time. If you ever try it, young whippersnapper, remember to get the motive force out first." He stopped and twitched his jaw as though trying unsuccessfully to cough. "But without that spell, it might have dissolved back into old bones and I'd be no better off than I am now."

He had been horribly broken, I knew, by being thrown to the cave floor, on top of the destructive final effort to transfer his spirit into the creature. "I'm going to try to lift you, Master," I whispered. "I don't want to pain you any more than I have to, but I've got to get you out of here. So if you—"

He interrupted me with what might once have been a snort. "I do like you, even if you are a whippersnapper. But if you're ever going to mature as a wizard you need more sense. Take my ring, but don't worry about the rest. I knew all along I would never leave the cave in this body."

He fell silent as though this speech had taken the last of his strength. I bent even closer and realized I could no longer hear or feel his breath. The light on the magic staff slowly went black.

IV

For a long time I sat motionless in the darkness, continuing to hold him, too full of sorrow to stand up or to cry. I may even have slept a little, for suddenly I jerked to attention as though abruptly waking from a dream.

The cave was still completely dark so that there was no difference between opening and closing my eyes, and the only sound was the rushing of the river. I feared for a moment that I had heard the monster coming back. Then, when neither my ears nor my magic could find any nearby movement, I decided that a wakeful corner of my mind had recalled me from unconsciousness when the first edge was gone from exhaustion.

I still felt almost unbearably weary. I stood up slowly, easing the old wizard's now cold body from my lap. When I turned on the image of the moon and stars on my belt buckle, it gave enough light for me to grope a short way down the slope toward the river and recover his staff. I illuminated the silver ball on the end, which gave a much better light than my buckle, and continued down to the river.

There I dunked my entire head under water and opened my mouth for a long drink. I came back up colder than ever and with my hair and beard streaming, but the water had certainly taken the last sleep from my eyes. The drink helped, too, especially since I had managed to take it without swallowing a cave fish. For the first time, I began to think about getting back out of the cave.

In spite of what he had said, I couldn't leave him lying here. There was only one thing to do. I put together a lifting spell and raised him slowly. The necessary magic distracted my attention from the staff, so that the light of the silver ball began to dim, but in a minute I worked out a compromise. If I supported him partly with my shoulder as well as with magic, I could keep the staff bright enough that I could find the way.

I started slowly up and away from the river. At least for the moment, the passage was wide enough that the wizard's body did not scrape against the sides. Because worrying that the monster was coming back would only take more energy, I decided not to think about it at all. But I could proceed only at what felt like a snail's pace, having to concentrate on my magic and, constantly distracted, in spite of my resolve, by seeing the confrontation between monster and wizard repeated in my mind.

I wondered vaguely what time it was in the outside world. It must be at least the morning after we had entered the cave, maybe the afternoon, maybe even night again.

At the first intersection where the passage forked, I propped the wizard's body against the wall for a moment while I said the quick words of the Hidden

Language to light up my magic marks. They glowed an encouraging blue, showing me that the way back lay in the direction from which I was already sure we had come. Feeling somewhat heartened, I reapplied the lifting spell and kept walking.

But soon I had to stop again, to work the spell to keep sleep at bay. My muscles found new strength as I lifted the wizard's body again, even though I knew my head would soon start aching. And the spell against headache would allow exhaustion again to claim me.

As I walked I seemed to see again and again the old wizard reaching out to touch his creature's hand and then slumping to the floor. I tried to decide what I should have done differently. Usually I had no trouble, after the fact, in finding my mistakes, but they did not seem as obvious this time. Certainly, I thought, there was something I could have done, even if I had to bind him against his will and carry him away by force.

But even that would not have worked. I might be Royal Wizard of Yurt, but my predecessor's magic had been substantially stronger than mine, right until the very end.

This thought did not make me feel any less responsible. I tasted salt and realized I had been weeping as I walked, large silent tears flowing unchecked and almost unnoticed down my cheeks.

Suddenly I stopped, lowered the old wizard's stiffening body as carefully as if I might still hurt him, and increased the intensity of the light. I did not recall having passed any of my magic marks recently.

There was nothing about the stone walls and rough floor of the passage to make it either familiar or unfamiliar. I tried the words of the Hidden Language to show my marks, but saw nothing in either direction, in the short distance before the passage curved out of sight. Could I, with my attention distracted, have walked right by a turning?

It seemed as though we should have reached one

of the very narrow parts of the cave by now and I knew we had not. On the other hand, it was almost impossible to judge distances, especially since I was now proceeding so much more slowly than we had coming in. Should I turn around and go back until I found one of my marks again?

But if I were still headed correctly, backtracking would only waste time and energy. And there would not be any magic marks anyway in a section of the passage like this, where no side tunnels branched away.

I lifted the old wizard again and determinedly started forward, then stopped, suddenly unsure if I might now be heading in the direction from which I had just come. The gravel showed no footprints and there were no landmarks to give direction.

I would have suggested the Devil could take the direction, but I did not want this thought to be construed literally. I tried a prayer instead, with little hope for an answer. But one direction now looked right, so I walked that way as quickly as I could.

Within a hundred yards, I came to an intersection where three passages came together, all equally broad. Stalactites, colored the palest green in the magic light from the staff, hung from the roof. I was quite sure I had not seen them before and there were no magic marks here.

"Then I did miss my way while worrying what I could have done differently," I said aloud and started back again. This time, I recognized the short straight stretch of tunnel where I had stood and hesitated.

The way back was longer, but in ten minutes the magic glow of the staff showed an intersection before me. Here, I thought, was where I had gone wrong before.

But there were no magic marks here, either, to show the way.

I put the wizard's body down and rubbed my pounding head, trying to think. If I had come through this intersection without noticing, then I only had to choose the passage which was most likely to have brought me here and continue following it back. But suppose I chose wrong? And suppose I really had gotten turned around when I stopped and the three-way intersection where I turned back was where I should be now?

I had no answers, only the need to get out of the cave. I put a new magic mark on the wall, lifted the wizard's body, chose the passage that seemed to lead upward rather than downward, and began to walk again.

After a while, it was hard to remind myself to put magic marks on all the intersections I passed. I knew I was lost, hopelessly lost, perhaps lost forever, but going back seemed no better for that would have been to descend again into the stone heart of the earth. I had again grown thirsty, but returning to the river would have meant going down rather than climbing. My only decision at each intersection, whether the tunnels were wide or narrow, twisting or straight, so low I had to bend or so high that the light from the silver ball did not reach the ceiling, was to take the passage that seemed to lead upwards.

Even when the angle of the floors seemed exactly the same, I did not hesitate. My head now hurt too much for any thought beyond keeping my spells going; at every intersection, I decided as rapidly as if someone else were deciding for me and I had only to obey.

And then, just when my mind was beginning to feel as closed and dark as the cave tunnels, a breath of air touched my forehead. I stopped dead, not daring to believe, but it was no illusion. Somewhere, not far away, was the outside world.

I staggered onward almost at a run. The air was growing fresher and fresher, a mixture of the real smells of trees and grass, not the cold absence of anything but damp which had for so long surrounded me.

And then I heard a voice. I stopped again, wondering wildly if it might be the spirit of the old wizard and if I should answer him, for the voice was calling my name.

But it was not the old wizard's voice. It sounded like a woman. "Upward, Daimbert," it called. "Look upward."

I raised the staff and looked above me. In the ceiling of the tunnel was a crack, just wide enough for a person, which I never would have noticed if the voice had not stopped me. But it was from this crack that the fresh air was blowing.

I took a deep breath, then another, to get that air into my lungs and gather the extra strength I needed. I flew slowly upward, squeezing through the crack and dragging the old wizard's body after me. I was now in a split as though the earth had shifted and, as I rose, I looked around feverishly, but there was still no light. If the earth shifted again, I would be crushed so thoroughly that I would not even have time to realize what had happened.

My head bumped on stone and I raised a trembling arm to aim the staff's light. I saw that I had reached the top of the crack in the stone, but a short tunnel now led horizontally before me.

I pushed into it, forced my feet along it for ten yards, then stopped again.

But this time I had stopped with joy, for before me was a sky hung with stars.

The relief was so great I could have sobbed. I realized now, as I stood with the wind in my face, that it had been the wood nymph calling me. "Lady!" I said softly, but she did not reply.

Off toward the east, the dim beginnings of dawn faded out the stars, but to the west they still shone bright. Below the sky lay the valley of Saint Eusebius, partially shrouded in mist. To eyes that had strained to see in the complete blackness of the cave, the darkness of land under an open nighttime sky did not seem dark at all.

After a moment, I determined I was looking out of a crack perhaps thirty yards up in the wall of the limestone valley. A few gnarled trees clung to the slope below me. I had been in the valley long enough that I quickly recognized the different limestone formations, even if it all looked slightly different seen from above. I was near the head of the valley, no more than half a mile from the Holy Grove.

I gathered the last of my strength, which wasn't a lot, put the old wizard's body over my shoulder and pushed myself out into open air. Very slowly, falling gently as I flew, I proceeded in the direction of the apprentices' huts.

I must have been in the cave for well over twenty-four hours. The priests would have finished their business at the shrine by now and left, but the apprentices would know where they had gone. At the moment I could not plan what to do next, indeed could think no further than collapsing into sleep, but I managed to tell myself sternly that at some point, very soon, I would indeed have to do something.

I was just thinking that the apprentices had already had enough trouble with strangers at the shrine without me waking them up this early, when I saw a yellow glow flick into existence. Someone had lit a fire.

I dropped to the ground in front of the hut where the fire burned, tried to speak, and managed only a parched croak on the first attempt but a passable "Hello?" on the second.

I expected one of the appentices, but the figure that appeared at the hut door was dressed in black linen. It was Joachim.

He looked almost as overjoyed to see me as I was to see him. But he did not say anything at first, only pulled me into the hut. I let him lower me and the old wizard's body to the dirt floor and press a cup of water into my hand.

In spite of the nearly euphoric sense of relief, drinking the water gave me enough of my senses to remind me how thoroughly I had failed.

"He's dead, Joachim," I said, although the chaplain had doubtless determined this for himself. "I couldn't save him. And the monster is still somewhere in the cave—unless it's found its own way out."

"The monster has not come out into the valley again," said Joachim with a sober look toward me. "Thank God one of you is back alive." The kettle of water he had put on the fire began to steam and he turned to pour it into a teapot. "Drink some tea as soon as it's brewed and I'll say the last rites for him."

Between sorrow and despair, I gulped down the tea, feeling it heating my throat and chest all the way down. A second cup, I thought, would finish taking the cold of the cave off me.

But sleep caught me in the act of reaching for the teapot. I slumped back against the hut wall, my eyes closing against the dawn light, just hearing Joachim's voice softly speaking the words of the liturgy as I fell into unconsciousness.

V

When I awoke, it was full daylight and Evrard was sitting beside me. I lay motionless for a moment, conscious of the heavy wool of a horse blanket spread over me and tickling my chin, but otherwise almost devoid of sensation. All my limbs would start to complain, I knew, as soon as I tried to move, but if I remained still forever this would not be a problem.

But I was now the senior wizard in Yurt and there was still a magical creature on the loose, one that had killed a man. I forced myself to sit up and immediately felt so weak that I almost collapsed again.

"Good morning," said Evrard. "You look terrible."

"I feel terrible," I agreed. I leaned against the wall

and rubbed my temples. At least the headache was virtually gone, but I was horribly hungry. "I don't think I've had anything much to eat for the last week, except for berries."

Evrard produced bread and cheese and a rather wizened apple. "This is about the end of the food the three priests brought with them." So the priests were still here after all.

I ate ravenously, thinking that I had never properly appreciated the meals in the royal castle. Then, no longer feeling I was about to faint, I pushed the horse blanket away and staggered to my feet.

"You're covered with blood!" cried Evrard in dismay.

I glanced down at myself. My clothes were indeed filthy, ripped and stained with quantities of blood. "Not my own," I said. "The old wizard's." But then I looked around in panic. "Where is he? Where have they taken him?"

"They took his body to the shrine," said Evrard, not entirely as though he approved but not wanting to disapprove, either. "The apprentice hermits and the youngest of those priests were all going to wash the body and lay it out."

"We'll have to take him back to the royal castle and bury him in the graveyard there," I said. "Evrard, the monster killed him. And it's still loose, probably stronger than ever. It has a real face now."

"Your chaplain told me you hadn't been able to catch it," he said in a low voice, as though afraid to suggest that he was belittling my efforts.

But I knew perfectly well I had failed, failed to catch the monster and to save the old wizard. I had to accept that now.

"I can't go up to the shrine like this," I said. "See if I have enough spare clothes in my saddlebag to keep me decent."

I walked down to the river, peeled the rags from my body and slid into the water. It was as cold as the cave, but bubbling beneath the brilliantly blue summer sky the water was only invigorating. I splashed and tried to rub off the worst of the grime and blood, then let myself sink to the river bottom. It was not deep enough for swimming, but lying on the stones two feet beneath the surface with my eyes open, I could see the green and white of the valley walls transformed into rippling slabs of color.

I jerked back to the surface, caught my breath and pulled myself up on the bank. Evrard had found me some clothes; I rolled on the grass to dry myself and pulled them on. For a minute I sat quietly, letting the sun beat on my wet hair, enjoying the fleeting sensation of peace.

"I'm trying to decide," I said then, "if we dare leave the valley while the monster's still in the cave. The old wizard said that he knew his creature would be drawn here, so it may not be able to get out. I would appear horribly disrespectful if I didn't attend the old wizard's funeral."

"Maybe it's lost forever in the cave," suggested Evrard.

"The creature can't see in there, certainly," I said, "and the cave itself is a labyrinth."

"It's terribly easy to get confused," Evrard agreed, "even with torches and a thread to find your way out." When I looked at him questioningly he added, "Didn't the chaplain tell you? When you and the old wizard hadn't come back by yesterday morning, he and I spent much of the day trying to find you. We unraveled my old tunic for thread." I noticed then that Evrard, too, had been improved by a change into spare clothing. "We didn't know which tunnel you'd taken off the large chamber, which made it difficult. I'd hoped you'd have left a magic mark to show where you'd gone, but if so you didn't use any spell I know."

I was touched that Evrard and Joachim had looked for us and wished that I had had the sense to unravel a thread as I went. "I'm sorry! I did use magic marks, but not until we were well into the cave. I only wanted to mark the way back out, even though as it turned out, I missed some of them and became lost anyway. I never thought anyone would try to come after us."

"We started by exploring the tunnels closest to the river, but they all went underwater very quickly or else became so small that we knew you wouldn't have been able to go through, unless of course you transformed yourselves into frogs."

"In fact, we left the great chamber by a passage on the farthest side—it's a wide, fairly straight way, at least at first."

Evrard shook his head. "We never got there."

I stood up carefully. "Even if we had dared transform ourselves into frogs, in the knowledge that our croaks would not be able to approximate the Hidden Language and that we'd have to be frogs forever, we wouldn't have needed to. The monster is human size, and all we were trying to do was catch it."

"Could you have summoned it, forced it to come to you?" asked Evrard, falling into step beside me as I started toward the grove. I had brought the old wizard's staff and leaned on it when even the short walk began to tire me. "Maybe a true summoning spell rather than the more general calling spell that got me all those sparrows?"

I shook my head. "It wouldn't have done any good to summon its mind if its body couldn't follow. And you know they always taught us that to summon a human mind, against its will, was the greatest sin a wizard could commit. I don't know about you, but the teachers refused even to teach us the spell." I and a few other young wizards had managed, on a late-night expedition to the Master's study, to get around that prohibition, but I didn't want to mention this.

"But in this case," said Evrard reasonably, "you wouldn't be summoning a human mind. That could mean, however, that there might be nothing there to summon! Not knowing the spell would certainly be an additional disadvantage . . ."

His voice trailed away. I didn't tell him that the monster had almost had the old wizard's human mind transferred into it.

As we approached the grove, I heard a distant hammering. I looked up toward the top of the cliff to see if the entrepreneurs were at work at their windlass but, if so, I could see nothing from below.

"How did you get out of the cave?" asked Evrard.

"I'm not sure," I said slowly. "The last few hours, it was almost as though someone else was guiding me. Then, at the very end, I heard the wood nymph calling me. If it hadn't been for her, I would have walked right by the way out and never even seen it."

"The wood nymph? Did she come into the cave?"

"No, but I think she must have been right outside, calling. Had you sent her to look for me?"

Evrard shook his head. "Maybe she just likes wizards."

When we reached the Holy Grove, the first thing I saw was the old wizard's body, lying near the pool with his eyes closed and his hands crossed on his breast. He had gone very far beyond the help of the wood nymph.

The apprentices had done a good job. The worst of the stains had been washed from his clothes, and his hair and beard were clean and combed. His twisted limbs had been straightened out so that, at least at first glance, he could merely have been asleep.

His dignity had been restored to him, but he would not have cared about his body's appearance when he was gone. He had wanted to create an undying monster and to live on in it and, if he had succeeded, he would have discarded this body deep under the earth.

I put my hand over my eyes and stood quietly for a moment to compose myself. I would have to live for the rest of my life with the knowledge that my abilities had been too weak to save him.

We continued the short distance to the Holy Shrine, where we found the old hermit and all the priests.

Joachim managed to look delighted to see me without smiling in the least.

"Good," said the thin priest. "You are here at last."

Before I could find anything to say in reply, the apprentices arrived carrying a roughly made coffin. This, then, explained the hammering. I helped them lift the old wizard's body in and arrange it. He still looked as though he were sleeping, but his flesh felt as cold as the stone a quarter mile beneath the earth.

Wizards, as a matter of professional pride, do not speculate about the afterlife, leaving that to the priests. But even the Church, with its prayers and liturgy, cannot say for certain what will happen to an individual's soul. The wood nymph might think mortality liberating, but I thought that a lifetime, even the long life of a wizard, might never be enough to finish with the questions, much less start on the answers.

He had died not fearing death, not worried about his soul, but irritated that he had failed in his spell. Looking at my predecessor's still face, I wished him well on his journey, wherever he was going.

"Were you going to bury him with this ring?" asked the round priest.

I had been staring without seeing and came back with a start. "No, he wouldn't want us to. In fact, he said I should have it."

The priest pulled the ring from the wizard's finger and handed it to me. I took it reluctantly, with the sense that it symbolized enormous responsibility.

It was quite a striking ring, made in the shape of an eagle in flight with a tiny diamond in its beak, but it did not in fact symbolize anything, being only a Christmas gift from the king after the old wizard retired. But I slid it onto my own finger as though taking up even heavier burdens than I already carried. Behind me, I could hear the apprentices nailing the lid on the coffin.

Joachim touched me on the shoulder and looked at me with his enormous dark eyes. "You're not a priest," he said quietly. "You're not responsible for anyone else's soul but your own."

This was probably supposed to be comforting. I nodded, took a deep breath, and turned to the thin priest. "Why did you want me here?"

He took a breath of his own. "Well. We need to determine the desire of the saint, to see if it is his will to return with us to the City where he first made his holy profession." The priest glanced quickly toward Joachim. "The Royal Chaplain thought it was important that you be here." He didn't add, "God knows why," but he might as well have.

The hermit, who had not yet said anything, suddenly spoke up. "The saint is very fond of this young wizard." We all turned toward him, priests, apprentices and wizards. "I didn't mention this before to anyone but the Royal Chaplain," he said with his gentle smile, "but the saint appeared to me in a vision last night. He had me send my daughter, the wood nymph, to look for him."

I staggered for a second with amazement, then felt Evrard's hand under my elbow and regained my balance. My prayers had been answered after all. This was so unexpected that I had to fight my initial impulse to say, "No, wait, I didn't mean it!"

This, then, explained the strange sense I had had that someone else had directed my path the last few hours in the cave. Someone else indeed had. But being unaccustomed to listening to saints, I had only turned to his guidance when faced with a clear choice between different tunnels. Voices could have spoken for some time in my mind without making me look up to see the crack that led to freedom. That had needed the voice of the wood nymph.

"I see," I said, which sounded highly inadequate.

But then I had another thought that made me as irritated with the saint as I had been overwhelmingly grateful a moment before. If Eusebius could save me from wandering to my death in the cave, why had he done nothing to save the old wizard? I leaned against Evrard, frustrated enough with all priests and saints that any wizard, even a marginally competent one, was exactly who I wanted beside me.

"Then perhaps it is indeed best for you to be here, Wizard," said the thin priest grudgingly. "After all, as Holy Scripture tells us, a little child shall lead them."

I had no attention to spare him or to feel insulted. I didn't know what the saint's plan might be, in which I appeared to feature prominently, but I felt a deep and unshakeable determination not to become a pawn in someone else's program. I would not be turned by gratitude into anyone else's creature, not even a saint's. I had more than motive force; I had a mind and a soul, and they were still my own.

Evrard interrupted my thoughts. "Are you all right?" he asked in a low voice, his blue eyes worried. "Can I get you some water or something?"

"Yes, that would be good." I sat down with my back against a tree, drank the cup he brought me and closed my eyes. I sent up a brief prayer, so that Saint Eusebius would know I really was properly grateful. The wizard had said at the end that he was glad I had never become obsequious. Well, I hoped that whatever characteristics had endeared me to a cranky old wizard had also endeared me to a cranky saint, because I had no intention of becoming obsequious to someone who let a monster roam his valley, killing respectable wizards.

I opened my eyes to see all the priests and apprentices clustered around. "Listen," I said. Something had just become obvious to me.

They turned toward me with surprising respect. I stood up on legs that trembled for a moment, then found enough strength to step forward. "This whole problem started when the entrepreneurs first put a booth on top of the cliff, inviting people to see the Holy Toe for a fee. I know why they're there."

And I did know. It had come to me not in voices,

not through revelation, but through my own reasoning powers. The saint, I thought, had been confident that I would find this answer and indeed hoped, in addition, that I would pass judgment, make the final decision of right and wrong. I had no intention of doing the latter. If I was barely competent as a wizard, a regent and a judge, I was even less qualified to be a religious arbiter.

But the first was important. "This may pain you," I said to the old hermit, "but they meant it for the best. Come here," to the leader of the apprentices.

He came toward me slowly, but not reluctantly, as though he had been expecting this and was determined to go through with it bravely. He even managed a certain dignity in spite of his rags and badly shaved head.

The round priest started to speak but I turned my back on him, addressing myself only to the young hermit.

"The first time the chaplain and I came here," I said gently, "you apprentices asked us if we had been sent by the bishop to take your master away—because of the entrepreneurs on top of the cliff. As I should have realized at the time, it was very odd that you might think that the bishop would hold an old hermit responsible for some disreputable entrepreneurs.

"And then the ducal wizard and I came to this valley to see the wood nymph, and he and I asked you more about them. All you would say then was that you weren't sure if your master, the hermit, had discussed their enterprise with the saint. Your unwillingness to talk about them contrasted strangely, I should have realized, with your master's quite open conversation when he and I spoke two days later.

"So far, you've kept it from him and I'm sure you felt you had very good reasons. Now I'm not going to accuse you or sit in judgment on you. But you do need to tell us all. Why did you apprentices invite those people to come make money off the Holy Toe?"

VI

In the ensuing confusion, I went back to sit under the tree again, to make it clear I was not passing judgment. The story came out somewhat incoherently, with the other apprentices hurrying to confess that they too were at fault, to say that it was their love and concern for the hermit that had led them into error and, at last, to fall prone before him and beg his forgiveness in voices racked by sobs.

The saint, I thought, could not have revealed this to the hermit, because the hermit might have refused to speak out against his apprentices. I presumed it was a compliment to my reasoning abilities that Eusebius had not felt it necessary to tell anyone else about this in a vision.

The story was fairly simple when the apprentices had finally told it all. They were worried about their master, who always gave them his last crusts even when he did not have enough himself. They were worried about the rather erratic appearance of pilgrims with offerings of food or coins and distressed because their own agricultural abilities had not progressed much further than goats and lettuce, although this spring they had planted a lentil crop for which they still had high hopes. When, earlier in the spring, a merchant traveler had detoured by the valley and asked for hospitality for the night, they had been more than willing to listen to his proposals.

The thought of obtaining a small but steady cut of the entrepreneurs' profits, of perhaps seeing more pilgrims once their shrine's fame began to spread, had been enormously appealing. It was only later, when they found that they were afraid to admit to the hermit what they had done, that they had realized they were trying to make money off the holy things of God. But by this time, their merchant contact had recruited Prince Dominic as a backer and the apprentice hermits had felt unable to back out. This was why the saint, after fifteen centuries, had begun to think of leaving the valley. Knowing that one of the apprentices would probably replace the old hermit at the Holy Shrine within a few years would have made even a less cranky saint irritated.

The apprentices had apparently made their peace with the hermit. Their leader rose, his face tear-streaked. "I'll go tell them now," he said. Refusing the priests' offer of a horse, he walked quickly toward the cliff and began to climb.

All of us fell silent, watching him. Although the trees of the grove hid much of his ascent, his small figure kept emerging into sight, climbing steadily up the white cliff face. I had a sudden fear of the monster bursting out of the cave and following him, but nothing of the sort happened.

The apprentice reached the top and disappeared. We waited for another ten minutes, then he put his head over the edge and waved, which could have meant anything, and started down again.

This was all Dominic's fault, I thought, though I wasn't going to say so. If he hadn't been willing to accept a cut of the profits, he would have turned these entrepreneurs out of the kingdom long before the saint decided he had to leave.

Twice while we waited, the thin priest said, "Well, since that mystery is solved—" but the hermit always silenced him with a smile.

The apprentice was back at last, tired and sober. "No one was there," he said. "But I wrote a message on a piece of paper I ripped out of the back of a booklet on the life of Saint Eusebius." I myself would have wondered if it was sacrilegious to do so; that the apprentice had not hesitated told me more than anything he had already said of his real attitude toward the entrepreneurs.

"I left it at the booth," he went on, "weighted down

with a figurine of a dragon. They must be nearby, though they didn't answer when I called."

"And what did you say in your message?" asked the round priest.

"I told them that we had all sinned against God and that this enterprise must be ended at once."

"Come here, my son," said the hermit. "You have indeed sinned, but God will wipe away the tears of the truly repentent." He blessed him and gave all his apprentices the kiss of peace, while the priests from the city fidgeted.

"I think now," the hermit said, still smiling, "there can be no question of removing Saint Eusebius from the grove where he himself served God and where hermits have served that same Lord ever since."

"We shall see," said the round priest in notes of self-importance.

The three priests from the City, accompanied by Joachim, brought out candles and a censer and began arranging them around the shrine. They lit the candles, and the youngest priest began to swing the censer. The pungent smell of incense drifted through the grove.

The thin priest went down on his knees before the golden reliquary of the Holy Toe. "Oh, blessed Eusebius!" he called as loudly as though the saint were in the top of a tree with the wood nymph. "Listen to our prayers, we beseech thee! We seek to do thy will, in Christ's name, but thy will has not yet been fully revealed to us. Show us a sign! Show us thy intention! Show us—"

A sharp crack rent the air, stopping the priest in mid-speech. I leaped up, convinced that the sound had been made by the monster, coming with its new mouth to eat us all.

But it was instead the sign the priest had asked for. A second later, thunder rolled across the cloudless sky and we looked up to see smoke beginning to rise from the edge of the cliff. Lightning from heaven had set fire to the entrepreneurs' windlass.

The thin priest, still on his knees, stared dumbfounded, as I'm sure I did as well. The Cranky Saint was beginning to be a little too active for my taste.

"I do hope those poor misguided souls had not invested too much in their figurines," said the old hermit mildly.

Joachim appeared to be almost transfigured by the sight and it took a minute for the three priests to recover their equilibrium. They did not seem to have expected anything this dramatic.

"This means—" blurted out the youngest priest.

But the thin priest silenced him at once. "It means the saint has listened to our poor prayers," he said. "This has become a valley of sinful activities, of those who have perverted Christ's pure purpose," which seemed a little harsh on the apprentices, considering that the hermit had just forgiven them and promised them God's forgiveness.

"Now that the sin has been rebuked," added the round priest, "there can be no doubt that the saint will wish to leave for a more virtuous site."

For a moment the old hermit looked stunned. "But the saint's sign—" he began, almost pathetically.

"Wait," I said suddenly. I had just thought of something. "You priests and hermits don't want to start squabbling in front of a wizard about interpreting a saint's intention." I hoped the Cranky Saint would go along with this. "Once before, fifteen hundred years ago, priests from your city came to take the relic of the Holy Toe and the saint revealed unambiguously his desire to remain. Test him again the same way!"

I stepped back, watching and waiting while they talked it over. The old hermit turned his smile full on me. The three priests brought out and lit more candles, then knelt in silent prayer for a moment. They then stepped up to the altar and all put their hands on the reliquary.

"Saint Eusebius, we wish to take thy holy relics with us, to honor them and serve thee devotedly," said the thin priest. "Therefore, we beg you to make your will explicit to us, your humble servants. We shall now most reverently lift your reliquary and ask that you express your desire to accompany us by making the Golden Toe as light as a feather in our hands. In the name of the Father and of—"

As the thin priest spoke, all three began to lift, but his voice faded as nothing happened. The reliquary remained as still as though nailed to the altar. It didn't look as though today's priests were having any better luck than their predecessors fifteen centuries earlier.

The thin priest bent down and looked at the base, as though suspecting a trick. "What's with this? Let's try it again," he said in an undertone, not sounding pious at all.

"—and of the Son—" They gave another, more violent heave. The reliquary did not budge.

The old hermit stepped up beside them. "Let me see," he said. He slipped one hand beneath the Golden Toe and lifted. It came up as light as a feather in his hand.

He set it back on the altar and turned to the priests. "Do you have your answer, my brothers?" he asked in genuine sweetness.

The round priest could not resist a last tug, mumbling "—and of the Holy Spirit!" but it was as ineffective as the first two.

Joachim cleared his throat. "The test has been clearly rendered," he said. "The saint's purpose may have been ambiguous before, but there can be no ambiguity now. Indeed—"

He stopped speaking and looked up. The sky above us darkened and a swirling wind suddenly surrounded the grove. The air touched us very lightly in spite of a force strong enough, I felt, to have lifted us from the ground. I would have expected the wind to smell of the trees and river, or even of the priests' incense.

But it smelled of neither, being instead of an almost overpowering sweetness, even sweeter than the king's best roses.

I stared although I could see nothing beyond the valley itself, gripped by emotion that combined great fear with great joy. Just for a second, although I could never reconstruct the explanation afterwards, I knew I did not need to question what the saint had or had not done, and felt overcome with awe and humility.

In the middle of the wind, I heard a voice, a woman's voice, high in the trees above us, and realized that it was the wood nymph. She called, "Eusebius!"

The echo of her voice murmured up and down the valley, and then the wind was gone as suddenly as it had come up. I felt a bump, mental rather than physical, as I fell back to myself out of the swirling air.

Joachim passed a hand over his brow. I knew how he felt. But the chaplain spoke calmly. "Indeed," he said, continuing where he had left off, "we can no longer doubt the will of the saint. He wishes his relics to remain in this valley, where they have been since the day of his martyrdom. I am sorry you had such a long and difficult trip, my brothers."

The priests' eyes came back into focus and they went from looking dreamy to looking highly irritated: with Joachim, with the hermit, with me and, most of all, with the Cranky Saint. But there was little answer they could give. The youngest priest began blowing out the candles that had not been extinguished in the wind.

I glanced around the grove, mentally catching my breath, and suddenly realized who was missing. "Joachim," I said, taking him by the arm, "where is he? *Where is Evrard?*"

"The other wizard?" said the youngest priest. "He went off in that direction a while ago." He gestured vaguely, but there was no question of the direction. He was motioning toward the cave.

PART EIGHT
The Monster

I

I turned from the priests and began walking as fast as I could, cold with fear, toward the cave. I realized I had not seen Evrard since the leader of the apprentices had begun scaling the cliff.

He had wanted all along to try to catch the monster on his own. He must have taken advantage of the rest of us being distracted, first by the apprentices' confession and then by the Cranky Saint, to slip away to the cave. If he thought I was being too deeply drawn into the affairs of the Church, then he might think it was his duty as a wizard to look for the monster without me.

Joachim caught up. There was no need to explain to him what had happened. "I've got the old wizard's staff for light," I said.

We reached the cave entrance and looked in. I did not sense the immediate presence of the monster, but there were fresh sooty marks on the limestone showing that someone had come this way very recently with a torch.

I illuminated the silver ball on top of the staff and

we hurried, bent double, down the first stretch of tunnel and into the great chamber. I had no time to waste admiring the walls glinting like jewels in the light. I went immediately to the passage on the far side which the old wizard and I had taken. Lying on the cave floor, almost invisible among the gravel, was a pale line of kinked thread.

"He paid out the thread yesterday," said Joachim, "and then wound it back up as we ran into each dead end."

We hurried along the tunnel, the wizard's staff tipped forward so that the silver ball showed the faint line of the thread we followed.

"Evrard!" I shouted inside my mind. "Where are you?"

I heard his answering mental voice at once. "I'm fine. I'll see you shortly."

I was only slightly reassured and we hurried on. But in less than ten more minutes we saw a light flickering ahead of us that was not the light of my wizard's staff and Evrard came around the corner, carrying a torch.

"Sorry if I worried you," he said, almost nonchalantly. "But with all that business about the saint, it didn't seem as though I was needed. I just wanted to explore the cave a little more. By the way, Daimbert, I *did* find your magic marks. Did the Cranky Saint ever make it clear what he wanted to do?"

Joachim told him briefly what had happened, Evrard tidily winding the thread back up while we walked. I tried addressing him sternly, mind to mind, but he now had his thoughts well shielded. I shrugged and gave it up. We knew, at any rate, that the monster was still deep within the cave.

Back in the valley, the three priests were grumpily packing, preparing to go. There was no sign of the hermit or his apprentices.

"I think we'd better go, too," I said. "I need to get

back to the royal castle to bury my predecessor as quickly as possible."

"It's already late," said Joachim. "We can't possibly make it there tonight."

"I am leaving this valley," I said as distinctly as I could. "I can use the magic light to show our way after dark."

The chaplain looked at me in assessment and shook his head. "You're already exhausted, in body and in spirit. And even your magic staff won't cast enough light for the horses. Let's go to the duchess' castle tonight and on to the royal castle tomorrow."

As we rode down the valley, the wizard's coffin strapped to the priests' pack horse, I wondered uneasily if my desire to be free at last of the valley had distorted my judgment. I had stayed even when I knew my duty as a wizard was to go in search of the monster. Now I had a duty to bury my predecessor at home and to catch the monster here and my strongest drive was to get out of the valley, not necessarily because it was the best choice, but because I had been unable to do so before.

I told myself that a saint who could summon lightning from a clear sky would not let a creature of magic and bone hurt those who served his shrine, that the monster might now wander aimlessly in the cave for weeks. But I also told myself that barring miracles, and miracles by their very nature could not be counted on, religion was primarily useful for dealing with the supernatural and the hereafter. The priests might try to explain to wizards the deep metaphysical significance of the forces of the material universe, but they always seemed to leave us with the full responsibility for dealing with those forces.

Evrard and I rode in front and, as we started up the steep road, a tree branch before us suddenly dipped. For a second we saw the wood nymph, who smiled and gave us a cheerful wave before disappearing again among the leaves.

She had called the saint's name as the wind had whirled around the shrine and, although I refused to speculate about whether that might mean she had a soul after all, I guessed that her old friend Eusebius had spoken to her at last.

At the top of the cliff, the wreckage of the booth and the windlass still sent thin plumes of smoke into the late afternoon air. As we approached, I was surprised to see the young man in the feathered cap. He and three others, whom I recognized as the men I had thought were pilgrims, were poking through the ashes. So far they had found half a dozen unbroken ceramic figurines.

The "pilgrims" stepped back rather self-consciously, but the young man looked up and gave his customary smile in spite of the ruins of his plans and, for that matter, Dominic's. "Greetings, Wizard," he said to Evrard, ignoring the rest of us. "I know I told you I'd get back to you about your offer to come help us with your magic, but I'm afraid we won't be able to start until later this summer and maybe not this year at all."

"Oh?" asked Evrard impassively.

"As you can see, we had a little accident. And the people who were sponsoring us seem to have pulled out. We aren't going to be able to make our 'overhead' costs, much less any profit at this rate. We haven't even quite made up our minds yet whether we should continue to try to set up here." None of us were fooled by this comment. "But if we need a wizard for another project, we'll be sure to keep you in mind!"

"Thank you," said Evrard gravely. "Just remember my fee scale." It was not until we were another quarter mile down the road that he began to laugh.

Shadows were long when we reached the duchess' castle. So far, it appeared, no one there had married anyone, but both Dominic and Nimrod were still at the castle, neither speaking to the other. Joachim hurried to the pigeon loft to send the bishop his message, but the rest of us sat down in the great hall in something of an exhausted daze.

Diana was mellower toward her wizard than I had expected. After she had set her constable to finding accommodations for all of us, she sat down to listen to his account of what had happened in the valley in the two days since she had left. Evrard told her most of the story, even though he had missed the Cranky Saint's miraculous demonstration of his intention to stay at the grove and had gotten the details from Joachim and me. As for any information about the death of the old wizard, other than the bald fact that the monster had killed him, I had not told anyone and did not intend to.

I hardly heard their conversation, giving all my attention instead to hot soup and new bread and butter. But I did rouse myself at the end of the meal to address the duchess.

"My lady, do you think it would be possible for you to send some food on a regular basis to the hermit and his apprentices?"

Diana actually looked embarrassed. "Of course. I should have thought of that myself. The valley *is* surrounded by my duchy," with a sharp look toward Dominic. "I'll arrange for them to get fresh bread from my kitchens every week, starting tomorrow."

When Evrard and I went up to the freshly repainted wizard's room at the top of the duchess' castle, I fell at once into exhausted sleep. But some time after midnight I awoke with a gasp, drenched with sweat and feeling my heart pounding with nightmare terror.

Listening to Evrard's peaceful breathing, I tried to persuade myself that it was indeed only a nightmare, that Saint Eusebius, after all that had happened, was unlikely now to send me a true vision.

Slowing my heart with long, deep breaths, I settled back down, but as soon as I closed my eyes against the room's darkness I could see it again: the monster roaring, wide-mouthed, as it had when it had killed the old wizard, but this time, standing helpless before it, were all the people I loved in Yurt.

II

We buried the old wizard at the royal graveyard of Yurt late in the afternoon of the following day. Joachim read the service while the rest of us stood silently, including the priests of Saint Eusebius who now threatened to become as cranky as their saint, and the duchess, with Dominic and Nimrod on either side of her.

They offered me the shovel to toss the first load of dirt onto the coffin. I was still young enough that even though I might fear violent death, I had no idea how I would react to the prospect of slowly growing old and weak. I couldn't be sure what I might think in another two hundred years, but I hoped fervently I wouldn't be tempted to try what my predecessor had.

The royal constable, who had nearly despaired of seeing any of us again after the knights of Yurt had come home with wild stories of the monster and of the duchess' two suitors, had been overjoyed when we rode up to the castle. He promised to have the old wizard's books and effects brought to the castle in the next few days and to find a home for the calico cat.

Dominic fell into step beside me as we started up the hill from the cemetery. I glanced at him in trepidation, wondering if I was going to be fired even before I had a chance to pursue the monster.

But the regent only seemed thoughtful. "Wizard, have you ever suddenly wished you could go somewhere and start over, leave all your problems and responsibilities behind, but discover you've said and done things which commit you far too deeply even to try?"

I felt a sudden and completely unprecedented burst of affection for the royal nephew. "I'm glad you understand," I said, patting him on the shoulder. "That's exactly how I feel."

The three priests refused the regent's offer of hospitality for the night, expressing the intention of putting ten more miles behind them before nightfall and of being in the episcopal city the next day. Joachim saw them off with mutual blessings and expressions of spiritual good fellowship that sounded sincere if not enthusiastic.

He urged them to give his personal greetings to the bishop. Since the bishop would already have received the chaplain's message, via carrier pigeon, that the relics of Saint Eusebius would stay in Yurt after all and that the wood nymph posed no problems for the sanctity of the grove, it was too late for the priests to tell him a different story.

Evrard and I also had somewhere to go. I was trying to decide if we should start back for the valley at once or if it would be too irresponsible to sleep in a real bed one more night before beginning our search for the monster when Dominic, fully back on his royal dignity, decided for me.

"You and the chaplain started this," he said, "when you claimed to be competent judges between Prince Ascelin and me." In fact, I thought, he and the duchess had started it much earlier by both deciding they needed their own real households. "You may have forgotten about the integrity and purity of the kingdom, but I have not. Tomorrow, the duchess must be married."

"Fine," said Diana, who was standing nearby. "It's even more dignified to be married in the royal chapel than in my own castle chapel. It's a good thing I thought to bring along my best dress."

After dinner Joachim asked me up to his room. He lit the candles, then sat down on one of his hard chairs. "Would you like to tell me," he said, giving me a long look, "what really happened in the cave?"

Even though I had earlier decided not to tell anyone, it was a relief to do so, a much bigger relief than I had expected. The act of telling moved the events into the external world, made it less of a continuing nightmare that affected only me. But, unfortunately, I knew that the monster was also part of the real world.

Joachim said very little while I told it. "Maybe I should never have become Royal Wizard," I finished. "All I've done is make other wizards act foolishly in trying to show off to me how well they can do magic. The old wizard, once he was retired, may have started making a monster in part to impress me. And you saw Evrard in the cave yesterday. He's going to get himself into trouble by trying to convince me he can have good ideas of his own."

"If it hadn't been you, it would have been another wizard."

"For the two years I've been Royal Wizard, I've always had in the back of my mind the thought that if I ran into a problem too difficult for my own abilities, there was another wizard to call on. Even though it didn't worked out like that, the thought was reassuring. And now there is no one to call on in the kingdom but me."

The chaplain shook his head. "I've already told you: Each person must answer for his or her own soul before God. We have to do our best not to lead others astray but, ultimately, we must allow them to sin or do good on their own."

Although I hadn't been talking about leading anyone into sin, Joachim's words were oddly comforting. Then I thought of something. "Wait a minute. When I first came to Yurt, you said that you'd had to take responsibility for *my* soul with the bishop."

Joachim looked at me as though I was speaking nonsense. "But that's different. I'm a priest."

There was one more thing that bothered me, that I had not before dared bring up. "It doesn't seem fair, Joachim," I said at last.

He lifted his eyebrows without speaking.

I took a deep breath. "If Saint Eusebius was willing to save my life, why didn't he save the old wizard?"

"There are several reasons I could tell you," said Joachim slowly, "and other reasons that lie beyond the understanding of mortals. The easiest answer would be that you had prayed to the saint with a contrite heart and the old wizard had not, but that would wrongly suggest that relations between living men and the saints were simply mechanical." His deep-set eyes met mine for a second, then he looked away. "I was praying for both of you."

He fell silent. I did not answer, waiting to see if he would go on.

"When we live and when we die," he continued after a minute, "is not ultimately due to the specific prayers we do or do not say, though the Bible tells us to pray without ceasing. Our destiny, rather, lies in the hands of God. You can't speak of what is 'fair.' All of us, ever since Adam, are sinners, and *deserve* death and damnation. That God, from His mercy, allows us to live and be happy at all should fill us with profound gratitude."

"I still don't think it's fair," I said. "If I were in charge of things, I would make them much less arbitrary."

"You sound like Job," the chaplain commented. He moved slightly and his eyes came out of the shadows. " 'My righteousness is more than God's.' " I had no idea what he was talking about. "But God answered Job out of the whirlwind, 'Where wast thou when I laid the foundations of the earth? Whereupon are the foundations thereof fastened? Or who laid the corner stone thereof, when the morning stars sang together, and all the sons of God shouted for joy?' "

"Well," I said grumpily, "I should have known better than to try to discuss theology with you."

Joachim did not answer, but the corners of his eyes crinkled with amusement.

I thought it ironic that he, who rarely smiled, should do so when I felt I might never smile again. "What's so funny?"

"You are. That sounds like what I'm supposed to say to *you.*"

In the morning, wearing my best blue velvet suit and feeling almost human again, I stood with the chaplain beside the royal throne of Yurt in the castle's great hall.

It had been an enormous comfort to be able to take a bath in my own bathtub and to fall asleep in my own bed. Even the illusory frog which Evrard had put on my pillow did not keep me awake for long.

Dominic now sat on the throne, glowering, waiting for the duchess to appear. His ruby ring in its snake setting glistened on his finger. In the distance, I could hear a great deal of urgent shouting from the kitchen; the cook and Gwen were madly preparing for a wedding feast they had only learned about last night.

The duchess appeared at last, dressed in a wide-skirted dress of white lace that she must have had in her baggage the whole time. The old-fashioned high neckline and the slightly yellow tinge suggested she was wearing her mother's wedding dress. The delicacy of the lace contrasted sharply with the hammered gold of her wide bracelets.

Dominic, too, was dressed in finery, black velvet trimmed with the blue and white of the royal coat of arms, and he wore a heavy gold chain around his neck. But Nimrod, who had come to Yurt as a huntsman and was much too tall to wear anyone else's clothes, was still dressed in rough green. But with a newly trimmed beard and a sober face, he managed to look more dignified than most of the court.

Several of the knights of Yurt seemed to have decided that they, too, might have a chance with Diana for they had put on their best and were laughing and teasing each other. But Dominic was absolutely serious and a deep frown quickly silenced the knights. He seemed, I thought, much sulkier than anyone should who would be getting married in half an hour. He beckoned to the duchess with a massive hand and she came quietly to stand before him.

"The purity of the kingdom depends on the purity of its women," he announced in a deep voice.

Joachim startled me by saying, "And the same is true of its men."

"A kingdom is not merely a piece of land," the regent continued, "or a political unit, but a group of people who are both guarded and guided by their aristocracy."

Diana's cheeks reddened slightly as she listened. Those who had stayed behind at the castle had received, I was sure, a highly speculative but nonetheless detailed version of what had actually happened that night on the plateau.

I tried to contemplate, difficult as it was, Dominic and Diana actually married to each other. The regent had maneuvered her into this position, of having to marry to preserve her honor, but she had been willing to be maneuvered. I still didn't know what her intentions had originally been toward Prince Ascelin, but now that she had—quite wrongly, I thought—decided he was a coward, she would certainly not marry *him*. But she would now have the household she had decided she wanted when she hired Evrard and she and Dominic could live in her castle on her rents.

"Therefore," Dominic continued, "any suggestion, any rumor of impurity by one of its leading women must be rectified at once." He paused briefly, as though overcome at the last moment with reluctance. But he thrust out his chin and continued. "My lady, you have already agreed that certain of your activities have become sources of scandal and that only marriage, immediate marriage, will wipe this scandal away. Do you still agree?"

The chaplain spoke before she could answer. "Think carefully before you give your response. Marriage is created by God, for the welfare of men and women. It is only valid if consent is freely given and it cannot be entered into by intimidation or force."

Dominic frowned again, but Diana shot Joachim a quick smile. "I have indeed thought carefully. You may be assured I have never yet been forced into anything."

She turned to face the rest of the court. The faint blush was gone from her cheeks and she appeared to be enjoying herself highly. "As all of you know, I have stayed single all my life because I never yet found a man who pleased me. But now, by the pleasantest coincidence, at exactly the same time when certain events might recommend a speedy wedding, I have decided that a suitor whom I earlier refused to consider is indeed the man for me."

Both Dominic and Nimrod stirred uneasily. Nimrod watched Diana intently, not daring to hope.

"Four days ago," Diana continued, "two men threatened to kill each other over me and then both tried to protect me when a monster unexpectedly appeared and attempted to carry me off. I, naturally, would have rescued myself, except that the monster had paralyzed me." I never had told her the source of that paralysis spell and never would now. "One of these men is the one who has won my heart."

She stretched it out for ten seconds more, looking back and forth between Dominic and Nimrod as though still trying to make up her mind. Both of them looked back at her white-faced.

Then suddenly she had pity on them. She turned to Nimrod with the assurance of doing exactly what she had always intended to do. "Prince Ascelin," she said formally, holding out her hands, "would you consent to be my husband?"

The tall prince smiled at last, a smile that transformed his face. He lifted her up and swung her far off the ground, so that her dress billowed out and she laughed breathlessly. He said loudly enough for everyone to hear, "Diana, I love you and always will, but you are the world's worst tease!"

I looked quickly at Dominic. He was caught between relief and wounded dignity, but relief appeared to be winning.

The constable pushed forward through the suddenly laughing and talking crowd to make himself heard. "If you would all like to proceed to the chapel for the wedding, I can promise you a fine feast afterwards!"

With good-natured jostling, everyone made their way up the narrow stairs to the castle chapel. The kitchen staff were still desperately cooking and preparing, but the rest of the servants joined the knights and ladies.

There was a moment's hesitation over who should escort the bride to the altar. I was afraid the duchess would ask Dominic, but she seemed to decide that that would push her luck too far for, to my surprise, she asked me.

"So, how did you finally decide to accept Prince Ascelin?" I asked in a low voice as we stood at the door of the chapel, waiting for everyone to settle down and for the music to begin.

She squeezed my arm and smiled. "I'd always intended to marry him. I know you realized that all along."

If she thought I had guessed far more than I in fact had, I was not going to disabuse her.

"That's why I had my wizard make the great horned rabbits, of course, so I could have an excuse to invite him into the kingdom. After refusing him five years ago, I couldn't very well send him a message by the pigeons that I had changed my mind! I had to have a

chance to see him, to hunt with him, to make sure
his own heart hadn't changed.

"When we'd known each other in the City, all I saw
was someone extremely handsome, an extremely good
dancer, who seemed to have a much too priggish
moral sense for any young member of the aristocracy.
He'd told me he was a renowned hunter, but I'd never
even seen him hunt. I *had* to turn him down. But in
the years since then . . . Of course, his seeking sanctuary when Dominic wanted to kill him, I at first thought
was cowardice. But then I realized it was both courage
and good moral sense, and maybe I need more of the
latter myself."

She laughed up at me, then turned it into a frown.
"There is one thing I still don't know. I'd had my
wizard make the horned rabbits so Ascelin and I could
hunt them together, but why did he appear in Yurt
even before I'd had a chance to send him a message?"

I smiled. "Once you're married, I'm sure he'll tell
you."

It was almost like a fairy tale in which the handsome
peasant boy woos and wins the lovely princess, except
that Prince Ascelin had never been a peasant and
Diana had never imagined that he was.

The chapel's brass choir began to play; I tucked her
hand firmly under my arm and walked with her down
the aisle. Joachim, looking sober, and Nimrod, looking
overwhelmingly glad, waited for us by the altar.

III

The service was short but dignified. The duchess
glowed and Nimrod's rough clothes became trivial
compared with his happiness. Dominic sat impassively
throughout, but at the end he did step forward to be
the first of the spectators to kiss the bride.

In the talking and laughing that followed, I heard
him say to young Hugo, "You know, I may indeed

take you up on your offer to go back to the City with you."

I slipped away from the knot of people around the altar with no attention to spare for Dominic. I had an idea.

In the great hall, the kitchen staff was still setting up the tables for the wedding feast. I went quickly by them with a nod for Gwen and into the room where we kept the magic glass telephone.

It took me several tries, including a call to the wizards' school, before I was able to get the magic coordinates for the kingdom far up in the eastern mountains where Elerius was Royal Wizard. Then it took several minutes for him to come to the phone. I realized my heart was beginning to pound, as though I might have only a few moments before the monster was on us, and the time was almost gone.

At first Elerius didn't remember me, although he tried politely to act as though he did. When he finally realized that, in spite of the white beard, I was the Daimbert, three classes behind him, who had always seemed so unpromising to the masters, he surprised me by congratulating me with apparently complete sincerity on the invention of the far-seeing telephone. But he then had trouble understanding what I wanted.

"It's been made with the old magic," I repeated, willing the tiny figure in the telephone base to know the solution. His black eyebrows made triangles over his eyes, which were a light brown, almost tawny yellow, and which I had always found disturbing in spite of their inevitably helpful expression. "Something similar to the spells you taught in that course at the school this spring."

"And you've already tried shooting it and paralyzing it?"

"That's what I said. And nothing works."

Elerius thought this over, looking troubled. He had always been very kind to the younger wizardry students and indeed seemed anxious, unlike most older wizards, to be friendly with everyone. If we hadn't always been so jealous of him, we probably would have liked him.

"There isn't a single spell to give sticks and bones the semblance of life," he said at last. "Your predecessor's magic certainly falls into a certain category of spells, the same category I learned from the old magician here, but at a certain point every renegade wizard who tries to create a living being must go about it differently."

"And there isn't a universal spell to dissolve such creatures?"

"I don't think so, Daimbert, or if so I certainly don't know it."

"How about the teachers at the school?" I asked urgently. "I heard—" I considered trying to explain about Nimrod and gave it up. "I heard that, some years ago, a renegade wizard made a whole army of creatures out of hair and bone and the school was able to catch them and destroy them."

"I'm afraid," said Elerius dryly, running a hand over his black beard, "that that was the old magician here in my kingdom. The masters of the school won't know any spells against creatures more complex than what young Evrard made. The magician had been in hiding ever since, until I found him up in the mountains only a month before he died. He knew he didn't have long and he taught me the spells before he went."

I closed and opened my eyes. "All right. Thank you. I'll see what I can improvise. Just promise me one thing."

"Certainly."

"If I fail, I'll telephone you again—or I'll leave word to have someone else call if the monster kills me. Should that happen, swear to me you'll get the best help possible from the school or from any other wizards there maybe who know the old magic. You've got to come to Yurt and stop this thing."

He nodded slowly. "I promise to try. But I'm

confident the creator of the far-seeing telephone will find a way himself."

I leaned my forehead against the stone wall once he hung up, wishing I felt as confident. My predecessor was gone far beyond where I could ask his advice. If the best wizardry student the school had ever had, one invited back to teach a magic none of the older masters knew, didn't know any spells more complicated than those to make great horned rabbits, I had no idea how I was going to stop the monster. But somehow I had to.

It sounded as though the wedding party was coming down from the chapel. I went to find Evrard, wondering if it would be more unsuitable to leave before the wedding feast or irresponsible to stay for it. But then a huge crash resounded in the great hall, followed by a scream.

The scream was repeated. It was a woman's voice.

In the chapel stairway I could hear the shouts of the knights of Yurt. But they couldn't help with what I knew I would find.

I raced into the great hall as Evrard and the knights burst in from the other side. In the middle of the hall, between the rose-decorated trestle tables, stood Gwen, clutching her baby, a trayful of silverware at her feet and an overturned bench blocking her retreat. Before her was the monster.

"Good," said Evrard.

"What do you mean, *good*?" I almost screamed at him.

The great hall was instantly a scene of panic as women and men yelled, some fighting to retreat up the chapel stairs as others fought to get out, and those already in the great hall ran in all directions. Only Gwen stood frozen; a creature as tall as a man but twice as broad slowly advanced toward her, its undead eyes staring fixedly at the baby.

One of the royal knights leaped forward, but the

monster lifted an arm, almost lazily, and dashed him to the flagstones.

Evrard sprang between Gwen and the monster, and it paused, then shifted its eyes to him. "My spell's working!" he shouted to me. "Come on! It should follow." He darted by the monster and out through the tall doors into the courtyard. Turning its back on Gwen and the dazed knight, the monster lumbered after him.

Evrard waited in the courtyard, but as soon as the monster came out he was off again, flying through the gates, across the drawbridge and onto the grass beyond. Again the monster followed and I flew behind. Out of the valley it moved relatively slowly, which was a relief. But seeing it again brought back vividly the last time I had seen it, as it had raced away from killing the old wizard.

"What did you *do*?" I demanded, dropping to the ground next to Evrard.

"I improvised," he said, panting but looking inordinately proud of himself. "I know they purposely never taught us the summoning spell, but a few of us young wizards found it in the Master's books, one night about a week before I left the school."

It was exactly what I had done myself. Maybe the Master had known all along what we were doing. The monster had stopped and was eyeing us, its head thrust forward between massive shoulders.

"I decided you were right," Evrard went on, "that I couldn't very well summon something without a proper mind, so I altered the spell. You're not the only person who can improvise!"

I had to admire his ingenuity, if not his good sense. I kept an eye warily on the monster. It moved slowly toward us and we backed away. It moved again, slightly faster, and we backed up faster.

"But how did you manage to put a spell on it?" I yelled to Evrard.

"While you were all busy worrying about the saint, I went back into the cave after it, remember?"

The monster was backing us down the hill toward the woods. Its eyes still seemed alive even without the old wizard looking through them. "You found it but didn't tell me?" I demanded furiously.

"Well, no, I didn't actually find it. But I went far enough back to be fairly sure I was going the right way. So I set up my summoning spell and added a few touches to your magic marks, which I hoped would help draw the monster in the right direction. Once it was out of the cave, I didn't doubt it would be able to follow us back here if I'd made my spell strong enough. And it looks as though I did!"

His spell was certainly working. The monster seemed fascinated by Evrard. Slowly and inexorably, it kept coming toward us.

We flew, at this point, down the hill to where the brick road from the castle entered the trees and paused again. "Evrard," I said, speaking slowly and carefully, "would you like to tell me why you called the monster out of the valley and brought it *here*?"

"You're not pleased with me?" asked Evrard in distress.

So he'd figured it out at last.

"And I'd thought you'd be impressed! If I hadn't summoned it, your Cranky Saint would probably have shipped it out of his valley and sent it after you anyway, since he seems to like you so much."

I ignored this jab. Overcoming the monster would need both of us. Besides, he might be right. "But why did you bring it *here*?"

The monster swung its arms as it advanced more quickly now. It would have been frightening enough if it was some sort of enormous creature, like a bear, but the mindless stare made it horrible, a force of nature given separate volition and evil intent.

"Well, I had to get it out the valley, of course," said Evrard, moving back into the woods. "It was able to move much faster there, so it was clear we didn't have the slightest chance against it. Since we were coming back to the royal castle ourselves, didn't it make sense to have it come here, too?"

"I wonder if it killed anyone on the way," I said grimly.

"It shouldn't have," said Evrard. "I deliberately made my spell so strong that it wouldn't want to stop."

He might be content to gloat over how well his spell had worked, but I could no longer stand the tension. "Come on," I said abruptly. "Let's take it down to the old wizard's cottage. He had it imprisoned there once; we may be able to bind it again."

I had become aware of the knights, led by Prince Ascelin, assembling on the castle hill. I couldn't risk letting him be killed on his wedding day.

Evrard and I flew along the road into the woods and the castle was lost to sight behind us. Almost immediately, we had to pick up speed as the monster pursued with a rapidity it had not yet shown today. It chased us with its arms extended, emitting a low roar.

Evrard, I was sure, was now flying farther and faster than he ever had before. We darted back and forth along the forest path, avoiding overhanging branches, but behind us we heard snapping and crashing as the monster plowed straight through.

We shot out into the clearing before the old wizard's cottage maybe a quarter mile ahead of it. Grabbing Evrard by the arm when he seemed to sag, I flew straight up and hovered twenty feet above the ground.

"Try to distract the monster when it gets here," I said. "I've got to look at my predecessor's notes." I dropped to the ground and went through the green door into the wizard's cottage.

The room was, if possible, an even greater mess than when I had seen it last. I looked around quickly, hoping wildly there might be something here to help. Most of the old wizard's books were dusty and appeared long-unopened, but a massive register was propped up on the table, ready if he ever came back. I glanced at the page to which it was open, then began to read. Here was the spell, written out in the old wizard's spidery hand, that had created his creature from dead bones. In the first three lines were two mentions of herbs of which I'd never heard.

I flipped forward. The spell went on for fifteen pages.

A wordless roar sent me diving for the window, which turned out to be locked. But the creature did not come in. In a moment, I looked cautiously out the door.

It was in the clearing in front of the cottage, circling below Evrard and ignoring me, at least for the moment. Evrard remained twenty feet off the ground, concentrating on holding himself up. "Keep it looking at you," I said quickly, "but don't do anything to excite it. If you can hold its attention for another two minutes, I'll try to find the herbs for the spell to bind it." I shot behind the old wizard's cottage.

My predecessor had always had an herb garden where he grew the most common magical herbs. I had thought I knew it well, but this summer over half the garden was given to a low, leafy plant I never remembered seeing here before. I plucked one, looked at it closely, and probed it with magic. This was the same herb the old wizard had found in the valley.

I flew back to Evrard and the monster, my fingers already starting to glow blue. "I'm going to try to put a special binding spell on it, but this will only work if the creature is absolutely still. Let's go over to the tree." Trying to fly and cast a complicated spell at the same time was too much for me. We flew to the enormous oak tree that sheltered the old wizard's cottage.

Evrard collapsed against the trunk, the sweat running down his face. In spite of my own greater practice in flying, I was not in much better shape. I wondered uneasily how well the monster could climb.

At first, it seemed content to circle the tree, appearing and disappearing from our sight. Its search for life had not been blunted by killing the old wizard. I hoped the cat had had the sense to hide.

I started trying to put the wizard's binding spell together, though if the monster kept on moving, it wasn't going to do much good. In the cave, I had been able to bind it only with the old wizard's help. I realized that I should have taught Evrard the spell immediately. Once again I had failed, this time in being too caught up the last two days in my own exhaustion and sorrow and sense of responsibility. I had neglected to look for help from someone who was, at least potentially, a perfectly competent young wizard and had, after all, once made a manlike creature himself. "Stop moving!" I muttered in the monster's direction. "Otherwise, I'll never be able to bind you."

In a moment, Evrard had caught his breath enough to sit up again. He turned to face me, his jaw set. "Well, Daimbert, I guess this is my problem and there are two ways to solve it.

"My calling spell has made it interested only in me. You said it was searching for life and the life it wants is mine. Either I can leave Yurt, which would make it follow me—" I started to speak but he didn't give me a chance. "—or I can go down to meet it. While it does to me whatever it wants to do, you can try your binding spell."

IV

"Good God, Evrard," I cried, "you can't be serious! You certainly can't spend the rest of your life flying around the western kingdoms with it on your tail, but there must be a solution short of letting it kill you!"

"Such as?"

"If it would just stand still for a minute, I'd try this binding spell. It *did* work before."

Evrard looked at me from behind lowered eyelids. "I've got another idea. How about if I try dropping things on it? I know I can't kill it that way, but with a boulder lying across it, it might be more susceptible to your binding spell."

"Good idea," I said, taking him by the shoulders to look at him and urgently hoping he had not been serious a moment before.

"As soon as I finish catching my breath, I'll go collect some rocks. The monster can't be stronger than a river, and I *was* able to block a river's course, even if only for a little while."

Evrard flew off toward the stream and soon he was back, carrying a good-sized stone with magic. He dropped it in the middle of the clearing and went back cheerfully for another. The monster poked at the stone with its hand, then hurried after him. It pushed straight and unhesitatingly through the dense brush.

In fifteen minutes, while I desperately worked on spells, Evrard had accumulated a fairly good pile. Twice he stopped on the oak's wide branch to rest and, all the time, the monster prowled back and forth, following him from below. I did not trust its intent expression.

It was some of the hardest magic I had ever done. Not only was the spell itself fiendishly difficult, but I constantly had to hold steady the part I had already completed. A spell I had worked very quickly with the old wizard now appeared interminable when I tried it alone.

Evrard's voice suddenly cut through the words of the Hidden Language. "Do you think these are enough rocks?"

I came back abruptly to myself, realized that it was probably very foolish to try such a complicated spell balanced on a tree branch, and shouted, "Let's try it!"

Evrard, still hovering, took a deep breath, squared his shoulders and began lifting his rocks with magic.

I couldn't help him and still keep the binding spell ready and he could only manage one rock at a time while flying, but very rapidly he started lifting and dropping rocks on the monster's upturned face.

The first few missed and, as the next bounced from its shoulder, the monster began to run in circles. But then Evrard got into the rhythm, saying the words of the Hidden Language so rapidly that the spell was almost self-sustaining, and two lucky shots in a row knocked the monster off its feet. With a whoop of triumph, Evrard piled another dozen rocks on top if it, so that at least momentarily, it lay still.

My turn now. This spell was too difficult to do while flying or even sitting in a tree. I came down to the ground, ignoring Evrard's warning shouts, and threw the binding spell at the monster.

The loops of the spell caught and held. Crushed by stone and held by the old wizard's magic, it lay looking at me with unblinking eyes.

Evrard's feet hit the ground beside me. "So is that it? We've done it? We've done it!"

"It's still very much alive," I said, "and if we aren't careful it—"

But I couldn't speak and work magic at the same time. And the monster's arm was starting to twitch, pushing upward again the stones that imprisoned it.

I threw another loop of the binding spell around it and again it lay still. But it was no longer looking at Evrard. It was looking at me.

We darted back up into the oak. We had a second to catch our breaths, but a very precarious second. Even the old wizard, who had created this binding spell in the first place, hadn't been able to keep his creature pinned down for long. I wiped my forehead with an arm. "We have to find a way to destroy it before it breaks free."

"Can you teach me the binding spell?" asked Evrard eagerly.

"I'll teach you the magic to keep it going." The monster twitched again, and again I renewed the binding loops. "There, did you see what I did?" I pushed drooping bits of plant into his hand. "Just keep saying that spell."

"Let's hear it again."

After hearing it once more and after one abortive attempt of his own in which both of the monster's arms threatened to break out, Evrard knew enough of the spell to strengthen it whenever it started to weaken, which seemed to be constantly.

"I might be able to improvise a way to dissolve the monster if I knew the spell that created it," I panted. "Quick, teach me the spell you used for the rabbits and I'll try to extrapolate."

It took twenty minutes for Evrard to teach me the spell, not because it was terribly complicated for someone who already knew a fair amount of the old magic, but because we had to keep stopping to rebind the monster.

I kept listening as we worked, wondering if the others were coming and praying that they weren't. Evrard and I, sitting high in the tree, were relatively safe but, if the monster broke loose from a spell that was becoming increasingly tattered, it could kill half the knights of Yurt.

Though I now could have made horned rabbits—or a soldier of hair and bone without even using dragons' teeth—I still couldn't dissolve this monster. The spell Elerius had taught was shot full of gaps, bridged almost tentatively by a few words of magic, so that anything made from it could be readily destroyed. The late Royal Wizard of Yurt had found a way to fill those holes.

I frowned in concentration, sifting through phrases of the Hidden Language. "Maybe if I looked again at the old wizard's spell," I started to say, then looked down to realize the monster had managed to kick all the rocks off one leg and was starting on the other. I couldn't take the time now to pore over the written spell, to find in it a way to dissolve the monster. I had to make do with what I already knew.

All I knew was the spell that had given the creature its facial features, and that I had heard only partially. But dissolving a spell might require only an understanding of its general lines, not all its details. Trying desperately to remember theoretic discussions of spell structure from lectures through which I had dozed, I tried reversing the spell, hoping that this might generalize enough to affect the entire creature. If not, I was completely out of ideas.

It was almost too late to try repairing the binding spell. I clung to the branch of the oak with both hands as the heavy words of the Hidden Language rang through the clearing.

Much more quickly than they had formed, the monster's ears, nose and mouth disappeared. The roaring stopped and, for a moment, it stopped kicking, but the eyes still glowed at us.

"Keep going, Daimbert!" yelled Evrard, renewing the binding spell. He piled on a few more rocks for good measure.

But I was temporarily halted. I looked toward Evrard. He was as exhausted as I was; only sheer will was keeping him going. I had maybe a minute before our weakening magic and the monster's strength freed it, either to climb the tree after us or go to meet the knights of Yurt.

I pulled together everything I knew, the spell to create facial features, the spell to make great horned rabbits, and the first few words of the spell I had seen in the old wizard's register; put on the twist that reversed spell structure; and tried it all in combination with the words that would break a normal spell.

It probably shouldn't have worked and, indeed, I could see no immediate change, but there was a sharp swirling in the local field of magic that suggested that a spell much more powerful than anything of mine was beginning to break up.

I tore my attention away from the spells just long enough for a glance at Evrard. Consciously or unconsciously, he had left the tree to move closer to the monster, as though trying to hold it immobile with the force of his personality as well as the spell that he was now working nonstop—or maybe he was now so tired that he didn't trust his ability to project a spell any distance.

"Now!" I shouted and threw what should have been the spell of final dissolution onto the monster.

And trembling, burning, spreading like fire, it began to dissolve the spells that held the old wizard's creature together. But first it destroyed the binding spell that had held it down.

The creature rose with a crash, stones and pieces of its body both flying from it. It flung out an arm toward me, started to take a step, and collapsed into a heap of bones—but not before the largest boulder that had lain across it had struck Evrard.

V

I had the boulder off him in a second, but he did not move and his eyes were closed. Trembling all over, I dropped beside him and tried to listen for his breathing.

Two wizards gone in three days and I couldn't save either one of them. I had a sudden, vivid and very painful vision of telephoning Zahlfast and telling him that Evrard was dead.

If I had been more systematic, if I had tried to instruct Evrard in a rational way instead of first assuming that he would be better at magic than I had been two years ago, and then scorning his quite real abilities when it became clear that he was not, he might have had a long and happy career.

But he *was* breathing, shallowly and rapidly. As I tried to brush back the hair from his face, darkened from red to brown by sweat, he moaned and opened his eyes.

"Daimbert," he whispered, "I couldn't hold it. What happened?"

"It's gone. I've turned it back into bones."

He closed his eyes again and weakly held out his arms. I was terrified that by shifting him I might kill him, if he was not killed already, but I could not hold out against that appeal. I pulled him toward me, trying to make reassuring sounds. I did not want to hold a dying wizard in my arms ever again in my life.

"It's my leg," he said faintly. "And I can't fly. All my magic has been knocked out of me."

"Your leg? Just your leg?" I said with dawning hope. Maybe I wouldn't have to make that telephone call to Zahlfast after all.

"I was trying to hold it down with that spell and, suddenly, it seemed to rise up and hurl a boulder at me. It hit me right below the knee." He stopped as his teeth began to chatter in spite of the warmth of the day.

"You're in shock," I said calmly, as though I knew exactly what to do. I let go of him for a moment, peeled off my now ripped and filthy velvet jacket, and put it over him. "Lie here quietly and get warm. In a short while, when you've rested, I'll figure out a way to get you up to the castle. Then we can send for a doctor to set your leg."

In a moment, Evrard gave a breathy snort and either fainted or slept. I looked up then for the first time at the pile of white bones that had once been the monster.

If the old wizard's magic had been a little more powerful, if he had found a way to hold the monster physically together and to transfer his mind into it at the same time, then those bones might have been the wizard's body. The creature would never now be able to receive the human life it had spent its short existence seeking.

At the edge of my thoughts I became aware of voices. I glanced up to see a group of riders emerging from the trees, led by Prince Ascelin, Dominic and Diana.

The duchess was still wearing her wedding dress, the skirt of which had become all bunched up by riding astride. She gave a cry of dismay as she saw Evrard and leaped from her horse.

"It's all right, my lady," I said, trying to smile. "He's still alive and we've destroyed the monster. It wounded him as we overcame it, but I could never have succeeded without him."

After Gwen and the cook had worked feverishly to have the wedding feast finished on time, it turned out to be delayed over four hours. The old cook was furious, but Gwen, recovering from the shock of meeting the monster in the great hall, used her nervous energy and the extra time to make cinnamon cookies. She had made them for her own wedding and had sent every person off afterwards with three wrapped in gold foil and she thought it would be a nice touch to do the same for the duchess.

In spite of the cook's dire remarks that the dinner was spoiled, everyone seemed to enjoy it hugely. It turned into a combination wedding feast and triumphal dinner in honor of the monster's destruction. Once Evrard's leg was set, he talked the doctor into letting him be carried into the hall to be hailed as a hero.

Late that afternoon, when the sunlight lay golden and heavy in the center of the courtyard but the shadows of the walls already stretched long, I went up to Joachim's room. Evrard was asleep in my bed and the rest of the castle was sitting around lazily, talking in some amazement of the day's events, feeling they had already eaten too much, and nibbling on cinnamon cookies.

Joachim threw his casements wide open and looked out into the courtyard. I had something important to ask him, something that I had managed to forget during the past few days.

Now that it appeared that Evrard was certainly going to live and indeed, according to the doctor, would be able to walk easily in six weeks, I had begun to feel that I might someday soon be cheerful again. Even the memory of the old wizard's death could not remain constantly before me, though I continued to feel I was more responsible than the chaplain seemed to think. But Evrard would be moving to the duchess's castle, which would leave me again as the only wizard at the royal castle. And even if Evrard stayed here, it would not be the same. Frustrating as Joachim sometimes was, he was still the closest friend I had ever had.

"What are you going to do?" I asked his back. "Does the bishop still want you to go to the episcopal city and join the cathedral chapter? How soon will you have to leave Yurt?"

He turned around, looking genuinely distressed. "Didn't I tell you when I met you down in the valley? That's why I felt so peaceful then. I know I said I'd talked to the bishop, that he'd reminded me that God does not give us burdens heavier than we can bear if we turn to Him. But didn't I tell you the rest?"

"What didn't you tell me?"

"I told the bishop that I hoped I had not fallen into the sin of pride, but that it seemed he might be preparing the way for inviting me to join the chapter. And if he was, I told him, I must request that he not do so. I explained that I felt I could do more in Yurt as Royal Chaplain than serving in the cathedral, where there are already many far better qualified priests."

"And what did he say?"

Joachim smiled. "It's not a desperate matter, Daimbert. He told me he understood and must agree with my decision."

I could see it all, even if the chaplain's humility kept it from him. The bishop was willing to let him remain in Yurt for now, but sooner or later, when they wanted a cathedral officer or even a new bishop, they would come looking for him again.

But that should be many years in the future. Almost reassured, I asked, "And he didn't try to tell you that you should guard against the untoward influence of friendship with a young wizard?"

Joachim smiled again and shook his head. "I think he's become reconciled to the idea. I should introduce you to him sometime."

I had one last question. "Could I possibly have been as callow as Evrard when I first came to Yurt?"

The chaplain smiled slowly but thoroughly. "Yes," he said.

I put my hand in my pocket and found Gwen's foil-wrapped cookies. "I'd thought after that feast we had that I wouldn't want to eat again for days, especially since I wasn't even hungry at the time. But these suddenly seem appealing. Shall we split them?"

The duchess and her new husband left early the next morning for her castle and were gone for a week. In the meantime, I went down to the village to find the young couple whose chickens the monster had killed and to compensate them.

They seemed delighted to see me and to talk about the resolution of the earlier quarrel even before I had a chance to ask them how much a new flock would cost. I decided not to mention that whatever cousin or uncle had been dug up and hidden in the woods as part of that quarrel had probably formed the bones of the monster.

At the end of the week, Diana and Ascelin were back at the royal castle. Prince Ascelin was now going home to his city, taking his bride with him, to tell his people about his marriage and to make the arrangements for the city to be governed by someone else for the six months of each year he and the duchess would live in Yurt.

In the morning, the duchess went into my chambers with Evrard. She talked to her wizard for over an hour before coming back out into the courtyard. "So, do you think you can keep an eye on Dominic by yourself?" she asked me.

"Of course I can. Now that he's decided that the big change he needs is a year in the City once his regency is over, rather than a wife, he seems fairly contented. He's so relieved that he didn't have to marry you after all that he shouldn't give us any trouble."

The duchess laughed. "If it had been up to me, I would have waited to go until the king and queen came back, but Ascelin is understandably in a hurry to get home himself." He came across the courtyard toward us and she looked at him affectionately. "It will be interesting seeing his City."

I was not fooled by her comment about waiting for the king and queen's return. Diana had always done exactly what she liked and what she liked right now was making her new husband happy.

In a few minutes she and her knights rode out over the drawbridge, Nimrod—as I still couldn't help but think of him—striding beside her saddle as he had the first time he came to Yurt. I wondered if they would ever find a horse big enough to carry him.

In my chambers, Evrard was hobbling back and forth, making a pile of some of my books by my best chair. "As long as I won't be able to move around much for a while," he said with a smile though not meeting my eyes, "I thought I should make use of the time and learn some of the magic the teachers at the school think they've already taught me." But then his freckled face became sober. "After all, it will be embarrassing always to have to ask them things I ought to know."

I sat down rather abruptly. "Wait a minute. I think I'm missing something."

"I've resigned," said Evrard, much too seriously to be joking. "I told the duchess just now and she agreed."

"But she thought you were a hero when we overcame the monster!" I protested, but Evrard wasn't listening.

"She never really needed a ducal wizard in the first place and she'll need one even less now that she'll be gone from Yurt for half the year. And let's be realistic, Daimbert. You and I both know that I'm really not competent to be out trying to practice magic on my own. I only graduated by the skin of my teeth and I could never have stopped the monster without you.

"There are always a lot of young wizards who stay on at the school for a few years, helping out as demonstrators and the like. Many of the City merchants also employ wizards, at least part time. Maybe Dominic will want some magical assistance while he's there! It won't be a disgrace to go back to the City, and maybe with a few more years of experience I'd actually be qualified to serve some duke or count somewhere."

I was caught between agreeing with him and feeling that he was much too hard on himself. "So you've fully recovered from the monster knocking all your magic out of you—" I asked tentatively.

"Oh, yes," he said as though surprised. "I'd forgotten I said that. The monster didn't suck my abilities out of me or anything so dramatic." He would have put a binding spell on my foot to show me how well he could still work magic if I had not stopped him in time.

"I think you'll be a very good wizard someday," I said, hoping I did not sound patronizing.

"I don't want *you* to feel you've failed me," he continued, looking down at the closed book in his hands.

"I've learned a tremendous amount from associating with you, Daimbert. And, of course, if I'd never come to Yurt, I would never have met the wood nymph!"

"I'll miss you," I said, entirely truthfully.

"There's one thing I do feel badly about," he said, looking at me fully for the first time since I had come in. "When I go, you won't have anyone here to talk to but the chaplain. Who will you tell your jokes to? Who will put illusory frogs on your pillow?"

I smiled, glad he could not stay serious for long. "I'll be all right. Joachim and I have been friends for a long time. Though I haven't taught him how to do illusions, I have hopes of giving him a sense of humor someday. But if you can get away from the school sometimes, I'd very much like you to come visit."

Evrard opened the first of the books and frowned at it as though he had never seen it before. "If you don't mind, I'd like to stay here until my leg is a little better. With all those young wizards, the school is no place for the wounded. And maybe by the time I go back, my beard will have grown out properly."

"Of course, of course. Stay as long as you like."

"I'll telephone the school, to tell them what's been happening, and find out if there's a particular branch of magic they think they'll need there so I can brush up."

But before Evrard could call the school that evening, our glass telephone rang. It was King Haimeric, calling us.

The constable answered and the king asked first about his roses, but then we all gathered around to talk to him. "I just got the message the duchess sent from her castle, via the pigeons, that she'd gotten married!" said the king.

"She and her husband left for his principality today," said Dominic. "But they plan to be back in a month or so."

"Well, then," said the king cheerfully, "I can look

forward to meeting him when they return. Has anything else happened?"

Dominic and I looked at each other. "The retired wizard, my predecessor, has died," I said.

"Oh, dear," said the king, sounding genuinely sorry, while also conveying the sense that this news would not trouble him for long. "Well, he'd already served, what was it, five generations of kings of Yurt?"

"He left me the ring you gave him," I said. "I hope you don't mind."

"Of course not, Wizard. Well, is that all the news? I hope things haven't been too dull in Yurt for you while we're gone!"

There was a short pause while Dominic and I looked at each other again. The regent, for one minute, came very close to smiling. Before either of us could speak, the queen appeared beside her husband in the tiny image in the telephone's base. She was even more beautiful than I remembered. She held the baby prince by the hand; he clung tightly but was indubitably taking steps on his own.

The queen's Aunt Maria smiled from behind them. "Did we tell you Baby Buttons has started to walk?" she asked.

"Dromnick! Gizward!" said the little prince, looking toward us with a broad smile. I hoped he never found out what chaos his birth had caused here in Yurt.

"Yes, sire," said Dominic, when the king's face appeared again, "a few other things *have* happened, but we can tell you all about them when you're back. Do you know yet when that will be?"

"Probably another week or two," said the king. "So nothing's happened that you can't handle?"

Dominic nodded slowly. "Nothing that the wizard and I can't handle."

There Are Elves Out There

An excerpt from

Mercedes Lackey
Larry Dixon

The main bay was eerily quiet. There were no screams of grinders, no buzz of technical talk or rapping of wrenches. There was no whine of test engines on dynos coming through the walls. Instead, there was a dull-bladed tension amid all the machinery, generated by the humans and the Sidhe gathered there.

Tannim laid the envelope on the rear deck of the only fully-operated GTP car that Fairgrove had built to date, the one that Donal had spent his waking hours building, and Conal had spent track-testing. He'd designed it for beauty and power in equal measure, and had given its key to Conal, its elected driver, in the same brother's-gift ceremony used to present an elvensteed. Conal now sat on its sculpted door, and absently traced a slender finger along an air intake, glowering at the envelope.

Tannim finished his magical tests, and asked for a knife. An even dozen were offered, but Dottie's Leatherman was accepted. Keighvin stood a little apart from the group, hand on his short knife. His eyes glittered with suppressed anger, and he appeared less human than usual, Tannim noticed. Something was bound to break soon.

Tannim folded out the knifeblade, slit the envelope open, and then unfolded the Leatherman's pliers. With them he withdrew six Polaroids of Tania and two others, unconscious, each bound at the wrists and neck. Their silver chains were held by some-*things* from the Realm of the Unseleighe—inside a limo. And, out of focus through the limo's windows, was a stretch of flat tarmac, and large buildings—

Tannim dropped the Leatherman, his fingers gone numb. It clattered twice before wedging into the cockpit's fresh-air vent. Keighvin took one startled step forward, then halted as the magical alarms at Fairgrove's perimeter flared around them all. Tannim's hand went into a jacket pocket, and he threw down the letter from the P.I. He saw Conal pick up the photographs, blanch, then snatch the letter up.

Tannim had already turned by then, and was sprinting for the office door, and the parking lot beyond.

Behind him, he could hear startled questions directed at him, but all he could answer before disappearing into the offices was "Airport!" His bad leg was slowing him down, and screamed at him like a sharp rock grinding into his bones. There was some kind of attack beginning, but he had no time for that.

Have to get to the airport, have to save Tania

from Vidal Dhu, the bastard, the son of a bitch, the—

Tannim rounded a corner and banged his left knee into a file cabinet. He went down hard, hands instinctively clutching at his over-damaged leg. His eyes swam with a private galaxy of red stars, and he struggled while his eyes refocused.

Son of a bitch son of a bitch son of a bitch. . . .

Behind him he heard the sounds of a war-party, and above it all, the banshee wail of a high-performance engine. He pulled himself up, holding the bleeding knee, and limp-ran towards the parking lot, to the Mustang, and Thunder Road.

Vidal Dhu stood in full armor before the gates of Fairgrove, laughing, lashing out with levin-bolts to set off its alarms. It was easy for Vidal to imagine what must be going on inside—easy to picture that smug, orphaned witling Keighvin Silverhair barking orders to weak mortals, marshaling them to fight. Let him rally them, Vidal thought—it will do him no good. None at all. He may have won before, but ultimately, the mortals will have damned him.

It has been so many centuries, Silverhair. I swore I'd kill your entire lineage, and I shall. I shall!

Vidal prepared to open the gate to Underhill. Through that gate all the Court would watch as Keighvin was destroyed—Aurilia's plan be hanged! Vidal's blood sang with triumph—he had driven Silverhair into a winless position at last! And when he accepted the Challenge, before the whole Court, none of his human-world tricks would benefit him—theirs would be a purely magical combat, one Sidhe to another.

To the death.

* * *

Keighvin Silverhair recognized the scent of the magic at Fairgrove's gates—he had smelled it for centuries. It reeked of obsession and fear, hatred and lust. It was born of pain inflicted without consideration of repercussions. It was the magic of one who had stalked innocents and stolen their last breaths.

He recognized, too, the rhythm that was being beaten against the walls of Fairgrove.

So be it, murderer. I will suffer your stench no more.

"They will expect us to dither and delay; the sooner we act, the more likely it is that we will catch them unprepared. They do not know how well we work together."

Around him, the humans and Sidhe of his home sprang into action, taking up arms with such speed he'd have thought them possessed. Conal had thrown down the letter after reading it, and barked, "Hangar 2A at Savannah Regional; they've got children as hostages!" The doors of the bay began rolling open, and outside, elvensteeds stamped and reared, eyes glowing, anxious for battle. Conal looked to him, then, for orders.

Keighvin met his eyes for one long moment, and said, "Go, Conal. I shall deal with our attacker for the last time. If naught else, the barrier at the gates can act as a trap to hold him until we can deal with him as he deserves." He did not add what he was thinking—that he only hoped it would hold Vidal. The Unseleighe was a strong mage; he might escape even a trap laid with death metal, if he were clever enough. Then, with the swiftness of a falcon, he was astride his elvensteed Rosaleen Dhu, headed for the perimeter of Fairgrove.

He was out there, all right, and had begun laying a spell outside the fences, like a snare. Perhaps in his sickening arrogance he'd forgotten that Keighvin could see such things. Perhaps in his insanity, he no longer cared.

Rosaleen tore across the grounds as fast as a stroke of lightning, and cleared the fence in a soaring leap. She landed a few yards from the laughing, mad Vidal Dhu, on the roadside, with him between Keighvin and the gates. He stopped lashing his mocking bolts at the gates of Fairgrove and turned to face Keighvin.

"So, you've come to face me alone, at last? No walls or mortals to hide behind, as usual, coward? So sad that you've chosen *now* to change, within minutes of your death, traitor."

"Vidal Dhu," Keighvin said, trying to sound unimpressed despite the heat of his blood, "if you wish to duel me, I shall accept. But before I accept, you must release the children you hold."

The Unseleighe laughed bitterly. "It's your concern for these mortals that raised you that have *made* you a traitor, boy. Those children do not matter." Vidal lifted his lip in a sneer as Keighvin struggled to maintain his composure. "Oh, I will do more than duel you, Silverhair. I wish to Challenge you before the Court, and kill you as they watch."

That was what Keighvin had noted—it was the initial layout of a Gate to the High Court Underhill. Vidal was serious about this Challenge—already the Court would be assembling to judge the battle. Keighvin sat atop Rosaleen, who snorted and stamped, enraged by the other's tauntings. Vidal's pitted face twisted in a maniacal smirk.

"How long must I wait for you to show courage, witling?"

Keighvin's mind swam for a moment, before he remembered the full protocols of a formal Challenge. It had been so long since he'd even seen one. . . .

Once accepted, the Gate activates, and all the Court watches as the two battle with blade and magic. Only one leaves the field; the Court is bound to slay anyone who runs. So it had always been. Vidal would not Challenge unless he were confident of winning, and Keighvin was still tired from the last battle—which Vidal had not even been at. . . .

But Vidal must die. That much Keighvin knew.

From Born to Run *by Mercedes Lackey & Larry Dixon.*

*　　*　　*

Watch for more from the SERRAted Edge:
Wheels of Fire by Mercedes Lackey & Mark Shepherd (October 1992)

When the Bough Breaks by Mercedes Lackey & Holly Lisle (February 1993)

FALLEN ANGELS

Two refugees from one of the last remaining orbital space stations are trapped on the North American icecap, and only science fiction fans can rescue them! Here's an excerpt from *Fallen Angels*, the bestselling new novel by Larry Niven, Jerry Pournelle, and Michael Flynn.

*   *   *

She opened the door on the first knock and stood out of the way. The wind was whipping the ground snow in swirling circles. Some of it blew in the door as Bob entered. She slammed the door behind him. The snow on the floor decided to wait a while before melting. "Okay. You're here," she snapped. "There's no fire and no place to sit. The bed's the only warm place and you know it. I didn't know you were this hard up. And, by the way, I don't have any company, thanks for asking." If Bob couldn't figure out from that speech that she was pissed, he'd never win the prize as Mr. Perception.

"I am that hard up," he said, moving closer. "Let's get it on."

"Say what?" Bob had never been one for subtle technique, but this was pushing it. She tried to step back but his hands gripped her arms. They were cold as ice, even through the housecoat. "Bob!" He pulled her to him and buried his face in her hair.

"It's not what you think," he whispered. "We don't have time for this, worse luck."

"Bob!"

"No, just bear with me. Let's go to your bedroom. I don't want you to freeze."

He led her to the back of the house and she slid under the covers without inviting him in. He lay on top, still wearing his thick leather coat. Whatever he had in mind, she realized, it wasn't sex. Not with her housecoat, the comforter and his greatcoat playing chaperone.

He kissed her hard and was whispering hoarsely in her ear before she had a chance to react. "Angels down. A scoopship. It crashed."

"Angels?" Was he crazy?

He kissed her neck. "Not so loud. I don't think the 'danes are listening, but why take chances? Angels. Spacemen. *Peace* and *Freedom*."

She'd been away too long. She'd never heard spacemen called *Angels*. And— "Crashed?" She kept it to a whisper. "Where?"

"Just over the border in North Dakota. Near Mapleton."

"Great Ghu, Bob. That's on the Ice!"

He whispered, "Yeah. But they're not too far in."

"How do you know about it?"

He snuggled closer and kissed her on the neck again. Maybe sex made a great cover for his visit, but she didn't think he had to lay it on so thick. "We know."

"We?"

"The Worldcon's in Minneapolis-St. Paul this year—"

The World Science Fiction Convention. "I got the invitation, but I didn't dare go. If anyone saw me—"

"—And it was just getting started when the call came down from *Freedom*. Sherrine, they couldn't have picked a better time or place to crash their scoopship. That's why I came to you. Your grandparents live near the crash site."

She wondered if there was a good time for crashing scoopships. "So?"

"We're going to rescue them."

"We? Who's we?"

"The Con Committee, some of the fans—"

"But why tell me, Bob? I'm fafiated. It's been years since I've dared associate with fen."

Too many years, she thought. She had discovered science fiction in childhood, at her neighborhood branch library. She still remembered that first book: *Star Man's Son*, by Andre Norton. Fors had been persecuted because he was different; but he nurtured a secret, a mutant power. Just the sort of hero to appeal to an ugly-duckling little girl who would not act like other little girls.

SF had opened a whole new world to her. A galaxy, a

universe of new worlds. While the other little girls had played with Barbie dolls, Sherrine played with Lummox and Poddy and Arkady and Susan Calvin. While they went to the malls, she went to Trantor and the Witch World. While they wondered what Look was In, she wondered about resource depletion and nuclear war and genetic engineering. Escape literature, they called it. She missed it terribly.

"There is always one moment in childhood," Graham Greene had written in *The Power and the Glory*, "when the door opens and lets the future in." For some people, that door never closed. She thought that Peter Pan had had the right idea all along.

"Why tell *you*? Sherrine, we want you with us. Your grandparents live near the crash site. They've got all sorts of gear we can borrow for the rescue."

"Me?" A tiny trickle of electric current ran up her spine. But . . . *Nah*. "Bob, I don't dare. If my bosses thought I was associating with fen, I'd lose my job."

He grinned. "Yeah. Me, too." And she saw that he had never considered that she might not go.

'Tis a Proud and Lonely Thing to Be a Fan, they used to say, laughing. It had become a *very* lonely thing. The Establishment had always been hard on science fiction. The government-funded Arts Councils would pass out tax money to write obscure poetry for "little" magazines, but not to write speculative fiction. "Sci-fi isn't literature." *That* wasn't censorship.

Perversely, people went on buying science fiction without grants. Writers even got rich without government funding. *They couldn't kill us that way!*

Then the Luddites and the Greens had come to power. She had watched science fiction books slowly disappear from the library shelves, beginning with the children's departments. (That wasn't censorship either. Libraries couldn't buy *every* book, now could they? So they bought "realistic" children's books funded by the National Endowment for the Arts, books about death and divorce, and really important things like being overweight or fitting in with the right school crowd.)

Then came paper shortages, and paper allocations. The science fiction sections in the chain stores grew smaller. ("You can't expect us to stock books that aren't selling." And they can't sell if you don't stock them.)

Fantasy wasn't hurt so bad. Fantasy was about wizards

and elves, and being kind to the Earth, and harmony with nature, all things the Greens loved. But science fiction was about science.

Science fiction wasn't exactly outlawed. There was still Freedom of Speech; still a Bill of Rights, even if it wasn't taught much in the schools—even if most kids graduated unable to read well enough to understand it. But a person could get into a lot of unofficial trouble for reading SF or for associating with known fen. She could lose her job, say. Not through government persecution—of course not—but because of "reduction in work force" or "poor job performance" or "uncooperative attitude" or "politically incorrect" or a hundred other phrases. And if the neighbors shunned her, and tradesmen wouldn't deal with her, and stores wouldn't give her credit, who could blame them? Science fiction involved science; and science was a conspiracy to pollute the environment, "to bring back technology."

Damn right! she thought savagely. We do conspire to bring back technology. Some of us are crazy enough to think that there are alternatives to freezing in the dark. *And some of us are even crazy enough to try to rescue marooned spacemen before they freeze, or disappear into protective custody.*

Which could be dangerous. The government might declare you mentally ill, and help you.

She shuddered at that thought. She pushed and rolled Bob aside. She sat up and pulled the comforter up tight around herself. "Do you know what it was that attracted me to science fiction?"

He raised himself on one elbow, blinked at her change of subject, and looked quickly around the room, as if suspecting bugs. "No, what?"

"Not Fandom. I was reading the true quill long before I knew about Fandom and cons and such. No, it was the feeling of hope."

"Hope?"

"Even in the most depressing dystopia, there's still the notion that the future is something we build. It doesn't just happen. You can't predict the future, but you can invent it. Build it. That is a hopeful idea, even when the building collapses."

Bob was silent for a moment. Then he nodded. "Yeah. Nobody's building the future anymore. 'We live in an Age of Limited Choices.'" He quoted the government line without cracking a smile. "Hell, you don't *take* choices off a list. You *make* choices and *add* them to the list. Speaking of which, have you made your choice?"

That electric tickle . . . "Are they even alive?"

"So far. I understand it was some kind of miracle that they landed at all. They're unconscious, but not hurt bad. They're hooked up to some sort of magical medical widgets and the Angels overhead are monitoring. But if we don't get them out soon, they'll freeze to death."

She bit her lip. "And you think we can reach them in time?"

Bob shrugged.

"You want me to risk my life on the Ice, defy the government and probably lose my job in a crazy, amateur effort to rescue two spacemen who might easily be dead by the time we reach them."

He scratched his beard. "Is that quixotic, or what?"

"Quixotic. Give me four minutes."

BUILDING A NEW FANTASY TRADITION

The Unlikely Ones by Mary Brown
Anne McCaffrey raved over *The Unlikely Ones*: "What a splendid, unusual and intriguing fantasy quest! You've got a winner here...." Marion Zimmer Bradley called it "Really wonderful ... I shall read and re-read this one." A traditional quest fantasy with quite an unconventional twist, we think you'll like it just as much as Anne McCaffrey and Marion Zimmer Bradley did.

Knight of Ghosts and Shadows
by Mercedes Lackey & Ellen Guon
Elves in L.A.? It would explain a lot, wouldn't it? In fact, half a millennium ago, when the elves were driven from Europe they came to—where else? —Southern California. Happy at first, they fell on hard times after one of their number tried to force the rest to be his vassals. Now it's up to one poor human to save them if he can. A knight in shining armor he's not, but he's one hell of a bard!

The Interior Life by Katherine Blake
Sue had three kids, one husband, a lovely home and a boring life. Sometimes, she just wanted to escape, to get out of her mundane world and *live* a little. So she did. And discovered that an active fantasy life can be a very dangerous thing—and very real.... Poul Anderson thought *The Interior Life* was "a breath of fresh air, bearing originality, exciting narrative, vividly realized characters— everything we have been waiting for for too long."

The Shadow Gate by Margaret Ball
The only good elf is a dead elf—or so the militant order of Durandine monks thought. And they planned on making sure that all the elves in their world (where an elvish Eleanor of Aquitaine ruled in Southern France) were very, very good. The elves of Three Realms have one last spell to bring help ... and received it: in the form of the staff of the New Age Psychic Research Center of Austin, Texas....

Hawk's Flight by Carol Chase
Taverik, a young merchant, just wanted to be left alone to make an honest living. Small chance of that though: after their caravan is ambushed Taverik discovers that his best friend Marko is the last living descendant of the ancient Vos dynasty. The man who murdered Marko's parents still wants to wipe the slate clean—with Marko's blood. They try running away, but Taverik and Marko realize that there is a fate worse than death . . . That sooner or later, you have to stand and fight.

A Bad Spell in Yurt by C. Dale Brittain
As a student in the wizards' college, young Daimbert had shown a distinct flair for getting himself in trouble. Now the newly appointed Royal Wizard to the backwater Kingdom of Yurt learns that his employer has been put under a fatal spell. Daimbert begins to realize that finding out who is responsible may require all the magic he'd never quite learned properly in the first place—with the kingdom's welfare and his life the price of failure. Good thing Daimbert knows how to improvise!